CRIMSON SON

CRIMSON SON

Russ Linton

Edited by – Heather Bungard-Janney
Cover design – Damonza
Promotional Artwork – Johnny Morrow

ISBN: 978-0-9903169-0-9

ACKNOWLEDGMENTS

For my wife and son who were willing to put up with a writer about the house. Without their support, Spencer might have stayed trapped in an icy hole forever. And many thanks to the gang at the North Branch Writers' Critique Group that inspired, shredded, and helped rebuild this little dream. Also, a special thanks to my beta readers who took their time to put a bit of well-needed polish on this tale. And finally, sincere appreciation to my first professional editor. I still have the fiddle and matches if ever you need some free time.

CHAPTER 1

I MIGHT AS WELL be lying in a coffin. I've seen them on TV before. The dead always looked so comfortable with their arms folded across their chest in those silky interiors. Peaceful, even though they're alone.

Unless it was a show where the dead happened to be vampires. Then they'd probably be smothered in women. Hot, vampire chicks and metrosexual Nosferatus, getting busy while luring mere mortals into their blood-sucking orgies of doom.

I don't need more of that kind of frustration. Smacking my head against the hatch doesn't clear the image. My thoughts drift to the half-naked diva who pops up on my iPod whenever her song starts to play. I don't even know how that crap got on there, but I listen to it. On repeat.

The escape pod I'm lying in isn't a coffin. The smooth metal interior is studded with switches and blinking lights. The hatch above has a tiny window, now smudged by the impact of my head. There's no ruffled silk to cushion the blow.

On my right glows the little red button.

Dammit.

Normally, the way the hatch seals out the charged air and

incessant groans of splitting ice is comforting. The pod is the only place in this prison where I can focus. Where I can hear voices I don't hear anymore, and even some which I might never hear again. Today, though, the space feels exactly how it is—cramped, restrictive.

When we first arrived, hearing the details from Dad about the escape pod was pretty cool. Essentially a hollow bullet, the pod employs a type of rail-gun technology. Blast off on the electromagnetically charged rails and leave an EMP in your wake. An escape, for when this frozen ass-crack of the world isn't safe enough.

That's what this is all about, safety; sanity is optional.

One push could end this.

I rest the tip of my index finger on the edge of the button.

One push.

Freedom.

But for how long? Only *he* knows where the pod lands. Operational details like that are deemed stuff I'm too young or too weak or too immature to understand. As soon as the capsule left the launch tube, he'd come flying to the rescue and I'd be right back here.

Of course, rewiring the emergency beacon so it doesn't alert him of a launch would take no time. But then what? I've got a running start? Like that matters against *him*.

Switching around a few wires won't save me. If it could, I'd be free already.

Tinkering has been the only thing keeping me sane. But I've picked through the guts of the bunker a hundred times over and imagined a whole series of escape plans, and they all end up with me either back here or in the clutches of a psychopathic super-villain. So none of that tinkering makes up for the fact that I'm a powerless runt.

Finally, those voices begin to stir. "It's an adventure," I hear her say. "The Swiss Family Robinson made it. Even Ernest, that little lazy know-it-all, did. Surely, you can too?"

But was he alone?

I'd kill for three brothers, a zoo full of animals and a tree-house right now. William, that self-righteous douchebag of a father, I could live without. But Elizabeth. Mother.

My hand falls from the button.

Forcing open the hatch, I breathe in the rush of cool air. Cold, always cold. And barren.

I sit up, eye level with the safe room floor. The escape pod rests on a sunken platform, with three small steps ascending to the grated metal plates that make up the floor. Shimmying out of the pod takes no effort because it was built for people three times my size.

Status lights blink on a control panel under the security monitors. Let's see—what's the forecast on *my* deserted island today? Wintry mix. Chance of snow a million percent. Temperature, ball-numbing cold. Perfect time for a hike.

First thing Dad had said two years ago was to never go out-side. I was seventeen, with over a dozen places I'd called home, and none of them had this much snow. One week into this jail sentence and I'd gotten the urge to toss a snowball—an opening pitch for my new life in the Icehole.

I tried to hide the blisters, but they were still raw and

painful when he got back. I was mainly glad I still *had* fingers. Dad was pissed, as usual.

Whatever. He's gone, again. He leaves any damn time he wants.

I exit the safe room and make my way through a spare parts room I like to call the library. Along the way, I grab my secret weapon off the shelf. It's only a TV, but most people don't have to make theirs out of a satellite phone and an old-school CRT monitor. They don't have to hide it from their dad, either. For months now, this baby has been my intermittent link to the outside world.

Intermittent is putting it mildly. My arctic life hack has more downtime than Windows ME. Not a design flaw though but more of a side effect of living where even penguins fear to tread. Atmospheric conditions here tend to wreck signals.

A single hallway connects each section of the bunker. The lights above click on and off, synchronized with my motion, as I walk into darkness with more vast nothingness behind. Dad says it saves energy because we've only got so much juice and we need all reserves on standby for the escape pod. But this is "home" and I have a constant urge to turn on every light in the place.

Between the library and my destination lies the living quarters, a bathroom, and Danger Bay. Danger Bay was cool on day one, and stayed cool for exactly one day. This only entrance to the bunker resembles the docking bay on a space station, designed to separate our living quarters from certain death. Of course, outer space is probably more hospitable—there's much less suffering before you die.

I continue past Danger Bay and drop off the monitor in what used to be an armory, rechristening that space "the living room". Whatever this place was before, people needed weapons; at least that's what the empty racks seem to say. Dad doesn't need them. If I had one... Whatever, the armory is the closest room to the exterior door.

Heading back to Danger Bay with the sat dish in hand, I punch in the code, then wade into the frozen air. Winter gear hangs on pegs along the wall of the narrow chamber. All the gear goes on: gloves, hood, liner, bib, shell, big chunky moon boots. The mask—I almost skip that.

He stopped giving me the code for the exterior door after the pitching incident. No problem. Disconnecting the security pad takes a few tries because my fat, gloved fingers won't cooperate. Eventually though, I get the job done.

A blast of cold pierces the marshmallow suit as the heavy door grinds open. Gripping the satellite dish, I trudge into the howling, snow-stirred landscape. Not for the first time, I wonder how far I could walk. Would anything ever rise up on the flat horizon?

Climbing to the top of our snow-covered pimple, I can see everything. A vast plain of snow and ice stretches into a veil of white. I don't think it's actually snowing right now, it's only the wind kicking up the tons of the stuff already there. On a calm day months ago, I thought I caught a glimpse of the ocean.

Even wrapped in the high-tech polar gear, my fingers start to get numb. And in spite of the mask, a snotcicle forms on my nose. I drop the antenna in what I hope is a decent place and head inside, reeling out cable as I go. Stripping off the gear, I shiver out of Danger Bay and partially close the door, bringing the heavy barrier down to rest on the cable without crushing it. I feed the rest of the cable into the living room where my homemade television awaits.

The results aren't great. They never are. Today there's only one station in range, and it isn't English speaking. At least there's a signal.

Bad enough that I don't know Russian, but the Cyrillic characters make even guessing at the text a lost cause. I've seen some of those characters around the bunker, printed on circuit boards or pasted on control panels. If I ever need to write tech-nobabble in Russian, I might stand a chance. It's not a big deal. Like every other news station on the planet, they'll eventually show what I'm looking for.

No sports. At least not by my definition. Baseball hasn't caught on in Russia. They've got hockey and full-blown features on chess, though. That helps pass the time.

I used to enjoy chess. Owen Ridley, the Grandmaster of the Terra Nova High School Chess Club, would go down in flames if we played now. I can practically hear "Eye of the Tiger" blar-ing as I sit in the Icehole, playing match after match on that lousy library computer. Apparently, whoever programmed the game didn't think to add difficulty levels, and I've been squar-ing off against the flawless logic every time. I'd give up if it wasn't the only game here.

Maybe I could live in Russia. Be some kind of chess master. Wonder if they get hot Russian chicks.

The news saves me from a trip to my iPod. Eyewitness video, probably from a cellphone camera, pops up behind the news anchor. Black, antique lampposts rise from a stone railing between a cobblestone walk and a river. Crowds mill about, and I hear the cameraman rambling in the background. He sounds American.

A giant Ferris wheel turns lazily beside the boardwalk. I'm pretty sure it's the London Eye. I recognize it from a documentary I watched years ago, back when we lived somewhere with cable.

The image jerks before tilting to the cobblestone. Terrified screams become background noise to the rending of metal. Shoes clip by and the walkway blurs. The cameraman shouts, "Oh my god! Oh my god! Hurry!" A fleeting glimpse of a massive figure beside the wheel slips by, then the camera focus goes to a clawed arm snapping the spokes. High-tension wires strike into the fleeing tourists.

With a tortured whine, the giant Ferris wheel tears off its moorings. It teeters and crashes into the boardwalk, sending cobblestones and a lamppost hurtling through the crowd, before finally pitching into the Thames. The cameraman hunches behind a wall. "Oh my God! Oh my God!" It's all he says.

Then, I catch a glimpse of him—a red streak in the sky leaving a wake of swirling clouds.

The news slow-mos the video, and a yellow circle highlights that crimson blur. It impacts the black mass with a crack of thunder. All the while, the giant wheel sinks, while Russian voices jabber in the news studio.

Dad says, you neutralize the threat before you save anyone. That's how it's done. He talks in this "wax on wax off" sort of way. He's so sure he's got to teach me. Prepare me to fill his shoes. The Augment process doesn't even work that way, he knows that.

But I can only wonder how many people are sealed up in their glass tourist tombs, while they sink to the river bottom.

The cameraman cheers and the video pixelates as he tries to track the action. Dad, a crimson blob, dances in the sky. Blurry or not, the black robotic shape needs no explanation either. It's another of the Black Beetle's battle drones.

I've never seen one this big. It must be five stories tall. They're usually man-sized, with the features of both a human and a bug. Pincers. Segmented armor plating. Eyes that reflect your helpless face in a thousand different facets.

Chunks of brick explode from a nearby building and the video ends.

News anchors with serious expressions mumble in their monotone voices over a live shot of the aftermath. Banks of spotlights sweep the river. Debris bobs in the water, and blue emergency lights ripple across the waves. Barges raise the wheel's remains.

The anchorman touches an ear, grumbles more Slavic gibberish and faces the screen behind him. A dark room replaces the earlier scenes of destruction. Visible only because of the sleek, sharp reflections cast from a hidden light, an insectoid face emerges. Multifaceted eyes break the feeble light into coarse shards: the Black Beetle.

A Russian translation drowns out his hissing English. I crank up the volume.

"… will rain destruction …"

"… Crimson Mask cannot …"

"… Earth shall bow to the Black Beetle!"

A strange heat floods my insides. My limbs shake, and my heart hammers out of a dead stop. I yank the power cable free, but the light tracing the helmet lingers on the dying screen. Even long after the monitor turns a lifeless gray, that outline remains.

The cold draft from the crack under the door in Danger Bay seeps into the living room. I ball up, huddled with knees to my chest and let the cold envelop me. I'm never getting out of here.

CHAPTER 2

I'M STARTLED AWAKE by the door from Danger Bay hissing open. The coaxial cable whips out of the monitor and the door grinds closed. For a moment, I wonder what's at the other end. Do I even care?

Dad stalks into the living room, back straight, head swiveling with the cable coiled loosely around his fist. He's still keyed up, scanning for hidden threats. His skin-tight black and crimson suit has seen better days. Dark black. A black that gets lost in the darkness of the hallway and a deep red vertical stripe from his forehead on down that's only a shade lighter than the shadows. Scorched and frayed, a small rip near his stomach shows a nasty gash along rippled muscles.

His eyes stop on the monitor, and I watch his jaw flex. He's got muscles where he doesn't need them. Deflection is never a good strategy. I might as well be waving a red cape in front of a bull.

"We're almost out of cardboard to eat." I sit up and scoot my back to the wall.

"You turned off the proximity alarm?"

I'll leave that as a rhetorical question. We wouldn't be

having this conversation had I left it on because we'd both be deafened by the ear-bursting klaxon.

He crosses the room toward me. I try to play it cool but my muscles tighten. He stops next to the television and stares at the cable held between his fingers. "We've talked about this, Spence. No signals except the secure array, and that's only for emergencies."

"I'm not transmitting, only receiving. It isn't a problem." Robot-fighting badass, maybe. Tech guru, he's not. But he never listens to me.

"You've got the heat working overtime without the doors completely sealed. No telling how much fuel you've wasted. You'll freeze to death in minutes if that gets overloaded."

I'm not going to respond to that either. I'm not sure I want to hear my own answer.

"Son…" He exhales. I feel the warm air strike my skin. Ice-blue eyes, cold as the bunker air, peer out of the mask. "We've got to be extremely careful."

"Don't you have the world to save?"

"We're not doing this right now," his neck stiffens and he starts to leave the room. "Clean this up."

"How was London?" Before he can reply I twist the knife. "I'm never getting out of here, am I?"

"I'll fix this." He's facing the hallway and a heat radiates off the words that could thaw this little prison. He's juiced up from his fight, muscles twitching, eyes restless.

The standard drill is to leave him alone. Let him disappear into his office until he reemerges with some new lead or the next group of complete strangers to rescue, but I can't let it go this time. Could be the frustration, the lack of any real sleep, or that taste of popsicle freedom when I stood outside in the howling snow.

"Keep telling yourself that. Tell it to Mom."

I don't see him move. He's hunched over me, his foot grinding the satellite phone into a fine powder. My heart pounds against my ribcage like a desperate prisoner. A fist hangs inches from my face, a fist that could hole-punch a sheet of titanium.

His eyes flare, wider than the mask holes will allow. Shaking with rage and whatever fuels his unbelievable strength, he growls, "Spencer, this is about keeping you alive."

"I'm already living in a morgue. What's the point?" I manage to speak without my voice cracking.

He snatches the mask off his head, a flash of crimson passing between us. A green welt takes up much of his cheek, and dried blood clings to the corner of his mouth. I'm not sure what kind of force it took to do that and I'm not sure I care.

"You don't know what you're saying. It's too risky for you out there." Talking quietly to the floor, he struggles to rein in his strength. I see a way out. I press.

"So I'm stuck here until you get your shit together? Is that it? You couldn't save her, what makes you think you can save me?" His eyes flare again and I stand and stride past him toward the hall. A raging furnace of anger rides the back of my neck. Without looking back, I continue down the hall, breath paralyzed, heart racing. I slip inside my room and lock the door. I huddle on my bunk and listen for the next sound I'll hear above the pounding of blood in my head. Heavy footfalls accompany the snap and twang of the floor's metal grating.

"Spencer, open the door."

A current of fear courses through me, but I let it pool and harden, casting it into the darkness where a dying light outlines an insectoid face. I can't move. I can't care anymore.

"Open the door. Now."

Metal bits cascade to the ground as the lock snaps. Dad's frame fills the doorway. No mask, but his face is a violent shade of red. He reaches out and grabs my arm between two fingers. My bicep crunches and wriggles against bone, sending burning pain shooting through my arm, but I let the dark vision in my mind devour the pain. With as much effort as a normal person might use to squash a bug, he lifts me from the bunk.

I close my eyes and think of the button. I wait for him to pulp my skull against a wall.

"You need to take this seriously." His voice shakes as he pulls me into the hall. He drags me through the library, shoving me into the safe room. "Do the drill."

He stands imperious in the doorway. I don't want to do it, but my feet shuffle zombie-like to the control panel as he repeats his mantra, "There's no thought, Spencer. It's all action. Training. Do it, now."

Clutching my injured arm, cool puddles gather on my eyelashes and I will them not to splash on the panel. I swallow and step through the sequence.

First, I mimic pushing the door seal button so he can continue to watch from the doorway. Next comes the emergency beacon. Sometimes we give this one a full test, but not often because it does transmit a signal. After the band on his wrist beeps, we'll quickly shut it off. I wait for a few seconds that flow like minutes. There's no response, so I mime these motions as well, wincing as I raise my arm. On the panel's opposite side are two flashing orange buttons labeled with a stylized flame.

"Thermite one away. Thermite two away," I mutter—these never get tested. They let loose localized charges that will melt the server into a silicon cinder. If the facility is compromised and I have to "evac" as he puts it, the information collected here needs to be destroyed. Every time we do this, thoughts of pressing the buttons race through my mind. I never did because of the fear he'd go ballistic. Now, I'm worried about the off chance that he wouldn't and I'd be condemned to live in the Icehole computer-free.

Finally, I walk to the far corner of the room and stare into the pod, my home away from home. Eyes dry and matted, I steal a glimpse at the doorway. Dad isn't there. Beyond the library it's dark and quiet. I climb inside and close the hatch looking out through the thick window, wishing I was anywhere but here, staring at the little red button.

I want to press it. I'm going to press it. But I need to see her one last time.

Sleep overwhelms me. Before long, I'm drowning, gasping for breath in a glass bubble and sinking slowly into murky waters. Nightmares, dreams, they are the same. For two years, always the same.

*

Home. I was seventeen. After years of moving, Mom put her foot down and we'd been in the San Francisco area for three years. She'd found a rental in an older neighborhood overlooking San

Pedro Valley Park, one of those stucco homes with a tile roof. Mom loved the place. I did too.

Mom sighs as she tries to feed a page into the fax machine.

"Spencer, honey, do you have any idea how this works? I think I might've broken it," she speaks without looking up and tucks a lock of dark hair behind her ear. She does that when she's frustrated. That mostly includes any time she's faced with gears, transistors, chips, batteries or so much as a stray piece of copper wire. She refers to herself as "technologically challenged." Really, she wants an excuse to get me to help.

I eye the aging fax machine with contempt. "I could figure it out. But, what about your phone?"

She looks puzzled as she asks, "What about it?"

"The phone takes pictures, right? I can take pictures of the papers and send those to Dad."

She smiles. My favorite part of this dream, nightmare, memory—whatever it is. I always try to stay at this point. Stop time. Freeze her face and burn it into my brain so I can see that expression, always.

"Honey, that's a great idea. You want to take over here?"

I've lived through this so many times, I know what she's thinking at this very moment. Nothing to do with sending papers, she's watching me work. She knows I'm happy with a new gadget. She gets me, even if she doesn't understand what I do. I miss that the most.

"What's this for?"

"Paperwork for the house."

"Are we finally going to buy it?"

"No, I don't think so." She turns away, busying herself with the fax machine again. The room empties without her smile.

I take the phone and spread the papers on the floor. More rental paperwork.

"I don't understand why we don't just buy the place. Didn't you say the owner wanted to sell?" I ask. She shrugs.

With careful motions I start snapping away, attaching the pictures to an email. I'm not sure where Dad is going to print these, but wherever he found a fax machine, chances are they'll have what he needs. I hit *send*. An hourglass pops up, followed by "Connection Lost".

This part always comes so fast.

I hand the phone back to Mom. "You'll need to send later, I guess. The signal dropped. Should be in your outbox ready to go."

As she takes the phone, the wall of the room explodes.

Here. Dream becomes nightmare. For a moment, I feel I can make it stand still, but why would I? Events unfold with the emptiness of the bunker gnawing at my insides. I can identify every stray chunk of plaster and splinter of wood in this time-robbed moment.

Fragments of home spray like a swarm of locusts. Mom screams and the world spins under her protective dive. I struggle to see through a haze of dust. Glimpses of the valley filter past a humanoid silhouette. A long, pincered arm lashes out. The arm clamps tightly around Mom's waist and retracts, drawing us closer.

"Release the boy and he will live," the Black Beetle speaks

with an unnatural vibration. "He can relay a message for your husband."

Mom squeezes tighter but her screaming stops.

I search her face, knowing what I'll find, all the while scrambling to find an anchor as we slide across the room. She's bleeding from a gash on her forehead and the pincer cinches tighter. Her eyes are full of fear, but focused. She's calculating, deliberating. A hundred times? A thousand? It always hurts.

"No, Mom, please!" I throw my hands around the leg of a toppled chair which drags uselessly behind us. Countless trips through this nightmare, I know I can't keep us here, but I reach out anyway. And always, she lets go.

I grab her arm, trying to pull her back, cursing my stunted size, my weak limbs, my feeble grip. Sweaty hands slip as the pincer continues to retract. Her trembling lips form a final smile and she watches me with a sad but determined expression. She mouths the words, "I love you."

"Mom!" I glance at the lifeless phone, shrouded in dust. The screen is dark and covered in spidery cracks.

"Tell your father it is time to turn himself in," the Black Beetle says. "Is that clear?"

With a pneumatic hiss the ebony battle armor backs into the afternoon sun. Blinding light floods in. The armor takes flight on a column of flame and the deafening roar rattles our battered home. I rush to the opening. She's an angel, floating away, the shadowy beast burning behind her. All I can do is stare and cry.

Only this time, the tears don't come.

Every time this nightmare strikes, I stand there, clinging

to that last glimpse as she's torn away. But this time, on her face, a different expression quivers through the waves of heat and exhaust. All of her fear is erased. Her eyes search mine as though she's seeing me for the first time.

I continue watching the brilliant rocket flares long after they dissolve into a sunless sky. Then, the points of light burst outward into the bright edges of an eclipsed sun. A ring of light that seems so close, yet so far from home.

CHAPTER 3

I'VE WANTED TO escape the pain of that recurring nightmare for so long, but this is somehow worse. Watching the relentless memory of that day drift into an insubstantial dream is like losing a limb.

Burned in my brain, I know every detail. A cloudy day, not clear. The sun was a blinding hole, not eclipsed. And her face always held the mask of bravery, not... something else.

The sweat-dampened sheets of my bunk don't help with the frigid air. Never have. I ignore the chill and try to clear my head.

Wait. I thought I passed out in the pod. Maybe I really am going crazy.

I look around the room, unsure about reality. The door is closed and the lock still mangled, but the pieces have been picked up. The bunker's quiet except the distant howling of the unchecked wind outside. Stumbling out of bed, I shamble down the narrow hall.

Dad's office is quiet and the security pad blinks red. When he's here, he doesn't bother with the lock. Light, dark, light, dark, I shuffle to the farthest end of the bunker, past the armory and into the kitchen. I'm pretty sure the island was made to support a body, or maybe a bunch of test tubes, and the sink wasn't for scrubbing plates. For me though, it's the kitchen.

A note hangs under a plain black magnet on the mini-fridge. Used to be, Mom would mediate those rare instances when planets aligned and I shared space with Dad. Now, that job has been relegated to a minibar reject.

> *Be back soon, went for supplies. For emergencies, today's code is 4RG677. Outer door is shut and proximity alarm reset. It will stay that way. The pod isn't a bunk. If you're in the safe room, you shut it up tight and hit the beacon immediately.*

Even after last night, it reads the same as every other note he's ever left. I'm not sure why he bothers. He could save time by printing one and changing the code. Reading between the lines today is easy: *"Failed again, need a breather, almost forgot to feed you and clean the cage."* I swipe the note off the fridge and let the magnet clatter to the floor.

I'm alive another day. I can't remember the last time I tried to choke down some food. Maybe I'll celebrate.

Opening the fridge, I'm met by stagnant air and the familiar hum is gone. Compressor's shot, again. A quart of lukewarm milk is all that's there anyway. I grab the container and head for the pantry. The cabinet contains mostly empty space and a couple of generic white boxes with even more generic names. They all share an "insert grain" plus "insert shape" theme.

I suppose this is nutrition, but I look like I'm on a hunger strike. At least Dad stopped saying I'd fill out. When I was a kid, he'd say I'd be tossing full-size cars around like Hot Wheels in no time. What bullshit. I pour a bowl of cardboard and get liberal with the room-temp milk.

Powdered milk was my biggest motivation to get the fridge running. Dad wasn't too happy with it disassembled and strewn across the floor. He kept repeating that the only reason he'd installed the fridge years ago was for a "mission". When pressed for details, he gave a vague response about antitoxin storage. That's all he would say.

When I finished, our "unnecessary power drain" was running like a champ.

And figuring out that "mission" wasn't exactly rocket science. News stations worldwide covered the "Anthrax Kid" incident. Everyone knew how Dad stopped that psycho, Jason Carver, who had filled a mosquito fogger truck full of weaponized anthrax and toured downtown Atlanta.

After Dad caught Carver, he didn't come home for weeks. My guess was he got quarantined in a bubble somewhere. He never said. Just another hole in his secret life.

Carver cooked up his own Augmentation formula while working at the CDC. He left journals detailing how he thought being immune to any disease, poison, or viral infection the planet had to offer might help him do his job. Other entries mentioned a failed marriage and trouble with his boss. Whatever the cause, he got his homebrew process wrong and went freaking nuts.

Not that he was the only Augment for that to ever happen to. Secret labs funded by governments used to crank them out by the dozens, and even with all those resources, accidents weren't uncommon. But still, they kept churning them out. By the time people knew the program had gotten out of hand, the Augments knew they held all the cards and started going freelance, for good and bad.

Following Dad's exploits used to be my favorite pastime. My dad, a freaking Augment. One of the good guys. Every kid wants a dad that cool. Too bad nobody could know.

Telling everyone your dad is an accountant (foreign currency and international markets so, no, he doesn't do stateside taxes), or an insurance salesman (global corporate insurance so he can't help you with your car), or an actuary (on-call and strictly does contract work for his employer), or any other profession which assures obscurity gets embarrassing.

But once I understood the truth, I kept up on everything related to the Crimson Mask. The strongest of them all. The best.

That was back when I was a stupid kid. What have those powers done for him? Or me? When they really mattered, they were worthless.

Raising the spoon, my arm throbs again. Maybe Dad's going off the deep end next? Maybe they all go crazy? For all I know, he knows exactly where she is. If he did, crazy or not, I'm damn sure he wouldn't tell me. Why else would it take so long? If I had all that power I'd find her.

Mom's face from the dream claws into my thoughts. No fear or resignation, but the look you might get from your teacher when you accidentally say something smart in class after managing to keep your mouth shut all year. What does it mean?

Before the dream, when I stood up to Dad yesterday, I

wanted to float away with her. I'd moved past any kind of pain he or this place could dish out. And then she changed. Why?

I leave my bowl of half-eaten sludge on the island and head into the hall. The milk carton goes with me. I pop open Danger Bay and set the milk in the colder air. The door rumbles shut.

Fine, so the fridge *is* an unnecessary power drain, whatever. He doesn't get me like she did. Taking that fridge apart, the keypads, the terminal, the server—it all kept me sane, at least until recently.

I thought I was out of options. But I'm not. As I tinkered, a plan percolated below the surface, born of wiring diagrams and circuit board landscapes.

It's time to put the secrets to rest. I need to see exactly what he's hiding. And I need to get the hell out of here before one of us misses the last stop on the crazy train. Might be too late for that, though.

CHAPTER 4

I PAUSE OUTSIDE DAD'S office and double-check the lock. Bypassing the door wouldn't be a challenge. I've disassembled and reassembled the keypads around here so often I'm surprised he bothers to lock anything. After last night, though, I don't know what he'd do if he came home and found me in there, and I'm not ready to die today. Not until I've done what he can't. Not until I've found her. Besides, I have a more elegant solution to the problem.

The library lights up that pale fluorescent blue, my sunshine. My own office of sorts. School room, game room, hobby closet. This cramped space contains a desk, computer terminal, and a wall of metal shelves covered in scavenged parts. A worn paperback sits on the shelf, bookended by a box filled with interface cards and a spool of coaxial cable.

I reach for the one item that transforms this room, the book, a copy of *The Swiss Family Robinson*.

Bullshit family values, a treatise on being resourceful, constant prayers and adulation to a higher power: pure old-school propaganda. Despite that, I used to think it was the best book ever written and I've read quite a few. Being lost in an exotic location and left to live on wit and sheer determination sounded fun. Jesus, I was such a dumbass.

I open it to the handwritten note on the inside cover: *"Happy Birthday to my adventurous teenager! Love, Mom."*

Mom was a "glass is half full and the faucet is nearby" sort of person. Even her handwriting in the note bubbles on the page. Moving around became our "adventure"; our ever-changing identities, part of some grand quest. By the time she gifted the book, we'd read it together, over and over. I knew the rose-colored interpretation of our life through that book was all an act. Constantly getting shipwrecked sucks ass.

At least then, I was being marooned in the civilized world.

I pull the book close to my face and breathe in deeply. It's got the scent of a real library. A smell of knowledge and learning. That musty, pulpy odor that speaks to the millions of printed pages filling those brick walls.

When every public library across the U.S. finally seemed to get internet access, my life was complete. We moved so much, we only rarely had our own service at home. The library became a lifeline to my real friends. We'd hook up online in chat rooms and forums, all hosted on hijacked servers, where we'd talk about everything from baseball to the latest tech.

This place is too quiet to be a library.

Goddamn memory lane. Dead end. Who knows, maybe I'll see a real library again soon?

I flick on the terminal, and underneath the metal floor, the server hums, sparking out of its sleep cycle. An awkward place to put a server, but heat rises and that dinosaur creates plenty. Of course, crawling around under the floor to do maintenance is a pain in the ass, but it offered challenge and exploration. In one particularly grueling month of boredom, I familiarized myself with every scrap of hardware under the floor and traced every cable to its source.

All the tech here is old-school stuff that's been repurposed. A lot of the hardware is stamped with Russian characters, another little mystery I have yet to be informed about. I do know there's absolutely no way Dad assembled this stuff alone. He can't tell RJ45 from co-ax. Lucky me; he'll never notice a few modifications.

The entry hall is dark. Through the open safe room door, the monitors stare back, cold and empty. I should have plenty of time—Dad hasn't exactly raced off to the convenience store. And if he walks in? I could care less.

I lift up an access hatch and shimmy into the crawlspace with one particular cable in mind. My multi-tool, some patch, a switch I cobbled together out of junk parts, and I'm done. As I work in the checkered darkness, Mom's curious face watches in some corner of my mind.

Sweat clings like droplets of ice as I emerge from the server's crawlspace. I switch the library terminal over to the new cable and stuff the old through the floor grating, out of sight. The screen flickers, and a login prompt blinks impatiently. No different than the library terminal login where I can access the equivalent of the bunker owner's manual and chess. However, the top of the screen displays the network address reserved for Dad's office.

Username:

There's a code I've seen on the pentagon-shaped necklace Dad wears. I try that first.

CM10288

I wish Eric were here. Hacking is not my forte. Sure, downloading programs and tiptoeing through the "how-to's" of hacking on virus-laden websites, I can do that. But my man, Eric, well, he takes it to a whole new level. He's Yoda and I'm the whiny farm boy.

We didn't even get to say goodbye.

Eric used to say most people use stupid passwords they can easily remember. Names of loved ones, dates. Of course, most people don't anticipate that kids who share their haunted memories will be hacking their account.

Password:

The password isn't hard to guess, but getting the order and format for the date is the tricky part. Actually, I have two dates in mind, but the least painful one goes first; Mom's yearly disappointment etched it into my brain—their anniversary.

Connie081287

Welcome, Crimson Mask. Please enter search phrase or file number.

"Jesus, even your computer calls you Crimson Mask." I type in the first name that comes to mind.

Connie Harrington.

Accessing...
0 records.

Staring again at the blinking cursor, I'm not quite ready to type the next name that pops into my head. I go with the guts of the Augment program, "Project Peacemaker".

Accessing...
1264 records. Sort by?

I sort the records by date and skim the titles. Most of it's stuff you'd hear on the news, or read in magazines and newspapers, but this is unfiltered, raw data. I check reality against what I already know, or think I know. There's always a gap between those. One file called "Peacemaker: A History" from a military journal catches my eye.

So far, nothing I didn't read about in Mr. Hutton's history class. During World War I, Germany tried to make soldiers that could breathe mustard gas. World War II saw America field the first Augment team. B-52, Minuteman, Fat Boy, Tomahawk, Hurricane; Augment Force Zero, the guys credited with ending the war with Japan. These were guys that had real powers, not just enhancements to stave off trench rot or keep their dicks from falling off from adding Europe's brothels to their tour.

Russia launched their Augment program, and tensions

escalated. Downtown Havana got turned into a parking lot. Chernobyl, where that mental patient Red Scourge left a trail of radioactive destruction across Eastern Europe. The world demanded change.

Didn't happen.

How do you end a program of that magnitude? That was the billion-dollar question. They said it was over, but it really wasn't. Some people thought of watching the Augments as a spectator sport, with property damage. Not until that day in September did everyone know the truth.

I was home sick, right after Dad had pulled his typical disappearing act. Convincing Mom I needed to stay home came easy those days. I'd complain about vague aches and pains. Stomach issues were good—not even your mother wants to confirm a raging case of diarrhea.

I remember having the TV remote in pieces. Watching the IR light flash as the buttons clicked had mesmerized me. I had started on a cartoon channel, but eventually settled on a local station in the middle of the "Good Morning" wherever-it-was-we-lived-then show. We might have been outside Dallas, I'm not sure. We weren't there long. Suddenly, the anchors veered off the petting-zoo script. Monitors behind them showed a skyscraper billowing smoke into a cloudless sky.

Mom came to check on me, and when she entered the room I flipped the remote's battery upside-down. I was only twelve, but even then I had grown tired of being protected. She never tried to change the channel, though. Not this time.

We stared in horror as the news played a clip of an Augment named the Djinn firing a molten ball of plasma from his palms clean through a smoking skyscraper. Dad beat the Air Force jets, but he didn't get there right away. By then, the unbelievable heat had melted through the supports on the building. It broke in half, spilling girders, concrete and people into the streets below even as the base collapsed into a cloud of dust.

Mom had never cried in front of me. But her facade of optimism collapsed with the buildings. Tears flowed when the cameras caught Dad flying amid the massive wall of dust that rode the New York streets like a white tsunami. She frantically searched the corners of the screen when the view panned to the towers' naked wreckage, jutting from the roiling debris cloud.

This was different than any other Augment attack. The Djinn came out of a program outside the normal government spheres. Secrets had been sold, or maybe a rogue group had gotten lucky with their own experimentation. He flew—not many of them do. And the destructive force behind his blasts was unheard of. Many of the shots the Djinn fired penetrated building after building and kept going. Missed shots cooked a flock of birds somewhere over the Atlantic, blinded an airline pilot, changed the temperature of the New York skies during the battle.

Talking heads speculated in the aftermath. But even though the Djinn disappeared into the clouds before the day ended, the media persisted, uncovering the use of Augments as proxy soldiers in Southeast Asia, the Middle East, South America. Cuba hadn't prompted any real change. The connections to governments had simply been erased. In that brave new cloak-and-dagger world, secrets were lost. At some point the invisible wars outside had boiled over and rained down on a quiet New York skyline.

Not even the media knew exactly what happened in the dense smoke and confusion that day. Dad never spoke about it either. When he'd gotten home, he'd been burned. Everywhere I could see, his skin was pink with patches of brownish blisters. One hand was mummified in cotton gauze. No one could find whatever remained of the Djinn.

Please enter search phrase or file number.

Djinn

Accessing...
Subject security level: Declassified.
1 record.

The enter key clicks.

Asset: Abdel Khalid Mustafa. Status: Terminated

Playing beneath the text is a video. Vomit rises in my throat and looking away isn't voluntary. It must be the Djinn. Or what used to be. His face is missing. As if punched into his skull.

Another one of Dad's "wax on, wax off" sayings comes to mind—in a war, which is what any conflict between two Augments is, you never pull your punches. You attack with overwhelming force.

A white sheet inches up over the face and several men hoist the body onto a flat board near the edge of a ship railing. Five men stand by in Navy whites, Dad's there too, his burns fresh and more gruesome than I recall.

The view pans out, and an aircraft carrier deck fills the screen. Planes arranged in tight lines crowd the space. A fade to black begins, and as darkness replaces the clear blue sky and neat rows of jets, one particular spot on the screen comes to life. Rocket flares hold back the blackness.

I stop the playback. Rewind. Playback. Rewind. Third time, I let it fade and the file closes. Twin rockets blasting into the sky. The Black Beetle soars upward from the carrier deck, only yards away from Dad.

CHAPTER 5

Please enter search phrase or file number:

THE PROMPT BLINKS, waiting for the next query. It should have been the first. My brain can't quite get the letters to my fingers. The thought of him and what he's done, reduced a place I wanted to call home to the backdrop of a recurring nightmare. He took it all from me. But was he really working with Dad?

Black Beetle

Accessing...
Subject security level Delta. Please enter passcode to continue.

Another layer. I've been at this for a while. I glance into the safe room and check out the security monitors. Snow, snow, more snow. There's no way my password-guessing skills will hold.

Copy the encrypted files, that's the best move. Popping a

thumb drive into a free port, I lean back and watch the file-names scroll. No reason to risk guessing at passwords. I can mess with decrypting the juicier files later, when he's saving the world again and not on a feed run. Not sure how long the transfer will take, but there can't be that much information.

What am I even doing? What has this turned into? Suddenly, this is more than a positional move to turn the tide on the deluge of secrets that have ruled my life. If he's linked to the Black Beetle, Dad has to know what happened to her. Maybe that's why he wasn't there. Why he can't find her. But if he is working with the Beetle why all the theatrics?

I lean back in the chair, trying to make sense of what I've uncovered.

As the transfer of data to the thumb drive grinds, my stomach rumbles. I haven't felt hungry like this in a long time. Digging through the well-stocked pantry at our old house was a subconscious activity. Going through the motions here is depressing, but my stomach apparently isn't as picky as my taste buds. I head to the kitchen to forage.

The crackers I settle on are dry and flavorless. About the only thing that will wash the sawdust down is a nice cool glass of milk. I start to open the dead fridge. Right—the airlock.

Walking to Danger Bay, I hit the activation button on the keypad and watch the fiery red digits come alive. My palm hovers above the keys and an odd sensation strikes.

You search for heat when you live in a place like this. If you stand there long enough, right before the pad resets, you'll imagine you can feel the heat behind the tiny LEDs, but it's never really there. A phantom sensation normally, but right now a warmth extends along my palm, all the way up my forearm.

My first guess is it's some kind of short. I sniff the panel. No telltale odor of burning wires, but there's a metallic odor I can't identify. With a fingertip I trace the keypad housing, the door jam, the seam. A whisper of warmth emanates from the unheated space of the airlock.

I punch in the code, and the door grinds open. That whisper of heat fills the central hall, pushed on by a thick, acrid smell. At the far end of the chamber, the exterior door remains closed and sealed tight. It won't be that way much longer.

A red-hot, molten trail of steel inches its way up the door.

Oh, shit.

Black metal pincers rip through the glowing trail. Molten metal drips from the claw as a tortured screech fills the small space, and the reinforced door peels away easy as a sheet of tin.

My hands won't cooperate. My eyes won't leave the claw. Sunlight reflected from the perpetual blanket of snow outside burns past the glow of superheated metal. Pure, white light wreathes a cancerous, insect-like figure.

It's him.

Got to get the code right. Fat finger the keys, reset. Double-tap a number, reset. The airlock door finally rumbles shut as the exterior door disappears into the blinding white.

Racing toward the library, I check the red proximity alert in the central hall. No way I didn't hear the klaxon spine-rattler. The red light stares vacantly from the ceiling. No alarm. I head for the safe room in a panic and I yank the thumb drive on the way by.

The exterior cameras in the safe room should show the problem. But, according to them, there is no problem. The front door is intact and the powdery white runs uninterrupted for miles. Then I notice the time stamp in the corner repeating, over and over. The security has been bypassed.

A feeble, orange light springs to life in the main hall from the top of the door to Danger Bay. Tiny sparks leap into the air and smolder on the floor. A dripping, molten line crawls down the door. It won't be long.

*

Before I've given any conscious thought, the safe room door is secured, the thermite released, the beacon activated, and I'm standing on the edge of the steps leading into the pod. A tortured moan signals the Danger Bay's door being peeled open and tossed aside.

Even behind the safe room door I should be afraid. But as I listen to and feel the mechanical death machine charge down the hallway, my body goes numb. I reach up and finger the bruise on my arm. Floor plates, shelves, spare parts clatter outside the door. The drone collides with the safe room door with the force of an artillery shell and a sound that vibrates in my head but I don't even flinch.

The heat, the cold, the residue of my dad's anger, the lingering pain, all disappear. I can't shake that surreal moment where I watched the outer door of this prison ripped to shreds and tossed into the vast arctic landscape. That door was torn wide open, never to close again. I'm free today.

I could leave. Right now.

Another one of Dad's heroic sayings is that bravery isn't

about taking risks. Being a hero is about executing the right actions at the right time. Careful planning, precision, training, you let it take over. You act without thinking and train so that those actions will be the correct ones.

But if I follow that advice, I'm in the pod right and ready to launch to safety. All that stupid talk about tossing cars around and here, he's been training me to run. To climb into a pod whose destination has never been revealed. A pod that could be my own little glass coffin for all I know. Melt the data, shoot the kid into space. Would he do that?

The door resonates again and the room shakes. I stare into the pod.

If he wanted me dead, I couldn't stop it. It would have happened long ago. Hell, he could've just flown off and not come back—it would've been that easy. Maybe he set up the robot attack? Why would that make any sense? He could have popped my head like a pimple last night. Do they even have CSI North Pole? Who the hell would find out?

An orange knot blossoms on the safe room door near the ceiling.

Whatever his plans, he'll find my steaming corpse back here before I blindly climb into his control ship. I'll show him exactly what I can do. Wait right here and confront him with the information. I'm not helpless.

I dig out my multi-tool and get to work.

During all the time spent daydreaming in the pod, I figured out I couldn't program the navigation system. The pod doesn't fly so much as fire. It's all a matter of adjusting the initial trajectory. The control software is also all in Russian. But between the language barrier, a lack of GPS coordinates, and no knowledge of good landing sites, if I tried to aim it into my old neighborhood, I'd probably end up in the Pacific or the side of a mountain.

So I leave the navigation alone and focus on rewiring the launch system. I'll dry fire the launch tube, keeping the pod on the loading arms. The EMP backwash will hopefully disable the robot before it disembowels me.

With the rewiring finished, I shimmy into the pod and slide the cockpit closed. There's the familiar hiss and click followed by pure silence. The quiet drives home how much noise, how much heat, how much atmosphere I was baking in out there: the odor of melting metal, the hiss and clatter of glowing shards skittering across the floor, the increasing warmth.

Warmth? Where has this damn robot been the past two years?

My laughter fills the pod. I haven't laughed like this in… forever. Even that's hilarious. My sides ache and unused face muscles are hurting all the way to the back of my neck. I can't stop. I don't want to stop. If this is one big fail, dying laughing in the Black Beetle's face isn't a bad way to go. Those pincers can pluck me from the pod and my final act will be a one-finger salute; the laughter amplifies. I *am* going crazy. I'm an Augment now, I'm Mental Man, nutso-supreme. Put me in a pair of fucking tights.

Eyes watering, I peer through the pod's tiny window. The safe room door is tougher going and the glowing metal has stopped halfway down. Strategic cuts begin to appear along the seams.

Laughter fades into the laser cutter's muffled buzz as the door liquefies. Glowing embers ping off the pod like fireflies dancing outside the viewport. One comes to rest on the viewport, throbbing with heat. I place my palm on the glass but it stays cool as the ember dies.

Finally. I put my finger on that freaking red button. I've left several wires dangling from the panel with their exposed coppery ends twisted together. It's a hack job. Might not even work. Only now does it hit me that this has to be the single dumbest idea I've ever had.

Cries of wrenching metal penetrate the thick hull of the pod. The glass is fogged over and I wipe it clean. A pincer pierces the bottom corner of the safe room door. The robotic hand shakes fiercely under the strain and a second pincer punches through along the glowing cut. Globs of molten slag slap onto the floor.

No laughing now. My hands are shaking. If this doesn't work, I won't have time to rewire the button to escape.

With a shuddering heave, a chunk of the safe room door breaks loose. This door doesn't peel neatly but shatters along the weakened seams leaving jagged, dripping edges. In the open void, a glowing, honeycombed eye peers inside.

Can't rush this. Have to wait. The EMP is a close-range side effect, not a directed weapon. The pod, the equipment in the safe room, that's all shielded. I'm only guessing Hannibal Gundam isn't.

It forces into the breach. I scream, a deafening echo in the pod, and mash the launch button. With a static pop, the pod rattles and the loose button whips out of my hand. Darkness floods the viewport, broken only by a diffuse, fiery glow.

CHAPTER 6

WILLIAM DRAKE SMILED the confident smile of a man with nothing to hide. It was a talent. "Gentlemen, ladies, I hope this presentation answered any questions you may have regarding your future investment. I'm afraid we're pressed for time, but I can perhaps address any minor concerns before the lunch break."

He attempted eye contact with each of the twelve investors. Impassive masks chiseled by innumerable business deals, shady and otherwise, stared back. A few bent studiously over crisp vinyl folders containing a decade's worth of his hard work. Nothing short of groundbreaking science, Drake mused. It would be impossible for them not to be impressed. There was little indication of this, however.

A sense of loss settled around Drake. This vague idea that something was amiss began with the enigmatic expressions of the investors and heightened with the cold breeze of an A/C vent on his exposed skin. His high-end cashmere business suit had been tailored in the finest Sicilian shops. But as far as Drake was concerned, the suit was merely a mat of dead goat hair and offered little of true value; no sensors for relaying breathing, heart rate, or perspiration of his targets. Any number of simple biometrics could have given valuable clues regarding the investors' moods—he'd need to consider constructing such a device. However, at this moment, he was stuck making less than scientific assumptions based on body language.

He'd purchased a book on the subject—after a quick skim, it was now collecting dust somewhere in his office.

Careful calculation rested behind Drake's selection process for the investors seated before him. Through years of research, planning, intelligence gathering, surveillance, other...tactics, an elite cadre of global billionaire financiers had been lured to his table. Now, the fate of his company rested on these more conventional negotiations, which Drake accepted as a necessity. Of the twelve, three were key to his success.

Sheikh Nabil Hamad met his gaze with a smile. Thirteen-billion-dollar net worth, owner of the world's largest construction conglomerate. Business and pleasure often overrode his more public religious sentiments. The sheikh was a closet wine connoisseur. Drake had learned this many years ago at the relatively cheap cost of a jilted wife; one of seventeen. Over the past four years, Drake had combined a steady flow of rare vintages along with his uncanny knack for predicting large scale downtown reconstruction projects. Hamad viewed Drake as a solid partner.

Next was Meredith Wainwright, the wealthy daughter of a media baron. She grinned vacuously, her folder unopened. Plump, no, absolutely corpulent, and a face adored only for the five-and-a-half billion dollars that had so recently been transferred into her accounts. He'd expended much effort into securing her support. Six months prior, her father had passed away due to exceptionally rare complications from an insect bite. A tragedy. Drake returned the smile.

Then there was Kerin Townsend.

Drake had debated Kerin's inclusion. Townsend's finances were abundant, his eye for innovation unsurpassed, but as a cutting-edge software firm's CEO, with contacts throughout Silicon Valley, Drake couldn't help but be concerned. Handing over even a rough sketch of his life's work to Kerin could be a fatal mistake. He could be courting either blatant theft or the creation of an extremely well-positioned competitor. That's what he would have done in Townsend's shoes. But Drake felt over-prepared for that scenario—playing dirty was his game.

The silence in the room became deafening. Drake wiped sweaty palms on the cashmere suit. He reached to his waist and when his hand did not wrap reassuringly around a certain small black box, he plunged his fist into a pocket.

Hands in pockets. He knew that would not do. This communicated dissatisfaction with one's self-image according to what he could recall of the book. No, he needed his hands in front. Confident. He tugged the collar of his jacket, smoothed his tie and pushed his shoulders back. The investors remained focused. Smart phones emerged, pens scribbled notes, but many sat in quiet contemplation. Drake examined the faces again, fighting to keep the corners of his mouth upturned and eyes relaxed.

Townsend peered up, his curly hair framing the face of a forty-year-old cherub tucked away behind chunky designer glasses. If the silence were to burst, Drake would not have chosen Townsend as the one to stick the pin. "Fascinating concept, William. This idea of a Distributive Hive on the nano-scale. I daresay, revolutionary, if it indeed works. However, will there be any—"

Ring. Buzz.

"Umm, will there be any chance for us to tour—" Townsend tried to continue.

Ring. Buzz.

Drake crushed an irritated scowl, making what he hoped was a passably apologetic expression. He reached into his pocket and fumbled with the phone. He'd hired administrative assistants to attend to his every need. Take calls, make appointments, adjust schedules, bring coffee, massage his feet, even, if the whim struck. But only he answered this phone.

Now, finally and unfortunately the center of attention, he pressed the buzzing phone against his chest.

"I do apologize, apparently our time is up. Save those intriguing questions, please, and we'll attend to them immediately after lunch."

A fragile smile stretched across his face as he backed from the room. The group watched with a mix of understanding, annoyance, and the seemingly favorite poker face. He turned and stalked into the hall, bursting into a small side office. Shocked, the girl at her desk swallowed a gasp. With a flare of his eyes, she was on her feet and then disappeared into the hallway. He snapped the phone to an ear and swatted the door closed.

"This had better be good. Earth-shattering," Drake spat into the phone.

"Yes, sir." A youthful voice with vowels stretched loose under a hint of colonial sophistication answered. "There is a thing you need to see."

"Yes, there is. I need to see several million dollars. Do you have that, Xamse? Do you?"

"N-no, sir. But I thought you would need to see this."

"You don't think. The drones are programmed, you monitor. That simple," Drake growled. "Mumbai?"

"No, sir. Mumbai goes according to your plan. The problem is U5345."

"The Arctic deployment? So, our client's intelligence proved useful?"

"Yes, sir. However, we lost contact, sir."

"What do you mean, 'lost contact'?" Drake spoke as he started for the door and then stopped short, bringing the phone back to his ear. "Xamse, if this is in any way operator error, you'll find yourself back on the front lines shooting at your playmates. Understood?" Faint static crackled on the line before Drake severed the connection and stormed toward an elevator.

*

An electric pulse hummed throughout the room as Drake stepped out of the secure elevator. The sound soothed his hurried thoughts and erased the unbearable atmosphere of the boardroom. Workstations lined the walls, their smaller screens scrolling with an endless parade of data. A single large display bathed the chamber in flickering light. On this central screen, a tiny metal room showed through a glowing tear in a heavy security door. A white halo stained the lower portion of the screen, bleeding out in a circle.

They'd received the intelligence about the bunker earlier in the day. The circumstances made Drake suspicious. Out of the blue, his client had procured information which Drake had spent nearly two years searching for. A breach of normal protocol, the information had come over a secure channel directly from Killcreek. Then again, what was normal for Killcreek? The facility was so classified, even his handlers barely knew more than the codename.

But just in case they were rethinking his contract, Drake had sent the single drone as a scout instead of personally attending to the matter. From the video feed, apparently the tip was legitimate.

"This." A young dark-skinned man motioned tensely to a computer terminal. His hair was cropped close on both sides and a ridge of tight curls grew down the center. From beneath a slender black band around his neck, a ragged scar stretched from ear to ear.

Drake devoured the space between them. "How did this happen?"

The boy spoke without looking up. "I am unsure. We lost connection. Video is only now reestablished."

"The nanomechs?"

"Yes, sir. They follow default protocols to restore the uplink first."

"I'm aware of their programming. I want full operational control. Now."

"Working on it, sir."

Drake's eyes flicked to a bank of smaller screens. Several feeds depicted scenes from across the globe. Calm blue skylines, cities half a world away twinkling in the night, the shattered boardwalk along the Thames. Another showed a stretch of highway along the business district of Mumbai. Beside that, a formation of drones cut through a cloudy sky, a timer counting down in the corner of the screen.

Placing his hands on the control panel, Drake leaned in to examine the main monitor. The image jumped erratically between an obscured view of the tiny space and a frozen picture distorted along invisible lines. Between the bouts of interference, he could see a small room with a metal grating on the floor. A workstation with several monitors. A chair. The room appeared empty.

A high-pitched whine blasted the air. Xamse cringed as the wail descended several octaves and settled into an annoying buzz. "Audio restored, sir."

"Obviously," Drake sneered. The view had also begun to clear. In the lower corner, no longer obscured by the slowly fading halo of interference, a metal door with a small window swung upward. The screen jerked and once again faded into a seizure of static. "Get it back."

From his suit pocket, Drake retrieved a black box. Xamse noted the movement and sweat beaded along his forehead. Drake's index finger tapped impatiently on the box. The sharp clicking drowned out the buzz of the speakers. Xamse's shoulders tightened and his keyboard rattled with frantic typing. "I'm trying, sir."

"Try harder."

The screen flicked back to life, and the blinding halo shrank to a fuzzy ring. A young man crouched in the corner of the room by the open hatch.

His sweatshirt hung like an empty sack from angular shoulders. Emblazoned on the shirt in large block letters was the word GIANTS. He looked toward the camera with wide eyes sunken into a pale face. A matted shock of dark hair sprouted at a slant from his scalp. His more masculine features, a broad jawline with a knotted chin, sat incongruously atop narrow shoulders. Keeping low to the ground, the young man crept forward.

"There's our little saboteur. My, how you haven't grown." Drake drummed his fingers on the control panel and scanned the room again, paying particular attention to the open hatch. "I see an escape route, perhaps, yet there you are. Curious."

"Sensors back up, sir. They're reporting—"

"The signature from an electromagnetic pulse?" Drake interrupted.

Xamse's cadence at the keyboard faltered. "Yes. You are correct, sir."

"Perhaps I should have gone myself. My battle armor is properly shielded. This drone evidently was not. Whose fault might that be?"

"Working on control, sir. Might have partial in three minutes. Nanomechs reporting now. Getting diagnostic feeds back online." Xamse rattled the accomplishments off with increasing urgency.

The young man onscreen walked forward, peering past the camera and cautiously reaching out until his hand disappeared out of view. With a defiant nod, he twisted his mouth. The screen flickered briefly and returned with a new obstruction sliding its way down the middle in a long, slimy trail.

Exasperation escaped Drake's lips. "Reports on anything useful at the location before I reduce it to rubble?"

"A data center was present, sir."

"Explain 'was'."

"Apparently it's been destroyed. The heat was tremendous. I'm registering an area behind the drone at several hundred degrees Fahrenheit."

The young man disappeared off-screen, and a wheeled office chair hurtled toward the camera. Drake's scowl deepened. "In that case, send a recovery team to be sure. In the meantime, when the drone's control is restored, kill the boy."

"Shall we not take him, like his mother…?" Drake's glare pinched Xamse's question into a trailing whisper. "Yes, sir."

Drake wheeled to exit, the looming business lunch seeping into his thoughts. He sighed wistfully and took in the control center, pausing to let the biometric scan complete and open the security doors. Now he'd have to return to a world of negotiations, pleasantries—of being willing to give ground in order to build his fledgling technology empire. The nanomechs would be a household name, no doubt, and the sooner he concluded his prior commitments, the better.

As the doors slid open, Drake turned. He crossed to the control panel and tapped an image on the smaller screen. It blinked and shifted to the large display. Sounds of rapid gunfire and screams echoed through the room. An orange flash of fire reflected in Drake's eyes, and a crimson streak zipped from corner to corner. "We *do* have a decoy on standby in Mumbai, do we not?"

"Yes, sir. All per your plans, sir." Xamse said, nodding vigorously.

"On second thought," Drake grabbed a headset draped on a nearby chair, "take the boy alive. We may wrap up ahead of schedule."

CHAPTER 7

"**A**RE YOU WATCHING this, you, bastard?" My confidence slips and the last word comes out jittery. That doesn't simply take the edge off the adrenaline, but completely dulls what's left.

I was pumped about the Black Beetle watching me spit in his face. But I've had up-close, personal experience with the real deal, and this has all the markings of another drone. Both have the same basic humanoid shape and pincered arms, but the drones are thinner, less articulated.

A gleam of greenish light sparks behind the eyes. There's power; an active process, or only a residual charge? Edging closer, I hear a faint crackle from deep inside. One of the arms twitches and I jump away. The robot watches mutely.

I creep forward again and risk trailing a finger across the exterior.

The skin is practically seamless, though along joints, booted hydraulics peek out from the sleek frame. A thin crack on the chest catches my eye as tiny sparks dance inside. I wedge the blade of my multi-tool underneath it and run the length of the seam. Without warning, the plate slides off and crashes to the ground, exposing the inner workings.

It's fucking brilliant.

Lifeblood flows through arteries of high gauge wire. Thick cables transmit signals along a spine of alloy and polymer. Actuators. Hydraulic pistons. Transmitters. Processors. The schematics are as clear in my mind as any tangle of valves and veins would be to a surgeon with their patient's chest spread open on an operating table. I knocked the drone senseless with the EMP, but I have a strange urge to resuscitate and coax it back to life.

A tiny shower of sparks cascades from the neck. I reach out and let them shower my palm. There could be some serious voltage running rampant inside, but I don't care. The bits of heat tingle as the embers strike and then fade.

Muted glows deeper in the chest cavity flash on and off, in a definite pattern and not the frantic spurts of a system gone haywire. A process booting? Internal repair? The last spasms of life?

I delve into the chest cavity and brush aside wires until I locate the main power supply. It's an enclosed cylinder the size of my own chest marked with a radiological symbol. Not even with all the digging around at this crazy, secret bunker have I seen anything remotely this cool. The genius mind that built this death machine has all the wires bundled, color coded, and easily accessible. I would have done it this way myself. Maybe I even could. A titanium bodyguard at my command.

No. Bringing this beauty back to life and reprogramming her not to smash me into a pulp won't happen before I freeze to death. So, unlike a surgeon, I slice an artery. Knowing the right one to cut is too easy. Those traces of light in the faceted eyes fade and I slip past the lifeless shell.

How's that, Dad? Eliminate the threat. Don't pull punches.

The library is destroyed, and the air is filled with pungent smoke. Beneath the grating on the floor lies a pool of liquid metal and silicon, pulsing with heat. On the side facing the intense heat of the melted server, the terminal desk has buckled. Left without solid footing, the monitor lies smashed on the floor. I check the thumb drive in my pocket, just to be sure.

Away from the library, the frostbitten air of the fractured bunker takes hold.

You'll freeze to death in minutes, son.

I head to my cell and my limbs lose feeling within the first few steps. With shaking hands, I grab my backpack and drop my multi-tool in the outside pocket. My cell has managed to retain more heat than the hallway, but a shiver begins along my spine and spreads outward. A few more essentials—iPod, a plastic collector's case with my few remaining baseball cards— and the thumb drive all go in my backpack. Used to be sad that my entire life could fit in a backpack, but now, it's damn convenient.

I head for the airlock, forcing myself to wade into the frozen air. I squint into the glowing snowscape and shove my hands under my arms, trying to squeeze every last ounce of heat out of my body. No sign of Dad. With waxy fingers I fumble at the parka and gloves on the wall. The moon boots, too.

The new layers of clothing seem to do jack and shit. I tear my eyes off the gaping hole in my prison wall. There's heat in the library. All the other environmental controls seem to be shot whether from robot attack or the EMP. At the library's entrance, I stop short and gag as I hit a wall of smoke. Air so thick, it feels like the vaporized computer is trying to reassemble in my sinuses. But there's one more thing I need. I zip the parka hood tight around my face and skirt the edges of the smoking pit.

The shelves are mangled. Some are melted together, others crushed beneath the robot's charge. I sift through the debris until I find it, splayed open, the edges blackened. I stuff *The Swiss Family Robinson* in my backpack, and the library is the spare parts room again.

I slip by the lifeless robot, giving it a swift kick as I pass. I tripped the beacon maybe fifteen, twenty minutes ago and 'launched' the pod. Dad should've had plenty of time to get to the far side of wherever this lands. I huddle on the steps to the pod to wait.

If I'm launching into his custody again, I might as well make him fly his ass here to pick me up. The server bonfire should stay hot for a while and provide a bit of heat. Maybe I'll roast some marshmallows while I wait. Of course, we don't have marshmallows. Wonder how tasty these boots are?

Cold builds. Heat from the destroyed server isn't reaching into the safe room anymore. I could move to the crater. Maybe hole up in the pod. Dammit. He needs to see this—me standing over the smoking remains of this drone. Spencer Harrington, his powerless mini-not-me, kickin' robot ass. I'll wait. My teeth might grind to nubs from all this chattering, but I'll wait.

I'm not sure how much longer. An hour? Two? I try not

to look at the time on my iPod. Watched pots and stuff. Heat. Heat would be good. Slowly, my brain starts to degrade into a grey matter slushee. Those were good. Ice. Sugar. Ice. Mom would buy those for me. I'd freeze my brain. Like now. Maybe I should let him find me here all curled up and blue. They can thaw me out when the world is safe.

Then her face comes to me. Curious. Waiting.

I dig out my iPod. There's enough battery life left for a picture or two. He can believe that. Finding the right angle to get a shot of my face with the robot in the background is tricky. Harder still is the pose, especially with these shakes. Smile? Thumbs up? I balance the camera on the control panel and settle for an arms crossed gangsta pose with the shell of a battle robot over my shoulder.

Okay, only one option left. Hopefully I'll get at least a taste of freedom. I want to see how far I can get before Dad shows up. With his record, maybe he won't show at all.

CHAPTER 8

I PRESS THE BUTTON.

A full body restraint balloons out of hidden compart-ments. I'm stuffed in a body-sized blood pressure cuff, the little pump in the hands of a sadistic nurse. A bright flash travels down the launch tube, then darkness, and finally a wash of pure blue.

I feel a dam breaking inside and my blood shifts course and runs upstream. Darkness creeps in, and the deafening roar I've only now noticed fades. Flames lick the window of the capsule. Fire gives way to black. Crushed in the restraint, a ghostly white ring fills my sight then shrinks.

I'm not looking at the launch tube lights anymore. Instead, I see the thin reflection of overhead fluorescent lights tracing a chrome surface. It's the metal hoop at the top of a clothes rack. Puffy winter jackets dangle from hangers, and I'm encased in a nylon and polyester cocoon. Tinny sounding Muzak plays over hidden speakers. I pull my feet up so my mom won't see them.

"Ready or not, here I come!" she calls.

Being small has advantages, if you want to be a

hide-and-seek ace. Hangers rattle on a nearby rack. I hold my breath. She's close, so very close. There's no way she'll find me.

I can't let that happen.

Bursting out of the rack, I shout, "Surprise!"

Mom whirls with a playful look of shock on her face. Her soft hair whips her cheeks before settling back above her shoulders. She grabs me, pulls me close and says, "You're it!" Then a look of confusion crosses her face. "Hey, I don't think that's how we play this game!"

Pressing close to her chest, I listen for her pulse and try to feel the warmth. I inhale, taking in every scent I can. I search for her own personal perfume. Fresh pancakes and grass stains and bliss. For some reason, it isn't there. Who cares, right? This is just a dream after all. I start to cry. I'm a little kid right now, though so I guess that's all right.

"What's wrong?" She tries to push away but I won't let go.

"I missed you."

She kisses the top of my head. "Honey, you weren't gone that long. We would've found you."

I can't respond through the sniffling. Wait, *we*? There's nobody else here.

"You don't have to play anymore if it frightens you," she says as she strokes my hair.

I step back and wipe my nose. She looks worried but happy to have me here, not worried and fearful, like when I last saw her. I swat her arm and take off through the racks shouting, "You're it!"

Her stunned expression explodes into a spontaneous smile. But the expression doesn't quite fit. Sure, it's playful, but in a raw, unbridled way. Then, her eyes flash into glinting pools that reflect my face perfectly. My heart races and I duck into more winter cocoons, diving through vertical layers of fabric. Her laughter echoes in the strangely empty store.

We dash between aisles, slide behind cash registers, and at one point she steals a hat and shawl from a mannequin and stands completely still. I try to creep toward her and she begins to count.

The infectious, playful energy evaporates. The numbers drone in a lifeless procession. I back away, watching her immobile form, and then rush headlong into another rack of clothes.

I fill in the gap burrowed through the clothes. Her counting doesn't stop. Wild-eyed excitement once again pulls at the corners of my mouth and I struggle to keep still. Muscles twitch until every last fiber is tight and shaking with strain, but the crazy smile won't leave my face, couldn't, even if I had to hide here for a hundred years. Hangers rattle and as I try to reel in my excitement, I realize not only is the clothes rack shaking but the floor too.

"Mom?"

I part the wall of clothes and she's there, standing on the display pedestal, the mannequin's shawl defying gravity and fluttering in the air like stalks of submerged kelp. Her head is tossed back, and she basks in the circular glow of a strange light that devours the color from her skin.

"Mom?" This creepy distortion of a childhood memory is hard to process, and I know I'm older but my thoughts are trapped in this bottled moment. "Maybe you should hide. I'll find you."

Her head rolls forward, mouth drawn open. Her lips barely move. "Maybe you shouldn't find me. Maybe you can't."

"No! I can. I will. I love you, Mom."

"You do?" Life returns to her silver eyes and I don't understand the surprise at those simple words.

"Of course I do."

The cloak of light around her disperses. In the expanding blast, the walls of the department store disintegrate. A flat stretch of beach lies beyond, facing a tranquil sea. Ocean water hangs mid-crest, frozen in the rhythmic lapping of waves on the empty beach. A green expanse of jungle rises on one side, surrounding a grotto beneath a waterfall on the other.

Puffy coats have been replaced by lush ferns. I force through the foliage and head for the grotto shouting, "Mom!"

I'll find a bridge, a clearing, a tent, and a small stream. A hill with a sail cloth-framed treehouse. She'll be there, too. I know. In my rush, I snag a root and tumble into the ferns. But I don't hit solid ground. I fall. The light fades into a soupy green mess. An eruption of sound fills the air. Cracking, snapping, and hollow, damp explosions. All the while green leaves streak by until, with a thunderous smash, it stops.

*

"Mom!" No answer comes, but I think I've left the dream.

Towering trees, broad leaves and a green canopy rise outside the tiny viewport of the escape pod. No more endless white. Only the brightest points of light piercing the foliage. I've gone from Hoth to Endor on the freaking Wonkatania.

The canopy won't slide open. Somewhere near my chest there's a release lever, but I can't quite reach it cause Nurse

Ratched forgot to completely release the cuff. Elbows jabbing, hands wriggling, I frantically search for the lever, eager to get out. The cigar-shaped pod rocks to one side. With a twist, I shift to correct the roll. Too little, too late.

Outside, the view swirls between sunlight, green leaves, and a coffee brown. The pod with me in it is rolling down a steep embankment. For all I know, I'm careening toward a cliff, or plunging into a deep cavern. Here lies Spencer, survived a psycho robot, killed by a rescue pod.

Wherever I'm headed, the blender's plug gets pulled, violently. My head smashes into the little window followed by a hollow "thud". I'm sent spinning like a top. Gradually, the motion winds to a halt. Before I can breathe a sigh of relief, two sharp explosions fill the cramped space. Ears ringing, I squint as the canopy flies into the trees. Air and light rush in and the cuff deflates with a hiss. I dive out, a drowning man lunging for a rescue line. The pod tilts, and I tumble halfway out onto bare earth.

If I had to pick, I'd go shipwreck. Out-of-control bullet ride is total bullshit.

Doubled over the lip of the pod, my numb head presses into the dirt while my stomach thrashes. I can taste blood. Barely audible above my screaming ear drums, a woman calls out, "Oh my God! Are you okay?"

"Mom?"

The sound of dry leaves cascading downhill gets louder. My forehead lies flat on the cool earth and stubbornly, my head refuses to turn when I try to get a better look. My eyeballs feel disconnected and keep spinning, no matter how hard

I focus. I see running shoes and black, ankle-length stretchy pants approaching. Maybe an Augment?

Wiry arms encircle my chest and start to pull. My moon boots catch at an awkward angle along the frame. As much as I'd love to, I can't get my limbs to cooperate. She lifts and shifts and twists, struggling with my dead weight until the boot comes free and we tumble backwards. Smooth, damp, cool skin envelops my face for an instant and despite the mental numbness, my thawing hormones recognize the source.

Real, honest to God, non-digitized *breasts*. Goodbye, iPod diva.

The mystery girl struggles to her feet and drags me away from the crash site. Gently, she lays me on my side and kneels. A highlighted strand of dark brown hair has escaped her ponytail, dangling down her cheek. Her eyes glow with green flecks in the woodland light. Her lips are parted as if she's mid-sentence. No makeup, just sweat and a smudge of dirt, all forming a stunning image.

I feel violently ill. Stabilizing my spinning head and lurching stomach becomes a priority.

I roll over and clamber to my knees, palms flat on the ground. Standing would be a good start. Impressive, even. Heck, it would impress the hell out of me if I can manage to get vertical with the earth moving this much. I stagger to my feet while she keeps her hands poised to stop the impending face plant.

Figuring out some ingenious way of explaining how I crash landed in the woods that a) makes me sound badass, and b) convinces her I'm not an alien invader (unless she's into that) isn't working out at the moment. I could say something cool: *"Me? I've seen worse."* Or go the funny guy route: *"I meant to do that."*

Opening my mouth is a big mistake.

I really hope she didn't like those shoes.

CHAPTER 9

I F SHE'S UPSET about the shoes, it's confined to a quick wrinkle of her nose. This is followed by her grabbing my face in a businesslike manner and checking first my eyes and then the knot on my forehead, which I had no idea was there until her finger found it. All the while, I attempt to casually wipe flecks of vomit from my mouth.

I'm staring, trying to see past the weird blob blocking my view of those eyes. After a while, I figure out she's running her finger back and forth in front of my face. Obviously, playing it cool went out the hatch on the escape pod.

"We've got to move, fast," she says as she drapes my arm over her shoulder and starts dragging me up the ravine.

Several questions fight through the fog. Where's here? What's the rush? Why does her voice sound like she's talking to me at the bottom of a pool? None of these stray thoughts get past my lockjaw vomit defense. Then I realize I don't have my backpack. After a terrible round of charades which consists of my free arm limply flopping in the general direction of the pod, she catches on. She heads over and peeks inside.

Eventually, she comes up with my backpack. Even the

blurred vision and head trauma won't cover up the flashes of tight yoga pants and bending. I could've died, and all I can think about is this cute girl and her cute ass. Sounds reasonable. Throwing my backpack over her shoulder, she hustles to my side and starts dragging again.

At the top of the ravine lies a trail of complete destruction. A series of deep furrows mar the earth where the pod skipped across the forest floor. Several thick tree trunks jut from the ground in bouquets of splintered fibers, with their upper halves strewn across the clearing. The precarious lip of the ravine where the pod came to rest looks like some fairytale giant ground his heel in the loose dirt. A trail of crushed plants and scattered leaves leads to the bottom, where the pod rests against a massive and now scarred tree trunk. I'm suddenly grateful I passed out for a bit on that ride.

Her grip shifts to my shoulders, pushing down and guiding until I'm sitting on the ground.

"Rest for a second," she says.

I can't argue and as I start to lean back, her hands catch me. "Don't lie down, just rest." She starts dabbing at the side of my head with her shirt. "I was so not prepared for this."

My stomach is settling, but I have to keep the reply short. "You think I was?" Is that what an Augment would say? There's a snort, or a huff… hard to tell through the constant humming in my ears. When the heck does that go away? I try turning my head to see if she's smiling and pain stabs at my neck.

"Your father warned me about you."

She knows Dad. Obvious, yeah. But she has to say it for the fact to sink in, and for me to even remember how I got here.

"Where is he? Where's my dad?"

I have to turn my entire upper body to keep the neck pain at bay. She blocks the movement, straightens my shoulders and puts pressure on my forehead.

"Ow!"

"Stop squirming, I need to get the bleeding to stop."

Stopping bleeding. Right. Sounds like a plan, but she hasn't answered my question so I repeat, "Seriously, where's—"

"You're not where you should have been," she interjects.

"What?"

"The trajectory was off." She dabs the wound lightly as she speaks, slowly increasing the pressure and incidentally the pain. "There's a clearing north of here where you should've landed. Would've been a rough ride, but not this bad."

"Okay, okay, but where the hell did I land?" I mutter through gritted teeth.

She's looking everywhere but my direction as she answers, "Wardensville Wildlife Management Area. Outside of Winchester, Virginia. There's a forest service road about a kilometer from here. That's where my Bronc is."

"Nice to know." And we're up for the second pitch. "Where's my dad?"

"I'm sorry, we've got to start moving." She faces me and hauls me to my feet. I hang limply in front of her. I feel like Pinocchio, without the strings. Definitely sans cricket, as my eyes fasten to her breasts. Really, I've got to stop doing that, so uncool. She doesn't seem to notice when she steps away, half-crouched, her arms extended, waiting again for me to eat dirt.

"Here." She yanks the parka zipper, sliding it off my shoulders. As the weight falls, so do I.

And I really don't mind. The air is crisp and cool on damp skin. Crisp and cool—not stale and freezer-worthy. I'm living in a dream right now. Laying down in the dry leaves with the parka for a pillow sounds perfect. "You could join me," I babble.

"What? No, no! Come on." She's pulling me to my feet again. "Someone has to have seen this. You could've been followed. We have to leave."

"What's the worst that could happen? Another robot shows up and I kick its ass? I need a nap. It's been a long day, um... who are you?"

"Emily. My name's Emily. I'm a friend of your father's."

"Right, you said that, but where *is* he?"

"My car isn't far from here. We've got to get you to a doctor and make sure you're all right. We have to get somewhere safe."

Strike three.

I hate safe. I'm done with safe. Put me on the Tilt-a-Whirl again without my seatbelt. Sounds good in my head, but the words don't leave my mouth. At least I don't think they do. Things start fuzzing over again, as she hefts me off the ground and starts the equivalent of a three-legged race with Stephen Hawking as a partner.

"That was *so* inappropriate."

I guess I am talking out loud.

"Yes," she manages between breaths.

The frantic energy that's been buzzing around since I first saw the bunker doors melt open has completely abandoned me.

My body hurts and burns behind a dull curtain of fatigue that I don't want to lift. I'm starting to slip to the ground again.

"Spencer… let's… move." She's getting tired hauling my useless ass around, so if she's an Augment, strength isn't on her power list. She's persistent, though, and soon I'm leaning heavily on her shoulder.

"Spencer, I can't carry you out of here," she pants, even as she flops my lifeless body through the woods. So maybe no super-strength, but the workout clothes aren't a joke. She lapses into an athletic trance and begins puffing to a cardio beat, synchronized with my dangling head.

A part of my brain feels bad and wants to help. It's also connected to that same part that's wired into my hormones and replaying the highlight reel of her retrieving my backpack. Yeah, it would have been nice to impress this girl by being a complete badass and shaking this off, but no—crippling reentry-vehicle ride for the win.

She's forging through the woodland brush. In between breaths, she starts cheerleading, "You can do it Spence, you can do it. One more step. Let's just make it to the Bronc. We'll stop by Hamburger Hut on the way to see that doctor."

That's it. That's her power. Some kind of mental manipulation or maybe a psychology degree. With the word "hamburger", my feet come back online.

CHAPTER 10

I DON'T EVEN BLINK as I dribble ketchup on the blood pressure cuff.

"Hey kid, do you have to eat that right now?"

"Yes," I say, wet, sloppy, and through a wad of half-chewed cheeseburger.

Emily's doctor friend's first name is Martin, last name, 'A' something. I can tell he's one of those guys that wears scrubs all the time. He's even got a surgical mask around his neck and he's not doing any surgery. He probably showers with it.

Besides, who keeps a blood pressure cuff in their study at home? Of course, the study is pretty well-equipped. The big, polished wooden desk I've parked my ass on is free of finger-prints and smudges, so I doubt he's putting the all-in-one, twenty-four-inch monitor/computer through its paces. Neat rows of books fill a tall, built-in bookcase under the vaulted ceiling—the kind of books that look old, might even be old, but nobody has ever so much as creased their spines.

About what I expected when we rolled up the drive. Some dude with more money than time. Although, I'd really been hoping Emily's friend was old. And fat. Instead, he's rich and in decent shape. Might even be good-looking if she's into that tall, dark and handsome look.

Fine, so much for getting the girl, but nobody is interrupting my assault on this hamburger. If the Black Beetle himself shows up, he's waiting for me to lick the cheese off the wrapper before I kick his ass and make Doc Abercrombie here look bad. I wonder if the defibrillator over there would fry any of the electronics in a battle robot…

"Where'd you say you found this kid?" Martin's looking more through me than at me.

"Oh, I was…" Emily prepped a cover story during the ride over here. It was lame. I should probably intervene. I'm an accomplished liar when it comes to personal details. All part of the son-of-an-Augment lifestyle.

"I was mountain biking, out on the trails." Emily glares from behind the doc as I continue, "She whipped into the parking lot at the trailhead and nearly ran me over with her rust bucket on wheels."

"It's a Bronco," Emily fires from the doorway.

"Felt like a freight train."

The good doctor decides to play ump. "Okay, kid, so you can't go to your own doctor because?"

"First, I'm not a kid. Yeah, I haven't gone to med school, yet, but after high school I wanted to get a taste of the real world before I cured cancer or whatever. The real world, unfortunately, doesn't include health insurance."

"What about your parents?" With that question from Martin, Emily's bemused stare takes on a whole new level of *shut-the-hell-up.*

"I moved out for a reason, Nurse—what's your name?" He doesn't look the least bit fazed by the remark.

"It's Alexander. Doctor Alexander," he says.

"Right. No insurance, and I figured your girl here would prefer a private consultation as opposed to a police report."

Martin flashes Emily a worried look and with a shake of his head grabs a penlight. He checks my eyes, maybe blasting my retinas a bit longer than necessary.

"Okay, so what's your name?"

"Spencer. Spencer Johnston," I say. Emily lowers her head and places her hand across her brow.

"And who is the President of the United States?"

I start to wonder exactly how long I've been shut up in an Arctic bunker. "Barack Obama?"

Martin steps back and gives an appraising sort of look that doctors must practice in the mirror. Either that or I just guessed the wrong President.

"What's the date today?"

I can't help but laugh and I take another bite of the hamburger. That, Doc, is an excellent question.

"Well?"

Emily's trying to curl up and hide behind her facepalm. Let's see, warm outside, might even be the middle of summer, or spring? I saw a lot of Maryland license plates on the way over, when I wasn't staring at Emily and drooling on myself. That was pathetic. She kept reaching over to wake me up. I'm not even sure if I was passed out or not. The entire ride is a blur of breasts, traffic lights, and buildings larger than a boxcar. Serious sensory overload for the bubble boy escapee.

Until the drive-thru at Burger Hut.

A triple cheeseburger, grande fries and Mega-Gulp soda all prompted the second coming of Spencer Harrington. I've never done drugs, but I seriously feel like I'm tripping balls right now. I'm free. I'm warm. I'm eating a cheeseburger and sucking down two thousand calories of pure sugar, while riding around with an exceptionally fine chauffeur. I should have climbed in that pod on day two.

I'm also doing it again. Staring. My upper peripheral vision shows me Emily is working her fingers on her forehead like she's bidding at an auction. Oh.

"Um, five… two… two… May. May twenty second."

Doc doesn't appear impressed. He gives the face again. The one that can say "Congratulations on your new baby" and "Sorry, you have cancer" at the same time. I shrug and cram the rest of the hamburger in my mouth.

"Well, I think you're going to be fine. You've got signs of a mild concussion, several contusions and lacerations—"

"Cuts and scrapes."

"Yeah, cuts and scrapes. You need to go to an emergency room and get checked out. Everything appears fine, but I can't rule out internal injuries. I was headed into work when you called, Em. If you want, I can take Mr. Johnston with me and run a few more tests."

"Actually, Doc, I'll have your girlfriend drop me by there on her way home." Disappointingly, he doesn't object to the girlfriend speculation. I slide off the desk and head toward the hallway. "Come on, let's get those X-rays. I might drop dead any second."

She glares, "Mr. Johnston, want to give me a minute?" Emily walks into the study, her lips pursed together and one hand on the doorknob.

"Fine, I'll be out at the car. Maybe I can buff the blood off the front fender."

"You'll wait in the hall if you want a ride." She has one hand on the door and her eyebrows are knitted together. Accepting her ultimatum with another shrug seems to satisfy her and she shuts the study door.

I debate eavesdropping but that's forgotten the second I peek into the living room. There's a 72-inch LCD TV just hanging there, all quiet and lonely. Hurdling into the leather sectional, I groan when I hit, and scan for the remote through pain-narrowed vision.

The rest of the furniture is a mixture of glass and chrome floating over marble tile. An elaborate picture frame surrounds the wall-mounted TV. This setup turns the TV into a prop that probably never gets watched. After what I've been through, I've got no respect for the waste of a good television.

"Where's the remote? You do watch this thing, right?"

There's no response until Emily emerges from the office and spears a finger toward the door. I get up, slowly, and glance into Martin's office as I pass. He nods with a puzzled look and I follow Emily outside. She doesn't say a word as we pile into her Bronco.

*

We've made it out past the tree-lined drive of the doc's estate and onto the rural highway that winds through idyllic countryside before Emily finally speaks. "That wasn't what we discussed." She sounds a little pissed.

"C'mon. A wounded hiker in the woods? I had to up the stakes a bit."

"I've spent months out there with my research. I hear about stuff like that from the rangers all the time. Besides, you practically told him your name."

"My first name. How many times have you had to change your name and relocate because some reporter got too curious, or some Augment groupie-stalker-weirdo got too close to the truth? You ever try to consistently answer to a first name that isn't yours?"

Emily frowns, her eyes glued to the road ahead. The rusted-out 4x4 rattles onward in a fury of roaring exhaust and wind noise. She shifts gears on the aging beast with the confidence of someone that's changed the oil, the brakes, done a few tune-ups, and isn't afraid to get some dirt under her unpolished, trimmed nails.

"How many times?"

As many as you want? I've launched into more fantasizing; mechanic's overalls, maybe a lab coat and not much else. Arctic isolation is an icy bitch.

Emily repeats, patiently, "How many times have you moved?"

"Oh, uh well, twelve, thirteen? Probably more."

She nods, eyes on the darkening highway. "Must've been tough."

"It wasn't that bad. You get used to it." I can sense more

questions of the type I don't normally answer. "So, how do you know Crimson Mask?"

Her expression stays the same. "We've worked together before."

"Are you… an Augment?"

A hint of a smile breaks her focused stare. "No. No, I'm not an Augment. No secret identity. Just me, Emily Radke, PhD."

"PhD? Right, you mentioned research."

"Yep."

"In what?" I say, sounding a bit more shocked than intended.

"What, surprised?" She glances my way. "Biomedical sciences and microbiology, with a focus in pathophysiology, thanks for asking."

"Is that how you know Abercrombie—"

"Who?"

"The good doctor back there, what's-his-face."

"Martin. Doctor Martin Alexander." Her emphasis is on "Doctor". "You were extremely rude. He was trying to help."

"It's a gift. I'll probably never see the guy again, who cares?"

"I've known him for years, so I care."

"Yeah, I sorta figured he was your boyfriend."

"He's not my boyfriend."

"That's too bad. You're probably not his type. Me, I actually prefer girls with PhDs running around the woods in yoga pants."

There's that awkward snort again. I knew she was laughing earlier. "Well, it wasn't my first choice. I've been practically living in the WMA for a few months now. The lake has been a

breeding ground for *Cryptosporidium parvum* since early spring."
She frowns. "I left a whole batch of samples and a decent tent."

"I got the impression you were waiting for me."

"Don't flatter yourself. The research was legit, if boring. But
yes, you were the main reason I focused on that area. Anyway,
you're lucky. The alert from the beacon caught me right before
my morning run. I was about to give up on waiting when the
pod hit. What took so long? I thought maybe the array had
been damaged or malfunctioned."

Now she's talking my language and I need a change of subject anyway. "How were you picking up the signal? A sat phone?
Immarsat maybe?"

"No. Think Iridium, only this is military-grade hardware
with a specifically nonmilitary encryption routine."

"Can I see?"

"Sure. Behind my seat. Careful, it's still plugged into the
laptop."

In the floorboard sits an open duffel bag cradling a bundle of electronic goodness. The satellite phone is sick. A sleek,
rubberized shell houses the phone, which is about the size of
a walkie-talkie. Aside from a speaker and a couple of buttons,
there isn't much else there. This is a far cry from the giant box
I converted into my TV antenna. A data cable runs to a laptop
that's also made for serious fieldwork—one of those housings
you can run over with a truck, drop in a pool, put through a
sandstorm, and still be able to get more than a Blue Screen of
Death.

"Correction, I prefer girls that run around the woods in
yoga pants with kickass tech."

"Honey, biologically speaking, I'm old enough to be your..." She stops, her face momentarily a paler shade, and her hands grip the steering wheel a bit tighter than necessary. "Your big sister."

"I don't have a big sister."

I'm surprised how much that hurts. I'm not even sure why it matters that she knows.

"Spencer, I'm sorry."

I close the laptop and try not to make eye contact. Outside, the city highway streams by in glaring neon and sodium orange, rising up to push the fading sun behind the horizon. The thrill of escaping certain death, the excitement of being out of my meat locker hideout, the tub of caffeine I sucked down, all slip away with the light.

Emily seems to know a lot more about me than I know about her. Dad. Mom. I don't understand why Dad, with all of his training and bullshit Augment lessons, wouldn't have told me about her. Telling me what to expect when the pod came crashing to earth seems important. Why am I always the only one who doesn't know?

I'm ready to confront him. Tell him what I think of his rules and his idea of "safe", and the strangers he's sent to drag me out of whatever mess he's made. Not to mention his attendance at the funeral of a terrorist psychopath, alongside an evil genius psychopath. I'll top it off with the picture in front of the fried Black Beetle drone and tell him he can stop protecting me.

"Last time. My dad. Where is he?" I can't look at Emily. I can only stare at the laptop case clenched tightly in my hands.

"Spencer, I don't know."

CHAPTER 11

"**S**IR." SOFT AND tinny through a hidden speaker, Xamse's voice blended with the hum of machinery in the lab.

Drake stifled a sigh before the breath could fog his face mask. He continued tracing the labyrinthine lines of a schematic floating on a sheet of light in front of him. He muttered a series of numerals and formulae, his eyes narrowed in concentration. At the wave of his gloved hand, the schematics slid by effortlessly.

"Sir..." The speaker crackled. Drake closed his eyes and moved his hand to his forehead as Xamse persisted, "The fifth circuit, sir."

"Excuse me?" Drake's iron tone faltered.

"You speak of the fifth circuit."

Drake returned his attention to the schematic he'd been muttering about only moments ago. Carefully tracing the wiring, he counted back to exactly five and sneered. "You know why ants are so fascinating, Xamse?" The laboratory buzzed in the background as Drake continued, "They are fascinating because their brains, smaller than the head of a pin, allow them to efficiently complete tasks with an absolute precision which would baffle the chaotic minds and actions of a collection of greater creatures. Do you know why that is, Xamse?"

"Ants are very smart, sir?" came Xamse's hesitant reply.

Drake strode across the lab, the swish of sterile coveralls breaking the monotonous hum. Brightly lit, the clean, white walls were empty with the exception of the single holographic projection. Tables lined the room, their surfaces covered with beakers, hoses, and blinking screens. Walking past a sealed metal cabinet in the center, Drake stopped at a table where thick glass sandwiched a column of dirt snaked with tunnels. He watched as a stream of ants ferried fragments between the see-through chambers. "Ants don't think. They simply do. They pursue a highly-focused group of tasks without question, deviation, or individual thought."

"I understand, sir."

Drake was entirely sure Xamse understood. "You, Xamse, are an ant. You do not think, you simply do. You complete the tasks I assign. Efficiently. Without thought. In fact, I prefer you not to use those words."

"Which words?"

"Think. Thought."

"Yes, sir."

"Now, did you interrupt my research to eavesdrop, or do you have a better reason?"

"No, no eavesdropping, sir. Only following your protocols to report on the Arctic team, sir."

"Ah, you're learning already. However, I'm quite sure they've failed to recover anything of use." Drake's dark eyes flicked to one side, and an inset video sprang to life on the hologram.

In that video, fire and smoke flared from a crowded highway full of blackened shells. Emergency lights strobed in the background. "There had better not be a problem with our cargo from Mumbai."

"No, sir. But the Arctic team reports the boy escaped the bunker, sir…"

"Inconsequential. The video of him already served its purpose. The team's main objective should have been securing any data that may have survived. Now, perhaps instead of interrupting my work for such trivial nonsense, you'd prefer to be back home, Xamse?"

A desperate reply crackled on the intercom. "No. No, sir. One report you will find important, sir. The last command I sent to U5345 was for a status update. I have only now received a reply. A signal from U5345. Inside the Eastern United States."

Drake folded his arms. "More specific."

Xamse began eagerly, "U5345. The drone sent—"

"Yes, the drone sent to the Arctic bunker. A glitch? Satellite echo?"

"No, sir." Xamse filled the silence that followed. "I checked. Three times, I checked. Duration was too long for an echo, and I sent a verification command exactly as you trained me. There was a link established. I received a reply."

Drake reached up to the holographic screen, flicking the schematic closed with a terse wave and revealing a liquid black background. Another stab, and a keypad appeared. As Drake's fingers darted across the surface, the screen blinked. A slowly revolving image of the Earth came into view encased in a network of red trails, each trail terminating at a separate triangular focal point. These points dotted the globe in several places, but a large cluster floated somewhere above the Indian Ocean.

"System, display U5345 at last status check."

The globe spun and the eastern seaboard of the United States exploded into view, re-centering on a single, blinking triangle. Numbers reporting the time, date, longitude, latitude, and signal duration scrolled beneath the triangle as it trailed along a stretch of rural highway.

"Only 47.8 seconds, sir."

"That drone was recovered several hours ago, was it not?"

The speaker squawked back to life. "Yes, sir. Per the report, the drone sustained severe systems damage due to—"

Drake interrupted Xamse's report with the suddenness and precision of a guillotine. "Terminate communication."

He stood motionless before the hologram, the blinking red marker pulsing in his dark eyes. As he considered the possibilities, a wicked grin burst across his face. He knew the preliminary damage report gave an account of extensive system failure. Improperly shielded, the EMP pulse had fried most of the inner circuitry, and this had been followed by a crude incision along the main power relays.

He could think of only one explanation for the contact. Was it possible that a tiny colony of his creations had survived the electromagnetic assault? A force too dispersed and too incredibly small to be bothered by the mere charged particles of an EMP? The line of reasoning made his stomach flutter and brought a fringe of dampness to his eyes.

As Drake stared at the screen, the triangular blip flashed again. Another wave of his hand, and the view centered again on the marker for U5345. With a brisk gesture, the area surrounding it filled the screen.

A narrow city block appeared, outlined by a square cluster of matching buildings. Each structure was rounded off on the inner corners, creating a courtyard dotted with vibrant flowerbeds. The red tracking triangle loomed large on the screen above the southeast building.

Drake addressed the empty lab, "System, resume communication, command center." Overhead, the speakers buzzed an angry tone.

"Yes, sir?" Xamse asked.

"Monitor the signal from U5345. Notify me of any changes and provide a full status before our cargo arrives."

He cut the connection before receiving an answer, certain Xamse would comply. That, and he could hardly maintain his composure. After only six months of field testing, the simple possibility that they, the nanomechs, his most glorious creation, had managed to contact him in an environment well outside their programmed role filled him with genuine pride.

Nanomechs evolving ahead of their original programming, his greatest threat neutralized; still, Drake found it impossible to shake the sense of unease from earlier in the day. There had been minor setbacks, the boy escaping for one, but he was hardly a threat to the plan. Yet uneasiness about the communication with Killcreek lingered. He called out once more.

"And track every transmission made over the secure channel to and from Killcreek. If someone so much as accidentally keys the mike, I want to know about it."

"Of course, sir."

CHAPTER 12

EMILY'S APARTMENT IS what people never trapped in an Arctic bunker might call an efficiency. The breakfast nook and the living area share the same space, separated only by a change from fake wood to linoleum. Right off the nook is the kitchen, complete with a dishwasher, microwave, and refrigerator. The pantry door is open and a stacked washer and dryer combo sits inside. Cozy, sure, but hardly "efficient" compared to the bunker.

Emily's in the pantry with a bag of clothes she brought in from the Bronco. The campfire and motor oil smell are being drowned out by the rich aroma from her coffeemaker.

"Whoa. A washer and dryer." At the bunker most of the housework was done with kilocalories. Not that I washed dishes or clothes often.

"Not sure how you could've made it without them," Emily says as she stuffs an armload of clothes into the washer.

I sniff my shirt: stale body odor, melted computer parts, and a hint of hamburger. The body odor is the kind you can only harvest in an environment made entirely of recirculated air. It holds its own versus the coffee and spring fresh detergent.

I wander into the living room, hopefully dragging the stench with me.

She's got a television and a well-worn couch calling my name. I would have immediately sunk into it and flicked on the TV had she not set the laptop on the kitchen table. Despite the wonderland I've crashed into, the thumb drive feels heavy in my pocket and I'm eager to find the time to get at the data.

On the living room walls are several seriously bizarre prints. Landscapes? Moonscapes? I'm not sure what they are. Maybe Lovecraftian acid trips committed to canvas. "Who's the, uh, artist?"

Emily looks over with a cup of detergent in one hand and a cup of coffee in the other. "Artist? Oh, me, I guess."

"You made these? Are they computer graphics?"

She nearly empties the coffee into the washing machine, stops, and dumps in the detergent before walking into the living room. "No, I just framed them. They're photographs."

"You're kidding. I mean, where'd you go to get a shot of Cthulhu here?"

"*That* is an image from an electron microscope of a blue bottle maggot. About one hundred times magnification."

"Most people put up family pics. Maybe knockoff prints."

Her expression is wistful while she launches into an explanation. "Hey, that maggot was a pretty big part of my college life. You spend years looking at that ugly mug and it grows on you."

"Wow." She's insane. I can't decide if that makes her hotter or not.

She walks toward me, absently folding a t-shirt from the

dryer and keeping her eyes on the freaky picture. "Once sterilized, those guys can be placed on wounds. They eat the infection, essentially."

"Jesus, that's twisted." I move closer to examine the picture, not sure what else to say.

"C'mon. It's got to be a little fascinating for a boy?"

Sure, the whole maggot artwork thing is pretty cool but, did she just say I was a *boy*? I've dealt with that bullshit my whole life. Teachers, friends, girls. Girls. Especially girls. Forget being a Lollipop Guild stand-in. "I'm not a boy. Doc and I went over that already."

"Sorry, my bad." There's a long silence before I hear her padding toward the laundry again. I glance her way and see her shutting the washer door. She calls out over her shoulder, "We can wash yours next if you like."

"Only if you're tired of the smell."

She laughs. "So, the real family pics are by the television."

Wondering how that could have anything to do with my "Eau de Bunkair", I check out the frames scattered around the entertainment center. Emily, with what has to be her parents. And then dudes. Lots of dudes. She's pretty attractive so it makes sense, but then I notice one picture with the whole cast of them. "Is that a family reunion?"

"The one in front of the house? Yeah, Christmas. My parents, brothers."

"Cousins? Uncles?"

"All brothers."

I whistle and make a quick count, "Eight brothers? Wow. What's that like?"

"Smelly. But fun. Always had someone to go digging around the creek for frogs with or play catch."

"Baseball?"

"Pigskin."

"Figures," I groan. "Contact sports and mud under your fingernails. Bet your parents were glad they had a girl."

Another quirky laugh and I wander over to the laptop on the kitchen table. "So, what's the password?"

"Nope."

"That's pretty easy. You should have eight or more characters and a mix of letters, numbers. Long phrases work best."

"I mean, no password for you."

"Why not?"

"You need to get some rest."

I head for my backpack, conveniently dropped in a chair on the other side of the kitchen table, and dig out my multitool. I flip out the screwdriver and start to remove the laptop's case screws.

"And what are you doing?"

"If I pop the BIOS battery, it might reset the initial password."

"Cute. I said no."

"Yeah, and you also said you didn't know where my dad is."

"Spencer, I don't. Honestly." Her voice trails into a whisper. "I wish I did."

"I see. More of the 'keep Spence in the dark and feed him shit' routine. Been there, done that. I should be sprouting mushrooms by now." My hand hovers over the keys.

"That analogy, I can appreciate. But I'm still saying no."

"C'mon. If I'm forced to start guessing passwords I might get you locked out."

She shrugs and keeps sorting clothes as she replies, "The laptop was for research mostly, but also to monitor the signal from Hotel One. So as of right now, I don't use it much." She's calling my bluff. I sigh, set my multi-tool on the table, and drop into a chair.

Through the kitchen window lies an open courtyard. The darkness shines with flared pools of landscape lighting. The colors on the flowers seem incredibly vibrant. Under the lights, they glow as if they're plugged in, too. So different.

"Hotel One? That's what you called the bunker?" I call out, but Emily doesn't answer right away. "I've got a few more names for Popsicle One if you ever want to hear them."

"No. I'm sure I don't," she replies, softly this time.

I can feel her eyes on me as I stare into the brick courtyard. With Dad, you can feel his gaze, too. A presence, a weight, that could crush you as easily as his inhumanly powerful hands. Her's is different. A feeling I'm not used to anymore.

"I just want to know what's going on. For once," I say as I switch from the flowers to the reflection in the window. Emily's standing right behind me.

She hesitates. "I don't know any more than you do." Her jaw flexes and she looks at me with a forced smile, "Go get some sleep. You need it. I'll come get you once I find anything out. I'm sure he'll be back by the time you wake up."

"I don't need anyone to protect me. Check this out."

"Spencer…"

Snatching my backpack, I pull out the iPod and bring up the photo.

There I am, hamming it up with that… beast… looming in the background. A shiver runs down my spine. The dark figure stands frozen in the breach of what used to be impregnable safe room doors. Doors that shattered like an eggshell. Then there's me, oblivious to the terror right below the surface of my skin.

She's already watching expectantly. It's a little late to put away the picture.

"Check it out."

She looks puzzled as she takes the iPod and stares at the screen. Puzzled goes to shocked at warp speed. She jerks the tiny screen closer.

"Spencer Harrington! What, what the hell?"

This is the part I've been waiting for—where I retell the glorious story of how I single-handedly took out a drone. The words won't form. My hardcore selfie was supposed to impress Dad, not her. Maybe get me out of the kid's club. But her scolding tone hits with an arctic blast of reality. No matter what I say, I *am* a kid to her. She's some biology genius that runs around with Augments and probably feels pity for "normal" people, like me.

"What were you thinking?" Her face is frozen. Shock, horror, I'm not sure what all is going on. I turn to the window as she continues, "You waited there for it? Were you trying to get yourself killed?"

"No. Well, yes and then no."

"I was going to ask why you had to leave. I mean, I figured

it was traumatizing. I'd give you time before prying too much. But I didn't know you had a death wish!"

"It was pretty friggin' easy, for your information!" My thoughts scramble farther away from sounding impressive, in control. Dad could always sound that way. If he was ordering pizza, it came out as an earth-shattering event. My voice is small and reedy. "Look, the EMP backwash from the launch disabled it. Then, I unplugged it like a desk lamp. No problem."

"That thing could have torn you apart!" Then her stare moves beyond the muted glow of the iPod screen still clutched in her hands. Maybe she's starting to see my sheer genius. Any minute now, she'll congratulate me on a job well done. By the expression when she looks up, I know I'm way off base and need to intervene.

"I fried a robot! Look, look at the photo! Me!"

"Once fired, the launch tube would require an adjustment or realignment. The slightest shift could translate into miles off-course." Her voice ratchets up in decibels, "That's why you missed the landing site!"

"What part of 'I took out a robot' are you not hearing? Come on, give me some credit!"

"When I saw the pod overshoot the field, I thought I was going to have to tell Sean you were dead!"

"Sean, huh?" Nobody calls him that. Except Mom. Even in his cover identities it was always "Mr. Insert-Name-of-the-Month-Here".

Emily stands absolutely still. Her lips part and she shakes her head before speaking. "Spencer, it's been a long day." Her brow is knotted and she clutches her elbows as her fingers clench and relax. She's suddenly radiating a helplessness which I'm intimately familiar with.

"You really don't know where he is?"

She turns away and makes the short trip to the living room. Motioning for me to sit, she lowers herself into the couch and reaches for the remote. "I was avoiding this, waiting for you to be asleep. C'mon, let's see what we can find out."

Nice. No direct link or high-tech communicator. She has to watch the news, too.

CHAPTER 13

I T DOESN'T TAKE long to find the reports. My family's well-protected secret is on network television 24/7 for everyone else to see. I've never been able to appreciate the irony. Worried about Dad? He's always as close as a tube, a mesh of LCDs, or a plasma bulb will allow.

The cable news channels run the story nonstop. Local stations scroll updates beneath their normal shows. A battle, death tolls, the Crimson Mask, the Black Beetle... Of course, he had to save the world again.

The tone is more frantic though. Right away, I can tell something else must've happened, something big. Emily settles on a channel and pulls her knees up to her chest.

A slick-haired anchor speaks with a calm voice and perfect intonation. He's backlit by scorched highway scenes straight out of a zombie apocalypse movie. "...continue following events in Mumbai, where earlier today, the Crimson Mask again went head-to-head with the Black Beetle and a small army of drones. The attacks left several blocks in ruins. At last count, one hundred and fifty-seven people are dead or wounded."

Images cycle behind the anchor. Explosions on a crowded

highway blossom into orange pillars writhing beneath tendrils of black smoke. Buildings wear the faces of war, gnarled maws of brick and metal beneath blasted, windowed eyes. Crowds run thick across rippled pavement strewn with the empty shells of vehicles.

"Our correspondent Krina Singh is live, speaking to witnesses of today's tragic attack."

A news anchor, her oval face framed by shiny locks of hair too perfectly draped for the devastation around her, steps into view. Beside her stands a dark-skinned man with a bushy black mustache, his mouth a tight purple band snapping rapidly as he spits a stream of harsh consonants and heavy vowels into the microphone. The correspondent nods crisply and retracts the mike, translating the man's words, "'They are all terrorists,' this man says. 'These men have dared to be gods and brought only death to peaceful people. They are shatterers of worlds, and the countries that created these monsters should be held accountable.'" The camera pans out to the wrecked city. "I've been hearing these sentiments from nearly everyone here on the streets of Mumbai…"

I grab the remote and start surfing. I don't need to hear this shit. One of these channels has to have footage of what went down. Stations float by wildly. Talking dogs. Laughing kids. A guy fixing his car with a blue pill floating in the background. Commercials—one thing I didn't miss in the bunker. Finally, I find another station with coverage.

"…battled with the robot forces of the notorious Black Beetle. The attack started in the early morning hours as millions of workers in the world's most densely-populated city were leaving for work. Our news affiliate from CNBC-TV18 brought us this footage live from the scene. We're still trying to contact senior correspondent Rafi Adani, and our thoughts are with him and all of Mumbai tonight."

The footage rolls into a close-in shot of Dad. He's rocketing full force toward the ground, a highway covered in death and destruction beneath him.

I've never seen news footage this clear of any Augment in action. A jigsaw line of jagged sheet rock is briefly visible along the edge of the frame. They're filming out of the upper floor of an office building from where a wall used to stand. Looking down on the chaotic scene gives a perspective like a chess board with the pieces arrayed mid-play. There's a familiarity about the actions of the drones, but I can't quite put a finger on it.

I'm anxious to see Dad again, but the view crushes that anxiety. There are dozens of drones. They're running rampant in the streets, hovering in the air, taking potshots at buildings, vehicles, fleeing motorists.

Two talking heads start jabbering, and the scene shrinks to an inset. The word "surrender" parses my hazy thoughts, but I focus past the talk.

"Go back to the video!" I shout. Pointless yelling at a TV, at prerecorded footage, I'm screaming into the past, but I can't help it. I realize I'm off the couch and hammering the volume to hear the inset's audio above the banter. News anchors' voices echo in the tiny apartment. Emily lightly touches my arm.

"Spencer..." Her voice is pleading, but I shake off her hand.

In the smaller picture, Dad collides with one of the drones

midair and it buckles, arms flailing under the force. The drone recovers quickly, and a torrent of sparks and errant tracers spew from a hidden cannon. Dad shields his face, palms out, forearms laced, and bullets ricochet across the dead freeway.

As the drone empties a cannon harmlessly into Dad's face, the other drones pause. It's brief but noticeable. Then, two break away while the rest go back to work, slaughtering people—people cowering in their cars, people running for cover, people being idiots and peeking around corners with smart phones in hand. Anyone is fair game.

While Dad responds to the nearest drone, the oddness I couldn't place my finger on starts to materialize—it's a storm of pawns. His opponent is twisting Dad's stupid mantras against him. Whittling down his defenses through blind sacrifice while bringing the most carnage possible. This threat cannot be neutralized and was never made to be. The important pieces have been kept out of reach, stalling for time. For this moment.

The lead-spraying drone lashes out with a clawed hand and Dad steps to the side, grabbing the arm and tearing it free in a shower of hydraulic fluid and metal shavings. A backhand smash, and the drone's head launches down the highway out of view as the knees go slack.

At that instant, Dad's eyes snap to his wrist. The beacon.

Motionless, he stares down while two drones blast in, rockets flaring white-hot from metal boots. They skip their cannons and careen into him, full force.

Dad and the collection of tin go hurtling toward the breach in the news studio wall. The melee goes off screen, above the shot. Brick and glass rain as screams erupt from a floor above.

Once again, the video inset takes up the whole screen and the talking heads fall silent.

"Get back, get back!" I hear a thickly accented voice calling amid cries of shock. It's all accented by a language with a hurried, frantic pace that only adds to the panic level. Vaguely, I'm aware of Emily's hand searching for mine and she grips it tightly.

"Spencer, you don't have to watch." Her eyes never leave the screen.

"Shhh!"

From off camera, a mangled drone cartwheels into the street below. The camera shudders—or is it the building?

A dark mass of twisted steel and crimson plummets by the hole. Rising, the camera jostles to the edge. The tangled ball hurtles to the earth and I see a drone peel away while the other wriggles helplessly between Dad and the approaching pavement.

The camera pans out and I stay with Dad. Pavement shatters as the drone becomes scrap. Dad's already assessing the scene before the powdered metal has even settled. I see him scan the carnage and check his wrist, again. There, street-level, surrounded by mutilated corpses, burning vehicles, homicidal robots, and the screams of the dying, Dad roars and wades in, flinging off robots with mighty shrugs and vicious maneuvers. He shouts in rage, mincing drones with bare hands at a furious pace. Eliminate the threat. Don't pull your punches. It's all the same, but a hidden fire burns behind every inhuman burst of strength as he plows through the drones. So furious are his attacks, the drones begin to hurtle at him, en masse. Dozens of fast pitches thrown from every angle, and Dad contacts each one with closed fists, feet, knees, forehead, elbows in a flurry of destructive force.

The camera swerves and shakes and for a second the view becomes a fuzzy patch of brick and blue sky. A dark shape hurtles by, jerking in and out of frame as the hurried voice of the cameraman sounds in the background.

The Black Beetle's battle armor lands atop a mangled car with all the grace of a falling meteor. Wheels fly out from beneath the tiny foreign vehicle as the remains crumple into a wafer-thin slice of cheap steel. Those drones that can fall back.

Only, this isn't the Black Beetle. No way it fits the strategy for him to be there in person. Besides, I've seen him up close and personal, picked apart one of his drones. This one's a cleverly disguised drone made to look like the real deal. A near-perfect imitation. Dad has to be able to tell. He has to see it.

Emily grips my hand tighter, "It's okay. It's okay. He's going to be fine." She sounds unconvinced.

The drones fade and the Black Beetle steps forward. Dad tenses and his foot digs several inches into the concrete. With bent knees he prepares to launch, but he holds back. Maybe he can sense it's a setup, too. Images of the Black Beetle and Dad on a Navy carrier come to mind. Maybe it's not a setup at all.

With a maniacal laugh, the Black Beetle extends a deadly pincer and a beam of light streams into the air, fading into nothing inches above his head. "Have you had enough killing today, Sean?" Light spreads from the focused beam to create a glimmering curtain. The curtain begins to separate into dark and light streams which slowly collect into a monochromatic image of ghostly white and dim blue. "Or shall I order one more execution?"

The camera zooms in. A face wavers on the surface of the hologram like a reflection in a stream.

It's me.

Emily lets go of my hand and covers her mouth. Her eyes finally leave the television.

Dad's tense shoulders fall. He stares at the image, unable to move, his response barely audible. I stand inches from the screen, soaking in every detail of his reaction. "How do I know he isn't already dead?"

"You don't. But I assure you, he will be unless you surrender. Now."

The Crimson Mask surveys the destruction. Cars and trucks continue to smoke. A remaining phalanx of drones stands ready to return to their mayhem. Muted cries and screams drift out of the wreckage.

He steps forward, head bowed. "It's time. Time to end this."

The Black Beetle nods and scans the predatory circle of metal. The circle tightens. Emily's tears stream unchecked.

I keep waiting for a blur of movement that never comes. Drones tighten the circle and latch on. Arms. Legs. He hangs defeated among them. They lift him into the sky.

Emily crosses the edge of my vision and the television goes dark.

"What are you doing?!" I shout, "Turn it back on!"

Fear shrouds Emily's face and she mutely shakes her head.

"Why did he do that?" I say it out loud, not expecting an answer. I need to know why he would surrender and go off with the Black Beetle. Is it an act? Are they popping champagne on a yacht in the Indian Ocean? Or did he really just surrender himself to the same guy that kidnapped my mom?

"I'll think of something," Emily says in airy breaths.

I'm numb and I can't fight as Emily guides me into the next room. She's nervously speaking, sniffling, saying over and over that I need rest. I'm not tired, but the numbness of the bunker is back.

A blanket, soft pillow beneath my head. On the other side of the closed bedroom door, Emily's crying seems to escalate. I let the cold consume me. The sobs fade and I'm alone. But not for long.

CHAPTER 14

THAT ODD RING of light comes again—the same ring that replaced the sun when I last dreamed about Mom. I want to talk to her. She's the only person that could help me make sense of all this.

My gut lurches and the light explodes. I'm moving, or flying, or my stomach is being ripped away. Then it stops.

"Jesus Christ," I say.

An almost familiar, lisping, whiny voice replies, "Why are you talking to Jesus?"

I'm standing in a well-lit garage. There are worktables with labeled jars, wall racks containing yard tools in ascending order of height, and two plastic containers, one marked "recycle" and the other marked "trash". This, even before they had curbside recycling in that neighborhood.

The centerpiece of the garage isn't a car. It's an electric race track. And not just any track, but a scale replica of the Formula One speedway at Monte Carlo. Classic French architecture lines the curves. Little trees and bushes fill spaces in the median. A harbor complete with yachts and wooden docks stretches toward an imaginary sea, and sand fills a construction site at the water's edge. Store-bought model building sand that you apparently can't just dig up in the back yard. A kid and his father spent hours together building this.

That kid is Kyle. The whiny voice is his, too. He's standing next to me. A little blond-haired boy with a dusting of freckles across a nose which is currently crinkled into a skeptical scowl. I say he's little, but when we were ten, he was bigger than me. Like everyone else. I look down at my hands. I guess we're both ten.

My words come out on autopilot. "Dude, come on! It would be *so* wicked!"

Kyle crosses his arms and glares at me. "No way! *No way!*"

"Don't be such a wuss."

"I'm not a wuss. I just don't want to burn down my track," says Kyle as his scowl deepens.

"You won't. It'll be awesome. Here, check this out." I pull the bottle of rubbing alcohol from my backpack. Strange, 'cause my backpack when I was ten wasn't the same black and orange backpack I'm carrying now, but here it is. I don't blink when I see the iPod or the satellite phone inside, but I keep digging. I get out the bottle, unscrew the cap and dip a finger. As an afterthought, I grab the cup of water on the table and place it closer. "Watch!"

His eyes are straight out of an anime as I light the match and touch it to my finger. Sure enough, my fingertip is bathed in flame and his mouth drops open. I smile and dip my finger into the cup. "See, no damage. All we have to do is put it out before the alcohol burns off and we're all good."

"I don't know," says Kyle, staring at my finger. "Can I try?"

"Yeah, why not." I push the bottle in his direction. Eyes still saucers, he dips his finger and reaches for the match. He fumbles with the matchbook, flipping it open and trying awkwardly to hold the book while tearing a match free with his alcohol-soaked finger. I remember, he will try, drop a match, and very nearly catch his pants on fire. That was comedy gold when I was ten.

I snatch the book of matches. Is this really a dream?

"Here, let me do that," I offer and he nods rapidly. I strike the match and he eases his finger forward, cross-eyed by the flame. With a quick breath I blow it out. "Maybe you're right."

"Hey! I'm not a wuss! C'mon, light my finger!"

"Kyle, I don't think you're a wuss."

"Well, maybe I think you're one."

"Am not!" I say. Great, now I'm arguing with a ten-year-old. Wait, aren't I ten, too? At least here? What the hell is going on?

"Do it. I dare you!" spits Kyle.

"Fine." With a scrape and a flick, the match springs to life and I light his finger. Kyle stares at his fingertip, wreathed in flame and turns it in slow circles.

"Dip it, Kyle." He's mesmerized by the flame even as I repeat more desperately, "Dip it in the water, Kyle." I'm starting to wonder why I was ever even temporary friends with this kid.

"It kinda tingles." Kyle turns his finger slowly in front of his face.

I grab his hand and shove it in the glass.

"Hey!"

"I didn't want you to get burned." Well, maybe I did, just a little bit.

"I was gonna do that." He scrunches his face again and blurts out, "Wuss!"

The indignation of a ten-year-old swells in my chest and the urge to play out this memory takes over once again, "Fine, let's do this."

I recall the bright idea that started it all. We were going to make burning tire tracks with the cars and try to get a picture with Mom's digital camera. It was like in a movie I saw, only this was going to be way cooler. On the highly detailed track, nobody would be able to tell it wasn't real. We'd have stock footage for our own killer action movie, with myself as director and Kyle the producer.

Once we get going, Kyle turns into a mini-pyro. He insists we do it over and over again until we get the perfect shot, using each and every car in the collection. Even now, I can feel my apprehension rise. Finally, one of the cars locks up on the track and Kyle reaches for it.

"This happens all the time. They get dirty and the connection doesn't close between the rails and the track," he speaks with the confident voice of his father's experience echoed in his tiny frame and I try not to roll my eyes. "I'll swap out the chassis on this and we'll get the last car."

As he flips the racer over, his eyes get wide again. He fumbles with the plastic chassis, turning the car over and over again. Tossing it to the track, he grabs another, then another. "Oh shit!"

At ten, a cuss word could mean only exactly what it means—serious shit. I grab the nearest car. The bottom is blackened, the copper contacts that connect to the track are warped and twisted. A black bubbly smudge melds the chassis with the frame of the car. We were so focused on not burning the track we didn't notice the damage to the cars.

"Oh shit! Oh shit!" Kyle can't stop saying it.

He's desperate, the look on his face isn't comical anymore. Fingers trembling, he's rooting through the cars again, checking and rechecking.

I know what I did back then, when this really happened, so I do it again. I grab the bottle of alcohol and douse the pile of wrecked cars along with a good section of track.

"What are you doing?" He's dumbstruck as I strike the match. I'm doing this for his own good, I tell myself.

Thick black smoke fills the garage. Kyle screams. I reach for the glass of water but I can't see. The smoke is billowing in a thick cloud and it wraps itself around my head. Unable to breathe, I'm falling, again.

Smoke clears. I stop falling, my stomach left about five feet above my head.

"Was anyone hurt?" Mom's voice. Pieces of conversation come from the living room. I'm seated on a stool in the kitchen. An apartment, like so many others. I ran home from Kyle's house and tried to pretend I hadn't just set fire to his little world. A faint ring of smoke which I didn't see until later surrounds my mouth and nose.

"I'm sure it was an accident," she says hopefully.

There's a long pause, and Kyle's father's muffled shouts drift out of the receiver of the phone a room away.

Mom replies, steady and quiet, "Oh. I see. I'm so sorry. We'll pay for any damages."

The angry voice blurts again.

"Yes, I understand. I don't know what could have gotten into him."

A soft click of the phone being returned to the cradle is the only reply. I sit waiting. Waiting. Dad isn't home, but I never had to worry about that.

Finally, she walks into the room. "That was Kyle's father."

I nod.

"What happened?" she asks, arms folded and eyes stern.

"We were making a movie."

"Why did this involve setting stuff on fire?"

"It was a dumb idea. Special effects."

She crosses her arms and I examine my feet perched on the rungs of the stool. "Kyle's father says you started the fire because Kyle didn't want anything to do with your idea."

Good. I remember. My half-baked plan sorta worked.

"Spencer? Is that true?"

"Yeah."

"I don't believe you."

My eyes leave my shoes. This isn't what she said back then. Off-script, I stammer, "What...what do you mean?"

Mom's face stays neutral, her arms crossed and a silver light gleams in her eyes. I start looking around for a sign that this truly is a dream, but it all seems so real. I'm hyperaware, and even the neutral colors of the apartment glare. Bits and pieces of the room start to become familiar. The stool and counter where I'd eat snacks at the apartment in Washington. The latticework on the patio door from a house in Florida. The simple design on the linoleum with straight lines and intersecting curves that I'd race Hot Wheels along from that house in... Kansas? Nebraska?

Above the table is a light. A fluorescent bulb, the tube is a bent cylinder forming a glowing ring in the sky.

"I don't believe you. I think I understand why you did that. Do you?"

"I... I wanted to see what would happen."

"Let's start over," Mom says, moving closer. I find I've inched away from her to the edge of the stool as she continues to question, searching with those silvery eyes. "Whose idea was this?"

"Well... mine." I hear the sink start to drip. I'm sitting straight up on the stool but the room feels like it's tilting backwards.

"For the movie? The fire?" She leans in and I can't answer as I stare at the corona of mercury around her pupils. "Don't be scared. I need to know."

"Why?" I grip the table to keep from toppling over. I try to rein in the fear I see etched on my face in the reflection of those strange eyes.

Her own expression softens. That should be pleasant and calming, but it isn't hers. "Because I want to understand. That's all. Don't worry. I'm not mad."

I swallow before speaking, trying to loosen my throat.

"We both wanted to do the movie. He was scared about my special effects idea, but once I showed him how it worked, he really got into it." Mom's smiling and shaking her head sympathetically and I keep talking now, unable to stop the flow of words I never said. "Kyle was gonna get busted 'cause of the cars anyway. My idea was, well, I could take the blame. We're probably moving soon anyway. Who cares if the crazy kid next door did it, right?"

Her face softens but the silver light flares. Her eyes and the ring of light above her are all I can see now. "You destroyed things. Put yourself at risk to help your friend."

"I guess."

"And you hated him for what he had." Excitement flashes across my mother's face as she says the word, *hate*.

"No." Hate Kyle? The kid was a dork, but I never hated him. But I can't ignore the stab in my gut when I think of him building that track with his dad. His house right around the corner from the same school he'd been going to since kindergarten. Their manicured lawn with the black iron mailbox etched with their last name. "I don't think so."

"Even though you were outside a cage, you still felt trapped. Strapped down." Her gaze darts wildly around the room and fixes on the light.

"This is getting weird."

Her eyes peel away from the light and burn into mine. "None of this is your fault, Spencer."

"Huh?"

She's smiling in a way that tells me she sees all of my pain. But this isn't a mother's empathy. She's lived that same pain of icy-cold isolation. And then, I catch a fleeting glimpse of the expression from the department store nightmare, memory, whatever it was. A look that so doesn't fit her face I can't describe it. Hunger? Anticipation?

"It's *their* fault, Spencer. Their fault, and they should pay."

CHAPTER 15

THROUGH WET AND blurry vision, I see a face inches from mine. A hand across my head. Cool, damp. I swat it away and roll. In one not-so-slick motion, I slip off the edge of the bed.

"Spencer..." Emily grabs my arm. I push off the floor and she pulls as I scramble onto the mattress. "It's okay," she says as she fluffs a pillow and places it under my head.

"I thought..."

"Shhh. Relax." She drapes a cold cloth over my forehead.

"Oh God. Mom?" I tilt the corner of the cloth and search the room. The same assemble-it-yourself furniture and a ceiling fan. Emily's eyes are next on the checklist. No weird lights.

She gives my hand a comforting squeeze. Light fades in the window of what must be her room. I thought it was already dark outside when we were watching television. She registers the confusion and tries to fill the silence.

"You've been asleep for a while. I'm not surprised. I was worried though, you started feeling feverish. I almost called Martin."

Rolling to face the opposite wall, I respond quietly, "Don't bother. This probably means I'm back to normal."

Night terrors, waking up drenched in sweat; bullshit from the bunker I guess I haven't escaped. Now though, the dreams keep changing. Always her and that weird light. I wonder if she's out there, hurting, waiting for me to find her. I suddenly don't know what's been real these past few hours and what's been a dream.

"What happened to Dad?"

Emily's voice quivers. "He surrendered."

I roll to my back and press my hands over closed eyes. Pushing, bearing down until rigid sockets stop the heel of my palm and stars burst in the dark. When Dad arrived the day Mom was taken, the only words I could manage were, "Mom's gone." The look in his eyes, I'll never forget it. The confidence, the intensity that always burned there, flickered. For a moment his armor had disintegrated. At least that's what I'd always thought.

Then that weakness had passed. He'd scooped me out of the rubble, and we'd left. We never spoke about that day again. He never pushed. But I wanted him to console or even interrogate me. At the same time, speaking about what happened was too painful.

On the surface, Dad adjusted. I'd thought it was because he was the strongest Augment ever created. Showing weakness got weeded out of his DNA.

In my gut, I know now this is all his fault. Mom disappearing. Me being trapped in an icy hell. And that Black Beetle bastard using me as a pawn in whatever bullshit scheme they might have going.

Emily leans back as I shift to the edge of the bed, the cool cloth in her hand held frozen midair.

"I'm fine. It's fine." My backpack sits on the floor next to the bed. "Perfectly fine." I try to switch off the painful scenes playing through my imagination, and start rummaging through the pack until I find the thumb drive.

"Do you... do you want to talk about it?" Emily sounds confused, her tone begs for information, a way to help. She doesn't know the rules.

"I'm going to need your laptop." As I rise from the bed, I avoid eye contact and cover the short distance to the door.

"Spencer, I know this is hard. Believe me, it isn't any easier..." Her words end in a ragged sigh. "I've been thinking about this for hours while you were sleeping. Right now, the best way I can help Sean is to keep you safe, like he asked." Her voice trembles.

There it is again. Everyone keeping me safe. Slumping against the door frame, my forehead comes to rest at a painful angle on the doorjamb. I grind my head against the corner. Pain, at least I've got that. Must have gotten that from Mom.

A tear burns my cheek as I face Emily. "May I please use your laptop?"

"You don't need to do anything. Let me..."

"No. I do. I'm the only one left that can find her."

Emily stares for a long time, swallowing her tears and examining my face. Tiny wrinkles mark the worry in her eyes and crease ever so slightly around the edges of her nose. When I take her hand, she pulls me in and strokes the back of my head. I let it happen.

For several minutes we cling together until she exhales. Her chest flutters against mine, and I can tell she's been silently crying. I step back. "Okay, okay," I say, rubbing my face to hide any evidence. "I'm good."

"C'mon." Emily steps into the main living area and heads for the kitchen table. The scent of java overpowers the room, and a half-empty mug sits next to the laptop. "We're going to do this together, Spencer. I'm right here. Are you sure you're ready for this?" I'm confused, but I nod anyway and sit.

Browser windows clutter the laptop screen and I mouse through them. News sites with footage from Mumbai, maps of India, lists of sightings on Augment fansites, news archives about Augment clashes.

"What's all this?"

"Research. It's the only way I feel I can help. I was hoping to find a clue to where Sean might have been taken. Find patterns."

"Any luck?"

"Sort of." Emily sighs and opens a spreadsheet. "The Black Beetle's attacks don't make sense."

The sheer organization and neatly color-coded rows is impressive enough, let alone the complex formulas peeking out of the cells. This must have taken hours, maybe days, to put together.

"Wow. OCD much?" No snort of laughter at my snide remark, just a "grow up" eyebrow twitch. "Exactly how long was I asleep?"

"Seven hours."

"Really? You did all this in seven hours? Why didn't you wake me?"

"You needed the sleep." She dives back into the data. "For a guy bent on world domination, Black Beetle's attacks appear unfocused. Plus, he's usually running into Augments along the way."

"What's so weird about that?" I ask, moving closer to the screen.

"You'd think he'd avoid them. Most don't have powers that facilitate transportation. And by his target areas, Black Beetle appears to have been intentionally seeking out encounters. The only data point these locations seem to have in common is proximity to an Augment."

"Taking out the competition?"

"That's been the end result so far. Extremely efficient, and with maximum mess." She points to a column. It lists a series of media monikers given to individual augments: Red Scourge, Titan, Fallout, Ember. The press had a field day when Augments went "covert". Without knowledge of the proxy wars, it was the perfect flashy, attention-getting crap that gives reporters hard-ons. Fancy names, colorful suits, explosions. Once all that was exposed and governments began to disavow and shut down the programs, Augments went "rogue", or "freelance"—depending on who your favorites were.

On this spreadsheet though, the only flashy part is the dominant color in the column of Augment names.

"Why are all those names highlighted in red?"

"They're ones that have been... eliminated, or captured."

"That many? Since when?"

"I keep forgetting how long you've been gone. Most of this happened in the past two years." She pauses before continuing, "There's something else. A statistically significant correlation between your Dad's activities and the Black Beetle's."

"Are you saying they're working together?" I try to sound surprised and I watch Emily's face closely.

Her response is immediate and she sounds shocked. "No! Correlation. That's all. You can't infer—"

"How much do you know about Dad's work?"

This time, her response comes more slowly. "We only worked together once. I know he was freelancing for the U.S. government, but he never gave details."

"Welcome to my hell," I mumble. She might be lying, but it sounds so familiar.

"All I can say is, based on this data, for a while every time Sean was rounding up a dangerous Augment for the government, the Black Beetle would strike, usually on the opposite side of the globe. But it gets really interesting here." She mouses over a date, exactly one day after Mom disappeared. One day after we fled to the bunker. "The attacks became less centralized. Drone swarms would strike anywhere. Everywhere. Augments were already thinned out. Civilians became the Beetle's targets."

When I first saw the raw data at the bunker, I tried to match dates up to Dad's "business trips" in my head. Presented here in perfect, color-coded columns, it's clear—flesh and bone Augments were being taken out of service on all sides; meanwhile, the Beetle was manufacturing more and more drones. Then, once I was incarcerated in my ice tray of doom, those drones were unleashed en masse. I'm reminded of the news footage from last night.

"Pawn storm."

"What?"

"Chess. You overwhelm your opponent's defenses with rapidly advancing pawns." None of this explains why or if he was working with the Black Beetle. I reach into my pocket and pull out the thumb drive.

"What's on there?" Emily slides a second chair over and sits as I pop the drive in.

"It's, um, well, complicated."

"Please. I can handle complicated," Emily scoffs.

Right. PhD, technophile, way too excited about spreadsheets, friends with an Augment. "Data," I say. "Data from the server back at, what did you call the bunker, Hotel Popsicle?"

"That's not what I called it, but you've earned the right to call it whatever you want."

"Fine. The Icehole," I mumble as I reach for the keyboard. "I copied some of the data before I melted the servers."

"Wow. Nice job… I think…" She sounds a bit stunned.

I kick the explanation into overdrive to try and derail any more safety lectures. "Part of the server held public data, like your Project OCD there. News reports, unclassified government info, that sort of thing. But that wasn't all." Emily nods and scoots closer as I continue, "Another batch, about the Black Beetle, was heavily encrypted. Probably whatever Dad uncovered trying to find him."

"We find the Beetle, we find Sean," Emily says hesitantly.

"Yeah." *And maybe Mom.* The screen blinks as a list of

scrambled files scroll by. "First problem, the old server interface isn't here."

Emily stretches across me and her fingers dance along the keys. "Your Dad's the one that gave me this laptop. It's got an emulator." Her index finger swirls along the touchpad. The files light up blue and ghost out as she drags them. Flicking her pinky to open a second program, a familiar prompt pops up, exactly like the terminals at the bunker.

"There!" She leans back, hands on her hips and a crooked smile. "Don't suppose you know the password?"

I stare at the familiar prompt in awe. "The one for the system was easy. Turns out even Augments suck at remembering passwords. It was Mom's name and their anniversary." I swivel to bask in her appreciation of my genius. A distant look in her eyes quickly dodges behind a tight smile. I manage a smirk and turn back to the laptop. Using the server emulator I load the data, but have to ask, "How the heck did you know what that program even did?"

"Well, I said I worked with your Dad before."

"Right, 'if you tell me you'll have to kill me' sort of stuff."

"Yeah. Let's leave it at that." Emily stands up.

"So, you've got to know other people he worked with, right? Augments? Shady government types?" I ask casually as I punch in the password for the login screen.

"Not many. Our work was very case-specific and had no connection with the Black Beetle. I don't see how any info I have can help." Emily's voice sounds farther away but I'm absorbed in getting the internet connection back up, surfing to sites with the right tools for taking a crack at this password.

"You say not many, so that means you know somebody. Why don't we call them up?"

"Remember the data, Spencer. The Black Beetle seemed to always know the right times to strike. And he found the bunker. He found your home. There's no telling who passed on that information to him. Who we can trust."

She's right. But I want more answers. Here's someone that shared in at least a part of Dad's hush-hush work. It's frustrating. Unfair.

"So, exactly how long have you known Dad?" I twist to face an empty room. Her bedroom door closes softly.

"Emily?"

Right. Leave it at that.

CHAPTER 16

IT'S BEEN AGES since I've had internet access. Within seconds of Emily's disappearing act, I'm like a crack addict handed a pipe.

After downloading some crypto software, hex editors and a few system tools, the time comes to locate the D3dm4n$ Ch3$t. Tracking down the site takes a while. The portal regularly relocates, piggybacking off legitimate websites until discovered and then relocating. Once there, you take a dive into the Deep. Since I helped create the site, I know ways to find it.

A Giant's game is running in another open window. Crash-landing in civilization couldn't have happened at a better time, 'cause the playoffs are in full swing and the Giants made the cut. Hacking, baseball; you gotta have hobbies.

I tried Little League one season, and Mom was supportive, but it was obvious I sucked. She wasn't any better, and I had to imagine that playing catch with Dad would have been the equivalent of dodging incoming mortar fire. So I settled on watching the Big Show.

We moved and changed names so often that satellite and cable rarely got hooked up. Reading about games in the paper or watching highlight reels online sucks. I needed real-time coverage, and the broadband connections at public libraries obliged.

Library card, headphones, a CD with enough hacking tools to disable the nonsense, half-ass filters they'd install, and I was set. If the less clueless, more vigilant librarians were on shift, I'd be happy with a book. When the shift change happened, I'd be in the computer lab, catching up on the games by hacking live streams or torrenting video files.

I only got ejected from the library once. The ump in that game, I swear, was blind, but unfortunately the librarian on duty wasn't completely deaf. He had no appreciation for a creative vocabulary, like you'd figure a librarian should.

Finally, between pitches, I get a fix on the D3dm4n$ Ch3$t. A familiar series of telephonic tones blares from the laptop speaker. Not the stereo speakers, but the system speaker tucked away on the motherboard. On screen, a pixelated pirate skeleton dances to the blaring sea shanty over a chest of green circuit boards. I log into the forum using a new alias and a throwaway e-mail account.

The guys here are mostly video geeks who decode DVDs. Usually huge collections of weirdo hentai porn, involving robots and tentacles and other messed-up shit. But there are also guys that can hack satellite receiver smart cards and pay-per-view in their sleep. Those guys are the real deal.

I search the posts for Eric's handle: "Enigma". It's there, all over the damn place. He's probably still running the site out of his parent's basement in the hills of San Francisco. A couple thousand miles away, but with the music playing, I feel so close.

The basement, the Throne; Babe, his liquid-cooled beast of a computer. *Our* computer.

Eric was a diehard Giants fan, a guy who didn't mind hanging out with a kid a few years younger—I was fourteen and he was sixteen when we first met. Quiet, a little nutty, but we had a lot in common.

I almost told him everything once. A crowd-drunk moment after an amazing Giants game. We were in the parking lot reliving each inning as if we hadn't both just left the stadium together. The booming hits, the key catches, both pitchers nearly throwing no-hitters until the last inning when an all-out slugfest ensued. The runs kept coming late into the night until the thirteenth inning, when a ball soared out over the center field bleachers and the crowd roared. Beyond late, the parking lot had nearly emptied by the time we headed to his car. Opening up and laying out the details of my bullshit life seemed right at that moment. He was a friend. He deserved truth.

Then, we both heard explosions downtown. He wanted to go straight home. I wanted to see it. No need for me to tell him, I could show him the truth. There were pops and screeches and the sounds of bricks toppling echoed through the streets. That excitement of the game, along with a mixture of pride and fear, hit me all at once.

"Dude, if it's bad, the Crimson Mask will be there," Eric said as he tore out of the parking lot. "I got my license less than a week ago and my Mom thinks I'm at your house."

I nodded and kept quiet.

I hadn't told Mom where I was going either. I figured that's what guys do. She'd never have let me go to a late game on a school night anyway, and it had ended way past curfew because of the extra innings. Mom had been pissed when I got home. Really pissed. Really anxious. Thinking about her face that day, her face from the dream comes to mind first, with those silvery eyes.

I've gotta focus. I browse the different forums; there's the Deck for your general posts, the Hold for links to digital booty, and the Captain's Cabin for Eric and me. It's been so long since we spoke, I've got no clue what he'll even think, but as long as I don't get quarantined to Davy Jones' blacklist, things should be fine.

I'm connected through a proxy and routing my outgoing transmissions through several legit servers. Standard procedure for a pirate site, but perhaps more important now. Capturing a snippet of a few of my login attempts to the bunker's encrypted data is easy. I grab enough to pique Eric's interest but not give away what it could be entirely.

> Subject: Looking 4 encryption type...
> By: s1ug3rGIANT
> IP Logged: 72.32.138.96
> **Can ne1 id this encryption? Bet u can't lol.**
> **XXXXXXXXXXXXXXXXXXXXXXXXXXXXXXXXXXXXXXXX**
> **XXXXXXXXXXXXXXXXXXXXXXXXXXXXXXXXXXXXXXXXXX**
> **XXXXXXX**
> (WARNING: This post has been modified by the moderator. Message: DON'T BE A DOUCHE)
>
> RE: Looking 4 encryption type...

By: 3n1g|\/|4 – Moderator
IP Logged: PRIVATE
Read the FAQ.

RE: Looking 4 encryption type…
By: s1ug3rGIANT
IP Logged: 134.29.231.1
Did. Long time ago. Wouldn't be here if I was following the rules.

RE: Looking 4 encryption type…
By: 3n1g|\/|4 – Moderator
IP Logged: PRIVATE
PM me if you know me.

RE: Looking 4 encryption type…
By: s1ug3rGIANT
IP Logged: 168.161.242.18
Don't have any of my old addresses, progs, tools, gear, etc. U know the encryption or not? Like I said, spent a long time away from civilization.

RE: Looking 4 encryption type…
By: 3n1g|\/|4 – Moderator
IP Logged: PRIVATE
WTF, prison?

RE: Looking 4 encryption type…
By: s1ug3rGIANT
IP Logged: 70.96.128.184
Yes.

RE: Looking 4 encryption type...
By: 3n1g|\/|4 – Moderator
IP Logged: PRIVATE
Sure. What was your old username?

RE: Looking 4 encryption type...
By: s1ug3rGIANT
IP Logged: 64.90.57.205
CR1ms0n8a11z. Been ages enigma.

RE: Looking 4 encryption type...
By: 3n1g|\/|4 – Moderator
IP Logged: PRIVATE
I went to pick you up for school and there was a hole in your fucking house. Prison – supposed to believe that?

RE: Looking 4 encryption type...
By: s1ug3rGIANT
IP Logged: 72.172.88.167
Yeah!!!! Look, not much time.

RE: Looking 4 encryption type...
By: 3n1g|\/|4 – Moderator
IP Logged: PRIVATE
Blocks are different lengths. Not a hashing algorithm.

RE: Looking 4 encryption type...
By: s1ug3rGIANT

IP Logged: 66.155.9.238
maybe some unreleased NSA shit?

RE: Looking 4 encryption type...
By: 3n1g | \/ | 4 – Moderator
IP Logged: PRIVATE
I ain't gonna follow in his footsteps, genius. keep fishin' fucker.

S1ug3rGIANT your account has been suspended. WELCOME TO DAVY JONES LOCKA' N008!

HTTP 404 – File Not Found
The page cannot be found.
The page you are looking for might have been removed, had its name changed or be temporarily unavailable.

CHAPTER 17

MY DRUM SOLO goes from a slick pulse-pounding roll to the lame sound of my hands slapping the kitchen table. I check the headphone jack on my iPod and it's dangling from Emily's fingers. Her hair's a little damp. She's changed, so no more stretchy pants. Now it's jeans and a navy t-shirt with green lines and letters on her... well, front and center. Could be a molecular structure.

"Caffeine," she says, following my gaze with a raised eyebrow.

"Huh?"

"Caffeine. The symbol is caffeine. Simplified a bit, but close enough." Emily turns toward the kitchen. "Want some? It's the best thing for late nights at the lab staring at computer screens."

"Sure," I say, even though I'm not sure if I'm a coffee drinker.

"Sorry for walking out earlier, but you were starting to get that look."

"What look?"

"The sucked-into-your-research-look. At the lab, you interrupt that at great peril."

"Yeah, I guess. Just needed a few programs set up."

"And I *really* needed a shower. I must have fallen asleep after that."

"No problem," I sigh, managing to hide the disappointment in my voice. But actually, there is a problem. I want more answers from her. Right now, though, I don't want to be reminded of how big of a cluster-fuck all of this is. My best friend made me walk the plank. To cope, I'd given up staring at the encrypted data a few hours ago and started downloading songs for my now-antique iPod. So when I add, "You haven't missed much," I'm hardly lying.

"No luck, huh?" she asks, returning from the kitchen.

"Nada."

She plops a can of soda next to the laptop and lightly backhands my shoulder. "Maybe you're not the computer genius your dad says you are, huh? Scoot over. You gave me an idea earlier."

I grunt with as much indifference as I can and shuffle to the side. Does he say that? That doesn't sound like him. He barely knows a hard drive from a motherboard and never seemed to care that I do. The clatter of the keyboard is white noise behind my thoughts. I catch a whiff of lavender and wood smoke as a damp strand of hair lingers near my face. It pulls me back to the screen.

Login failed.

"Wait, stop!"

"Relax, let me try one more."

Login failed.

"Ok, Dr. Biology, hands off the keyboard!" It's hard to keep cool. One more failed attempt in that short of a time frame and we're locked out. I thought she would've known that?

Emily straightens, speaking in a soft and far away tone. "Sorry. I thought maybe…"

I kill the background hacking program before the brute force hammering trips the third and final attempt. The animated icon of a black boot bashing on a door comes to rest. Yeah, pirate humor. Arrrrgh.

"Guessing at the password is exactly what I have this program doing. But more efficiently and, best of all, set up so we don't get locked out."

Oblivious to the reprimand, she responds with a demanding edge that's entirely new. "How long will it take?"

"Honestly?"

"Of course."

"I can't do it."

"What?" Her eyes flare.

I hadn't quite figured out how to tell her about the forum post. But Emily's parental tone has returned, with a little bit of crazy thrown in. I mumble, "I've got a friend working on it." Of course, I'm pretty sure he didn't believe a word I said.

"What do you mean 'a friend?'"

"No, no. Hold on."

"We went over the not trusting anyone."

"Hey, this dude can hack anything. He's the patron saint of hackers."

"Who is this 'dude'?"

"I've known him a while, well, longer than I've ever known anyone else." A skeptical squint pinches her face and I say, "A lot longer than I've known you."

"Fine," she relents. "Who?"

"A guy I went to school with. He's an expert and he's got plenty of reasons not to run his mouth."

"School? You mean high school?"

"No, I mean the Remote Academy for Ice Sculpting. Yes, high school."

Emily touches her temple and bows her head with a sigh. "Spencer, we don't need more kids involved."

The chair scrapes and teeters, crashing to the ground as I stand. Slamming the laptop closed, I start to cram it and the cables into my backpack. My iPod, the sat phone, it all gets dumped in along with the remains of my life from the bunker.

There's a thump on the ceiling from the apartment below.

"What're you doing?"

"You've got the PhD, you figure it out."

"Spencer Harrington, don't you dare!" The mom imitation cuts deep this time. I grab my shoes off the living room floor and stomp into them, tucking the laces against my feet. She stares as I stalk toward the apartment door.

At the last second, Emily slips in front of me, her arms spread like she's trying to contain the unseen force dragging me forward. "You can't go! I told *him* I'd keep you safe and I told *you* I'd stop protecting you and... I..." she stammers. "Now he's... we need him! And I don't know what to do, but I can't keep you *and* your friends safe!"

"I'm not asking you to! Goddamn, why is it everyone is out to save me! I'm *nineteen*!" I roar. A double thump replies from the apartment below, and I stomp madly on the spot.

Her arms drop. She sucks in air as she shakes her head. "Damnit. Damnit! I'm sorry. I know, you're not a child, but you've got to calm down. Please, give me a second. One second." As quick as it came, my flash of anger dissolves while she searches for what to say next. It's easy to see she's freaking out inside too.

"Okay," she says. "I know a few guys at the university. Computer science, crypto, top in their field." She's chewing on a nail as she talks.

"No good."

"Why not? If we're bringing in outside help, might as well be people with actual training."

"Eric's learned more about cryptography in the wild than anyone ever could sitting around a lecture hall."

Emily looks skeptical as she replies, "I bet these guys have similar backgrounds to your friend."

I adjust the backpack on my shoulder and fix my gaze on the door. No longer angry, I'm starting to think my life would be less complicated if I was doing this on my own. "No, I trust Eric. Excuse me. I'll find a way there myself."

She's speechless. Judging from the power hike in the woods, as pathetic as it sounds, I think she might have the upper hand if she wanted to place me in a submission hold, but then what?

She can't keep me here forever and she knows it. Finally, a situation where I feel I've got some kind of control.

"Fine. We'll talk to your friend. Where is he?"

"San Francisco."

"Wow. Wow." She's chewing on the same nail again and from the looks of it, she's talking to an end table, not me. "How's that going to work?" she mutters. Her head snaps up. "I can…" Then, her eyes go wide.

She tackles me to the floor as the window behind us explodes.

CHAPTER 18

THUMP.
Thump.
Thump.

My ear is pressed on the floor right where the downstairs neighbor has been tapping out S.T.F.U. in Morse code. Emily's face comes into focus.

"Emily?"

She's laying on the floor beside me, her eyes closed. I put a hand on her throat, blindly groping for a pulse. She's got to have a pulse. Somewhere? I don't know what the hell I'm doing, but I feel a shallow breath on my forearm. Glass shatters and I peek over the couch to see the robot shouldering through what's left of the window.

I grab Emily's arms and drag her closer to the couch. Broken shards of brick clatter onto the breakfast nook's linoleum while the drone rips through the wall.

Awake, asleep, how many times do I have to relive this scenario? People diving on me, surrendering for me. Maybe this time, we can both get carried off into the sky. All of this can end.

A fog of mortar dust hangs in the air. The swaying shadows are sharply outlined against light from the busted overhead lamp, its naked bulb swinging wildly. Outside air rushes in as the robotic arms gouge more chunks from the wall.

The aromatic scent of the flowers in the courtyard carries on the breeze. I recall their bright colors, the complete opposite of the frozen hell I came from; a place I will absolutely, positively never see again. *Never.*

With that thought, I'm juiced. Alive. The entire world is waiting. Waiting for me to prove I don't need to be locked up and praying for someone to come save me. If anyone needs to be saved right now, it's Emily. She needs my help, and carrying her out of here isn't going to work. You've gotta work with what you've got.

I'm going outside and the drone is coming with me.

Jumping to my feet, the distance to the apartment door closes fast. Glowing eyes in oversized sockets lock on to my movement.

"Why can't someone program you morons to use a door?" I shout, trying to keep its attention focused on me.

With a final swat, the drone clears a chunk of the wall big enough to fit through. Its head turns slowly as it scans the interior of the apartment and the eyes flare when they sweep past me. My sudden clarity of purpose wavers. But Emily, she's still lying motionless on the floor.

"That's right, I'm talking to you. Your backup better be a Roomba, bitch!" Sounding brave works better if you aren't desperately fumbling with a deadbolt.

The drone hovers through the opening, and boot rockets

extinguish right as the faux-tile floor blackens and melts. It lands with a squishy thud and the cloud of pulverized mortar thickens. Head swiveling, it scans again. I'm looking over my shoulder as the deadbolt clicks. Bug-like eyes lock on once more and the drone starts to pound across the apartment. Past Emily. Straight for me.

Scrambling out the door into the stairwell, I get maybe half a dozen steps before the landing shimmies as the robot tears through the door frame in one long stride. Two, three stairs at a time are left behind in frantic leaps. I nearly fall face-first in the foyer. An angry old woman with a hairnet and a Hawaiian muumuu glares out the doorway of the apartment below Emily's.

"Have some respect! You know what time it…" her voice dies as the entire building shakes.

Our fearful eyes connect and she disappears inside. I shout and ram the push bar of the courtyard door, stumbling into the cool night air. Cutting to the left, I leave the walkway and crush a trail through the flowerbed.

There's an enormous crash as the foyer door hurtles into the courtyard. Sure, being a non-Augment right now sucks, but I've practically got a degree in running from lumbering bullies. Sharp turns are the best option, keeping obstacles between us to slow my pursuer down. I head for a row of parked cars along the street.

The sounds of rending metal and raining shards of plastic and glass fill the air as I duck between parked vehicles. A few cars zip by on the road, swerving madly as the drivers catch sight of the cyclone of metal behind me. Further away, cars screech to a halt, engines gunning desperately in reverse. If I stay out here much longer, someone else is going to get hurt.

A car flips end-over-end along the street as the drone searches the parking spaces. I dive under a nearby SUV, shimmying on knees and elbows to the other side and trying not to hook my backpack on the undercarriage. Heat blossoms out as the drone takes to the air.

Unfair.

Up and running, the street is my only option. Bright lights whip around the corner. The air screams with tortured tires. A hood emblem looms large and I roll away, eyes closed. My foot catches the curb and the pavement comes up, hard. Whatever impacts next, hopefully it'll be big. Maybe a dump truck or a semi, and this'll end quick.

"Holy crap! Kid?" A man's voice, tinged with panic, separates from the idling engine noise. He stumbles out of a dangerously-close box truck in slow motion. Why the hell is this guy getting out?

Two bright points of light flare above the truck. I stagger to my feet and fling a floppy arm at the man and sputter, "Get out of here!"

Hot blood streams down my face and throat. Pain shoots through my ankle but I race down the sidewalk. There's a shout of surprise but I don't look back.

Flames roar and spit behind me. The distance to the corner might as well be a million miles away because the robot will catch me before I can get there. Light from a store streams into the gray street. Glass doors unlocked, I barge in and the drone jets by, inches off my shoulder.

A guy that can't be much older than me looks up. His face pulls into a scowl between chunky earphones. He's pushing around a big floor buffer that's whining as it scours the tile. He swats the headphones off his head, tossing the cord over his shoulder. "Hey! We're closed!"

Checkout counter to the right. Shelves to the left. I take off for the floor-to-ceiling aisles shouting, "Get down!"

The Zamboni driver, or whatever the heck they call it, flicks the machine off and starts toward me. Before he can take a second step, there's a high energy whine from the street.

He's barely got time to shriek before he throws himself behind the counter. The exterior doors explode in a shower of glass fragments and twisted steel. I slip behind a pegboard display on a sturdy shelf. Through the tiny holes, I see the robot scuttling around on all fours. And like those time-lapse movies of a plant sprouting, a third pair of limbs comes writhing from the trunk.

With an unnatural twist, the head swivels, first toward the counter then the aisles. I hold my breath. It might be necessary to make some noise if the robot decides to try to finish buffing the floor with Zamboni-guy's face. But no need. It charges straight for me.

What? X-ray vision? Infrared? How can it even tell me apart from that dude? Doesn't matter, I can only run like hell. The drone crashes through the pegboard and slides on the freshly waxed floor.

I zigzag up and down aisles, overturning a rack full of garden tools. Floor cleaner, fertilizer, power tools; no loose display is left standing.

Despite the trail of debris, this thing stays close. To get more speed, I slip off the backpack and hurl it overhead in an arc. The pack hits the warehouse ceiling above and bounces onto the top of a shelf full of insulation. When I round the next corner, the rapid-fire clank of gaining drone appendages stops.

I skid to a halt and flatten against the shelves. Across the aisle is a kiosk with a cash register and a paint-splattered terminal. Several paint cans litter the counter.

"*What color is home for YOU?*" belts out a cheery baritone.

Spinning toward the voice, I see a display covered in a rainbow of color sample strips. In the center, a monitor displays a bearded, handy-looking guy. He's shouting. Loudly.

"*Bay Breeze? Colonial Red? Winter Sun?*"

No volume control. No off switch. Just a tiny motion sensor mounted under the monitor. I shove a desperate hand over the speaker and peer around the corner. Two aisles down, the shelf sways. It shakes again, and I see a clawed arm grip the outer support bars. The drone is in the aisle where I ditched my backpack.

It wants my backpack?

"*Our specially formulated radiant barrier paints beautify and protect...*" Mr. Snitch continues his muffled shouts into my palm.

I can make a break for it. While the drone screws with the backpack, I might stand a chance of escaping. Instinct says to get the hell out of here while it's still possible.

But I can't.

Every hope I have of finding her is in that backpack: the

thumb drive, the laptop. I lose those, and there's no hope. And the book, that's in there too, the only thing I have left from her.

"…thick, premium coating that protects against harmful UV radiation, insulates, and provides ultra-bright colors with one-coat coverage…"

I grab the nearest can of miracle paint this guy is spazzing about and a church key from the paint desk. I race the row of street-facing windows, running perpendicular to the aisles. Through the glare on the windows, only ghostly motions are visible outside, and sirens wail in the distance. Headlights flash next, followed by the hiss of heavy-duty brakes.

I grab onto the shelf. As a toddler I had my own special powers. Mom said I'd climb stuff, make ladders out of the drawers and run around on the kitchen counters. Once, I got on top of the refrigerator where Mom hid my old pacifier. She called me Nips, after the monkey in *Swiss Family Robinson*. Climbing these shelves should be cake.

With a gallon of super paint.

With the entire aisle being rattled by an angry drone trying to reach my backpack.

Halfway up, I remember they also used Nips as a food taster. To make sure stuff they foraged wasn't going to make them sick or kill them.

Yeah. Not cake.

Despite the difficulties, I make it up the backside of the shelf. About three feet of crawlspace exists between the top and the ceiling. The shelf continues to shake as I push through a gap between fuzzy rolls of insulation.

It'd be more fun to roll in poison ivy. Every inch of my

skin, clothed or not, prickles under invisible thorns. Crawling only makes it worse.

My tattered backpack pops into view, inches from a clawed appendage anchored to the top shelf. Fumbling with the key, I start to loosen the lid on the paint. A whole hardware store, and this is the best idea I've got—straight out of a fucking cartoon.

The upper deck lurches with a tortured crack. The shelf sags, folding inward under the pull of the drone's arm. Everything slides—me and the backpack included. Bales of pink, fuzzy insulation disappear over the edge. Grabbing the shelf with one hand, I manage to hook the backpack under a heel before it topples to the floor. The wire handle from the gallon of paint slips. Caught in the last rigid bend of my fingers, all the weight settles in a thin, stabbing line.

I let go of the paint can. At the last second, I direct it with a solid kick from my free foot. The loosened lid pops free and paint splatters across the multifaceted eyes. With both hands, I grab the shelf, twist, and secure the backpack.

I can almost see the subroutines firing in the blinded drone, searching for an appropriate response. A second arm snakes up from below, then a third. With a buzzing hiss, the pincers retract and small round ports appear in the palms.

Oh shit.

My flailing legs shake loose a bale of insulation that slides toward the blinded drone. With a wild, backward kick I send the backpack tumbling into the opposite aisle. A high-pitched whine fills the air, and tufts of insulation ride glowing tracers. Bullets sear through the shelf. Grabbing a bale of insulation, I dive to the far side.

My insulation ride strikes the concrete floor with the slap of a painfully failed cannonball. Air floods out of my lungs on impact. I roll, gasping on the cold floor.

Tracers continue to streak in javelins of orange fire above. They punch through the insulation, pushing out thick, pink cores that break apart and trickle down. Vision blurs. Sound fades. There's only the strangled wheeze of my lungs. Maybe now I'm free.

A distant horn sounds. Through the threaded haze of pink snow, lights flash. An engine growls.

I try to look toward the light. An arm's length away is the backpack. *My* backpack. My chance to end this bullshit. My chance to know the truth.

Light spreads across the store window and for a split second I see two distinct globes. The growl becomes a frenzied wail and the horn a steady blast. A big white box truck barrels toward the windows, aiming right for the aisle with the blind, backpack-obsessed robot.

I grab the shoulder strap of the pack and run down the aisle. Away from the windows. Away from the flying glass.

Doors, people. Doors!

CHAPTER 19

W'RE RATTLING DOWN the highway in Emily's beat-up Bronco. This beast's suspension is straight out of a covered wagon. Everything hurts, again, and I'm reminded of this fact on a regular basis by the ride. But that's not the worst problem. With each little bump, my skin screams.

"It itches so fucking bad!"

Every inch of skin I have, had, or might grow in the future squirms and prickles as though I've been buried in a nest of ants.

I remember getting halfway down the aisle and the world exploding, and next, Emily was dragging me out the newly installed drive-thru. I might've even passed out. Not sure. It all seems like a blur of pink fuzz. Dreaded, horrific, pink fuzz. I should have let the robot shoot me.

Emily casts worried looks, finally forcing out a breath she's probably been holding since she gunned that dude's box truck through the store window and into the backpack-obsessed robot.

"You've got to think!" Her shrill voice does not help the constant prickly, tingly, writhy, please-make-it-stop feeling.

"I don't…" *squirm* "…know…" *twitch* "…what you mean."

"Damn it, Spence! You attacked a piece of military hardware with a can of paint!"

"High quality, single-coat, UV resistant." I jam a hand down the back of my jeans and itch furiously as I add, "It protects and beautifies."

"Are you serious? Think, Spence!"

"I'm completely serious…" *thrash* "…I'd die to be coated in it *right now!*" There's sympathy in her eyes but I can tell she's not going to give this up, so I plainly say, "I did what needed to be done."

"What needs to be done is you staying alive!"

"I needed that data."

"Tell me, how are you going to find your father if a robot blows your head off?" She shakes her head and says, "You're exactly like him."

"What?" I stammer as I rake my fingernails down my back.

"Your father. You're just like him!"

"No. No way! I bet he's *impervious to itching!*"

"Exactly like him," she repeats, with much less sympathy this time.

"No!" There's a twitch on my upper thigh. Did it really get through my jeans? Does this shit move? "*No!*"

She's shocked by the emphatic scream, but shakes her head and keeps at the lecture. "Racing off into the nearest mess without a thought for yourself or what anyone else might be feeling—"

"Wait a minute! If I hadn't left," *My God, the bottoms of my feet are itching! How the...* "...the robot would've hurt you."

"It was probably after you, Spencer. How can you not get that after what we saw on the news? He surrendered because of you."

A silence descends filled only by the rumble of the engine and scrape of blunt fingernails on skin.

"It wanted the laptop," I gasp. For an instant, the itching seems under control.

"How do you know?"

"I dropped the backpack and it left me alone."

"That forum you posted to, that got tracked, I bet." She thankfully says this without sounding too satisfied.

"No, I covered my tracks. The site is crazy hard to find."

"Fine, how else did the killer robot find us?"

We hit another bump, and every subdued inch bristles with fresh itching. I lean back and try to focus. Or meditate. Some kind of yoga guru shit. Yeah, doesn't work.

"What about your friend?" She says slowly between the fresh string of curse words I'm polluting the air with. "The one who's going to help with the code."

"Eric? No way. He doesn't even know Dad's an Augment." I dig my fingers into my scalp, chasing an elusive twitch. "Who would he tell anyway?"

"Maybe he's got new friends? It's been a long while since you've seen him."

She's right, and his reaction online was... weird. But there's no way Eric would do that. I've got to believe there's at least one person I can trust. "C'mon. He's just another kid, right?" I have to force that last part out as a fresh storm of itching erupts. "Oatmeal! I read something about oatmeal!"

"What?"

"You rub it on? Swim in it? Stops itching!" I grab a handful of skin on my side and squeeze. *"Tell me we're going to see that Quaker bastard!"*

"We'll get help, soon."

"No! *No! Now!"*

Emily glances out the window, frustrated. "We're not quite there. Forty minutes, tops."

"Then here!"

"Hang in there." Emily squints at a passing road sign. "We're close to the university. I could swing by the office, drop off the few samples I have. Keep things business as usual. But is that even safe right now?"

"I don't care about safe. How many times…"

Emily's quiet, her face fading in and out under passing headlights. I clasp my hands together until my fingers start turning colors then close my eyes and think happy thoughts. Kiddie pools of oatmeal. Cold ice cubes on my skin. Hydrocortisone. Calamine! That's right, that's the stuff. "Drive faster."

*

The George Mason University biochem lab is pretty much what I would expect from a top-notch research facility. Cabinets with glass doors line the walls, filled with opaque containers, their labels turned squarely toward the room. Others hold tubes and vials along with a bunch of technical equipment I've never seen. Recessed workstations dot the spaces between all the cabinets. It's a nerd playground.

In one corner, there's a glass partition that houses that bad boy Emily mentioned at her apartment: the electron microscope. A large vertical cylinder studded with dials, the microscope platform attaches to a workstation with two monitors.

Emily marches across the room and starts digging through a row of lockers, "What size are you?"

"What?"

"Pants, shirt. What size?" She's pulling clothes out and checking tags, returning them without bothering to close the doors before she moves on to the next.

"Medium," I lie. After a certain age, you get tired of saying "small". "Pant size, whatever you can find." Good luck with that. I usually have to find a belt and roll them up anyway. The college guys that probably use those lockers aren't lamenting the loss of adjustable straps in kid clothes.

With as little movement as possible, I place my backpack on an empty table. The itching is only really bad now when my clothes shift. It's why I refused help while limping up the stairs. Maybe Emily thinks I was acting tough, but really, I needed complete control over the movement of my clothes. "Hey, that was badass, back there."

Emily twists my direction for a split second and goes back to peeking in lockers. "What do you mean?"

"The store. The truck."

She doesn't respond right away. "You kidding? It was insane. I didn't know what else to do."

"How'd you get that guy's truck anyway? Was he..."

She holds up a pair of sweatpants between us and squints. Her hands are shaking. "He was fine. A little shocked, but fine."

I nod.

"This will have to do," she says as she crosses the room, glancing out the windows. "Ever been in a Decon room?"

"No. Went to Comic-Con once. That was freaking awesome."

"This, this is not nearly as awesome." She disappears into another locker and grabs a collared shirt. "I need your clothes."

My eyes lose focus, and my mouth stops accepting signals.

Emily's business-like demeanor shifts, and her mouth bursts into a fierce grin as her eyebrows swoop upward. "You're blushing! And speechless!" she gasps. "God, I need to remember how to do that!" The delight in her face makes my cheeks burn even more.

"Uhhh…" I grunt in an unsuccessful attempt to refute the "speechless" part.

"Come on," she says, and jogs by with the scavenged clothes draped on her arm. "I don't have keys to the gym and it's one in the morning. Not many options, but we'll get you taken care of."

My anti-itch shuffle doesn't keep pace, but I don't get too far behind. She stiff-arms her way through a set of double-hinged doors. I follow, carefully avoiding contact with the doors on the return swing.

We enter another stark lab room, but this one's got a weird, ceiling-height caterpillar tent in the center. She pulls aside an opening in the first section and I see that the whole tent hangs on a circular rod suspended from the ceiling. She points inside. "Strip."

I gulp. Her finger raises to point at the far side, where a

second parted curtain reveals a chrome shower tree and a floor drain. "Flush." She then raises the fresh clothes to eye level. "Cover."

I begin to roll up my sweatshirt. She turns, heads to the far end of the tent chain, and drops the fresh clothes. "I'm going to run to my office, I'll be right back."

As soon as she's out the door, I tear off my clothes and fling them aside even before entering the "stripping" tent. The shower head at the flush station isn't any more than a shiny pimple, but it'll do. I smash the button and scream.

She could've said it was cold water. Icehole-bunker-on-a-bad-day cold. It doesn't matter. Undeterred, I take the spray full-on, and it strikes with enough force to leave little waves of skin in its wake. The pressure also makes me incredibly familiar with the location of every bump and bruise I've collected over the past few days, too. Between the cold and the pain, I'm positive I sound like a wounded monkey. But the itching is going away. That's worth all the pain in the world.

The shower dribbles to a stop and I tiptoe into the next section. My scavenged clothes lie next to a towel on a small table. I should be feeling miserable—dripping wet, beat up, half-frozen. But I'm not.

Strangely, the world feels normal, for the first time in days. The curtained walls form a tight space. A chrome showerhead drips behind me. Goose pimples pucker on my skin. It's so close to home. Well, the bunker.

How messed up is that? The bunker: my new gauge for "normal".

A ticking sound creeps through the room. A noise that

couldn't have been heard over the shower spray, or my squeal-ing for that matter. I don't remember if I could hear it when I started or not.

The doors clack. I slip into a very loose pair of sweats, cinching the waist to the point I have to tie the cord in a knot and tuck it away somewhere around my knees.

Emily calls out, "I've heard primate mating calls that were more attractive." See. A monkey. There's the start of a snort but then silence, and the weird ticking takes over. "What's this?"

I slip into the shirt and slide through the curtain. "I don't know. Wasn't it going on when we came in?"

"No." Emily crouches over one of the tables where my Giants sweatshirt landed. She moves the shirt around and the time between clicks shrinks. "Strange."

"What is it?"

"Geiger counter."

"No way!" I watch as she puts the pants I was wearing next to the counter and the clicking increases again. "I'm, what, radioactive?"

Maybe I *will* be tossing cars soon. Or cookies.

Emily picks up the counter and starts exploring my stuff, testing distances, ranges. She checks me and comes up blank.

"The trip in the pod?" I ask hopefully.

"Pod's shielded," she mumbles as she methodically picks through my backpack.

"Well, there was the time I opened the robot and checked out its guts." I say this with ripping-off-a-Band-Aid speed.

Emily barely swallows an instinctive response and main-tains an attempt at a neutral tone, "Go grab your backpack."

Through the swinging doors and up the hall, I return with the pack in seconds and she places it at a workstation. The Geiger counter clicks ferociously as she dangles the wand inside. "Okay, then."

"We're not going to get cancer, or lose our hair or anything?"

"Sieverts aren't that high, but this isn't normal."

Sorting through the contents, she quickly narrows the source of the radiation down to the laptop and the attached sat phone. The clicking blurs into a rapid pulse. She looks on, confused.

"I'd like to point out, that's your stuff." Frozen in thought, Emily ignores my jab. "What do you think it is?"

"Not sure."

"Any way we can find out?"

She snaps on a pair of latex gloves and carefully arranges the backpack's contents on the table. "Maybe, but we shouldn't stay in one place too long. Besides, our flight to San Fran is waiting."

"Nice. That was quick. How?"

"I've got a friend, he owns a plane." She splays my Giants sweatshirt across the table next to the laptop. I tense up, waiting for her to pin it down and reach for a scalpel.

"That's my favorite shirt, you know."

She only continues to wave the counter, adjusting knobs and listening carefully to the clicks and beeps. "If that's the point of first contact, based on decay and what you're telling me, it doesn't make sense that it's stronger on the laptop." My stomach sinks as she wiggles the end of the sleeves. My favorite shirt, contaminated by robo-guts.

"Unless it was on your laptop first. Any way to figure that out?"

"We don't have time for a thorough test. We need to keep moving."

"What about that electron microscope? Think we could see whatever is there?" Flicking off the Geiger counter, Emily chews on her bottom lip. An almost pained expression scrunches her face and I try to persuade her, "C'mon. You know you want to play scientist."

Emily rolls her eyes but the tight expression doesn't change. "I can't explain this. There's no way the radiation would transfer with that kind of strength from simple contact with the shirt."

Breathing a sigh of relief, I snatch the sweatshirt off the table and speed limp toward the door. "Sweet. Dibs on the microscope!"

CHAPTER 20

"SPENCER, YOU DON'T call dibs on a half-million-dollar piece of equipment." Exasperated, Emily flicks on the monitors. "Give me your sweatshirt."

One monitor displays the inside of the electron microscope's sample chamber, the other shows an interface with a mouse pointer and drop down menus. It appears to be a standard piece of software. "Come on! A motivated kindergartner could operate this. Let me try something cool first. Here, what about this?" I dig the iPod ear buds out of my backpack. "I wanna see Mount Earfunk!"

She snatches the sweatshirt. "I admit, that could be interesting. You never know what could be between those ears."

My eyes haven't left the sweatshirt. Emily confirms my fears and reaches for a scalpel. "Whoa, wait... Nobody said anything about dissecting the G-shirt."

"A little piece. It'll be fine."

I wince as a chunk of the cuff gets sacrificed in the name of science. Emily places the cutting on a disk and into the microscope chamber. A steady hum that sounds like a fluorescent bulb on its last few candles fills the office as she snaps the chamber closed.

I've read a little about this stuff. That noise would be the vacuum. Something about colliding electrons and the vacuum keeping the cathodes from arcing during operation. And the smell. That's definitely the smell of a slot car track from when Kyle and I were kids. Not the burning track—that was god-awful, what with the thick black smoke and choking odor of plastic. No, this smell is the cars as they'd spark along the embedded rails. A good smell. Clean.

"You might be surprised at the stuff living in and on your body. You get over that in Microbiology 101," Emily says. It takes me a bit to realize she's still seriously considering the earfunk idea while she works. "Okay, let's see what we've got here."

An image appears on the interface screen; a forest of twisted bare trunks. A whole new world inside my favorite sweatshirt. Something scuttles across the view. "What the fuck was that?"

"*Dermatophagoides farinae.* Dust mite. And you should really work on your vocabulary."

"You're the one talking dirty."

"Har har," Emily scoffs. She leans forward and adjusts the screen positioning. "You never quit, do you?"

As if to prove a point, my mouth shoots off without much input from my brain which is currently entranced by the tech show. "Dad says I'm a pain in the ass. Mom said I was tenacious."

Without turning from the monitors, Emily nods

appreciatively, "A pain in the ass for the world's toughest Augment? That's an accomplishment."

"Not like he didn't cause his fair share of trouble." My voice cracks.

"What do you mean?"

"Nothing." I keep staring at the monitors. I can't make eye contact with Emily. Dad's a freaking Augment. The toughest, she said it. But he never did find Mom. Maybe never wanted to. Because of those weird dreams, I'm seeing Mom so clearly now, it's almost like she's here, watching. I don't care if I find him. He can take care of himself. But I'll find Mom.

Another multi-limbed beast scuttles by on the monitor. No, this is different from the first. Multiple legs and a tiny glowing strip of pulsing light. It quickly slips into the upper right corner. "There! What's that?"

Emily turns, "Where? What? Probably another dust mite."

"It was right there. I'm not sure it was even alive."

"What do you mean, 'not alive'?"

"Looked like a microchip. With legs."

She presses her face inches from the monitor and her hands perform automatic motions of routine and experience. Within seconds, she pulls the creature up dead center. The image freezes and resumes several times. Her eyes dart back and forth between the monitors. She glances at me, then back again.

"That's not a living creature, Spencer."

"Is there an echo? My guess, you guys probably aren't working on tiny robots here."

"If anyone in the university was building this level of

nanotech, I think I would have heard about it. Besides, we don't have the facilities to pull this off." She zooms in. "Nobody does. I mean that can't be more than fifty micrometers across."

"Standard English, please. I suck at the metric system."

"Smaller than an amoeba." Emily leans forward and gasps, "Oh my! More!"

We both stare as Emily maneuvers the display, revealing more and more of these tiny invaders crawling through the wilderness of my sweatshirt. Maybe a dozen are on the viewer. They seem to be moving in formation, a tiny platoon exploring a jungle of cotton fiber trees and hunting dust mite wildlife. Every so often, one will stop and search the immediate area with needle-like limbs.

"The way they're moving. Their interactions appear... complex. They might not be alive, but they're behavior suggests otherwise. Like ants, maybe. Some sort of hive mentality."

A mental curb stomp follows. Hive, behavior, electronics.

Leaving Emily to her amazement, I rush to the table with my backpack. Spreading the contents across the table, I slide out the laptop and follow the connected data cable to the sat phone. The power LED glows a steady green. Pissed off, ready to storm out of her apartment, I never turned it off. I click the power button and the light fades. I stare at the extinguished lens.

It winks back to life.

"What the fuck?"

"Spencer, language." The scolding tone drifting from her work station lacks any sincerity.

I press the button again, holding it down for several

seconds before releasing it. The light sparks to life, only this time faster. "The phone won't shut off."

"Huh?" Emily finally turns.

Flipping the case over, I slide the battery off the back and watch as the light dims, staring to make sure it doesn't reignite. A single green glow lingers, but it's only in my imagination. "We've got to get out of here."

CHAPTER 21

"**N**OT THIS GUY."

We're pulling up in front of Doc Abercrombie's little estate again, somewhere between the suburbs of Pretentious and Retired. The house is probably ten times the size of the bunker, or Emily's apartment. An estate, complete with a manicured yard that could be a state park. In the early morning light, the house has a lonely glow.

"He lives!" Emily half smiles, but her eyes continue to scan the skies relentlessly as we make our way up the gravel drive running between the meticulously spaced trees. "You haven't said much since the lab."

It was too intense, waiting for a drone to drop out of nowhere. I'm out of EMPs, paint cans, and places to bruise. "Sleep. I'm trying to kick that habit," I grumble. "What are we doing *here*?"

"Spencer, this is the only way."

"Who lives in a castle alone besides Dracula or Doctor Frankenstein? This guy has body parts in the basement, I guarantee."

"He got the house from his parents when they passed away. And there is no basement."

"Great, body parts in the freezer. It's Dahmer or Major Force. Can't you just buy a plane ticket, or does this guy have to buy it for you? Maybe I can hack into an airline reservation system."

"No, he's got a private plane," I bet she can feel my eye-roll as she says "private plane", "and we want to avoid getting on anybody's radar." Emily whips the Bronco around the circular drive and jams it into park. She slumps on the wheel and tucks her hand under the side of her head as she sighs. "Yes, I'm paranoid. You should be too, after everything that's happened."

I check the sky again. We both jump at a rap on the glass. With another sigh, Emily rolls down her window. In the darkness, the white surgical mask around his neck gives him away. Martin. He's wearing scrubs. Douchebag.

"Come inside, Em, uh, Mr. Johnston, right?"

Yeah, genius, you figured it out. I'm not who I said I was. Congrats.

I slide out of the Bronco, or mostly ooze out of the Bronco. My battered muscles have started to stiffen during the drive. Best if Doc Abercrombie doesn't notice. I've already got one babysitter. I can put up with her for now. She's cute, smart, and put a truck through a wall. Two babysitters? Not sure that works for me.

"So, what's really going on here, Em?" Martin's voice trails me toward the door. I hear her reply, but can't quite make it out.

Martin attempts a whisper but I hear it loud and clear. "He

looks worse than yesterday. Do I need to call Child Protective Services? Is that what this is about?"

"If only you knew how stupid a question that is," I mutter.

Emily's alarmed eyes glow in the dim light. "Not now. Let's go inside and talk this over, alright?" She sounds tired and that same sense of fatigue washes over me. One pleasant memory of my earlier visit to Chateau de Douche was that fancy leather sectional with the hi-tech television. Maybe we can spend some quality time together. I shamble toward the door, pushing my way into the entry.

"Make yourself at home, Spencer." Martin sounds a bit annoyed.

"Yep."

"On second thought, stop by the office first and let's see how you're doing."

"Nope." I keep walking, headed to the living room.

"Spencer! We're Martin's guests," Emily scolds.

I wheel and make for his office but keep my head down. "Sure, but let's make this quick. No probing and turning my head to cough, okay?"

Martin watches, unamused. Emily steps closer to me and whispers, "He's agreed to help us. Play nice."

"Come on. Doc here has probably already called the cops," I say at a normal volume.

Emily starts to reply and her eyes go to Martin. Without any further hint of annoyance, Martin strides past me into the office. "Doctor-patient confidentiality." He looks at me. "I do have a patient, right?"

Before long, I've let Martin check my bumps and

bruises—everywhere I let him poke around, that is. He bandages a few of the worst scrapes and wraps my ankle. From the kitchen, the rich scent of coffee floats through the air.

He's staring into my eye through one of those handheld scopes that ends in a disturbingly pointy cone for what seems like way too long. "Do you need to blind me every time?" I imagine I can see his eye, enormous and unblinking, past the reddish-purple halo that has replaced my vision. He lets up and steps away.

"I do when you keep ending up with head trauma." He tucks the retina scorcher into a pocket and folds his arms, saying, "Emily didn't want to say much on the phone. You can wait until she gets back in here to talk, but knowing what's going on here can only help me out."

"Well, I'm being hunted by a super villain's military hardware."

His expression doesn't change.

"And I keep kicking ass. Mostly singlehanded."

He nods, stone-faced.

I hear footsteps in the hallway.

"But Emily's no slouch either. We're like a team." Emily clips into the room with two cups of coffee. I smile and extend a hand, continuing to give Doc the lowdown, "A robot-ass-kicking team. Of two."

She keeps walking and hands the extra mug to the Doc. Without taking his eyes off me, he accepts the cup and nods with a dimpled smile. "My initial diagnosis is that he's delusional. I think he's been playing too many video games."

Emily turns toward me, cradling the mug in both hands

and takes a sip. She closes her eyes and breathes in deeply. Once open again her eyes light between Martin and me, and eventually roll toward the ceiling while she takes careful steps into the hall. "The testosterone is harshing my caffeine buzz. I might regret this, but you two talk this out. I'm going to try to do some productive thinking. Or maybe nap. And Spencer, remember, Martin can help us get to your friend." With that, she's gone. In the silence that follows I hear the television click to life.

"Well?" Martin sits in the chair behind the desk. He leans back and rests sneakered feet on the edge of the dark-grained wood.

She's right. He's maybe the only person that can help. Driving would take days.

"Can I use your phone?" I ask.

"After I know what's going on." He's not going to make this easy. Calm, relaxed, patient, he starts by asking, "What happened to you?"

"Robots."

"Right." He takes another sip of coffee and puts the mug on a ceramic coaster, then folds his arms against his chest. We enter into a quick staring contest neither of us wants to lose. "Spencer, I've seen some bad situations in my life. There's no sense hiding what's going on here."

"Honestly. Robots. You watch the news?" Since when is an ER doctor a shrink, anyway?

"Watch? No. Usually I'm too busy. But they've got it playing on one TV or another up at the hospital. There was something about Mumbai?"

"Do you sleep in those?" I've been dying to have that question answered, and I'm not so anxious to start telling him about my problems.

"I have. Can't avoid it in the ER when you've been on shift for twenty-four hours, and it slows down enough to get some shuteye." He reaches for the mug and takes a long draw before setting it neatly on a coaster. "I came straight here from the hospital when Emily called. Had to cash in a favor and get my shift covered, but it's all good. Take all the time you need to tell me what's up."

Time. I can almost feel it. Pressing down, hard. A weight precariously balanced between sleeping for an entire day and finding out what happened to Mom. Keeping ahead of the Black Beetle and these robots—microscopic and otherwise. Is this a typical day for the Crimson Mask?

He'll probably refuse to answer any questions until I've answered his, but I'll start with them anyway. "So, how long have you known Emily?"

"Eight years now. We met in undergrad at George Mason. I went on to med school and she stayed for her doctorate, but we kept in touch."

"You guys dated?"

"Yeah, for a bit. It got tricky with our schedules, they never seemed to link up. Then she started working on an off-site project with the CDC and she suddenly had even less time than I did."

"When was that? The CDC project?"

"About six years ago." Martin reaches for the mug and takes another sip and I do the math. Six years, the Anthrax Kid. He interrupts the revelation. "What about you? How long have you known her?"

This math is much harder. I try to count hours in my head, then days, and I'm figuring out I don't have a clue how much time has passed. "Several days, or so."

Martin's expression finally changes as his eyebrows raise over the steaming mug. "Is it okay if I verify that with her later?"

"Yeah."

"For now, I'm going to assume you've got problems with your family—"

"Sure you're name isn't Watson, Doc?"

"—let me say, I get it. I do."

"No, you don't. Seriously. There's no possible way."

"In the ER you get a close look at how messed up stuff can get. Life is crazy. Hell, I've been through it myself. I wasn't much younger than you when I lost my parents."

"Look…" I'm about to dig in on the incessant kid references, when what he just said punches me in the chest.

"It made me into the person I am today. Not having them around was hard. Making all the decisions, growing up before my time. I mean, I wasn't completely alone. I had good caretakers, people that'd been with my family for years. I lucked out, too. Most of them seemed to have my best interests at heart. Not everyone does. So I get your reluctance to talk to me. But letting those people help in the first place was the only way to find out who I could trust."

"What happened to your parents?"

Martin sets the mug down again and stares like he's considering the empty space around it. He keeps staring as he speaks,

"It's fine. It was a long time ago. A carjacking gone bad. They were both shot and the perpetrator fled the scene without even taking anything. Dad died instantly. Mom, she bled out in the ambulance."

The scrubs look a bit different on him now.

"Why are you telling me this?"

"Because I need you to trust me, Spencer. I do want to help. Emily is a good friend, and I can tell she's in trouble. I can also tell there's plenty you're not sharing with me."

"All right. Let me start with the robots…"

CHAPTER 22

MARTIN'S EXPRESSION WAS priceless after he returned from "verifying" what I said with Emily. Yep, my Dad's the Crimson Mask. Yep, I'm apparently being hunted by killer robots. And last but sure as hell not least, *yes, I'm legally an adult.* Right about now, though, I imagine my expression matches that same Cubs-won-the-World-Series look he had.

"This is yours?" I sputter.

"My parent's company needed a bigger jet. I took this one," replies Martin matter-of-factly.

On the wet tarmac sits a sleek private jet with a pointed nose and swept back wings. Chrome glistens along the leading wing edge and the intake of each engine. A half dozen rect-angular windows break the white surface. The narrow cockpit window peers down the runway like a knight's visor on the jousting line.

I so hate this guy.

Getting the flight set up was easier than I'd imagined it would be. We parked Martin's Beamer next to the hangar and walked into the office. He waved at some dudes while I grabbed about three *free* donuts, Emily a cup of coffee, and next thing we're standing by a plane. No x-rays, no security checkpoints, no tickets, no trail. I guess Emily made the right call. Not only do we have a direct flight to San Francisco, but we're going in style.

"When she said you had a plane, I was thinking more along the lines of prop engines and sardine seating," I say.

"Well, you're in luck." Martin heads for the stairs leading up to the open cabin. An attendant hustles over. He matches the private plane terminal atmosphere that we just came from with his spotless, crisp overalls, clean hands and professional smile.

"Welcome, Dr. Alexander. Everything's ready to go," beams the overly cheerful attendant while he extends a hand and helps Emily up the steps. Martin returns the smile and motions to me unnecessarily—I'm right behind her.

Once on the plane, there are two captain's chairs to my right, facing a glossy wooden table between them. The aisle continues, flanked by plush armchairs, with the last five feet or so taken up by a cream-colored padded bench. To my left is the cockpit. I let out a low whistle. I've only seen the inside of big commercial airliners. While the massive rows of gauges, switches and jeweled lights on those always looked pretty cool, this is A-mazing. Three large LCDs take up most of the instrument panel, and a thin line of switches and buttons frames them. The yoke is closer to a go-cart steering wheel than what I've seen on a plane before.

"You like?" Martin's voice is right over my shoulder.

"Meh."

Brushing past Emily, I sling my bag to the ground and sink into the leather bench. "Well, it beats a cross-country trip in Emily's banged up beast!"

Emily flashes a hurt look. "Don't knock the Bronc." The pouty lips switch to a playful smile. "I've known it longer than I've known you. And it's a lot less trouble." She stows the giant purse that she'd dug out of her locker at the university. A colorful striped bag with woven handles. In it are the electronics—sat phone, laptop, even my iPod—hermetically sealed in hazardous waste bags.

Martin steps inside, waves at the attendant and pulls the cabin door closed. "Your next stop, ladies and gentlemen, California." His relaxed tone is in sharp contrast to the disciplined professionalism of Doctor Alexander and he disappears into the cockpit. Emily follows.

I swing my feet onto the couch, dig out the *Swiss Family Robinson* and prop up on the armrest. "Where's the flight attendant button? A pillow would be nice." The only answer to my question is the whine of the engines warming up for takeoff.

A silky smooth rise into the air, and the landing gear are tucked away before I even know what's happening. Clouds race by, and as we pierce the top layer, they settle to a steady crawl below us. Open, boundless sky competes briefly with Mom's birthday message on the book's first page.

I peer over the book into the cockpit and see the top of Emily's head angled on the headrest. Engines whir—not too loud, not too soft. I close my eyes to try and clear my head. Pain from the bumps and bruises fades with that pre-sleep numbness. My head dips. Eyes surrender. I twitch on the couch, only vaguely aware of the book slipping out of limp fingers.

*

My eyes flutter open, then closed. From that brief glimpse, I open one again, wide. This isn't Martin's jet. I'm in my bedroom. An apartment in Omaha, I think. The walls are covered in Giants posters for the '03 season. I was excited then. It was a good season, but they'll choke in the National League Series against Florida. If this is a dream, I'll pretend they won.

Doing duty as a bookend on a wall shelf is my consolation trophy from an aborted Little League season. Beneath that, a desk with a computer tower. Ancient technology, a Pentium 4 Northwood core. I'm lying in bed, the worn copy of *Swiss Family Robinson* in hand.

A tray clatters in the hall, and my door opens.

"Good Morning, hon. Hope you're feeling better," Mom says brightly.

Breakfast in bed the day after our two-person party for my thirteenth birthday. I had the "flu". It was that, or going to yet another school and fighting through the new kid routine. Besides, Mom gave me all kinds of creative birthday presents. Usually the toys and stuff were "from Dad". The books and sick days came from her.

"Better. I bet I'll be ready for school tomorrow." The words slip out without any thought.

"Yes, sir, I think you might be." Mom sets the tray down—pancakes with a chocolate chip smile and whipped cream eyes. "Your first day as a teenager. Figured I'd sneak this in one last time. Of course, if your stomach isn't up to it..."

I lock the tray in a death grip. "I'll suck smiley-face pancakes through a feeding tube when I'm one hundred and thirteen. Don't ever stop making these!"

She laughs, smiles. My throat cinches up and I think I might cry. Lines of worry crease her forehead and she asks, "What's wrong?"

"Nothing. I'm fine. I mean, I'm, um, sick, but nothing's wrong. Nothing else." I stare into her face, trying to memorize every detail, again. It's even clearer than the last few dreams. A tear creeps down my cheek.

"Honey, what is it?" She sits down and places her hand on my head, stroking my hair.

"Nothing."

"Spencer…"

"Is this real?"

"What do you mean?"

"Uh. Real whipped cream."

She squints an eye, "Yes, why?"

I always start eating the pancakes by carving an outer circle around the face. I save the eyes and mouth for last. It's where all the sugary bits are, but mainly, I always felt a bit weird eating those first. When I was younger, I'd talk to the face and tell him about the adventure he was going to have in my stomach. Sometimes, he'd talk back to my mom for being such a horrible person, feeding a poor defenseless pancake to her child.

It's a bit pathetic at thirteen, let alone nineteen—I'm not sure which I am now. I want to skip the jokes and enjoy the gooey sweetness. I want to savor this bizarre, panic-free moment. Dream or memory, doesn't matter.

Perched on the edge of the bed, Mom smiles, looking somewhere beyond the plate, and tucks her hair behind one ear.

"No, not my left eye! There's no love for pirate pancakes!" I attempt the high-pitched pancake voice, but it doesn't sound the same.

"Oh, Spencer." Her grin is forced, but she reaches out and pats my knee. Her hand stays.

It was my job to cheer her up when Dad was gone. This time it isn't working, and it didn't work then either. I'd overheard a conversation and figured out he'd gone to New York. Gone six weeks this time. The news broke about the Anthrax Kid's capture three weeks ago, but he still hadn't come home.

I can't ignore it anymore, no matter how much I want to. Answers I have now that I didn't then keep gnawing their way into my thoughts. I recall Dad's explanation about the bunker refrigerator. It was only there so he could keep samples for a case. The anthrax case. Samples a biologist would make. That happened six years ago, the same time Martin said he stopped seeing as much of Emily. And the look of concern now on Mom's face about Dad, missing—a perfect reflection of Emily's when we found out he'd surrendered.

Looks like she's more than just a worried colleague.

"You're not worried about Dad, are you?" I try to hide the anger in my voice.

"Always." She doesn't make eye contact until after she says the word. Her irises have changed again. Under her mirror gaze, the room shrinks. Her hand tightens on my knee. "Where is she?"

The air feels wet, too thick for my lungs. I try to breathe

and the dense air forms a skin over my lips. She? Images of Dad lounging around the bunker with Emily assault my mind. Enjoying his cozy little getaway while Mom and I tried not to wonder whether or not he was coming back this time. Next, I see Emily standing on the plane with her bag slung over her shoulder and that worried expression on her face. I struggle to speak. "What the hell?" I gasp.

"Spencer! What's gotten into you?" Her expression is flat but her eyes are their normal color now.

I can breath again. My room, the birthday breakfast in bed, all return, but any feeling that this place was ever home has been erased.

"We should go. You don't have to live like this. Maybe you won't—"

"Live... live like what?" She turns to stare absently at the wall. "Spencer, he needs us. We need him, too. Don't we?" Her question rides a wave of genuine confusion.

"In a couple of years you'll get kidnapped by a psycho that Dad managed to piss off. He doesn't do shit about it."

She peels her eyes from the spot on the wall and reaches out to take the tray. The intensity in her face returns. "We'll be okay. You'll make sure that man can't hurt us. Then we can all be together. A family, Spencer. We'll be a family and nobody will ever take that away from us." Her irises are empty, colorless, and the whites are living mercury.

Uncomfortable under that hungry glare, I look down at the book in my lap and it's changed. The manila cover carries a single line of type:

KUBARK.

CHAPTER 23

FOR A MOMENT, I can't move, can't scream. Agony squeezes out as a strangled whimper. Then, I'm released. A thin blanket clings to my damp secondhand shirt. No posters. No desk. Empty walls are broken only by the narrow row of windows along the fuselage. My copy of *Swiss Family Robinson* sits on the table. Through the open cockpit doorway, I can see Emily and Martin's heads poking above their seats and bobbing in a conversation I can't hear over the engines.

I need to tell them that she's alive. She needs my help. Time to activate the hyper-drive on this jet and get to San Fran, yesterday. But there were other revelations in that dream, too. Maybe it's time to make my own plans.

Swinging my feet off the leather bench, I peel off the blanket and start down the aisle. Emily's bag peeks out from under a seat at the far end of the row. As I approach, pieces of their conversation become clear. Made strong by a harsh tone, I hear Martin first.

"Then what, Em? You can't keep running," he says as he scans the skies. Emily's reply is muffled, but she stays fixed on whatever distant cloud she's considering. She curls up in the copilot's chair, her feet underneath her and arms pulled tightly out of sight. I kneel next to her bag.

Martin continues his lecture. "You're going to get hurt, or get that kid killed." If my hand weren't digging around Emily's purse, I'd launch a verbal smackdown. "You've got to stay out of this and tell the authorities." Martin shifts in his chair and I can no longer see him past the door frame.

Emily's head snaps his direction, her full profile coming into view. I freeze. She's too focused on Martin to notice me.

"No, we can't go to the authorities. We've been over this. Sean was in that bunker for a reason. He didn't want to be found by anyone. Not until he'd taken care of the Black Beetle."

"You honestly think you can do that?" asks Martin, bewildered.

"No… but he can. I need to find him. Set him free somehow." Her head turns back to the window and whatever else she says gets lost in the jet wash. My hand sinks into the purse letting only the barest whisper of bio-bag slide along my fingertips while I grope for familiar edges and corners, my eyes locked on the cockpit.

"I still think that's a job for the cops, the FBI, the CIA, whoever. Not you."

Emily shakes her head. "I last spoke to him before the London incident. He said not to trust anybody, especially his government contacts."

At least now I know where he was. The lull in the conversation dissolves and Martin's bedside manner voice returns. "Those experiments have been shown to cause neurological damage."

Half my forearm buried in the purse, I again fight off an urge to jump up and kick the doc somewhere near the proctology department. Dad may be a jerk, but that's *my* dad he's talking about.

"Do not go there," Emily warns.

"I'm worried about you, Em." After nothing but silence from Emily, Martin continues, "You remember the attack in downtown Alexandria, three years ago? Right? That idiot, Captain Dynamite took on Black Beetle. The ER was packed. I amputated a lady's leg that had been crushed under a chunk of concrete..."

My fingers brush the slim shape of the thumb drive, sealed behind a thick barrier bag. It slides against another object stuffed in the same container. I follow the edges until I feel the unmistakable antenna of the sat phone.

"...same as her dog. She was still clutching the leash, screaming, when they brought her in. The paramedics had to cut it and drag her into the ambulance."

I pinch the bag between two fingers while maneuvering my other hand past the laptop and spreading the purse open far enough that I can lift the bag without crinkling the stiff plastic or brushing against the other contents.

"There was this other guy with a piece of rebar through his skull. We saved him, but he's lucky to be speaking in single syllables. That's not even the worst of it..."

I rise cautiously, staring into the cockpit where Martin's matter-of-fact tone has Emily's head turned away from him and shaking vigorously. Every ache and overtaxed muscle complains as blood tries to find its way through my legs. Before I knelt down, there'd been only a dull sensation, but now my leg muscles ache. I bite my lip and turn to the back of the plane.

"Stop!" Midway to the leather bench, I've half-turned before I realize she's talking to Martin. "Sean isn't like that! I'm going to find him!" Wild desperation in Emily's voice only further explains why she waited in the woods for weeks, or months as a favor for her "colleague". She slumps forward, resting her forehead on her palm.

Two words escape Martin's lips, "I see."

"I don't want to talk about this anymore." Emily's voice is pained and she buries her face in her hands.

I make it back to my seat in the deafening silence without being seen. I'm zipping up my backpack when I hear Emily say, "Hey. How'd you sleep?" She places a hand on an armrest and kneels beside me.

"Fine. Just putting my book away."

"You doing okay?"

"Fine."

Her hand touches my shoulder and she sits on the bench next to me. She massages her temples and her face pinches. "We'll find him, Spencer. I promise."

You do that.

"I'm going to check out the cockpit, if that's cool."

"Sure. Martin won't mind." Worry creases her face behind a mask of genuine pain. "My head's killing me. I'm just going to rest for a bit."

She's really attractive. Smart. A total geek, even. I can see why I was stumbling over myself when I crashed into her arms. I can see what Dad probably saw. But she isn't Mom. Not even close. My eyes linger too long, letting my own mask crumble enough that I can tell she watches my entire trip up the aisle to the cockpit. Martin's not my first choice of company, but it's the only other place to go.

Martin twists to face me and his lips spread into a warm smile. "So there's the patient. How's the ride so far?" He stands and puts a hand on my shoulder. He has to bend a little at the knees so he can stare "deep into my eyes". Awkward, but I should be used to it by now.

"C'mon, Doc, really?"

"Have a seat." He motions to the copilot's chair. "Any pain? Headaches?"

"Nope. I'm good." I drop into the high-backed chair. "How long until we get there?"

"A couple hours." He reaches over to one of the touch screens and taps. An ETA of one hour and forty-seven minutes shows under a GPS heading. Extremely cool, but unsettling.

"Anybody could track the GPS signals," I say.

Realization dawns slowly on Martin's face. "Oh, yeah, I guess there's a way to do that. I'm not sure how they'd know to find you here." He must be able to tell that his vague statement is not reassuring, so he explains, "I registered a flight path, that's it. No passenger list. It isn't required like a commercial flight."

Not that I had a bunch of travel options, anyway. Like I told Emily, playing it safe won't find Mom.

Martin works in a precise manner, like I figure a doctor might. A roving eye on the sky, the slightest adjustments, and diligently recording flight information along the way. Most of the functions seem to be handled by the hardware, though, and it doesn't come across near as intimidating as flying should.

"I could do this," I say.

"You think so, eh?" Martin laughs. That's the first time I've heard him laugh and it's a deep rolling sound that makes me smile.

For the next couple of hours, Martin scratches the surface on flight school 101 and I'm completely taken off-guard by all the technical details. It's a conversation comfort zone I gladly slip into. Back to hanging out with friends discussing tech or baseball with borderline obsessive detail, and staying clear of anything remotely personal.

At one point, he shuts off the autopilot. "Go ahead," he motions, "take the controls." Aside from waking Emily with a sudden course correction, it goes pretty smooth. Okay, so that happens twice. I'd do it a third time, but I don't want Martin to think I'm not able to do this. In fact, I must be doing pretty good. Martin lays off the "kid" bit and actually tells me he's impressed. I'm having to dial down the doc's douche status by the minute.

"Are you a teacher?" I don't generally like those either, so his answer might help get the "Martin is a spoiled, overly hand-some tool" train back on track.

"Flight instructor? Oh no, all this is only a hobby," he replies.

"Well, you could be one," I muse.

"Must be the ER." Martin explains. "I'm the guy that gets tapped to talk the interns through procedures."

"Why's that?"

"Mostly a rookie gig. I found I don't mind so much though."

"Rookie? You haven't been a doctor for long?"

"No, a medical degree takes a while. Not to mention, I took the scenic route."

"I would too if I had this baby." My hands slide back toward the controls and I loosely grip them, careful not to interrupt the reengaged autopilot.

Martin chuckles. "No, I mean scenic, as in, I started in the College of Business with my eye on an MBA."

"Why'd you do that?" I ask through an involuntary scowl. "Your parents left you a fortune. Heck, why even go to school?"

"I felt obligated to their legacy. The business had been running for years without me, but there was always this standing offer to take the helm. Stocks, trading, pretending a bunch of numbers had actual value, never interested me."

"So, med school?"

"Yeah."

"Why not a pilot? You seem to know this stuff," I ask, thinking that getting my hands on a plane would be much more interesting than getting my hands on somebody's appendix.

"Well, sure. I've always loved flying. I'd hate to do it for a job, though. Shuttling people like you around the country would get old," he says with a smile.

I return the smirk but hold off on the normal Spencer-sized helping of snark. We silently watch the clouds float by, scanning an empty, endless sky together. After a few minutes and a few false starts, Martin breaks the silence.

"I know this is maybe a weird question, Spencer, but did you ever go flying with him?"

"Yep. Lots of times."

Martin stares into the clouds. "That must've been...
awesome."

I turn back to the windshield and nod. Up here, the world
looks so small and vast at the same time. Yet, you're always aware
you're in a different place where the aluminum fuselage around
you is the only thing keeping you here. It isn't like you're actually flying through the sky, more like you've scooped out a piece
and forced yourself into the gash.

But when you're flying in someone's arms, you *are* a part of
the sky. A part of something greater.

"Yeah, it was awesome."

Once. Only once.

CHAPTER 24

DRAKE SAT FUMING behind a holographic display projected from his desk. He swallowed his rage and called calmly into the granite office, "Xamse, my office, if you please."

"Yes, sir," Xamse's anxious voice floated down from the intercom.

The film footage of the delivery confirmed that the drone escort had indeed reached Killcreek with Crimson Mask, so Drake should have been able to relax. But now, this. He stabbed the air where a rewind button hovered. From the projected image, a chaotic scene of gunfire and airy pink blobs retreated into a rather mundane view of an aisle inside a hardware store.

He flicked the play button and watched the video as the drone's claw grasped a shelf, slowly bending it down. The contents tumbled toward the screen, but a backpack stuck stubbornly in the middle of the crease. A flashing triangular beacon on the drone's HUD illuminated the backpack. Digital gun sights flickered on and chased after each item that careened off the shelf.

Drake jabbed again, his hand passing unnecessarily through

the pause button. He pinched at the edges of the floating image and spread his hands to enlarge the view. The backpack's shoulder strap was hooked on a tennis shoe attached to a scrawny leg. Flexing his jaw, Drake resumed the video.

Next, from behind the bales of insulation, a trembling arm and a can of paint emerged. The can dropped flush with the shelf and slid to the middle. A foot lashed out, kicking the can toward the camera. An amorphous white blob spattered and obliterated the view. Drake tented his fingers and pressed his chin to his thumbs while glowering at the hologram as it looped again to the beginning.

A soft tap at the door, and light sliced into the office in a harsh wedge that slowly narrowed again as the door closed. Xamse called out, "You wished to see me, sir?"

"Yes, do come in." Reaching into a drawer, Drake placed a small black box in the center of his desk. Xamse walked hesitantly into the vast office, where dark granite walls absorbed the hallway's light. The hologram's feeble luminance provided a glowing beacon in the center of the room. Drake peered through the hologram as he addressed Xamse, "Have a seat."

Xamse settled onto the edge of the chair opposite the desk.

"What is this?" Drake spoke smoothly, gesturing to the animated image that floated between them. Xamse's eyes glowed in the coruscating light as he examined the hologram.

"Video feed from Unit 324, sir," replied Xamse, slowly.

"And I see the retrieval of the information was unsuccessful," Drake said.

"Y-Yes, sir. I performed exactly as asked, sir. I let your programming control the task. Your programming is always the best alternative." Xamse squirmed and awkwardly added, "The boy has lucky spirit. Next time…"

Drake's eye twitched and he slammed his fist on his desk. Too late, Xamse noted the box and his white eyes became haunting specters floating amid the blackness as he cried out, "No, please!" Flicking the switch on the box with his thumb, Drake calmly rose while Xamse clawed at the band around his throat, arching his back with such violence that the chair shot out from underneath him and he collapsed to the floor.

"'Lucky spirit'? You want to return to your land of absurd superstitions?" Drake spat.

No answer came as Xamse wailed.

Drake's voice was smooth and clinical as he asked, "Tell me, how did that feel? Your throat being slit ear-to-ear by your commanding officer?"

"No!" Xamse sobbed.

"Watching them rape your mother? Your sister? Hack your brother to pieces and feed him to the hyenas?"

"No! No! Please!"

Eyeing the button as Xamse writhed, Drake sat in his high-backed chair and swiveled to face the rear wall. "Computer. Open vault."

Amid tortured cries, a section of the granite wall slid open. Bathed in a muted red luminance stood an ebony juggernaut. Multifaceted globes peered into countless horizons. The jagged claws were poised to crush. Every visible surface was sleek and precisely angled to deflect radar, high explosive rounds, and even larger projectiles. Sensor arrays gave near omniscience on a battlefield, and hidden weapons, capable of dicing opponents into tiny hunks of metal or flesh, lurked behind shuttered ports.

The screams continued.

Drake admired the armor, his first invention. An attempt to level the playing field. Battle armor which could make any normal human the equal of an Augment. Originally, he had hoped to secure his fortune by selling it to the "lesser" nations of the world; those who needed a response to First-World Augment technologies.

But a different opportunity had arisen instead.

Drake missed the days when he'd suited up to personally prove his plan which was indeed the only way to disarm the Augment nuisance. He'd been a wiry scientist who had no business taking on men and women with the powers of gods. But he'd succeeded beyond even his own expectations.

In the end, the use of an automated drone force was ideal. Operator weakness and hesitation to pursue the necessary action could be eliminated. Drake's own will and determination could be imposed on each drone. Unfortunately, some human oversight was still necessary. A deeply flawed human oversight.

Xamse gurgled from the floor.

Fighting wars was costly, dangerous. True security and fortune, Drake mused, rested in the private sector. With his talented, complex, industrious nanomechs.

But now that security seemed to be in constant jeopardy. Earlier, the shock of finding the Crimson Mask's hiding spot after two years of searching had forced Drake to adjust his strategy. He'd been concerned that perhaps his clients at Killcreek had set an elaborate trap. That matter settled, now a boy was roaming the streets with a collection of sensitive documents that could potentially derail his plans yet again. Was there ever an end to such inconveniences? If only he wasn't surrounded by incompetence.

Another strangled cry interrupted his thoughts and Drake swiveled, tapping his finger on the edge of the black box. Xamse's pleading face strained upward and his twisted hand reached out. Casually, Drake flicked the switch. Xamse collapsed.

"I remember finding you that day while searching out my fallen drone, to figure out how it had gone so far off course. And there you were, impudently digging through its delicate components."

A soaked, wretched mass, Xamse breathed heavily and pulsing clouds of condensation collected on the granite floor.

"Fate, Xamse. A week later, and I would have already signed a contract that left my 'decommissions', my cleanup, to our client. I would have had no concern about a downed drone. Even so, I was going to vaporize you, you know. It was an important mission and these were secrets for which you had no clearance and no reason to lay eyes upon."

"I'm sorry..." Xamse's thick reply crept along the floor. "I did not mean to fail you."

Deaf to the pleas, Drake continued. "You sat there. Staring. You didn't run. Here was a boy savage, staring down Death incarnate. You didn't even bother reaching for your rifle." Drake stood and paced around the desk. He knelt, placing his lips close to Xamse's ear. "I let you live. I saved you."

Barely mobile, Xamse's head twitched.

Drake stood and looked into the darkness wistfully. "You showed promise. You'd actually figured out a few basic repairs. It reminded me of myself." Drake half-smiled. "Do you remember what you said to me?"

"'Help me kill them'." Xamse's words were a whisper of pain.

"Yes," Drake hissed softly. "That's right. You couldn't have done it on your own. I repaired the drone and sent it to your camp, even though my mission lay elsewhere. I killed the man who'd put the gun in your hand. Who'd slaughtered your family."

Xamse nodded, rubbing the skin beneath the collar, his forehead still planted against the floor and his breathing becoming steady.

"This is only so you remember the pain *I* saved you from." He reached down and gently took Xamse's arm, lifting him to the chair.

"Xamse never forgets, sir. Never," sputtered the boy as Drake stepped away. "I always remember. How you made my dream real. Stopping the murderer. Bringing me here. Letting me help you do your work for this great country. Xamse is grateful. Please, no more of the pain."

"I do this to remind you, because often, I feel you forget. Only you are to blame. Do as I instruct, and all goes well." Words of protest formed on Xamse's lips and then died as Drake turned and stared through him. "We need to retrieve whatever information this boy has. It is very important. You do understand?"

"Yes. I will do my best for you, sir."

"No, not your best. You will succeed. So far, I'm ahead of schedule. The number of drones have dwindled faster than my calculations, but they have served their purpose. I assume you have not?"

"My purpose is to repay my debt to you."

"Good. I will give you one more opportunity, Xamse. Then I will have to see to the matter myself. It will interrupt my business negotiations and jeopardize the future of the Nanomech Initiative. That is unacceptable. If that happens, well, I'm afraid I will know then that you have completely forgotten all I have done for you."

Drake turned to the alcove, red light spilling out like an open wound. The battle armor's only flaw, in his eyes, was the anthropomorphic configuration. Inefficient and vulnerable, a human bipedal form was his last choice of design. Drake's earlier designs had been more influenced by the deadly efficiency and grace of the insects he loved, but his client had insisted on more human designs for reasons they refused to disclose.

However, one of his earlier prototypes was still in storage.

"Retrieve the Mantis from the warehouse. Prep it. Find the boy, dispose of him, and secure the data. We cannot have any links between this corporation and the Black Beetle out in the open, understood?"

Xamse departed the room with his head bowed. "I will make you proud, sir."

As the door closed, Drake muttered, "I should hope so." He backhanded the holographic screen and it collapsed into a bright vein of light.

CHAPTER 25

NOT SURE HOW long Abercrombie and Bitch will be arguing at the rental car kiosk before they notice I've bailed. They'd been giving each other the cold shoulder ever since the conversation in the cockpit. Pretty sure Martin figured out that bullshit with Emily and Dad, too. No way Mom knew. Just goes to show I'm in this alone. Ditching them was easy. They didn't stand a chance. I almost feel bad.

Melting into a crowd was as easy as curling up in a coatrack. Hopping on a bus to a random remote lot. Hotwiring the little pickup I found. None of it took much time. I've never done any hotwiring before, but it turns out to be an extremely simple hack.

Stealing a truck, *that's* what I should feel bad about. I don't even know this person and here I am, in their truck. They shouldn't have left the parking gate ticket on the dash for the world to see. Either that, or maybe I should feel bad for the twenty bucks I borrowed from Martin to "get a bite to eat" when I wandered off. Nah, he's loaded. And hey, when the owner finds their truck, at least their parking ticket is paid.

But I can't help remembering how on that private jet

something strange happened in the universe. The Earth's poles reversed, the moon landing turned out to be a hoax, or maybe Justin Bieber wasn't all that bad. Some sort of complete meltdown of the laws of nature. Over the course of the flight, Martin had ceased to be a tool.

In fact, I sorta figured out I wanted exactly what he has. Sure, his parents died, that's pretty horrible stuff, but I can only think that would make my life easier right now. I wouldn't be hauling ass down the 101 in a stolen pickup, for starters.

Besides, they'd died but they'd also left him millions of dollars, an estate, a private jet and a functioning company that keeps lining his pockets. Now he runs around actually saving lives and not ruining them. My parents leave, and I'm left dodging bullets and picking up the pieces.

It's been a long time since Eric showed me how to do donuts in the school parking lot. Driving isn't so hard though. So far, a few angry horns and a couple one-finger salutes from other drivers are the worst of it. I'm getting the hang of it again and have avoided any cops. I should be in the clear. Emily will keep Martin from telling the police, at least for a while, and whoever dropped this truck off, there's no telling when they'll get back to the airport and find it gone.

Anyway, Martin was a liability, I've got to remember that. Every time he looked sideways at the TSA guys at San Francisco International, the hair on the back of my neck stood up. He was dying to dump this problem on the "proper authorities" from the start. They can't be involved just yet. Dad might've been lying to me and Mom, but I'm pretty sure what he told

Emily is right about not trusting anyone. He should've given me the same option and let me decide who I wanted to trust.

More honking. I salute like a pro and swerve back into my lane.

The exits slip by. No flashing lights. No helicopter blades humming in the fog overhead. No sign of Emily and Martin in hot pursuit. No drones, yet, either. In the clear as I take my exit and wind toward the old neighborhood.

An urge to cruise the block stops cold at the mental image of my house, ripped open to the sky. I pull into the Qwik Stop right outside the neighborhood entrance. This place is the exact same rundown dump it always was. Dingy stripes run the length of the building, the colors borrowed from a popular national chain. Faded cardboard cutouts of big-breasted girls hold beer cans and smile toward the empty sidewalk. A few cars sit at the pumps with people talking on mobile phones or riding out the foggy day in their vehicle while they fill up. I edge toward the corner by the ice machine and the payphone.

I almost have to pull out the seat to get it all, but there's nearly three dollars in change spread around the truck, mostly in the ashtray. Eric's phone number is burned into my memory, more than my own. I blow out through pursed lips and grab the phone before plunking in a string of coins.

"Hello?" Eric's voice is a ghostly echo from the past. I could almost hang up now, I'm so relieved to simply hear him. He's half-asleep and the annoyance at being woken sometime before noon is obvious.

"Hello?" he repeats, alert and cautious now.

"What up, Jint?" I manage.

There's a pause so deep, I check the receiver.

"S-man, that you?" He doesn't have a trace of excitement in his voice, so I bury mine.

"Yup."

"Really, who is this?"

"It's… it's me."

The line goes dead.

I press the phone painfully to my ear and listen closely. Maybe bringing him into this was a terrible idea. This Augment bullshit is dangerous. Martin said it, the random guy interviewed on the street in Mumbai said it, even that gung-ho cameraman filming the destruction in London would've agreed. Good for ratings, shit for sanity.

But there's Mom. Those aren't just weird dreams. They're way too real. I've got to follow this through to the end, and I need his help for the next move. I feed more change into the phone and dial. It rings. It rings again. Again. I don't plan on hanging up and I let the ringing go until I think I'm about to get that operator timeout.

"Who are you?" Eric hisses.

"You know who this is."

"I'm not falling for it."

"Seriously, it's me."

"And who might that be, huh?" I hear a faint beep on the line.

"C'mon, you suck at this spy game shit. Now you're going to stall me and trace the call?"

"You aren't who you say you are."

"I'm the dude that hacked the Diablo's scoreboard at the

homecoming game to make it say 'Mr. Ennis is a Pennis'. Remember that?"

"Too public. Anyone could've heard about that."

"Yeah, but no one ever figured out who did it. Just you and me knew, that's all."

"And you were the prime suspect. Your parents went ape-shit."

"Yeah, see!"

"No, I meant to say Spence was the main suspect. All you have to know is he liked to tinker with stuff and you can put two and two together."

"C'mon, man." Another beep.

"Frak!"

"Yeah, I'm up the street, I…"

Again, the call drops.

I slam the phone down and turn toward the truck. I left the driver's door wide open and the engine running. Not that I care, but I didn't even notice when I hopped out to make the call. The idea was to ditch the truck here anyway. Stolen truck, friend's house, maybe not the best combo. But I suddenly don't feel like walking.

I gun the engine, squeal out of the Qwik Stop parking lot and in minutes, I'm parked in the street out front of Eric's house. His parents', really. An earth-toned stucco and tile roof home like most of the houses in the neighborhood, it has a garage and a basement carved out of the steep hillside. His compact shoebox looking car slouches in the driveway. It's seen better days. A concrete stairway leads up through a weed-choked lawn to his front door, but I'm focused on the wooden fence next to the garage.

I've made the walk through that gate to the basement door a thousand times. When Eric turned thirteen he begged his parents to turn the basement into a game room. By the time I met him, he was sixteen and had moved his bedroom down there, living in his own personal Nerdtopia. I made sure to come over as much as possible.

His parents both worked long hours to afford a Bay Area lifestyle and were rarely home. Now, midafternoon, they're probably both gone. But he'll be home, as always.

Grabbing my backpack, I hop out and head for the gate. A camera at the corner overlooks the walk. That's new. I smile and wave before practically face planting into the wooden gate. Locked. That's new, too. I fire my best W.T.F. face at the camera, then start to climb.

On the other side, a knee-high labyrinth of electronics awaits. Scattered remains of computers, televisions, radios, cell phones, and miles of spare wire. The front yard was always a mess, mostly because his parents worked so much and Eric was supposed to mow, which never really happened. Back here, the yard consists of a narrow stretch bordered by the house and a concrete retaining wall. There'd always been a few bits and pieces scattered around, but not like this.

I pick my way through the narrow path to the basement door. The glass inserts have been blacked out with maybe paint or tape, though the weathered wood and rusted handle don't scream "high-security". I knock, loud. "Hey, dude! C'mon, it's me!" A few swift kicks to the base of the door and I shout,

"Hurry up! It's cold out here!" Actually, this is a heat wave compared to what my body chemistry has adjusted to, but I remember these foggy days in the Bay getting chilly.

A click from the other side is followed by a metallic slide and a five-part series of sharp clacks. "Fuckin'-A, man. What if there's a fire in there? You're dead before you get the door open."

The door creeps inward and my smug expression disappears down the barrel of a gun.

CHAPTER 26

ERIC'S BLACK T-SHIRT stretches tight across his round belly and absorbs the mid-morning light. A flattened slant of blond hair only emphasizes the jarring contrast between skin tone and dark clothing. His face is more round than I remember too. Somewhere beneath the funhouse mirror is my friend. For maybe the first time ever, I'm worried I'll say something offensive, or that the look on my face will give away what I'm thinking because, well, he's got a gun.

He straightens his glasses with his free hand. I look him dead on and try to smile. He stares back, eyes tinged red and floating above dark circles.

"Get inside." He motions with the gun.

I don't argue. The basement is lit by a single lamp. Light scatters into a mosaic of white shards on crinkled silvery walls. The whole place reeks of stale body odor and mildew.

"Are you living in a TV Dinner?"

"Shut up." He pushes me toward the center of the room and I put my hands in the air. I can't help but stare at our old hangout as he fumbles with the locks, keeping the gun trained shakily in my direction.

Beyond the foil covering every scrap of wall space, not much has changed. I check out Babe first; our pride and joy, she's a liquid-cooled beast of a computer. A never-ending process of upgrades and attachments, she comes complete with a power supply that could jump-start a truck and enough fans that you'd swear there was a helipad nearby. She sits on the same metal garage-sale desk, but the neon case lights which used to glow Giants orange are dead.

My eyes trace the bundle of wires snaking out of Babe to the server rack. The rack has been moved to the wall farthest from the door. A giant silver disk rests on top of it. Next to this, his bed occupies the same alcove, but gone are all the trippy techno-rock posters that used to line the walls there. I wander forward, my hand absently reaching out for the Throne, our dilapidated leather chair. I run a finger along a crack where the white backing peeks through the leather.

The clicking parade of locks stops and I see Eric in the corner of my eye, gun raised. Locked in here with him, this place so unfamiliar to me now, I should be more scared than I am but I'm having trouble processing the image of him pointing the gun at me. Is it even real?

"Is that a giant magnet on the server rack?" I ask, trying to draw attention somewhere else.

"Shut up!" he stutters unsteadily. I keep my hands up and nod as he demands, "Who are you?"

Maybe my looks have changed for him too? But how could getting scrawnier make me look that different? Maybe the do-it-myself haircuts?

"Relax, man; it's me, Spencer."

"And how can I tell?"

"Do I honestly look that different?"

Eric advances and shouts, "That doesn't mean shit! There have been exactly two Augments documented with the ability to change appearances—Doppelganger and Shifter." He holds up two fingers. "How do I know you aren't one of them?"

I take a chance and ask, "Are they still alive?"

"No." He hesitates. "But you could be a different one. A new one!"

Maybe all the lies have caught up to me. Who am I really? Lost, I cast around for anything to prove I am in fact, Spencer.

I gesture to empty spots on the wall and start to paint a picture from the past. "Alien Vampires, Pendulum, The Medic Droid—your posters, they're gone, but they used to be right there." I walk to the alcove and look up at the ceiling above the bed. "A poster of the UC Supercomputer Center. You hung it there as a joke." I turn to the cracked leather chair, a faint moldering odor of parmesan cheese still wafting from it after all these years. "The dumpster behind the Pizza Pie. You said I was a dumbass for diving in to drag the Throne out, but you helped. And, and it's the best seat in the freaking house!" The gun begins to lower and I keep going, "Babe, our rock star, overclocked beast! Named after Babe Ruth... but that's maybe too obvious, though she was never a guy, a she, like a ship, a pirate ship." I turn wildly to the server rack, shouting now, "We bought the rack online from a 'wholesaler'. And, and remember, not long after that we heard about the university computer lab getting broken into? You spent weeks staring out the window calling every car 'an unmarked cop car'. Remember?" Despite the gun,

I round on him. His arms hang limp at his sides. He's staring at a ghost, and the gun dangles from a fingertip. "C'mon, nobody knows that. We never told a soul!"

The gun clatters to the tile and I wince.

"Spencer! Holy shit!" he cries. Eric devours me in a hug and squeezes, tight. As his weight hits, I force the pain of all my bumps and bruises into a constricted laugh. He chuckles nervously, "WTF, man! Did the Feds put you in a concentration camp?" He pushes me to arm's length and inspects.

"Look who's talking!" I say. "That time I said you needed to be behind home plate, you must have misunderstood."

He takes in every detail as he shakes his head, his expression pained and excited at the same time. "Spencer Fucking Harrington!" Then his face switches to panic and I tense, not sure what to expect. He shoves me aside and races first for Babe. Then he stops in his tracks and jiggles back and forth between there and the server.

I rush the server and grab the magnet, grunting under the sheer weight. It fees like it weighs about fifty times more than it should. "What... the?"

Part of his dilemma solved, he slaps furiously at the keyboard as I chunk the magnet to the floor. He doesn't answer until he surfaces from the typing frenzy, panting. "Was... scrapping the data... thought you were setting me up."

"Why the hell would I do that?"

"Dude, you were dead, Spence. They came and got you and I knew I was next."

"What did you ever do?"

Eric grins, his eyes twitching. "I'm an Augment, too."

CHAPTER 27

"WHAT?" I'M NOT sure I heard him right.

He turns toward the desk and won't say a word.

"Eric?"

The silence stretches on longer than it should. He stares at the fractal screen saver exploding on Babe's monitor. I can't see his face, but I can tell I don't want to force my way into whatever thought is riveting him to that spot; a place where I, we, were once safe from the craziness that was life. But after what seems like several minutes, I have to say something.

"So, how's the Bride of Frankenstein? Damn, I've missed her."

"Runnin' smooth. Three gigahertz on four processors. But systems are pushing five to six gigahertz now. Never-ending upgrade, man."

Silence returns. I'd rather he said something. Explain this Augment business. Tell me what a shit friend I am even.

I walk forward with enough noise he can hear me, but cautious—like approaching a wounded animal. It takes everything I have to reach out and touch his shoulder. A weight seems to pull his body into a defeated slouch, and the stale atmosphere in the basement becomes oppressive.

"What did you mean about being an Augment?"

Still no response, and I watch his thick knuckles crease as he leans on the computer desk. He glances toward a manila folder under a stack of anti-static bags and technical docs. A photo peeks out, containing a patch of green grass in the corner punctuated by a rough chunk of rubble. The sandy edge of a building sparks vivid memories. I reach over and tug at the edge. Eric grabs my hand.

"Stop!" he shouts, his face a twisted mask of pain.

I pull away slowly. "What's going on?"

He shuffles the folder deeper into the pile, keeping his eyes down. "That day. Only Mrs. Crumley saw."

Mrs. Crumley. She was my old neighbor, not his. A real pain in the ass. Mom always said she was charming. She was like one hundred and fifty years old and probably had stories of growing up trading beads with the Ohlone Indians.

"The nosy lady," I say.

"She came at me with a broom that day." He glances up to an empty space on the wall. His face forms a distant smile.

"How much did she see?"

"Cell service out, power down." He continues, as though he never heard my question. "I didn't hear a damn thing about it until my parents got home and let me in on the rumor mill. 'Old Mrs. Crumley saw Augments running around the neighborhood.'" A huff of disdain escapes his lips. "I tried to call you. Figured you'd get a laugh out of it, but you didn't answer the phone."

I recall Mom's phone shattered in the rubble. My eyes drift back to the folder.

He wanders over to a small refrigerator next to the desk, opens the door and crouches, speaking into it. "I waited until the morning, you know, to pick you up for school. I was too damn busy farming shit on Swords of Legend to go see for myself." He turns empty-handed and lets the refrigerator clamp shut. "Man, they said she saw Augments. That was all. If I knew something happened to you, I'd have been there. I would."

"I know. I know. Don't sweat it."

With heavy feet, he makes his way to the Throne and perches on the edge of the armrest.

"She was gonna attack you with a broom, huh?" I give a half-hearted laugh.

"Broom, yeah." He swats at the air trying to shoo away the question. "I showed up to get you for school, like always. I couldn't believe what the fuck I was looking at. Hole in your house, police tape. Had to talk to Crumley from behind the car door. She was rambling about me stealing the copper or some bullshit."

"It isn't like you haven't been to my house a million times before. She'd have seen you there, peeking out through her curtains like she did every day. Anyway, you'd steal my Kirk Rueter autographed mitt first."

"You can't joke about this, Spence." Eric's eyes meet mine. "She saw it all. The Black Beetle blasting a hole in the wall, taking off with your mom. Crumley didn't know you were there until your dad showed up. She was too scared to leave her house."

I never said Crimson Mask was my Dad.

Eric either doesn't notice or ignores my unhinged jaw as he slips off the armrest and wanders toward the desk. "All I could think about was that dumbass voicemail I left the night before. 'Watch out Spence, Augments invading the 'hood!'" He returns, staring past me, through me. "What a goddamn thing to be joking about, right?"

Now that invisible weight is mine and I drop into the Throne. When he finally speaks again, his voice is fast and animated, his fingers flexing repeatedly.

"I ditched school that day. Day after. The next day. I don't know, maybe a week, until my parents started getting on my ass and counselors at school started calling. Here you were, gone. And there was absolutely nothing on the news, *zip, nada, nothing*. Cops, they responded to Crumley's call, she had to make it from the Qwik Stop—I got the 911 transcript, here," He whips the folder out of the stack and thumbs through more papers. "Middle of the day, nobody else home. Nobody. I talked to people up and down the street—everyone had been at work, school, one dude said he was home but listening to some dub-step too loud to hear much else. Dumbass thought the explosion was a bass drop. Cops poked around and left, never followed up. They didn't even care, man, nobody. Everyone thought it was drugs, you know, that's what the cops started saying. They found drugs in the home, meth lab explosion. Man, I knew that was bull and I was the only one. Your damn parents, always keeping to themselves."

He shoves one of the papers in my face. "See? Drugs. Right there," he says as he points.

He's tapping on a police report that details the crime scene, my old address. All the so-called evidence they found, blood collected, results of a search, and a neighborhood canvas. I take in as much as I can while Eric tears through more pages.

"Took these when Crumley was away at Bingo," he mumbles, stuffing photos of the ruined house in my direction. "An FAA Report, no unidentified craft. My own damn report I filed with the police, right here. Missing persons, no information ever surfaced. All of it got sunk to the bottom of a magic pile of bullshit."

By the dates, we're several weeks past when Dad and I left the neighborhood and still, Eric's pawing through a thick stack of documents.

"That's when I started to dig up stuff on you, Spence. Your family. People don't just disappear. If you moved somewhere else, there'd be a trail. If you were in prison, there'd be a record. If you were dead, a body in the morgue." He's speaking as he digs deeper, rattling off scenarios with each paper. Intensity burns in his cheeks and desperation tightens his throat. "Life is digital. There's always a trail. Always breadcrumbs, always.

"Then I found these," he says and rattles a handful of printed webpages. DMV records. They're the same photos over and over, with names beginning with Sean and Connie, and ending in the lies we'd told over the years. Why wouldn't he have doubted who I was? "And I'm thinking 'WTF?' Federal Witness Protection? Undercover Spies? Aliens, man? Yeah, aliens." He spins a finger next to his temple but his "isn't that crazy" expression reads way too true.

Documents begin flying out of the folder so fast under Eric's trembling fingers, I barely have time to register he's handing them to me, let alone read. Dates continue to pile up along with the papers. "But Crumley and her story started to make sense. It fit perfectly, you know?"

Then the thought drives itself to deep center field. Two years, and he never let go.

I thought I was in a bad situation being stuck in the Icehole. The whole time, I never thought of what Eric might be going through. I always thought of him here, in the basement, pirating tunes and playing games. At Candlestick Park catching a game or driving around in his car. Enjoying a life I was whining about not having.

No, he was going through his own little hell. Because of me.

I know I need to say something, but no idea what. "Man, I…"

"You weren't the first," he says. Pupils larger than the possibilities, he plows through my attempt to apologize. He gives up on the papers and turns to Babe, backhanding the mouse to wake her. The sudden gale of cooling fans is startling. Madly, he's opening folders and mining through directory trees. With a click, a program loads, displaying a chaotic scrawl of colored lines and boxes.

Augments. Names, places, sightings, powers all displayed on a version of Emily's OCD spreadsheet but on speed, crack, and steroids. Well past obsession, the sheer volume of information veers into mental-case territory.

"You couldn't have just kept collecting Pokemon?" I manage to say.

Eric checks over his shoulder with a knowing grin. "Yeah, isn't it awesome? I know everything. You. Your dad. Everything. It's my power."

I nod and make sure the gun is lying on the floor by the door.

CHAPTER 28

FOR HOURS, ERIC drags me through his data that supports his rat's nest of thoughts and the logical sense he's made of it all. He's right on with the information I can confirm, and the stuff I can't, which is most of it, all sounds plausible. As he speaks, the old Eric starts to come back, so I don't dare interrupt. He's talking with the casual excitement of giving a play-by-play of last year's World Series.

"So, your theory…"

"No, dude, this isn't theory. This is absolute truth. Documented, one hundred percent truth. We find truth here." He pats the computer and "old Eric" slips away.

"Fine. So, Crimson Mask…"

"Your dad."

"My dad, was the last Augment in the field as of a few days ago?"

"Technically. There are a few that were voluntarily 'decommissioned' and seem to still be floating around."

"And you say they're trying to wrap up the program? What about the Black Beetle?"

He holds up a finger and grins as he opens a document. Marked across the top of the page are the words TOP SECRET.

"Jesus, man." The paper header refers to a Pentagon Psy-Ops department. It's from just after the Cuban incident in the Sixties, the one that made the world think twice about Augments on the battlefield. The document outlines the whole Proxy War concept and the best ways to use media sensationalism as a cover for continued Augment operations.

"Journalists figured this out years ago," I say with as little interest as possible. Eric smiles, wags his finger and attacks the keyboard again. Another file pops up, this one twenty years newer than the first. This file describes ways to use a similar process to systematically pit Augments against one another.

"Why?"

"Because we were getting out of hand," he says.

For a while, Eric seemed almost back to normal, so I don't get the "we" right away. He means "we Augments". I sigh, letting him finish his thought. "Once we got shuffled to covert programs we became an even bigger problem. Now the U.S. and Russia had a bunch of thinking weapons on their hands, trained with freaking spy skills. It was too easy to start bucking the system and making our own rules. The government even tested an alternative." Keys clack again and a collection of diagrams hits the screen. Outlines of complex circuitry with an unmistakable symmetry fill the monitor.

I can only stare open-mouthed at the schematics of the bunker busting drone I pried open not so long ago.

"Yep," he smirks. "About seven years ago, an unnamed contractor got caught up in a sting where he was shopping this bad boy around the Middle East and other countries that didn't have Augment programs. But, get this. The documents don't refer to him by name anywhere. That's been redacted. When you can read it, it says bullshit like 'A source' or 'Anonymous'."

"Black Beetle."

"Exactly."

"What else do you have?"

Eric latches onto my excitement and returns to the keyboard, almost cackling. "He signed on with the government for a few years. Then they changed tactics." He clicks and another document opens with a new, later date at the top.

"That's right after the Djinn hit New York," I say. Eric nods. "But why would the Black Beetle be a problem for them now? Did he go rogue?" Could this be an explanation for the carrier footage? Maybe Dad only worked with him when he was one of the good guys.

"Keep reading."

The document appears to be from that same "anonymous" source. It's stuffed with complicated statistics, psychology and tactics. But the end result seems to involve maximum carnage and bloodshed, specifically designed to turn public opinion against every Augment. This would give the ones operating in secret even fewer places to hide, make them more cautious, and throw them off their game. At the same time, the Black Beetle would be built up as the villain and the face of the death and destruction. A face without nationality that would become inextricably linked to every single one of the Augments. A businesslike conclusion projects "containment" of the Augment program within five years. But where does this put Dad?

"And the pièce de résistance," he adds with a flourish of his hand on the mouse. This new bit of information details a secret mutual disarmament agreement between the United States and Russia. Both were on board with the plan.

Eric folds his arms across his chest and beams.

I don't know how he did it, but his confidence isn't overplayed. He'd probably be given a death sentence for looking at this stuff sideways. It must have come from some seriously secure servers behind the world's toughest cryptography. Maybe he does know everything?

"Tell me where the Black Beetle is."

Eric squirms. "I don't know...yet."

"How? You got all this!" His eyes are wide, and I realize I'm standing over him wadding his shirt in my fist. I let go and back away.

"Sorry, man," he smoothes his shirt and turns to the monitor, his eyes darting nervously in my direction. "All I can tell is that information has got to be stored on an internal network without so much as a telegraph wire linked to the wild. My guess, most of the guys in on this program don't even know. They were so desperate to round us up, it was a no-questions-asked situation for the guy that could do it."

"Reality check—there is no 'us' in Augment, Eric."

A hurt look crosses his face. He stabs a finger in the air and dives back into the data. Newspaper clippings pop up about Chinese girls being abandoned, or worse, by their parents.

"You also aren't a little Chinese girl."

"No, dumbass." More furious fingers and windows pop open. "See!"

"The Foundation for a Brighter Hope? Ending Infanticide? What the hell does this have to do with anything?"

"The foundation isn't real! It's a cover! They were snatching babies for some kind of experiment!"

"Even if you're right, last I checked, you still weren't a *little Chinese girl*."

Maps fly onto the screen along with more scanned news clippings, and websites splashing open. "The hospital I was born in is right here! They used to have an office, here." He points wildly a few blocks from the Hospital symbol on the map.

"What does that prove?"

"They lost me in the hospital, the day I was born. The nurses couldn't find me when it was time to check out. Everyone panicked. It was two hours and twenty-six minutes." Under Eric's direction, a hand written note scrawled on hospital stationery shows onscreen. The times are readable, but that's about all. More incident reports from the hospital cycle by. "My parents talked about this all the time!"

Up until now, despite the conspiracy vibe and the crazy insistence he was an Augment, his information made enough sense that I could at least see where he was coming from. This switched-at-birth crap, though, isn't even in left field; it's in the parking lot for the next stadium over. That, and the crazy look in Eric's eyes has come back.

"That's what the experiments at the Foundation were all about. They wanted to replicate an earlier experiment and create Augments that had special brain powers. I'm exactly like you, Spence."

I peer at him out of the corner of my eye, trying to gauge his hopeful expression and get a feel for exactly how much insanity might be in there. "Eric. I'm not an Augment."

His face pinches in disbelief.

"No, seriously. I'm not an Augment."

Eric sits there, his hand lifeless on the mouse and a great pressure builds behind his eyes. His mouth opens and closes in abrupt bursts before he blurts, "You're not?"

I shake my head.

"But, but your Dad."

I gesture at the screen. "How many other Augments did you research that have little Boy Wonders running around?" All this information, all these classified documents, all the lists of Augments with their powers, yet he's blind to this single, obvious fact. He doesn't respond, and this is too close to home for me to stop the assault on his delusion. "Why haven't they come to get us? Huh? You just showed me how they killed and rounded everyone up. Why not us, too?"

His mouth works limply but no sound escapes. I can't watch him struggling with the truth.

"I was only ever a stupid kid. A kid with a fucked-up family and an equally fucked-up life. I've got nothing left that my dad's Augment bullshit hasn't picked up, crushed and hurled through a brick wall. My friends, my family..." Family. The word sticks in my throat. I grab his shoulder again, hard. My turn to go batshit crazy. "What about my mom? Where's my mom? Show me!"

Eric's eyes widen and he turns to pull up more information

from his digital conspiracy files. Mom's face appears on a photo from the DMV.

I let go of his wrinkled shirt and stare. Unlike everybody else in the world, she liked her license photo. That fact alone captured her perfectly. Carefree. Making the best of life, even a rushed headshot in the ghastly light of a DMV office.

Eric is speaking but I can barely hear him. "Her birth certificate. Places she's lived. Places you've lived. That trail ends on that day. She disappeared as soon as Beetle got her."

"What?" I hiss.

"Beetle's an outsider, Spence. A ghost. Nobody wants to be linked to him. I explained that." His voice drops to a whisper. "Information even I can't find." This hole in his "power" is a source of pain, I can see that. And seeing it helps me remember who really caused all this. Why I have no reason to be mad at a friend who has sacrificed so much.

"Maybe I can help you fill that gap." I head over to my backpack. Once my hand closes on the bag, I find it hard to pull out the thumb drive. A voice tells me I should stop. Let all this go. Leave Eric alone and tell him to get on with his life. This is way too big for him. In his current state, maybe this won't save him but wreck him completely. I look up to check his expectant face.

But Mom's eyes are smiling at me from the monitor.

As I remove the bag with the thumb drive, Eric sees the biohazard symbol. With tiny shuffles of his feet he rolls his chair across the room. "Relax. It's not smallpox or something. It's data. Stuff my dad collected."

"Why the bag?"

"It's sorta infested."

"Infested? Virus?"

"No. Like tiny nanobugs the size of a gnat's testes."

With the same short shuffles of his feet, Eric scoots forward. "Really?" He sits gaping at the bag for several seconds and then wheels hurriedly to the outside door. "Why didn't you tell me?"

The afternoon sun has shifted. Dust motes drift across a ray of light seeping through a chip in the black paint over the door's windows. He stands and reaches up to the top of the frame. Ferreting out the main coaxial cable for the ISP, he traces it to a nest of wires and cables near the server rack.

"I really need to label these someday."

"Never heard that before."

"You're the one that did the wiring. You could have done it just as easy. Make yourself useful. Hand me a pen and some tape."

Excavating the desktop, and finally scrunching my head against the wall to peek behind the monitor, I find a pen on the floor but no tape. A sticky note gets torn into a strip. "Why bother doing this now?"

"Never went wireless. I pull this cable, there's no way we get compromised."

"You're not planning on hooking up that thumb drive?" I can't help but sound incredulous.

"Hell no. But I can't see nanotech and Babe is monitoring all incoming and outgoing traffic. The second she detects an anomaly, she'll let us know. I want it clear which cable we yank when that happens."

"Sure, but this thumb drive is where that snippet of code I posted came from, so we need to get in here." I hold off on telling him exactly how right he is to be paranoid. Maybe I'm the one who is crazy?

"Oh, yeah, that." Eric drops into his chair and glides to the computer desk. "A memory dump of a failed login. What a great place to start, said no one ever."

"Yeah, pretty weak. Was it enough for *you*?"

"Uh, no." He turns his head, fingers continuing to jump between the keyboard and mouse.

"So the NSA guess wasn't far off?"

"Dude, closer to NSA meets E.T." He calls up a site I've never seen before. It's a forum with a simple black background and above that a flaming eye stolen right out of Mordor burns across the header.

He stops with one finger on a key and the cursor on the login screen. Old Eric has left the building, again. A suspicious glare from him and I cross the room to sit on his bed. The keys click as he asks, "You never answered my question. Where did you go?"

"What?"

"You dropped off the radar completely."

"A bunker at the North Pole," I say as he nods and shrugs, unimpressed.

"Arctic bunker. Scary good encryption. Makes perfect sense, you know," he mumbles and opens a thread. He wheels to the side and makes a sweeping gesture at the screen.

I return to the computer. A picture of a middle-aged guy, greying hair tufted around a bald spot, looks out from a neatly formatted rap sheet of sorts. It's only a portrait shot, but twenty-to-one says the guy has a pocket protector.

"He's one of us," says Eric. "And I know exactly where he is."

*

George Carrick Walker aka Polybius.
*from Conspirapedia, the only – free – encyclope-
dia of the New World Order*

George Carrick Walker (June 23, 1948 – ?) was a cryptanalyst for the National Security Agency during the Cold War. Much debate surrounds this clandestine Augment and his role in a number of what became high-profile incidents of divulged Soviet secrets. Walker presumably masterminded the communications crack behind the к северу звезда *(North Star) initiative. The break led to the exposure of a series of bunkers inside the Northern Hemisphere, designed to rapidly deploy Augment strike teams into the continental United States.*

Walker was reportedly one of the first Augments to manifest increased mental ability from the secret Augmentation process. Early Air Force military records describe an above-average intelligence and physical ability, but gave no indication of the future level of genius into which Walker would finally evolve. Even among the Augment program, the results were reportedly astonishing.

As an Augment, Walker took on the code name

"Polybius"—an ancient Greek who created an early form of cryptography using a matrix of letters which were assigned numerical substitutes. His work with the NSA was highly classified; however, it is speculated that he was involved in the following:

British Spymaster Anthony Tobias' exposure as a Soviet double agent.

Annihilation of the Soviet Augment team, Iron Hammer, in a skirmish over Northern Afghanistan.

Successful compromise of Syrian communications and the evacuation of the Iraqi Embassy during the 1996 Israeli Offensive.

Most controversial was perhaps the hacking of a series of privately-owned email accounts after an online service provider failed to comply with a United States government request for access. The break led to the deaths of a number of foreign nationals reported to be part of an Islamic terrorist cell with links to the rogue Augment, Djinn. A Foreign Intelligence Surveillance Act court secretly convened to give the green light to the Augment strike force which killed the presumed terrorists.

While most of America supported the outcome, the controversy surrounded the ease with which Walker reportedly hacked the account system. Several sources quoted that within three hours of refusal of coopera-tion, the system had been compromised. At the time, company officials confirmed they were using the lat-est encryption routines, which, by private industry standards, should not have been susceptible to such a rapid attack.

This led to an enormous outcry for more transparency in government operations. Privacy organizations feared that ordinary citizens' data would be compromised in sweeping mass surveillance programs. With the U.S. Augment program already under increasing fire, Walker's exploits and involvement were continually downplayed until he appeared to have left active service.

An anonymous leak to a website in 2008 indicated that Walker had slowly been becoming mentally unstable. The identity of the leak was never confirmed, nor the veracity of the claim. However, Fredrick Paulson, well-known author and expert on worldwide espionage, asserts that the claim was from a legitimate source. This has led to speculation that while many Augments' abilities center on physical strength and power, which reportedly leads to early retirement from service, Walker's mental abilities may have placed unusual stress on his cognitive processes.

Walker's current status and whereabouts are unknown.

CHAPTER 29

"SO THIS POLYBIUS guy is in a retirement home?" I ask.

A new site is on the screen. Another old dude, this one with a grill full of perfect, too-good-to-not-be-polymer teeth, smiles at us from the website header. His teeth match the groomed cloud of hair on his head. He's on a patio in a lawn chair, reading a book. A log-cabin style building sits behind him, complete with a window box full of flowers. Tall trees rise on the horizon.

I check Eric's face for any signs of crazy. Yep. The smug grin is out of our high school yearbook but a bit too broad, too excited. The sound of a door closing upstairs saves me from what can only be an awkward conversation.

"Shit, my mom! Hang tight." He rolls his chair to the bottom of the stairs before hopping out and stomping up them.

Must be later than I thought. Eric's dad was like a project manager, and his mom was a nurse at the local hospital. They never made it home before five. Barely ever in time for dinner, even. And often, his mom worked weird shifts. When the rest of the world was sleeping, she was checking vitals and inserting catheters. When he wasn't herding cats, his dad was wasting time navigating the BART system to get downtown.

Usually when I'd stop by, I'd never set eyes on his fam. I don't think they ever came down here. If they did, well, maybe it wouldn't smell like it does. Anyway, it never bothered me that his parents kept out of his stuff. Sorta every teenager's dream, really. They were a nonentity in our secret world of pirating and stolen baseball broadcasts.

Heh. Maybe I have more in common with my dad's top-secret bullshit than I thought.

I wander the room in a haze, trying to absorb all the new information. This place seriously used to be our own Bunker. Once we salvaged the secondhand microwave and his parents got him the mini-fridge, we were set. Then came the never-ending computer upgrades. I still don't know where he got the money for that. Well, I knew, but never asked. Credit card accounts weren't tough for him to crack.

My eyes fall to the gun on the floor.

I pick it up. A revolver of some kind. It looks old, the metal surface pitted with rust. I check the cylinder. Fully loaded.

Voices chatter upstairs. If the age-old pattern holds, his mom will have been up since three A.M. and be headed to bed. Not a bad thought.

I shuffle across the room to the bed and toss the gun underneath. When I sit this time, the bed has the power of that super magnet, locking onto the tiny particles of iron in my blood stream. I drop and even though the smell is worse here, my sore body refuses to right itself.

Voices continue upstairs, humming through the sub-floor

and droning into a hypnotic buzz that gets simultaneously louder and farther away as my consciousness begins to drift. Laying here, I'm closer to that one true home than I've been in years.

I wonder if she's close, too.

*

Pretty soon, I'm floating. There's no odor, no distant hum, and the room's light is a single round pool, etching ripples across the surface of my skin. I look above and see a shape. A person maybe? It's so small and so far away and then, nothing. I strain to see past the light until my vision becomes an amorphous, glowing blob.

The light shifts and the shape above me mars the center. Details of a person emerge, their arms pointed forward, legs arrow straight, and a face shrouded in darkness.

Closer, and I see it's a man.

Closer, and the muscled form is unmistakable. Dad.

He's wearing his costume, but no mask. His hair is swept back by the motion and reflects the liquid glow. A red film covers him from forehead to chin, his glacier eyes floating in a sea of blood. Expressionless, he wraps an arm around my waist as he passes. We hurtle toward the darkness below.

A pale hand breaks the outer column of light, grasping at us as we pass. From the shadows, the withered corpse of my mom emerges. Her skin is shriveled and her face clings to raw bone in thin, torn sheets. Her mouth falls open as she reaches out. "Spencer," she calls from somewhere between the curtain of light and the dark oblivion.

"Mom!" I grab for her hand, but she's already out of reach.

Soon, she is a tiny speck sucked into the darkness. I'm crying, beating on my father's shoulder, but he dives deeper and his speed increases. Faster now, until my cheeks burn and my blood pools. His face turns to me, stretched tight with effort. Determination and another emotion that catches me completely off guard—fear.

"Let me go!" I grab his arm. All of my muscles lock and strain against his titanic strength. Futile, like trying to lift a mountain, but as I push that mountain quakes. My throat burns as I yell. I shake and quiver on the edge of a collapse where the massive weight will slip and crush me.

He stops and his arm slips away. The momentum fires me into the darkness; an escape pod from a tube, or a bullet from a gun, I can't tell. Before the shock wears off and before I can cry out, he's nothing more than a speck wheeling to face the light racing toward him. Defiant, he's completely absorbed by the energy. The great maw of the bloating star collapses around me and deep within, I feel a presence, watching.

An incessant beeping interrupts the nightmare. But, no, I'm still asleep. A dream within a dream? What's going on?

I slap wildly to the side and miss the alarm clock. Opening my eyes isn't on the priority list. I grope around the nightstand. Finally, defeated, I start smashing every square inch of the dresser until it collapses and the beeping stops.

Dad's standing in the door to my room. Yep, my room again. The Giants posters this time are from the last team I saw in action which was the same crew Eric and I braved that curfew-busting game to watch. I'm home. The one place we ever lived that I could give the name to.

"See, Dad? I did it!" Maybe he'll overlook the pile of kindling that used to be the nightstand. Surely he had problems like this when he got Augmented? Ripping apart doors he meant to open? Crushing a can of Coke and spewing it all over the place? I never saw that if it ever happened, that would've been before I was born, but he has to understand.

No smile or nod of approval. He doesn't look pissed even. No, that fear is still etched on his face.

"Dad, come on! I'm an Augment!" I give the former nightstand another whack and splinters scatter into the air.

"I'm sorry. You'll have to clean this up on your own," he bows his head and disappears into the hall.

Maybe he's as shocked as I am. Once it sets in, he'll see how cool this is going to be. No way am I going to be his goofy sidekick though.

"What's all the racket?" Mom's voice seems to come from the walls, the vents, everywhere and I can't help but smile in spite of the creep factor.

"Mom! Come quick!" I shout.

She steps into the room drying her hands on a kitchen towel. They're stained red and the white towel is smeared with scarlet splotches. I start to ask why, but she interrupts, "Did your Dad—"

"No! It was me!"

She smiles knowingly. "Oh, honey, what happened?"

As she picks her way through the mess and sits on my bed, the knowing smile never wavers. I'm excited to show her, but confused by her reaction. I decide to up the stakes. I leap up, extend my fist and imagine blasting off through the ceiling. The bed settles under the sudden movement and my feet sink into the mattress. Mom balances on the edge with her hands folded neatly in her lap.

I pump my fist upward and toss my head back, trying to will the next step. My feet sink further.

"So, maybe it's not all there, yet. But Mom, I've become an Augment! I'm strong like Dad!"

I plop down on the bed next to her, frantically search the room, and see the Robb Nenn autographed baseball "Dad" brought to me a week after my thirteenth birthday. I snatch it and toss a heater at the wall. White ribbons of dust drift out of the hole.

"Spencer!" Mom sounds amused and not the least bit surprised.

"Okay, okay. I'm sorry. It's just... just..."

"What?"

"Well, I think... I don't know," I ramble. It's getting difficult to form a thought. Both Mom and Dad are reacting so strangely to my news.

The bright shimmer in her eyes wavers like the light on the bottom of a pool, and with that shift comes the silvery sheen. "You can tell me, sweetie."

"He just walked off. Didn't say a word about my powers. He used to talk about this happening to me, even though it can't." I start to shake off the dream. "How *did* this happen?"

"Don't you want this?" she asks.

"No. I don't. I never wanted this. Dad wanted it. Not me."

"Why does that matter, Spencer?" She's closer now. Her stained hand grips mine and her gaze devours me.

"I'm not sure." I want to look away, but I can't.

"Dude." A whispered voice inserts itself between us. Right next to my head even, but I can't look away.

"What if we were all Augments, Spencer?" she says.

I nod.

"Dude!" The whisper persists.

"The whole family. Wouldn't that be nice?" The light in her iris intensifies and becomes the source for a ring of pure brilliance on the wall behind her, bleaching the baseball posters into white emptiness. "Come find me. We'll be a family. Again. We're waiting for you."

I'm shaking. Uncontrollably. Sweat. Body odor. My body odor? A wave of tomato sauce and oregano fights off the stench.

Eric leans over me, gruffly pounding a fist on the bed. He has a paper plate in his hand and the microwave on the wall is open behind him.

"Hot Pocket?"

CHAPTER 30

DRAGGING ERIC OUT of the house had been as easy as convincing a vampire he needed some vitamin D. When I told him to bring a laptop, he seemed less squeamish. When I told him to make sure it was a laptop he didn't care much about, he looked torn. I don't want to do any more damage than I already have, but there isn't a choice.

"Why can't we take the truck?" he whines as he bends protectively over his shoebox on wheels. I glance back into the crowded mall parking lot, and the beat-up pickup's bumper peeks out from a row of mini-vans and tiny hybrid cars. "Why am I even doing this?" he mumbles.

"The truck is hot. And if you can't break this code, I need to talk to this Polybius guy."

"There's no telling what they've got at that facility," he says. "We need to keep clear of the hunters. We're the prey here."

"I said you can wait in the car. But I still need your car. Someone'll be looking for that truck, eventually."

"*And* my car! You keep forgetting, they're watching all of us, Spencer!"

I grit my teeth to avoid attacking his little fantasy for like the umpteenth time. "I'm done hotwiring cars, so it's yours or we walk." Without waiting for a response, I climb in the passenger's side and slam the door. Eric stares at me through the windshield. His face tightens and he spits a string of curse words that fail to penetrate the glass while his arms jerk tightly around his body. Finally, he storms around the front and plops into the driver's seat. Forearms heavy on the wheel, he leans forward.

"Man, this is such a bad idea," he groans.

"You have a better one that doesn't involve hiding in your basement?" I grumble.

He shakes his head but refuses to make eye contact.

"I'm asking a lot, I know that. But remember the picture I showed you? My reinforced bunker that Beetle's drone wrecked? If you really believe he's after you, you can sit around and wait for him to find you, 'cause he will. Or, we can act like Augments and go on the offensive. Get him first." I can't believe I'm using his ridiculous story to talk him into this. He deserves a better friend.

Eric nods. He stretches his seatbelt across his belly and starts the car, cruising out of the lot without a word. I turn on the radio and he immediately shuts it off, no explanation. Only his continued hyper-vigilance, I guess. The trip should take five hours and leave us in another state. It's going to be a long drive.

As he makes his way to the highway, his eyes are everywhere but the road ahead: on ramps, the rearview, scanning the skies. Been there, done that. The feeling that Mom might be out there overrides fear with a sense of urgency. I want to be there, now. He's fighting a flight response, I'm just fighting.

I've got no reason to believe in those dreams any more than I do in my friend's personal delusions. They aren't exactly coherent. Simply real. Intensely real. Like I'm having a conversation with her after all this time. I can't be sane either, I've already thought of that. Two years in a bunker, being chased by killer robots, and finding you've driven your only friend to the brink of insanity should be enough to push somebody over the edge.

"What's KUBARK?" I ask. The question draws a flick from his roving eyes.

"A cryptonym, for the CIA." Eric turns his head, "Why? Where'd you see that? Your Dad's stuff?"

"No. I think I saw it on a book of some sort," I lie. I'm not ready to talk dream interpretation with Eric.

"Plain cover, manila, maybe a field manual?" As he asks for the details, another glance in my direction but it slips toward the glove compartment. The glance is subtle, but as part of his increasingly weird vibe, it makes me worry. He insisted on bringing the gun.

"Yeah." I say, trying not to sound too nervous. "What is it?"

"You, the Beetle. Both were gaps in my knowledge. Once you left, anyway. I never figured that out." His tone is detached and I can't find an answer to my question in his response.

"I told you, I was in the Bunker."

"Uh-huh."

It could be the trance of the open road, but Eric's twitchiness has stopped. We're northbound on a stretch of interstate between areas of civilization. The sun is high and the heat in the air condition-less car stifling.

"It occurs to me," he continues, "this could all be an elaborate trap. A way to pull us into the open."

"C'mon, man. How would they know we were going to drive up and knock on Polybius's door?"

A piercing glare and Eric asks, "I don't know. How would they?"

"No, Eric. No. No. No! We talked about this. I'm Spencer. Not an Augment with shape shifting powers. No powers, nada! I want to find my mom, that's all. I don't want to see anyone get caught or get hurt."

Maintaining that withering gaze, he isn't answering and I feel compelled to start watching the road ahead for him. "If the Beetle is chasing me, he's only after this." I dig out the bag with the sat phone and thumb drive. "He wants this information. Beetle could give two shits about me."

"He's rounding us all up…"

"Not anymore. But this data might tell us who he is and what he really wants. You said it yourself; he's not a part of the Augment program, he's an unknown. A player that even you, Eric the Omniscient, doesn't know dick about." From wild suspicion to an almost maniacal stare, he considers the backpack. His face is intense and I can't watch. Facing the passenger window I say, "Dude, just pull over and drop me off."

No answer.

"I can hitch from here. I never should have gotten you involved," I say.

"I was already involved," comes the reply.

Now I can't turn away from the window, because my eyes start to water. "I know. I'm sorry."

"Don't be, Spencer. We didn't choose to be this way."

"We didn't."

He sags against the wheel. "It's an interrogation manual."

"Huh?"

"KUBARK. Manila cover. A field manual for interrogation." I wipe my eyes and risk a glance. He's absorbed by the road as he speaks, "Typical stuff. Electric shocks, isolation, whatever will make people talk. Softer techniques such as getting people to trust you work best."

"Eric, you can trust me. I swear."

"I hope so. Probably too late for me to turn around anyway."

We continue on in silence. Mountains rise ahead, giving a vague impression of distant thunderheads floating on the horizon. As we get closer, the mountains flank the highway in jagged walls. Pretty soon we're signaling for an exit.

The world shrinks as we enter a labyrinth of hills, valleys and towering pines. On the highway, everyone seemed so close. The sky smothering, the traffic an angry swarm, and the road behind a lurking presence. Here, trees stretch up beyond the top edges of the windshield, and we're driving through a tunnel draped by a blue and feathered sky. Camouflaged from the world, I've returned to a kind of isolation. Never thought I would want it that way ever again.

"Get ready. We're almost there." Panic tinges Eric's words. "You have a plan?"

"Yeah," I say, taking in the last bit of calm from the wilderness. "Let me do the talking."

CHAPTER 31

WE PASS A weathered sign on the side of the road. Raw wood and a bit of peeling paint sport the words "Whispering Pines Living Center". The sign is graced with an angular, jagged logo, maybe a tree someone with safety scissors and a helmet might cut out. It's a far cry from the almost up-to-date website. Next to the sign sits a guard shack and a striped wooden gate arm blocking the road. On the other side of the arm, embedded in the pavement, is a thick strip of metal that gives the impression there's a hunk of steel buried flush with the pavement. Next to the guardhouse lurks a black SUV.

A thick-necked guy blocks the road, sporting a military haircut and a handgun. The white shirt, black pants uniform has "mall cop" written all over it. That's fine, maybe we're wasting our time here. He's pretty buff, though, and his expression says he takes the job way too seriously.

Eric creeps forward and rolls the window down. Super Mall Cop is already posted in the middle of the road with his palm out and jaw set. He's staring down Eric's shoebox car, daring us to run him over. Eric lurches forward as he goes for the brake while fumbling with the window controls at the same time. The front end gets awkwardly close to the guard. He doesn't budge.

"Put it in park, please," the guard commands. The last word has no hint of politeness. He walks over to the driver's window and bends down to look inside. His movements suggest some sort of ritual born of the same rote training Dad always hounded me about. He's not too close, and keeps his hands off the car while his eyes somehow simultaneously lock with ours and search the interior. He's checking hands, the bag in the floorboard, along with scoping out the laptop. "Can I help you?" Again, no sincerity.

Eric's whole body stiffens and his face starts to change color. I lean over him and say, "Yeah. We were looking for a place to camp and got lost."

Unyielding eyes drill into mine and the guard responds, "Take the road there back west and you'll find the interstate."

"Oh, right, but, I was hoping maybe to use your phone? Mine's out of juice..."

Eric's color goes from rosy to virulent. He might explode soon.

"I'm afraid I can't help you."

At this point, the guard is watching Eric as well, probably judging the distance he needs to be so he doesn't get spattered with bits of him. If Eric pops, his eyeballs are going to go first because they're practically protruding out of their sockets.

"What about an internet connection? Surely the old folks chat with the grandkids. I can Google a campground. I'll be quick, promise."

"Going to have to ask you to leave, sir," Super Mall Cop says. He doesn't flinch.

I don't look like a "sir". Something else he must be doing out of habit. This has to be the place.

"Well, thanks anyway."

I backhand Eric's leg and he grinds through the gears into reverse, eventually whipping around in a cloud of dust. We're out of sight of the main gate before he sputters, "That was your plan?"

"Well, sort of."

"I said I trusted you, Spencer. Not that I was an idiot!"

"We have the right place, I can guarantee that."

"No shit, I told you this was it!"

"Excuse me for not trusting that website."

"Are you mental? He could've grabbed us right there!"

"Yep. And he didn't."

He can't form a response. In my world, I was pretty damn sure whatever government Augment program that was maintaining this place could care less about me and Eric. A couple of dumb teenagers lost in the woods, that's all Super Mall Cop saw. I saw a military trained hard ass, with instructions to turn away anyone and everyone. Hopefully, Eric found a bit of the truth as well.

"Pull over here." I point to a flat area on the shoulder between a couple of trees. He guides the car between the thin piney trunks and slams it into park.

"Now what?"

"You wait here."

I'm shouldering the backpack and have one foot out the open door when he says, "No way."

Once I'm out, I hang on to the door and peer at him. A good long stare and I close the door, dipping back in through the open window. "Yes way."

Without hesitating, I turn and head for the woods. I hear the driver's door open and close, followed by a frantic scramble through the gravel near the roadside.

"Stay here. Stick with the camping story. If I'm not back in a couple hours..." I'm not sure how to end that because I've never planned that far in advance.

"Bullshit! You've... you've got my laptop."

"I hope that's not a problem. Might need it," I call out as I push into the undergrowth.

"You... I... what are you doing now?"

He's close behind, crashing through the brush and I whirl to face him. I grimace when I see the gun in his waistband but lay into him anyway. "What am I doing? Breaking into a covert facility to talk to an Augment. It's stupid. Probably won't work. Might get me arrested, or worse, killed."

"What says he'll even talk to you if you do get in?"

"Nothing. I don't even know if he's there. But if he did make this encryption and my dad was using it, well, maybe he helped set up the system at the bunker. Maybe he wants to help."

"So a wild hunch and you're off on your own?"

"This is why you stay in the car."

I watch the inner turmoil play out on Eric's face. Our old friendship is there battling the theories he's been sucked into since I left. Is he worried that, as a still-unconfirmed piece of his past, I'll sell him out and the black helicopters will descend as he waits, or concerned for the safety of his friend? I can't sense which way he's leaning. All I know is that I want him to be safe, and if I find what I need, my next step will be to hitch a ride out of here without him.

"I want to go. You don't believe that I'm an Augment. But I'm telling you, I am. You can't do this without me."

Christ, here he goes again. "You aren't an Augment. How many times do I need to say that! You aren't. Can't be."

"But the Foundation? Getting lost at birth? Weren't you listening?"

"A coincidence. That's it."

"Then how do you explain my insatiable thirst for knowledge? My ability to break through any firewall that stands in my way? Man, I don't even know how I do half the stuff I do. I can have an army of hijacked computers at my disposal in an instant. If it's coded, I can crack it." I point at the backpack with a raised eyebrow, tapping the pocket with the sealed bag and thumb drive. Eric rolls his eyes. "Fine, fine. Not that. But that's classic Polybius, man. He's, well, he's—"

"An Augment?"

He slouches in defeat and I put a hand on his shoulder. "Eric, you're a fucking genius. Not an Augment."

"Damn it," he exclaims. With a halfhearted chop, he brushes my arm aside. "Let me go with you. You find out about your mom, I find out if I'm an Augment. Maybe Polybius knows."

"I can ask him," I reply, still pressing forward.

"Bullshit. I want to hear it for myself. I want to see your face."

Raw determination and utter sincerity are blazing through the schizo fog that's been surrounding him. In lots of ways, I can't think of anything better that could happen. Why anyone would *want* to be an Augment is beyond me. I got over that real quick as a kid. Seeing Eric suffer like this is too damn hard.

"Fine. You can come. But put the gun back. If we get into a shootout, we're as good as dead anyway."

CHAPTER 32

"THAT'S WEIRD," I whisper. I don't know why I'm whispering. Eric and I belly crawled up the small hill overlooking the retirement home with all the stealth of wounded animals. Special Forces, we are not.

"What?" Eric pants as he claws his way up beside me.

"No cars," I say. "The parking lot is empty."

He peers over the rise and scans the grounds. "Helicopters. They use those, I bet."

The area below is lifeless. It's a sprawling one-story brick complex with high windows along the arms of each wing. Trees are cleared in all directions for maybe an acre or so, but not nearly as far away as the photo on the website. There are no patios with old guys reading the paper in the fading sun. A mundane sliding glass door entrance faces the parking lot.

One wing, however, is windowless and solid brick from top to bottom, with a different material on the roof. It's thicker and the door appears metal with massive hinges. I point it out. Nodding and huffing, he starts to scramble down the hill.

I grab his arm. "It'll be dark soon, let's at least wait until then."

"Oh, yeah, good idea."

Light slips away as we huddle behind the crest of the hill. What few attempts we make at conversation are awkward at best. Short, barely audible exchanges that can't hope to encompass all the stuff I want to say.

Once the sun's set, we're set to creep down the hill when the sound of an engine flattens us to the ground. The black SUV from the guardhouse makes its way up the main road and a figure emerges from the glass door entrance. A tall, lean man in a form-fitting white T-shirt walks out to meet the SUV. In the gathering darkness, it's difficult to say, but I'm hoping it's the SUV from the gate and I'm really hoping it's only the one guard and not backup. They exchange words and as the vehicle departs along the main road, the man in the T-shirt scans the horizon. Before disappearing inside, he leans his head back and inhales deeply, twisting his head in an arc.

"What was that all about?" I ask.

"Maybe they found the car?" He says. "This is strange, man. No other guards, only the dude at the gate and whoever that guy inside was. Did he have a piece?"

"A piece? What are you, the Pillsbury Mafia boy? No, I don't think he had a gun. Wait here. I'll see if I can get that door open." A word of protest sticks in his throat as I scramble to my feet and shuffle down the hillside.

In the dark, lights have winked on, but their pale pools of illumination are easy to avoid. I keep an eye out for cameras and don't see one until I'm almost to the reinforced door. It's right above the doorway. I flatten against the brick wall, hopefully out of view.

Cameras aren't my specialty, but as I stare at the tinted globe, I can see there's little to worry about. The wires are cut. Creeping even closer, I see the exterior lights shining right through the bubble. No trace of a camera, even. Still cautious, I slide toward the door, a single hunk of metal with a latched handle similar to one on a walk-in freezer. An irregular lump sticks out from the center. To the right on the wall, there's a keypad.

I run a hand along the door as I work toward the handle and I can feel the lump, about the size of a fist—like someone on the inside was pressing against a sheet of plastic. I'm amazed by the damage while I fumble for my multi-tool. By the time I'm ready to crack open the keypad, I notice that's missing, too.

I pull the handle and the door opens.

Why is "easier" so much worse? Hoping Eric can see me, I raise a palm in the direction of the hill and slip inside.

I enter an empty hallway with dim lights near the floor. The hall stretches out to a "T" intersection. Other heavy doors line the walls. I avoid checking them as I move. I'm not sure I want to know if they are occupied, and I need an idea of how this place is laid out, first.

Reaching the corner, I can tell a bit more light fills the hallway to the right. That's as good an indication as any of where the occupied areas might be. I continue sliding forward, flat against the wall. Light floods the next intersection. Frozen, I try to steady my breathing and build up the nerve to peek.

The air gets dense and my ears pop painfully. I start to shift for that peek and that's the first time I can tell I'm held against the wall. A hand clamps down on my mouth. Another grips my shoulder. I kick against the wall, my scream muffled by a leathery palm.

A man's bald head gleams in the light from the hall. He holds a finger up to sunken lips.

"Calm down, son, or the Jerrys'll hear ya!" He sounds like he's talking with a mouthful of peanut butter.

His finger trembles in front of a reddened and chapped face. In fact, in the dim light, his whole body looks that way—everywhere not covered by a standard hospital gown. I do a quick double take to see that yes, he isn't wearing pants, and I see only a thin shadow where his right leg should be.

He leans across me and peers around the corner. There's a sharp aroma of Ben-Gay and a rotting stench beneath that. With his finger hovering in front of his mouth, he pulls his hand from my face inches at a time, all the while nodding up and down. I nod back.

"Whew, a mess out there, yeah?" the man says, his chest rattling. "What the heck's a kid like you doing here?"

"Nothing. I mean, well, who are you?"

"The name's Hurricane."

"*The* Hurricane? Augment Force Z—"

His hand is back before I can finish, or blink, or move. He squints one eye, taking me in head to toe. "Who gave you that information?" He casts a nervous glance at the corridor as he tips his hand away from my mouth.

"Indian Springs Elementary. And I read about it way before then," I manage to say.

"You been hit in the head, kid?"

"Lately? Yes." What other way can I answer that?

"We don't have time for fooling around. How'd you hear about Force Zero?"

Why he's denying the existence of information anyone can get off a night on the couch with the History Channel, I'm not sure. But I need to play along, because old or not, sane or not, this guy means business. If he is who he says he is, he's totally serious business. "I'm on a mission. I came to talk to Polybius. They said Force Zero could help me find him."

He shakes his head in contemplation, grinding his jaw. When he starts to speak, I notice why his voice is so strange; he's got no teeth. "You're in the know, kid. Let's say I can take you, but what do you need Polybius for?"

"Code breaking. I've got to break a code and nobody in the world can do it except him."

"Sounds legit. Hop on, son, I'll run ya into HQ and we'll see what we can see." Hurricane sticks his right leg straight out in front while he bends the other. The gown cinches up and that thin shadow catches the light. The lower part of his thigh is fitted into a flexible cup. From his knee down, his leg is a metal rod that ends in the molded shape of a shoe.

"What happened?"

"Huh? Oh, my leg gets stiff every so often. Jus' gotta wiggle the toes a bit and it all works out. See?" His foot and the shoe remain motionless in the shadows. He bends forward and sticks his elbows back. "Come on, hop on."

"You're kidding, right?"

"Nope. You can't weigh more than what, a buck and a quarter? Might slow me down some, but unless you want to hump it through the battlefield out there, you best saddle up."

"A buck fifty." I lie as I clamber onto his back. He's thin and frail, but his muscles and bones feel like granite lurking beneath a sheet of leather. "And speaking of humping, this is awkward."

"Don't get fresh, kid, just hang on."

The world streaks by and I can envision my insides flopping around in the dark corridor somewhere behind us.

CHAPTER 33

"HEY, HOUND, WE got one in from the front!" Hurricane announces.

We're facing another room with empty walls and a concrete floor. A caged fluorescent bulb runs along the ceiling, providing sanitized light. There are three hospital beds, each beside narrow tables; two on the closest wall and one on the far side. Of the two on the closest wall, the one nearest the door is occupied and a formless mass fills the other.

Despite being only as loud as a strained whisper, a commanding voice comes from the closest bed. "What the hell are you goin' on about now?"

Propped against the wall with a pile of pillows behind him is the guy Hurricane is calling Hound. Hound pulls away from an open newspaper and glances our direction, his nose twitching. He's peering at me through bushy eyebrows as white as his T-shirt. He's an old guy with a sheen of salt-and-pepper hair combed in thick lines against his head. Clean shaven, the skin on his face is rugged and bronzed. His nose continues to wriggle.

Hurricane hobbles into the room toward the unoccupied

bed, leaving me in the doorway. "Nazi codes. Maybe some of that Jap Purple crap. We'll get one over on the Bletchley gang, for sure!"

I try and ignore Hound's gaze and check the bed in the far corner. A glistening, liver spotted bulb juts from a mound of sea-green blankets that rise and fall in mechanical waves.

"Is that Polybius?" I ask.

Hound twitches his head in the direction of the corner bed. He takes in a long draw through his nostrils as he asks, "Who the hell are you?"

"My name's Spencer."

"Where's your friend?" he scowls.

"What friend?"

"That's not an answer. Is your friend in here or not?"

"No."

He lowers his head, glaring through the wiry eyebrow tufts with a silent demand. Without thinking I add, "No, sir."

Hurricane creaks into the empty bed and pulls the artificial leg from its socket. The stump beneath is raw and bloodied. Where his leg rests in the fitting is a bunched-up cloth streaked in scarlet, copper and black.

"'Cane, you keep that bullshit up and you're gonna wear your leg down to your nuts," barks Hound.

Hurricane laughs. "Maybe I'm trying to lure the nurses up here, eh? You see the one Echo Company has working with the field medics? Finest little French girl I ever saw."

Hound rattles his paper and dives behind it, turning the page with a grumble.

"How long has this place been here?" I call from the doorway.

Hurricane answers with a smile as he binds his leg, "Since the start of the War."

"Which war?"

Hound slaps his paper closed and tosses it re-folded onto the bed as he swings his feet off the mattress. "*The* War, son. There's only been one. Rest were an 'undefined action' or 'insurgency' or some other bullshit." Standing with arms crossed, he glowers at me. He doesn't look old enough to be a World War Two veteran. Back straight and eyes needle-sharp, his broad frame stretches at the white T-shirt. Peeking out from his sleeve is what might be a bruise… or a tattoo. "Suppose we should call Chuck," Hound sighs.

"Chuck?"

"Guy at the gate you talked to earlier," Hound mumbles as he makes toward the doorway where I'm standing.

"Wait! My mom's been kidnapped by the Black Beetle and I have to get her back." Hound scrunches his face and I fumble over the words, "Mr. Dog… Hound… sir."

"Stick with 'sir'. How old are you, son?"

"Nineteen."

He frowns incredulously.

"Oh yeah, Hound. You remember Blaise?" Hurricane's cheerful voice plummets into a whisper. "Heard he bought it by mortar last week. Good kid…"

Hound walks forward with slow, deliberate steps. "I've heard of him."

"Blaise? That French Resistance fighter. Had his dad's ol' powder rifle when he—"

"Not Blaise, you senile old fart, this Black Beetle the kid's goin' on about."

Hurricane shrugs off the name-calling with a smile. "Oh, stop yer growling, Hound."

I take a gamble and step into the room toward Hound. "I don't have much time. I think Polybius can help…" My eyes trail to the occupied bed in the corner. There's a metal tree hung with bags of fluid, and a heart monitor standing at the side of Polybius's bed. The shrouded body rises and falls rhythmically. "Is that him?"

"Son, only thing he's good for is catheter practice."

"You mean, he can't talk?"

"Not payin' attention? He can't even piss for himself. Not sure how much help he'd be."

"Maybe I should go and fetch this friend ya mentioned?" Hurricane stuffs a handful of fresh gauze in the prosthetic and swings his damaged leg to the edge of the bed. Affixing the prosthesis, he stands and presses his thumbs into his lower back leaning with a groan and a crescendo of popping joints. "Be back in a jiff."

"Dammit, 'Cane…" Hound starts but too late. Hurricane's white bed sheet settles to the bed which is now pushed back several feet. For a heartbeat, Hurricane just isn't there.

I wince as my ears pop and a blast of air drags the door to the hallway closed. Hurricane's back, inches from my face, squinting. "Hey, Blaise, where's this friend at anyway?"

"He's hiding in the trees. I don't think we need to get him."

I call out the last bit as the door swings open again with enough force to bounce closed. Hurricane's gone.

Hound groans and strides to the bedside. "Damn fool."

"Do you think he'll find him?"

"He'll find him." Hound opens the paper. "That was his job—recovery and delivery. Idiot thinks he's still doin' it."

"Are you going to turn us in?"

No answer.

"What about you? What was your job, sir?"

"Sniffer." Between lazy turns of the pages, Hound rattles off his resume. "Findin' unexploded ordinance, Jerrys in bunkers, Japs in tunnels, landmines." Hound's eyes travel to Hurricane's empty bed before slipping back into the Local News section. "Keepin' soldiers outta trouble."

"Are you, uh, in charge, here? In charge of Hurricane?"

"You ever try to grab a rocket in flight?" Snowy eyebrows that remind me of caterpillars come together as Hound peeks over the paper. "I've been tellin' him for months that we're awaiting deployment at a captured German HQ. I think that's why they put me with 'im. They know I'm stupid enough to keep doin' my job. But nobody gives him orders. They tried strappin' him down for a bit, but he thought he'd been captured and caught his bed on fire wiggling at the restraints."

"You haven't been here since the War, have you, sir?"

"Hell, no. Not me. Stationed here a year or so. 'For my own safety'. That Black Beetle menace was tearing up the world. Old tunnel rats like me were just gettin' in the way. Was kinda hoping we'd be assigned to kick his bug ass." Hound sighs and nods toward the empty door. "Hurricane's been here longer. Ever since his mind started going. Might be ten years."

I can't stop myself from asking, "Who else was brought here?"

"As far as I can tell, all of us in the program got the same marching orders. Can't say they all responded."

"What about the Crimson Mask?"

Hound inhales again and his eyes go wide then quickly settle. "Guess he had his orders, too."

"Such as?"

"You'd have to ask him," Hound says matter-of-factly.

I really wish I could. Maybe he was supposed to do the same, turn himself in to the government. Maybe then the Black Beetle would have left us alone. Dad couldn't stop him anyway. How was he even a threat to whatever bullshit plans that guy dreamed up?

"Why are you here? This place looks deserted." I press for more under his piercing stare and when he finally answers, he's no longer sizing me up.

"The few that showed up, they moved out in small groups to another facility. Me, Hurricane, Polybius were gonna be the last. All this happened while they were taking this place down around our ears. Probably a goddamn paperwork problem, why we got left behind. Always paperwork problems."

"But why relocate everyone?"

Hound sees the confusion and twitches his nose. "I don't ask questions, son. I just follow orders." He reaches to the bedside table and picks up an older, faded newspaper. He tosses it in my lap. It's folded to a page—the obituaries.

At first, I find I'm reading the entries and focused on the younger ones, to see what might have killed them. Twenties or thirties, with a normal life, a normal job. No traipsing through war zones or obvious signs of Augment parents that dragged them into a world of shit. How does someone like that die? Then, those same intense eyes currently studying the newspaper are staring back at me. Captain Arnold E. Raffens, born April 15th 1928, died January 23rd, 2011. World War Two veteran, awarded the Congressional Medal of Honor for action in the European and Pacific theaters. Father, husband, grandfather.

I check his face to compare the details before asking, "Mister Raffens?"

"Sir is fine."

"What about your kids? Do they know, sir?"

He's speaking in a gruff whisper now. "Hell, I didn't know until my superiors handed me the paper. I'd already come in as ordered. I suspect my family was given a cover story."

"Then you got left here to rot?"

Hound squares up and glowers at me as he rumbles, "When you're part of the program, you sign your life away. It's right there in the fine print. They make sure you read it. They make sure you understand it. They get shrinks to poke around your head and really make sure you understand. Only after all that do they juice you up."

"But they can't own somebody!"

"They don't own anyone, son." He sighs and shakes his head. "Nobody nowadays really gets it. I signed up for it. I signed up to serve my country at any cost. I was ready to dry up to dust in the Sahara, be blown to shit in a snow-packed Alpine pass or lay down on a grenade on a Godforsaken hunk of rock in the Pacific. I asked to serve and will continue to do so."

"But dragging you out here and locking you up until you die? How is that—"

"I'd die for this country a hundred times over, son."

"Sounds more like a death camp than a retirement home."

Hound grumbles but can't manage a full response. I walk toward Polybius's wheezing form. From a distance, his bulbous head was hairless, but closer I see thin wisps sprouting from the top and waving in an unseen breeze. Featureless pearl globes fill the socket of his eyes and split lips bubble with phlegm.

Hound crosses the room and swipes a rag off the table, gently wiping Polybius's face. "Guess he was the reason you came here?"

My sinus cavities vibrate and the door slams shut with a rush of air. "Yeah, right where I thought he'd be," Hurricane proclaims, now standing at his bedside smiling. Eyes closed, lying on the bed, is Eric. "Took me a bit longer, he ain't no buck fifty."

"What happened to him?" I rush to Eric's side.

"He passed right out when I found him on the hill! He'll be fine, won't be the first person I scared the daylights out of."

"'Cane, sit down. Get your weight off that leg of yours."

A heaving cough can't erase Hurricane's smile as he slides onto the edge of the bed.

Hound eyes Eric then me, and his gaze lightly touches upon the paper in my lap. With a sigh, he asks, "So what's it about this data you've got?"

I fish the laptop and the sealed bag from my backpack. "The data on this is my only lead."

"And you're relying on him?" Hound hooks a thumb toward Polybius's inert form.

Hurricane hops across the room, prosthetic in hand and hovers over Polybius. Reaching into a pocket of his gown, he pulls out an inhaler and takes two long drags. Vapor curling out through his permanent grin, he sees me staring. "Gettin' old is shit, kid. Avoid that as long as ya can!"

Hound slaps at the air and growls, "Go on and get outta here with your friend. Chuck found your car and told me to keep a look out earlier, but I see no reason you need to be hauled off."

"No, sir. There's got to be something here that can help!"

"You're not hearin' me. They stripped the place down. Evacuated all personnel and it's just us." Hound motions lifelessly to the room.

"Don't listen to him, kid. Polybius there's a genius when it comes to numbers and codes. Never met him 'til I got here, but I'd swear he's worth fifty of them damn vacuum-tube countin' machines them Brits have!"

"'Cane, shut your mouth. Stop getting this kid's hopes up."

"You're just too proud to admit he's better at them Jap puzzles than you. I'll never understand that, but they're some crafty yellow bastards, I'll give 'em that."

"Jap puzzles?" Sure, he sounds completely insane, but I have to ask.

"Yeah, the ones they started putting in the paper."

"'Cane…" Hound's glare is icy and a powerful jaw twitches beneath his cheeks.

"Soe-doo-kee. Sow-duck-oh. Whatever the hell you've been calling it. Solves them in a jiff when you done lost your wits."

"Sudoku?" I exclaim and stare openmouthed at Hurricane, who's absently itching at his leg.

"Yeah! That's it! Crafty little guys."

CHAPTER 34

"WHAT'S THIS ABOUT Sudoku?" Eric sounds groggy as he rolls to one side and leans on his elbow in the hospital bed.

"He's comin' to!" Hurricane calls out from the bedside. At the sound of Hurricane's voice, Eric flies out of the bed, causing a spine-tingling screech of the metal frame on concrete. In his bewildered state he staggers away from the door and traps himself in an empty corner. From the look on his face, he'd bolt if he had a clear path to the door.

"Relax, man!" I put my arms out front and make myself seen as quick as I can. Eric hones in on the movement of my approach.

"Spencer, they got you, too?"

"Uh, no. Nobody's got us," I say and glance at Hound. "Right?" Hound snaps the paper open and a low harrumph rises from the business section. "We're safe."

"Okay." Eric nods slowly. His wandering gaze settles on Hurricane. "He, he came out of nowhere, Spencer."

Hurricane smiles the same toothless grin. "You didn't see

me. Happens all the time." Hurricane, at a volume the whole room can hear, adds, "He's shell-shocked. He'll get over it."

"Eric, this is Hurricane." I know Eric has heard of this guy. Everyone has. But his wide-eyed freak-out face doesn't change. Shell-shocked, huh? "Augment Force Zero Hurricane," I say, hoping to get some sort of reaction.

"A pleasure," Hurricane says, hitching up his gown and digging a pair of fingers between his leg and the prosthesis.

"And the guy behind the paper is Hound." Neither Eric nor Hound responds. Desperate, I lean in close to Eric, hopefully out of earshot and whisper, "They're Augments, like us."

That generates a blank nod. I steal another glance and Hound has lowered his newsprint barricade, glaring with narrowed eyes. Great. Super hearing, too? Does he piss with one leg in the air? I sigh and turn my attention back to Eric.

This was supposedly all part of his imaginary world, and now he can't even speak. I wave Hurricane away from the bed and guide Eric there. He sits with all the sincerity of a coiled spring.

"So," I say at a volume I hope is loud enough to pierce Eric's mental breakdown, "that was a good question, Eric. What was that about Sudoku? Hurricane?"

Hurricane's face lights up. "Oh, come on, Hound, the guy can solve 'em in his sleep. Just show the kid. You won't bother him none."

When I'm sure Eric is sitting under his own power, I move to the stack of papers on the nightstand and start digging despite Hound's sideways stare. Doesn't matter if Hound won't talk, I'm going to figure this out. Snatching the "Games and

Puzzles" section, I spill the better part of the Sunday edition onto the floor.

Hound grabs my arm. "Kid, you leave him alone." His voice is gruff, and his grip, while strong, couldn't quite rip my arm off.

"Why?"

"He's done his duty."

"So you're seriously going to tell me that seeing if he can help save my mom is a bad idea? But using him to solve Sudoku is a noble cause?"

"That isn't how it happened," Hound says and flashes a look at Hurricane. "I used to read the paper to him. One day he started spoutin' out numbers. Thought it was gibberish until I noticed the puzzles were facin' his way."

"Maybe if I show him the data he can do the same?"

Hound stoops low, nose-to-nose, and his grip tightens. "I said no. They find out he's got an ounce of juice in that scrambled brain of his, they'll come back for him. They want him in service. Either that, or he's got information locked in there they needed." He releases me and starts peeling away the blankets, which are tightly wound around Polybius. As they unravel, Polybius's form shrinks into an emaciated shape. He's covered in bruises, broken by odd lumps and projections where bones shouldn't be. Cables run the length of his left arm, burrowing somewhere into his chest through puckered patches of skin. Several panels with LEDs blink on his abdomen. A plate on his arm displays more lights and numbers.

The puzzle section that I held flutters to the floor. Another pop of pressure, and Hurricane is maneuvering a limp Eric onto the far bed. Hound takes in the impact crater that is my face and starts tucking the blankets around Polybius again. He growls, "He's done his duty, son."

I'm only vaguely aware of Hound as he finishes covering Polybius. The battered form shows through the careful tucks and folds. Hound grumbles, "If they coulda put his brain in a jar and made it talk, they would've."

"Is this what they do to Augments? You?"

Hound's eyes flit up from his work. "He's the only one. A failed program. They sent him back from it this way. Die in peace."

"But you don't even know where that is! How can you not be sure this isn't what they were going to do to you?" I ask.

Hound finishes smoothing out the blankets around Polybius and starts to pick the papers off the floor. "We talked about this. Whatever they do, I signed up a long time ago."

Once again, Polybius is wrapped in comfort, or a death shroud; I can't say which. I watch the blankets rise and fall with a perfect rhythm. Causing someone unnecessary pain isn't what I'm after, but I've got to get Hound to let me at least try. "Nobody will ever know what happened here, Hound. I—"

A vicious stare shuts me down. "Wake up your friend and get the hell out of here!"

"No."

The stare intensifies.

"No, sir."

"Hurricane, carry these guys out of here. They aren't cleared for any of this!"

"But, what about Blaise's code?"

"Are you questioning my orders, soldier? These kids are a security risk, they gotta go." Hound's got to be almost eighty, ninety? But standing there, straight-backed, his chest puffed out by impeccable posture, his white sleeves cinched up tight around his biceps, he may as well have stepped off the battlefield yesterday. The mark on his arm is fully exposed—a tattoo of an eagle perched on a globe and anchor, with the words "Semper Fi".

Hurricane wobbles over. I step back, even though trying to play keep-away from this guy would be pointless. I can at least glower at him defiantly while he runs me halfway across the state. Maybe I can struggle a bit, wiggle free somewhere close enough to walk my no-power-having ass back here and do this song and dance again.

Our eyes meet and I see a similar fire burning behind his. A little gleam that shimmers behind the craziness. Not defiance but anticipation. "You said you were nineteen, kid?" Hurricane asks.

"Yeah." I can let the kid reference slide.

"Same age I was when I started my scenic tour of Europe and Southeast Asia. I had to protect my country, my family. Never regretted it. Right?" He squares up with Hound, who puffs up under his crossed arms. "But that was a long time ago. Right now, I'm not here 'cause anyone asked me to be. I'm not even here 'cause it was the right thing to do. I'm here 'cause this is one of those things that once you've found it, you can't let go. And it won't let go of you. But at least I'm man enough to admit that."

In this moment, Hurricane's mind seems free from whatever

prison the past has walled him into. Hound senses the change, too. His imperious posture relaxes and his jaw muscles form hardened wedges.

"Please," I say. "This is for my mom. We never signed up for this."

Hound stoops enough that his face is level with mine. Unblinking, he takes in every detail and his chest expands with a sharp inhale through his nostrils. "Make it quick. Hurricane, watch the hall in case Chuck does his rounds."

"Yes, sir." Hurricane salutes and hobbles to the doorway.

In seconds, I'm booting up the laptop, ripping open the bio-bag and slipping the thumb drive into an empty slot. Now what? I hold the screen up to Polybius's face. I didn't notice before, but his eyeballs are rolling back and forth beneath the lids. Without lashes, they'd seemed melded together in one smooth surface. The lids part, but only a white sliver ever peeks through.

I flip the laptop toward me and pop open the server emulation program that loads the login screens. After digging down to the password prompt for the Black Beetle's files, I turn the screen toward Polybius. There's no response. I enter a bogus password. "Polybius, I need the password." The empty eyes continue to scan, his mouth hangs open.

"He can't answer you," Hound says. He's trying to sound uninterested even as he's leaning over my shoulder.

"No shit, sir."

Hurricane wheezes out a chuckle from the doorway, "Easy now, Blaise. You aren't supposed to know his bark is worse than his bite."

Without turning I mutter an apology and dive back into the laptop. I know the guy laying in front of me is little more than a pile of wires and a breathing machine, but I'm willing to try anything at this point. Putting a bunch of code in his face to decipher seems legit. Desperate, but legit.

I open the first hodgepodge of coded files. At first, Polybius stares blankly at the screen. Then, his eyes crawl open revealing empty, pale orbs. A blunt, hammering voice fills the room, echoing letters and numbers in bizarre sequences. Hound stares open-mouthed, and Hurricane leans on the door frame, watching us, not the hall.

My jaw is clenched shut and I swallow, trying to loosen my tongue enough to speak. "Yeah, I'd say we've outclassed the vacuum tubes." The inert form of Polybius rattles off information in a continuous stream. Sometimes binary and sometimes hexadecimal, I begin to decipher that much, but it's never plain English.

Right about now, Eric would be really useful. There's no table space nearby, so I gently rest the laptop on Polybius's bed and cross the room to stand by Eric. I shake him and call his name. No response. I try again, a bit harder this time. "C'mon! Wake up!"

He opens his eyes and they roll back in his head with a groan. "Nooooo! I'm still here? I was hoping someone laced my weed."

"Get up! You don't even smoke."

"I will. As soon as we get home, I fucking-A will!"

"Come on!" Wedging a shoulder behind his back, I push

and shove to get him on his feet. "You're an Augment! Act like one! Get off your ass and help me out!"

"No, Spence. I'm not an Augment. I'm an idiot. An idiot!" He's putting up less of a fight as I force him off the bed. Once his feet touch the ground he begins pointing wildly. "That toothless mental patient in the nightgown! He's an Augment! And that guy! Frankenfreak! *He's* an Augment! The dude reading the paper? I don't… oh shit, that face, he's one too! What am I doing here!"

"Dammit, don't fall apart again, Eric!" It must be the influence of Hound's barking, but in that moment the words rumble from deep within my chest, lending a presence way outside my weight class.

Polybius speaks.

CHAPTER 35

"SEAN? IS THAT you?" The voice doesn't match any-thing—Polybius's frame, the bare acoustics of the room we're in, or even the normal range of a person's vocal chords. It's utterly inhuman. Bony thumbs press the laptop into his palms. His eyes cycle at warp speed as the screen blazes with information.

"You know my dad?"

Lines of code crawl up Polybius's unblinking eyes. Wide, dark brown irises descend from his forehead. His pupils relax from tiny specks and he measures me with an awakened gaze.

"Spencer. Yes." His speech matches the cadence of the breathing machine, interrupted by gasping mouthfuls of air.

"You, you know my name, too?"

"Your father. Spoke of you." Several clicks of the mechani-cal lungs pass. "Where is this?"

"Whispering Pines facility," Hound responds. He's close enough to my shoulder that I can smell stale cigarette smoke on his breath.

"How long. Like this?" Polybius wheezes.

"Long time before I got here," Hound continues cautiously.

"You dropped off the radar in '08. There were rumors about your... condition."

"Asked too many questions. Interrogated. Mental augmentation kept me from compromise." Polybius's eyes flick unnaturally. "Your father. He's here?"

"He surrendered to the Black Beetle."

"Black Beetle." Polybius faces the open laptop.

Code races across the screen. Eric is powerless to resist the technology, the revelations. I feel his thick fingers on my shoulder.

"No way. How are you doing that?" Eric rarely speaks in awe while watching a computer. Contempt, enjoyment, utter confidence, but not amazement. Whatever is happening on the display, I can't begin to understand. Tantalizing bits of code, programming syntax are all wrapped in a peculiar data structure which cascades by in uneven rows. There's a sort of repetition, an almost readable pattern.

"I do not. Understand." Polybius strains as he answers.

"What is it you see?" I ask Eric.

"A dude controlling a laptop with his brain. Either that, or the laptop is talking to itself." Eric puts his head next to mine. In the blue glow, the earlier fear is washed away.

"Talking to itself?" Hound asks, mesmerized.

"Well, chunks keep repeating. One command pops up, gets echoed rapid-fire, and eventually another piece gets added. It repeats and then the focus shifts to another system." Eric sights down a finger and runs it up the screen to follow a particularly elusive chunk of code.

His description makes me worry, but I lose the feeling as

more deciphered data appears. Among the documents, a few are even scanned and handwritten notes—the same handwriting on those damn refrigerator notes he used to leave.

A text file labeled "Killcreek Initiative—Black Beetle Link" opens.

The only sound in the room is the hiss and click of the breathing machine.

"I'll be damned," Hound says in awe.

I'm reading as fast as I can, tapping impatiently while waiting for the scrolling words to catch up. Answers to questions come slow at first, then in a raging torrent. The notes in the margins, scrawled or typed, get the most attention.

Orders to Dad from the Killcreek Initiative flicker across the screen. Augments were going rogue. They needed to be neutralized. The reported goal: to round up rogue Augments and prevent another disaster like the Djinn.

And then we see the field reports show up. Codename Crimson Mask being ordered into operations around the world. But soon, I'm seeing Dad's signature on documents requesting clarification on his orders. Documents that ask why he's not being tasked to deal with the Black Beetle. But he never got a straight answer. The people deciding his marching orders were the same ones protecting the Beetle. A puzzle that super strength and nigh-invulnerability couldn't solve.

Soon, we're scouring through scanned documents with chunks of data missing beneath bold black lines. From what I can tell, one of these is a contract. It mentions money sent to a bank account. I see Dad's handwriting with the words "BB shell" circled. The date at the top of the page is from a little over two years ago. He got suspicious. Got too close to the truth.

Then she was taken.

"What else on BB?" I'm not even sure who I'm asking until Polybius intones an answer.

"Cross-reference indicates BB synonymous. Searching." The screen goes nuts and more contracts flash by with thousands, millions, maybe billions of dollars sent to one fake company after another.

"Matches up with my 'crazy' theory, eh Spence?" No longer lost in the code, Eric reads the documents as they flash on screen. "They sent outclassed Augments into the drone meatgrinder. Meanwhile, your dad was rounding up the rest on orders and being fed a different story."

I remember Emily's spreadsheet, her correlation which stated the now-obvious truth. "All while Dad was intentionally sent in other directions, away from the Black Beetle."

Eric nods appreciatively, "Yep. Crimson Mask is King of the Augments. After the battle with the Djinn, people wondered if he could even *be* killed. They saved him for last."

"A bunch of pussy asymmetric warfare," Hound scoffs. "That goddamn bug couldn't finish Crimson face-to-face, so he wore him down. Made us look bad in the process. People thought we were all reckless mass murderers."

"But the Black Beetle was the murderer, not my dad," I say.

"Guilt by association. The government wasn't officially claiming Crimson Mask. As far as anyone else knew, he and that bug were tearing up the world 'cause of a personal grudge.

First sight of blood nowadays and people get squeamish," Hound snarls.

"Years ago I uncovered this possibility. Sean refused to believe. I had restored the bunker. One I failed to report in Northstar. Intended for myself. Told him the location. I asked questions, too. Was sent to Killcreek for 'rehabilitation'. Experiments." Polybius's burst of communication taxes him and he closes his eyes, while mouthing the start of more words that never come.

The laptop screen flashes and goes dark, replaced again by the dizzying rain of code. Eric presses in, a moth drawn to a flame.

"Beetle planned it this way. My dad *was* trying to stop him." I'm looking at Hound, but I could be talking to anyone. Myself even. I have to hear the words leave my lips. Hound watches and his jaw tightens. This whole time, I haven't known what to think about the insanity exploding around me. I can feel heat rising into my cheeks and a flutter in my stomach. Hound stays stoic, but there's a slight change in his military stance, an invisible weight pressing on his shoulders.

"Whoa. It's hitting the NIC now."

"Who's Nick?" Hurricane calls from the doorway.

"Network Interface Card," I translate. "On the laptop. But that means…" The concern I pushed aside while piecing together the information comes back and comes back hard. I whirl toward Hound. "What did they strip from here? Did they leave any computer equipment? Phones?" I move to an empty bed and dump the contents of my backpack.

Confused, Hound tries to answer but Hurricane cuts him

off, "They took it all, Blaise. I must've been round this place a million times since they left, and there ain't a scrap of equipment 'cept what's in this room and some med supplies."

The light on the satellite phone is still dead and the bag with the battery is sealed tight. But there might be another problem. "Eric, tell me, what's going on now?"

Even with the lure of the data, he's trying to keep his distance from Polybius, but since I stepped away, he's inched closer to see the screen.

"Latched on and tried to ping an IP address. That and…" His voice trails away, slow and measured while he squints at the screen.

I give him a few more seconds but he stays lost between thoughts. "What? And what?"

"It's changing," Eric stammers.

"What do you mean, changing?" I demand.

"It's getting weird now. I could make out the code every now and then. Almost got used to it. Now, gibberish," he mutters.

"But you got the IP address?" I ask, my mind racing with the possibilities.

Eric taps his temple and then turns to me. "Spence, what's going on?"

"I think I know, but I hope I'm wrong. Bring me the laptop, quick."

Eric practically falls off the table and backs away. "Uh, nope. You're the hardware guy, you ask Cyberveg for it."

"Eric, get it."

Hound places a hand on Polybius's forehead and his brow

furrows with concern. He grabs the laptop but as he pulls, the wiry muscles in Polybius's arms tighten. "George, it's me. Let go." He pulls again and the bed shifts. "George?"

Polybius's eyes fly open. He springs up, straight-backed with the laptop held in front of him. Eric tumbles into the wall and slides into a quivering crouch. From the doorway, Hurricane coils, ready to fire, while Hound watches helplessly at the bedside.

"He spews pea soup, I'm outta here!" says Eric and he inches up the wall to his feet.

"Blaise? What just happened?"

I turn to Hurricane. "The nanobugs. I think they infected Polybius."

CHAPTER 36

ERIC HAS A pretty brilliant idea. Not that this is a rare event. He was practically inhaling code I couldn't make sense of, processing it as mindlessly as lungs convert oxygen. But in his current freaked-out, emerging-from-delusion state, I'm amazed he can think clearly at all.

"Eric, you can do this. It's a good theory you have. The best one we've got."

I can't blame him for being freaked out. After trying to pry the laptop out of Polybius's grip, we discovered he was physically connected. A port on his right wrist, maybe meant for an IV or maybe more tech, had lashed out and freaking attached itself.

"Only a theory!" exclaims Eric. Hound's holding him by the scruff of his neck at Polybius's bedside.

"Don't be a pussy, son. I've seen men your age stuff their guts back in a belly wound so they could keep fighting," barks Hound. "If you can help this soldier, you sure as hell better start asap!"

"Aw, give him a break, Hound. He looks paler than those

sheets. You might make 'im woozy again." Hurricane's perpetual smile looks really awkward right about now.

"Neither one of you are helping," I say.

I do my best to get between Eric and Polybius. There's plenty of space, because even though Hound is pushing him forward, Eric has contorted his body in the opposite direction. He won't make eye contact.

"Why can't *you* do it, Spence?" Sweat dampens Eric's forehead as his eyes cut accusingly my way.

"I'm not sure I even can. Besides, you can get this done in half the time. Or less."

"What if Frankenfreak attacks me?"

"His *name* is *George*," growls Hound.

"Or Polybius, even," I add, trying not to look at the mangled cyborg beside us. "We'll be right here."

"I'll pull ya clear in a jiff, son!" Hurricane cackles. Eric's knees buckle and I give Hurricane a disapproving glare. "Err, I'll go watch the door some more, eh, Blaise?"

I touch Hound's arm and he grunts, roughly letting Eric go. He stumbles, so I grab his forearm and plant an arm in his back. More weight than I'd expect pushes against me at first and I'm afraid he'll fall, but his knees stiffen and soon he's standing on his own. "We've got to do this. The sooner we do, the sooner we get out of here, okay?"

Eric's eyes meet mine. He sounds wounded when he asks, "How the hell can you be so calm about all this?"

"I don't know…" Emily's voice echoes in my head, *You're just like him.* "I've been locked in a bunker for two years, maybe I'm fucking insane. All I know is that I've got to figure this out. I've got to find Mom." Eric accepts my explanation with a nod. "Get in there and make this happen, man. I'm right beside you."

Eric begins a series of about five shuffling steps to cross the foot long gap to the bed. I fight the urge to push. When he gets closer to the laptop, he tightens his lips and his fingers inch their way to the keyboard.

"Nice job." He's trying. I'm trying.

He henpecks the keys at first, but as he sinks into his zone, the typing becomes fluid and furious. Code streaks across the screen, and Polybius maintains his rigid posture. Fear lost, Eric flows to a feverish pace and again, it becomes impossible for me to keep up.

I understand the gist of his idea—he's talking to the nano-bugs that may or may not have taken over Polybius's systems. Their last commands seem to have been an attempt to establish a connection of some sort. He plans to make them think they've done that. He figures that might break whatever loop Polybius seems stuck in. But that's not even the most interesting part of his theory. The best part? This could be a two-way connection.

What we don't know is what the hell happens to Polybius next. He was awakened from his coma; will he go under again? Will he be up and about, ready to help with the next part of my plan, which I haven't dared yet tell everyone?

From the waist up, Polybius is sprouting more hardware than a Google server farm. The more I examine him while Eric works, the more familiar each little wire and board looks. Most of the components are amazingly similar to the hardware inside the drone I popped open.

If I'm right, this explains how the nanobugs could even interface with him at all. When he first woke up, it might have been an autonomic response, akin to the Sudoku trick Hurricane mentioned which got all this started. But now, his consciousness, or maybe his life, could be dependent on these the tiny invaders.

I never thought I'd admit this, but I'm wishing Martin was here. With his hyper-concern for patient care, he might have kept me from exposing Polybius to whatever was in the bag to begin with. Minus this lead, though, I'd be stuck with zero information.

"Okay, I got it!" Eric steps back, smiling with pride and gazing at the computer puzzle in front of him instead of Polybius's broken form.

Hound steps forward and checks Polybius's vitals. His eyes are closed, but restful—no more REMs measured in RPMs. A sideways glance at everyone then Hound reaches forward and slowly tugs the laptop away. The arm tethered to the laptop falls limp and a thin wire, or maybe a vein, zips into the port on his wrist. Eric shudders.

"Sweet!" I say. "Man, you're amazing."

"Yeah," he agrees, lifelessly.

Hound sets the laptop beside my bag and returns to Polybius to help him lie down. The broken form unfolds with a mechanical motion. Polybius lies inert and speechless, as Hound gently tucks a pillow behind his head. All signs of the coma he was in have returned, and the rhythm of the oxygen machine fills the hollow space left by his voice. Hound continues to work, smoothing the sheets down with a concern that suggests the battered man underneath them might snap under too much pressure.

"Sorry if you didn't get what you needed, kid."

Too many people have been destroyed by this Augment program. Shutting down the whole thing, maybe that was necessary. But Polybius shouldn't have to suffer. Or Hound. Or Hurricane. None of them deserve this.

And then there's Eric, Mom—what did they ever do? My anger burns inside and thrashes around, seeking a target. What about Dad? Was he selfish? Did he put us at risk for his own sake? Why? For Emily?

But every scrap of data I find leads back to one single guy. A guy hiding behind a suit of armor and a fleet of robots. A guy who doesn't care who he slaughters as long as he gets his payday. Black Beetle. That sadistic piece of shit took my life from me—my home, my mom. Crimson Mask couldn't find him, but I can.

"I'm going to get him." All heads turn as the words erupt from my mouth.

"Who?" Eric asks. Hurricane rises, his flapping grin expanding. Hound returns to his work at Polybius's bedside.

"The Black Beetle. I'm going to find him and make him tell me what he did with my mother."

"Ooh! Ooh! I'm in on this, Blaise!" Hurricane practically pogos on his metal leg.

Eric swallows and nods, checking his shaking hands. "Okay."

Hound doesn't take his eyes off Polybius as he asks, "What do you need me to do, son?"

Despite the emotions thrashing inside, my face breaks into a full grin to rival Hurricane's wind-stretched face. "Hound, I need you to keep Super Mall Cop busy. Send him on an errand if you can. Hurricane, I need you to keep the drone busy."

"Damn, Blaise! I love this plan already!"

"Drone? What drone?" Eric looks feverishly toward the ceiling.

I stride across the room to pick up the sat phone and laptop. "The one we're going to call."

CHAPTER 37

W E'RE HALFWAY DOWN the hall when Hound emerges, sprinting after us. Behind him, the room roars and exhales a cloud of debris. A chattering of knives slices the air, and a gleaming shape the size of a compact car explodes from the doorway.

I'd love to shout, "It worked!" at this point, but I'm suddenly doubting my sanity again. Operation Phone-A-Friend? Probably my second worst idea ever, maybe third, and all of those ideas were hatched in the past few days. I'm starting to wonder why every single one of these ideas involves killer robots that get scarier and scarier every damn time.

The beast scuttles up the hallway on four legs, each long and slender and ending in vicious points. Two shorter arms in the front sharpen their sword-like projections. A cluster of amber lights fans out above a mouth full of razors flanked by mandibles slicing the air in excitement. There's a buzz as the terror drone turns to face us and thin metal sheets flutter along its back.

Eric squeaks and takes off in a dead heat, clutching the laptop.

I'm scared shitless and can't move. At the same time, I'm hypnotized by the stunning assembly of tech poised to shred my insides. The glowing green-eyed drone that ambushed the bunker isn't visible in this profile. The vaguely humanoid shape of the one that jumped us at Emily's apartment is missing as well. The long tentacles of the massive robot that tore a swath of destruction along the Thames are absent, too, thankfully.

I hadn't thought of that until now. Hell, an army of those giant beasts could have shown up this time. But this doesn't look any more promising. And this time, there's no television screen between me and the destruction.

"A German cockroach, yeah!" Hurricane laughs and his face lights around the toothless grin. "Get moving, Blaise! Be there shortly." A final maniacal cackle, and the sheet rock on the wall behind him explodes into powder. He's gone, followed by a crack like gunfire that echoes up the hall. At the sound, Eric screams and finds another gear, and I run to catch up.

Another crack issues behind us, and Hurricane's voice whistles out, "Take that one to the Führer, ya Jerry cockroach!"

We round the next corner into the Whispering Pines lobby with Eric screaming the entire way. I flash back to his lost-in-the-hospital, I'm-an-Augment-no-really story. Maybe he does have a little Chinese girl inside. An odd noise bubbles out of my mouth, a laugh, that causes Eric's bulging eyes to turn as I pass him.

We're so close to death, I can taste it.

Hound's propped up behind the reception desk with a Glock in his hand. At least that's what he called the handgun. He said he borrowed it from the guard shack after sending

Chuck out for "some grub". Even Chuck, Super Mall Cop extraordinaire, was tired of the MREs that got left behind.

There's a flash and a muted popping noise that pounds out in an even rhythm as Hound unloads on the creature. I grit my teeth, grab Eric's arm, and dive through the sliding glass doors that we jammed open earlier.

The gleaming, VW-sized cockroach, as Hurricane called it, careens into the room and perches on the reception desk as Hound falls back firing. The bug stabs a spiked forelimb down, skewers the desk, and tosses the battered remains aside. Hound, visible in the wreckage, stands to run, pushing an office chair toward the beast. It tosses the chair with a vicious swat, and Eric yanks my shirt. I'm pulled behind the corner with him as the chair flies past us into the parking lot.

I brace against the corner and shout at Eric, "Do it! Now!" His frantic nods seem to shake his entire body as he fumbles the laptop open.

In that instant, the air thickens as a familiar shockwave rattles in my chest.

"Pussy!" Hurricane is outside at the edge of the parking lot hefting the discarded office chair. There's an eardrum-inverting pop, and drifting brown pine needles fill the air as he disappears inside. I peek around the corner in time to see the chair appear out of nowhere, smashing into the bug with enough force to send it toppling over what's left of the reception desk. Hound races for the exit.

Clicking angrily, the bug rights itself. I see a dent where the chair impacted at Mach whatever, and what at first glance appeared to be an extra antenna, I can now see has the wheels of a portable IV tree. The shiny metal pole juts out right behind the creature's head and above the enormous eyes that are tracking Hound as he races toward us.

"C'mon, ya tin cockroach!" Hurricane appears across the room, away from the door. In a blur of motion, a food tray launches toward the bug and shatters in a puff of smoke, showering the room with plastic shrapnel. The drone scuttles to face him. "Got a sack full o' DDT next."

As Hurricane shouts, I can see he's bent forward slightly, one hand on his thigh above his prosthesis. His chest constricts in tight breaths.

"Eric, hurry," I shout.

Eric mumbles to himself behind me, his face lit by a greenish cast on the screen. He's in a meditative trance, reading off the indecipherable collection of letters, numbers and, symbols. He doesn't look up, but the mumbling escalates and words form between recited chunks of code. "Found the carrier signal." His fingers join the trance, flowing across the keys with unerring certainty.

I stay low and peek under Hound's bent knee as spent casings drop from his gun. Gunfire so close to my ear is muted by the ringing left in Hurricane's wake. A dervish of pure destruction, Hurricane devours the beast from all sides and it lashes wildly, taking giant chunks out of the foundation and leaving furniture in shattered heaps. As he ejects an empty clip and reaches for another, Hound shoves my head around the corner.

"Hurry up, boys. We can't hold this son of a bitch all day!" he shouts. As another spent clip drops, he loads another before the empty one strikes the ground.

Looking at Eric, I can tell asking him for more is pointless. Already, his stare has taken on a transcendent quality. He's lost in that world of digital bits and bytes and all things numeric where we first met. A leap to baseball and centuries of stats wasn't far. Number crunching, memorization, hacking other people's systems to avoid talking about our own. Now though, I'm staring into the face of a Zen master of code-fu. As the world literally explodes around him, he tames digital chaos.

"Forget being an Augment! You are a fucking god, Eric! Get it, man! Do it!"

An unfamiliar grunt comes from the reception area followed by a sharp snap. Hound presses me against the wall even as I try to see past him. A metal prosthesis skids out through the doors.

"Hurricane!" I start to stand but Hound pushes me down and rises, stalking down the entry hall in plain view of the beast. Another clip strikes the concrete floor, and while he reloads, I make a break inside.

Hurricane lies flat on his back wheezing with the ginsu machine whirring above him. Blood trickles in a thin line along his arms and another across his chest. Defiantly, he grabs a nearby piece of desk and his arm becomes a blue blur as the chunk splinters in the beast's face.

"Beetle! Over here!" I shout. "I'm the one you're looking for! Come get me!"

The monster rears and when it settles, the bug eyes are locked on me. Unfortunately, I've got nothing to follow up the taunt.

"Drop, kid! You're in my fire!" Hound yells.

Bullets whiz past and spark on the side of the metal beast's face as I drop.

"Run!" Hound yells and before he's finished I've scrambled to my feet and made several strides to the exit. As I get even with him, I feel him grab my arm. My feet practically leave the ground. I start to protest but see Hound standing perfectly still, his smoking gun level.

I regain my balance and whirl to face the reception area. Hurricane lies on his back, scratching his chin. Several hundred pounds of sharp, pointy drone loom over him, completely frozen in place.

"Well, good thing that worked," mutters Hurricane. He fumbles in his gown and digs out his inhaler. He primes the cylinder with shaking hands and only gets an empty hiss. With a shrug, he tosses it aside and lays down, staring above and wheezing.

"How bad are you? Can you get over here, 'Cane?" Hound is half-crouched and eyes the drone suspiciously. "Or you need me to come get you?"

"Been worse. Lost a leg once, even," Hurricane cackles. "Gimme a minute, I'll come to you."

I slip out of Hound's grasp and turn to see Eric standing in the doorway. His face drained of color, he speaks in an empty monotone, "I fucking pissed myself." He stares absently in the direction of the drone. "Believe that? Pissed myself."

Hurricane belts out another cackle from the floor behind me. "Told ya, gettin' old sucks, boys."

CHAPTER 38

"I DON'T KNOW how the hell you did that." My voice drifts upward as I stand in the robot's shadow. Killer insect drone or the world's creepiest lawn ornament; it's a tough call at the moment. Eric refuses to get any closer. Hound took Hurricane off somewhere to patch up that nasty gash. Might've even cracked a rib, Hound says. Hopefully he's okay.

"Well, the machine language for the nanotech kept trying to hit that address, the one I saw in Polybius's room. I spoofed it and told the nanos that the laptop *was* that address. That gave me the opening to communicate with them," Eric calls out from the doorway.

"You're a genius, dude. A complete genius."

Eric creeps forward taking slow, measured steps, the metal beast in his eyes. "Yeah, and you are crazy as balls."

"I completely agree. So what the heck do you have the drone doing now?"

"Diagnostics. The nanos wanted to contact their base and give some sort of report. Checking all the systems for a diagnostic digs pretty deep into the drone's resources. So I made it do that. Like a jillion times."

"You fed a denial-of-service attack to a Black Beetle drone?" I say in awe. "Keep that in mind, forever."

"Yeah." He blushes.

"Will anything break the loop?"

"Not until you shut this down." He waves the laptop. He then sets into briefing me on the syntax, and I start to see the labyrinth he was peering into more clearly. "You've got twenty percent left on the battery. That goes, I think the robot starts trying to kick the shit out of everyone again. So, you might want to plug that in."

"Leave me with the laptop and the power cable. You go meet up with Hound and Hurricane."

Eric checks the display. "Nineteen percent. Why don't we both go see what they're up to? Or maybe we can just get the heck out of here."

"No, go. They should be down the hall, getting Hurricane bandaged up." I shrug off my pack and dig out my multi-tool.

"What are you going to be doing?"

"Part two of Operation Phone-A-Friend."

I snatch the laptop and he backs away. Eric looks down the hall where Hurricane and Hound disappeared. He sets his jaw and nudges a busted section of particle board, kicking a thin layer of dust into the air. Under his breath he mutters the same mantra of cuss words he spit out when I first talked him into this road trip. "Fine. But you better not be diced into little Spencer cubes when I get back, dude."

"Don't worry. Go check on Hurricane for me, those cuts didn't look so good."

He nods and disappears down the hall toward the infirmary.

Soon, I'm alone with my project. I nod and stride deeper into the shadows, eyeing the expanse of metal beneath the meat grinder mouth. The edge of a panel is visible, but with no obvious release. Walking behind the bug, I see the IV tree still jutting from its back.

I set the laptop down and scale the back leg. The metal plates are both impossibly thin and incredibly strong. This close, I can see fiber optic hairs covering the entire surface of the drone. I run a hand across them and they flex against my palm. Amazing. These filaments must act as some kind of external sensors. Maybe that's how the one in the hardware store detected me?

Using the bent leg as a foothold, I climb to the base of the drone's head. I'm sure Emily would have some kind of bug term, but she's not here.

The IV tree has gouged out a perfect hole. I recall reading stories about hurricane-force winds, and tornadoes putting straws through telephone poles. It was all bullshit, I'm pretty sure. But not for *the* Hurricane. The IV tree is wedged solidly into the skin, carapace, whatever. I grab hold and shake, twist, yank then try standing on it. There's finally a little give and the panel loosens.

A beep from below grabs my attention. Hanging on the IV pole, I lean out and see a light flashing on the laptop. Hopefully the battery in there isn't a piece of shit. I go back to throwing my weight into loosening the panel until it gives way.

Even though the outside is one shade of insane killing machine past the other drones I've seen, the systems inside immediately appear familiar. The guts of the drone at the bunker are splayed open before me, only they're configured slightly differently to fit the insect form.

All this time spent hating the Black Beetle—well, still hating the asswipe—but it's impossible not to marvel at his creation. Tiny nanobugs are impressive, but most of the time, they don't seem real. You can't see them, smell them, hear them. This, though. This you can't ignore.

About time someone put it to good use.

*

I strike a triumphant pose, one sneaker on the slicer's head and my fists on my hips. Eric and Hound have competing expressions of skepticism on their faces.

"Say hello to my little friend." I try to add a bit of Sicilian accent to the announcement. No laughs. Tough crowd.

"Spencer, you're going to get yourself killed." Eric's skepticism is laced with fear.

Hound only shakes his head. His brand of skepticism pretty clearly shouts "dumbass".

"Me?" I ignore the looks. "Cuddles and I'll be just fine."

"'Cuddles'?" Eric stammers.

"Yeah, I named it." I flash a smile as I shimmy down the back leg. "Cuddles. It's friendly and feel-goody. Might keep me from shitting myself while we're in flight."

"While you're what?" There he goes again with the bulging eyes and the gaping mouth. While Eric's face has moved on to abject horror, Hound keeps his cool.

It dawns on me, Super Mall Cop hasn't shown back up. We've been alone here for a few hours while I wired up Cuddles. "When's Chuck getting back?"

Hound starts to speak, but a fist of pressure slams into the room. Hurricane appears, clutching a wad of bandages to his naked chest. He's wearing hospital scrub pants at least, but they've already started to fray along the inner thigh.

"He'll be a while. Gave him a slow leak in both rear tires while he was yakkin' with Hound," says Hurricane.

"How are you?" I ask, keeping my eyes above Hurricane's chest level for a couple of reasons.

"He'll be fine." Hound tries to sound nonchalant, but he's checking out the bandages as he speaks and Hurricane pushes him away, his permanent grin growing wider. "He's got skin thicker than cowhide. It didn't open him up much. Ribs are bruised up pretty bad though."

"Polybius?" I ask.

"He's back to sleeping. Something us old farts need to do more of, eh, 'Cane?"

Hurricane ignores him. "I hear you right? You gonna ride that bitch?"

"That's the plan." When I first had this idea, it sounded great, but seeing the excitement scrawled across Hurricane's crazy face confirms he's probably not the only one that's lost his marbles.

Eric's eyes are still locked on Cuddles with the same terror. Even so, he manages to speak. "How are we going to follow you?"

"You're not."

"What?" Eric advances into the shadow of the drone. "What is that supposed to mean?"

"You're not coming." I check Hound and Hurricane's faces. "Neither are you guys."

While Eric mutters incoherently, Hurricane jumps in. "Damn! I was really wanting to put my good foot up that Beetle's ass!"

Hound only nods and reaches out a thick hand. I try a typical shake but his calloused palm slides up to my forearm. Staring down, his eyes narrowed, Hound says simply, "Good luck, son." A final crushing squeeze and he's walking down the hall toward the infirmary calling out behind him, "You aren't goin' anywhere, 'Cane. Get back here so we can change out that bandage."

I stare after Hound as he disappears down the hall, his solid physique bent slightly now, and suddenly he's wearing his actual age. Hurricane hobbles up next to me.

"Aw, don't mind him. He ain't any good at saying good-bye, yeah? Not to soldiers anyway." Hurricane's gnarled hands enclose mine. He looks at me with that permanent, toothless grin and whistles, "We'll be rooting for ya! Come home in one piece, eh, Spencer?" Before the wink of his eye registers, I'm staggering backwards and he's gone, the only sign of his passing, a light ripple in Hound's stark white shirt.

"Did he just call me 'Spencer'?"

CHAPTER 39

"DUDE, I CAN'T let you do this," Eric hisses, still standing with me in the shadow of the metal beast and its razored limbs.

"What do you mean? You just *helped* me do this!"

"Run off, alone, like you're some kind of Augment."

"I thought we were, man?" I'm not sure how that remark will play out the moment it leaves my lips, so I smack his shoulder playfully. The swat lands with a dull thud.

Eric blushes. "This day, this week, has been…"

"Batshit, off-the-rails insane?"

"Yeah," he nods. "Look, maybe we aren't. You aren't. Maybe I… I don't know what to think. Spencer, I spent two years trying to find you. Why should I let you run off and get squished by the Black Beetle?"

"Because you're not going to get on the back of that." Eric glances up and realizing how close he's come to Cuddles, takes his first half-step away before locking his feet in place.

"How do you know?"

"I know. And besides that, I don't want you to get on there. This Augment crap has ruined my life. I've been trying to get away from it for years. Don't let it ruin yours." I don't wait for the response as I scale Cuddles, but he only stares open mouthed. "Besides, I need you to do something else."

"Yeah, man, sure."

I dig through my backpack and toss him my iPod. "I've got a video on here. The one with Black Beetle and Crimson Mask on a Navy ship. All the data's there too. Maybe Polybius can finish decoding if he ever comes to again. If you don't hear from me in a few days, put this out there. Follow the trail to the IP you have, too, and get a name, address, whatever you can. Make everything public. I'm not even sure what the heck this Black Beetle is into, but people deserve to know the truth."

Eric mutely nods and stares at the iPod.

"Now, go hang with Hound and Hurricane a bit while I start her up. I haven't exactly tested this yet."

I can't watch as he backs away, so I check my handiwork on Cuddles. For power, I'm using a makeshift cable I've pieced together from the charger cord and some sort of maintenance outlet on the drone. All of this is taped behind Cuddles's head with spool after spool of surgical tape. So far, the battery hasn't exploded, the cable remains cool to the touch, and the charge warning has shut the hell up, so I must have gotten that much right.

Eric watches from the hallway.

"Go on! Give me a few minutes to get her moving and then you should be clear to head for your car. Okay?"

At first, he doesn't move, he only stares with unblinking eyes. Then, he starts backing down the hall, slowly at first, until he's halfway to the infirmary and he turns and jogs away, clutching my iPod. I swallow the urge to call him back.

This may not even work. Cuddles might decide to dice me up when I hijack her. Best if he's clear of this. If anything goes too wrong, Hurricane and Hound will get him out of here. I don't doubt that.

Only one way to find out if my crash course in psycho-robots paid off. I interrupt the diagnostic loop Eric set up, and start entering a simple routine that should have Cuddles returning to base as part of the maintenance protocol.

The stiff bristles on Cuddle's back spring to life and metal sheets along the frame flutter. Reflections of my face are scattered across the upper ridge of eye facets, a flock of disembodied heads staring. Behind my reflection, a glinting silver crescent pierces the facets, a needle through a bubble, slipping closer. I risk a glance over my shoulder.

A leg hovers high above me guillotine-style, ready to reap a nice fat harvest of overconfidence. I rattle commands across the keys without taking my eyes off that razor edge. The first series of commands should, in theory, cancel the last directive she received before we hijacked her.

The leg wavers.

Drops to the side.

Cleaves through the thin industrial carpet and into the foundation.

"Good girl. Nice Cuddles." My full attention turns to the laptop. "Now, let's go home."

I enter the next series of commands. Cuddles responds instantly.

With a buzz that vibrates the air, the thin metal sheets spring to life. Cuddles has sprouted wings, beating with hummingbird ferocity. I wince as the leading edge catches on my backpack. I'm forced to crouch low across the head and rest my chin between the bulbous eyes.

Cuddles makes an abrupt turn and we shoot down the entrance hall, clipping the wall and shattering the doors as we go. We're airborne in seconds. Soon, we're skimming above the pines, and needles rake against Cuddle's legs, filling the air with their fragrance. The retirement home fades away, and the road flashes between the trees in a silver vein of moonlight.

Hoping for a gentle descent, I watch the road closely and at the right moment order Cuddles to land. In the dark pine boughs, Eric's shoebox on wheels comes into view.

I swing down off Cuddle's back, head to the passenger door and pop it open. A feeble dome light winks on and I grope for the glove box handle. Compared to the metal blender behind me, the gun is laughable. But when I remove it from the compartment, the sheer weight is evident in my hands. A small, snub-nosed handgun that has more density than it even should. Cool, nickel-plated surfaces drink moonlight into the ridges along the cylinder and spit the light out along straight lines down the barrel. This, the massive robot: both were designed with one intention.

My first thought is to chuck the gun in my backpack. However, I've got an idea of how this will all go down. I take the gun and, with a bit of extra surgical tape, I strap the gun to my leg under the oversized sweats.

"All right Cuddles, let's roll." Even in the dark, I'm getting better at mounting my ride. With a quick command, Cuddles launches through the whipping branches and explodes into the open air.

As we fly, the temperature drops. It's not arctic cold, but it's still a chill my baggy clothes can't quite keep out. However, Cuddles finally lives up to her name. Her metal skin radiates an inner heat. Probably the radioactive power source if I had to guess, but once I hunker down behind her head, I'm happy to grow an extra limb, lose some teeth, whatever it takes to keep from freezing. I'm done feeling cold.

Untarnished by the light of civilization, the night sky is breathtaking. That sodium chemical glow that felt so strange when I first rode into the city with Emily doesn't exist here. There's only a blanket of night, pierced by a steady pulse of stars. The stars seem close enough to scoop up a handful and stuff them in my pocket.

I sit into the wind, careful to avoid the drumming wings, and I lock my knees around Cuddle's neck. I try it, reaching up with one hand, and close my fist around a handful of the night. Wind rushes in my ears, cedar and pine aromas wash across my senses; I'm free. For the first time in two years, maybe more. It took a parade of angry robots to finally make this happen, but I'm free.

My problems will still haunt me, track me wherever I'm headed, but for now, it's just me and the sky. Cuddles got me up here, the very thing meant to kill me, but even that seems distant. For a while, I'm sharing a moment with Dad. The ability to fly and leave it all behind. I'm amazed he ever came back in the first place.

Sure, I can't fly on my own. I can't raise a fist to the sky and launch into the air. I need to hijack a robot and get more than a little crazy myself. But as freaking scary as my ride is, it's *my* ride. I'm in control. And here I'd stay, if it were only that easy.

Never is. That's what I'm learning.

CHAPTER 40

"MORE WINE, SIR?" The waiter's towel-draped arm held the bottle at the perfect angle to display the label.

"You have exquisite tastes, Mister Drake, but I'm afraid I must again decline." Sheikh Hamad nodded with a wink, his mouth framed by a tightly groomed beard that dimpled under flushed cheeks.

Drake's selection of the wine, a Sicilian vintage, had been calculated to entice Hamad into indulging in his taboo hobby. While Drake knew he would not partake in public, he had already ensured that a bottle would be delivered to the sheikh's suite later that evening.

"Madam? Mr. Townsend?" Drake said, turning to the table and noting two empty glasses while calculating the body weight of each individual. Drunkenness could pose problems. Questions of diminished capacity for any business deal they may finalize. A lightheaded buzz, well, that could break the ice.

Drake was less concerned about Meredith's capacity. She held her glass out with a broad grin. He had arranged a special surprise, awaiting her in her penthouse suite, to attend to her peculiar desires. Questionable, but unlikely to derail his plans. Suddenly awash in her father's money and without his doting supervision that had carried on well into adulthood, Meredith was experiencing a whole new world for the first time and embracing it with carnal gusto. Her father's unfortunate "accident" had perhaps been a positive event for her, Drake assured himself.

But Kerin Townsend was different. Townsend had sipped at his wine contentedly all evening and placed a hand above the rim of the glass as the waiter swooped his direction. This man was proving to be infuriatingly single-minded. Business and technology were his sole motivations in life. Drake had an urge to reach out and crush his larynx, but such energy needed to be saved for the negotiations. Perhaps later, when Nanomech, Inc. had matured, he would stomp the life out of Townsend in a more socially acceptable way. Hostile takeover; he loved the sound of it.

Besides, without Kerin's approval, Drake sensed that several of the investors would have backed out during the meeting. In fact, the principals at this table would have declined his invitation altogether. His technical brief had been indecipherable to the other investors who had turned him down one by one. But the details had astonished Townsend. True, the sheikh was a longtime partner, but he needed Kerin's technical seal of approval all the same. Meredith was a sheep and needed to follow a lead and Kerin had been her logical choice.

Drake understood human psychology, but not so much humans themselves. Years of hunting Augments, drawing them out into the open with calculated cruelty and barbaric precision, had accustomed Drake to ruthless success; always outthinking his prey while maintaining personal risk as close to zero as possible. Kerin Townsend was proving to be another animal entirely, in an elusive hunt for which he was starting to feel ill-prepared.

However, Drake knew he needed to do his best to work within the rules. Corporate conflict was surprisingly and pleasingly flexible. Bribes, insider trading, and creative accounting were all commonplace. In the case of Meredith's father, Drake had overstepped the bounds, but he couldn't risk any more such ventures.

"I'll need a tour of your facilities." Kerin said, as the waiter settled the bottle into the table-side bucket and walked away.

"Oh, that sounds positively fascinating," Meredith interjected, "Do tell us when!"

"Absolutely. I wouldn't think of proceeding otherwise." Drake tabulated the areas his investors would be granted access to as he spoke. "Certain proprietary limitations notwithstanding, of course."

"Naturally," replied Kerin.

"This has been so exciting!" Meredith babbled. "My father was never much for inviting me to meetings!"

Drake longed for the tiny black box. "Yes, I'm sure he had his reasons. Rest assured, he was quite enamored by the project when I first introduced it to him, many years ago. He'd be proud of your continued interest."

Meredith returned a tight-lipped smile.

Sheikh Hamad ran a finger along the lip of his empty

glass. "The money, friend. Quite a sum required to bring this to market."

"Yes. However, we've cleared our research and development stage. The technology is field-tested and ready to move. You have zero risk at this point."

"What of your R&D backers? Why haven't we met or heard from them?" Townsend eyed Drake speculatively.

"Thus far, financing has come through private investments. Mostly my own."

"A lab capable of that level of fabrication and precision seems outside the scope of a single investor."

"I was lucky, as Sheikh Hamad can attest." Drake raised his glass and the sheikh's beard parted in a smile. "At any rate, my personal finances are on the table with the rest of the data. You'll find everything in order." Drake stared at Kerin. He would indeed find the financials to be rock solid. The money siphoned from the covert programs had been thoroughly obfuscated by intelligence agencies intent on hiding their activities, and then further buried by Drake himself.

Buzz Buzz

Drake froze in surprise as his pocket hummed again. "I'm sorry, you'll have to excuse me. The lab again. They're running a series of tests on the second-generation tech." Placing his napkin on the table, Drake rose and turned to leave.

"I've got a plane to catch, Drake. Don't be long." Townsend wet his lips with the wine and glanced at the other two investors. Drake smiled over his shoulder, continuing into the hotel lobby before bringing the phone to his ear.

"What?" Drake demanded.

"Sir, we've lost the Mantis, sir." Xamse's tone was tight and restrained.

"Is the data secure? The boy eliminated?"

"No, sir."

"Explain."

"He has control of the Mantis, sir."

"He has what!?" The concierge glanced up from his kiosk as Drake's menacing shout echoed in the marble lobby. Drake clenched his teeth and turned away from prying eyes. "Control of it? How does he have control of it, you incompetent worm."

"It is not answering my attempts to communicate. A diagnostic appears to be running. I was able to force a positional update from GPS, and the data indicates the Mantis is moving."

"Where?"

"To Northbase, sir. It will be here within four hours."

For Drake, it was as if the entire lobby stopped, froze, melted and started again.

"Northbase? *My* Northbase?"

"Yes. Here." The soothing music of the lobby filled the pause. "Sir."

Drake cursed and devoured the space to the concierge in cutting strides. He slapped the desk, causing the white-jacketed employee to jump and knock over his stool. "My driver. Find him." Glaring, Drake turned toward the lobby, and the concierge slipped out the door.

"That is not all, sir."

Openmouthed, Drake gaped at the ceiling, barely able to restrain his reply, "Not all? Do elucidate the matter for me,

Xamse, before I rip out your intestines and—" A passing guest wheeling a suitcase from the elevators stuttered in her steps and a furtive glance strayed Drake's direction. Her pace quickened.

"The secure signal from Killcreek," continued Xamse. "It has sent a broadcast on all military channels. It is urgent, sir."

Drake slammed the phone on the lobby floor where it shattered into several pieces. A thin black chunk glanced off the black patent shoe of the concierge at the same moment he raced back inside. Eyes wide, the concierge let his momentum carry him to the full open arc of the door ahead of Drake's fury. He flinched as Drake stopped and jabbed a large bill into his jacket pocket.

"Tell my guests something has come up and send my regrets. Let them know I will provide them with further documentation in the morning. Understood?"

The concierge nodded eagerly. Drake cursed again as he stalked to the waiting limo. His lantern-jawed driver held the door and stared straight ahead. Drake shrieked, "*Privacy!*" and disappeared into the backseat behind a tinted window as the driver closed the door.

Inside the limo, Drake pulled the center console forward. It hummed and rose along a slender arm, stopping at chest level. The leather trim flipped back, revealing a sleek touchscreen. Drake's fingers danced across the panel, and a holographic display sprang to life. "Incoming Communication" flashed impatiently onscreen. Drake stabbed the panel.

A nondescript man in a lab coat appeared. Blood smeared his face. It was a tight shot, but what could be seen behind him had the appearance of a slaughterhouse. There was a short hallway lined with doors and scattered with corpses. Motionless figures wore lab coats, fatigues, environmental suits, and blood. Errant sprays and streaks of crimson blossomed on the walls. Despite the carnage, despite the barrel of a handgun pressed to his temple, the man appeared calm.

But Drake was hardly unnerved by the death. What bothered him and drew his full attention were the man's eyes. His pupils swam in mercury. A soul gazing outward. So fine was the reflection, that movement from behind the camera swam across their surface.

"I am not the only hostage. There are more. Our demands are three. We require the code. The code to release the failsafe." The man's jaw tightened and the liquid eyes narrowed. "Next, we request your presence. We require witness to our new family, which we have waited so long to find."

"Finally, we demand you be punished." Veins stood out along his neck, and the man's mouth twisted in agony as he spoke. The gun next to his head began to shake. "Those who stole us from family and enjoyed what we never had. Those who used us for their own ends. Made us pry out the secrets from inside so many. Prying and prying until they could take no more. You will pay! You have taken her from us! You did this!"

Spittle flew from his mouth and the man, the gun, continued to shake as the camera steadily panned out. He stood alone in the hallway, the gun gripped in his own shaking fist.

"No!" The gun fired. His cries ended. As the transmission died and the body fell, the man's irises faded into a lifeless brown.

Drake raised an eyebrow. He leaned back in the seat, steepling his fingers beneath his chin. As long as the mess could be contained, this event could provide an opportunity. Perhaps the Black Beetle could offer his services one last time. Drake rapped on the dividing window, and the limo pulled away from the curb.

"Rewind transmission. Four times speed… now two. There. Stop. Zoom."

Drake examined the reflection in the silvered eye. It was difficult to tell. Female, green t-shirt. Another hostage, perhaps. Most likely whatever Augment was behind this would not allow themselves to be seen. Of the dozens he had delivered to the Killcreek facility, the profile, the powers matched none of them.

The limo raced down the streets, headed for his offices. With the Crimson Mask's son controlling one of his drones, and the Crimson Mask himself possibly freed given the state of Killcreek, it was time for a new strategy. Xamse had failed for the last time. Drake would need a new assistant, and the Black Beetle needed to be removed from service, for good, in as highly public a way as possible. Then he could focus on patching things up with his investors.

Efficiency in spite of human frailty. It was what drove Drake and had gotten him this far.

*

Kerin Townsend watched Drake melt down from a safe distance. The wood-paneled waiting area right outside the hotel restaurant offered a decent view of the lobby through stained-glass windows. He'd hoped the odd lighting and rippled glass would make him hard to see, though he wasn't a master spy by any means. He'd intended to confront Drake away from the other investors, to try and pin down a date for the tour. But by the time Kerin reached the lobby, this genius inventor, who'd shown up fully operational and ready to go public, virtually out of nowhere, was maniacally shouting at his phone. Kerin had ducked behind the glass mostly out of embarrassment.

Kerin had seen this before. Well, not quite like this, but similar situations. A highly skilled inventor would make a widget, and then decide he was also a businessman. From personal experience, Townsend knew the combination was rare.

So far, Drake had only borne out that observation. The man seemed distracted, flighty, and now either insane, over-stressed, or both. A stable business partner he was not.

Yet, the technology was utterly, undeniably brilliant.

Once Drake had stormed outside, Kerin crossed the lobby to the concierge who was busy sweeping the remains of the cellphone into a dustbin.

"Excuse me."

"Mr. Townsend, yes." His eyes dropped to the shattered pile of circuitry and he swallowed. "Oh, yes, your colleague, he wanted me to extend his regrets. He had urgent matters…"

Kerin raised his palm and nodded. "No need. No need. However, do you mind?" He motioned to the bin.

The concierge gave him a puzzled look, but after a second gesture from Kerin, he raised the bin in the air. Townsend squinted and fished through the pieces, pulling out the phone's SIM card. He smiled and added a large bill to the one peeking out of the concierge's jacket.

"If my colleague returns, let him know the lobby was swept and the trash taken out, hm?"

The concierge frowned and considered the proposition. Another bill entered his jacket pocket.

"Of course, sir."

CHAPTER 41

CLINGING TO CUDDLES for hours in the blasting wind with no solid handholds went from fun to mind-numbingly painful a ways back. The deep emptiness of unlit wilderness below has transitioned into the spider-web lines of street lamps, growing denser at the core. We've been flying mostly south, that's all I can tell. I have to wonder if I'm close to home.

I wish I would've swung by our old house one last time. It was right around the block. Eric said the bank took possession, fixed the hole, and sold it to a new couple. Three kids, a dog. On second thought, maybe I didn't want to see that.

During the flight, I've tried to figure out more commands to send Cuddles. Breaking the "return home" command and dropping out of the sky like the two-ton hunk of metal she is sucked, so I gave that up.

I remember swearing I wouldn't do it again, but the flight's long, boring, even with the amazing view. Once again, not a lot of thought went into this plan. I decide to risk it again and see if I can get Cuddles to do some tricks.

This time my attempt is cut short even faster. I'm locked out. I no longer have control; somebody else does.

Frantic, I go back through the steps Eric drilled me on. The little bugs are still trying to find their way home, still tying up Cuddles's resources, but my attempts to access their communications keep getting blocked by an external source, originating from the same address I'm blindly headed to. Skewering the Black Beetle with his own robot is now a distant dream. Living another day might be too.

I hang on tight. At any moment, whoever it is could probably introduce my face to the ground at terminal velocity. Either that, or let Cuddles do the job. But I can only clench my cheeks for so long before they get sore. The flight goes on, as scheduled.

From up here, I see a dark patch far to the west that might be the ocean. Below, the outskirts of a city races by. A sprawling campus comes into view surrounded on all sides by acres of woodland. Cuddles aims for a helipad on top of a four-story building. A small room with glass walls sits next to the helipad. The lights are on, glowing bright against the night sky in the room, empty except for an elevator. Not what I expected. Cuddles lands with a jolt and a dull clang.

So, here I am, on a rooftop in the middle of the night. Instead of whoever it was finishing me off, I've been allowed to arrive for my little showdown with the Black Beetle. At least I have a gun, which suddenly seems too small. I slide down Cuddles's back leg.

My own legs shake uncontrollably. That's from either the extended ride or the fear, but I don't think I'm scared anymore, as dumb as that sounds. I feel… pumped. Alive.

An elevator chime drifts through the door and I move toward the glass. A kid walks out. Dark skin and large, alert eyes, his curly hair cut so close to his head that only a thicker strip down the middle reveals he even has any. Jeans, t-shirt; I'm not sure if this is a minion or the janitor, but there's no way he's the Black Beetle. Right? He leans against the glass door and eyes me, one hand on the door handle.

"Um, you're a kid," I say.

His face pinches and he steps out, letting the door rattle closed behind him while he points a hand my direction. A crackle. A blur of motion. I fall rigid onto the helipad. Every muscle in my body tightens and contracts. My gun comes to mind, the robot, a million other things I should've done differently flash between pulses of pain.

"Stop!" I stutter.

The kid is standing over me with an expression of hatred. The pain fades. "It only stops because I want it to," he says. He points the taser toward me and I see the wires trailing off into my leg.

"Fuck! Fuck! Hold on!"

He pulls the trigger.

I flop and drool and hurt.

The pain goes away.

"Wait! Wait! I've got information you want!"

His expression changes and he kneels down with a hungry stare. Closer, I see he's wiry but bigger than me, although that's not saying much, and has a hardened stare that overshadows his youthful features. A jagged scar wriggles behind a thin black collar on his neck as he asks, "What information?"

"I'll only give it to the Black Beetle," I say through convulsing breaths.

He checks the taser and my pulse explodes. "I should punish you again. I am not a kid. I am the Black Beetle's *wäras*—I am his heir."

"Man, whatever you want. Just take me to him."

"Give me the information," he demands and holds the taser up for me to see.

"No. Only—"

There's no warning. No getting used to it. The same intense fire rages through my muscles and my body won't respond. His face jerks by and I see the expression soften, briefly. I'm losing focus and the world starts to slip away into a watery, jittery mess of hurt. My head arches back and the light from the door streaks and separates forming an irregular, silver ring.

"Mom!" I gasp.

The pain stops. I'm in a pool of sweat, panting. The boy's spotlight eyes stare, and there's hesitation as he reels in the wires. I can't put up a fight as he slips off my backpack.

I also can't move while he pats me down. He finds the gun, pulls a knife from his boot, and cuts it free. My brain wants to panic—the gun taken, a knife inches from my junk—but I can't move.

"You are lucky he asked to see you. I won't throw you from the building." He drags me up and puts a boot in my back, and I stumble toward the door. Once we're in the room, he waves a badge clipped to his jeans at a card reader, and the elevator doors spring open. He shoves me in, and I slide down the back wall as he punches a button.

"You should never have stolen Black Beetle's secrets." He adjusts my backpack now slung over his shoulder.

"I don't care about the secrets," I groan.

"Why are you here then?"

"I want to know where my mom is. That's all."

The kid faces the elevator buttons, his arms crossed. He seems comfortable with the taser in his hand and Eric's gun stuffed in his waistband. I can see he's watching me in the chrome button panel.

"Weird accent. You aren't from around here?" He responds to my question with more staring. "Heir, huh? Must be a big job." My voice cracks as he turns around and I realize I'm watching the gun and the taser more than his face. I glance up and see his eyes narrow, but he doesn't reply. "I cracked open one of his drones once. It was pretty sweet. You do that all the time, I bet."

"Shut up."

Great advice. Really good. But the mouth's on autopilot again. "Sorry. Just thought I saw what looked like a Multicore Delta chipset in there…"

His taser hand twitches. Every muscle tenses and I'm in a ball, squinting with anticipation. The pain doesn't follow. The taser is pointed my way but he's staring at the wall as he finally speaks, "There are many of the Black Beetle's wonders inside the drones. He brings them life. Gives them purpose."

The doors open and he steps back, keeping one foot in front of the sensor and leveling the taser. "Get up."

Using the back wall for support, I slide to my feet and stagger forward. He yanks me into a deserted hallway. We walk in silence and each time I check over my shoulder gets me another rough push. At the end of the plain, white hallway is a set of black double doors engraved with a complex geometric pattern.

"Your gun is uncared for." A click and a spin rattles over my shoulder. "Might not even fire."

"Guess I'm lucky then. Right?" My nervous laughter has too much desperation.

He grabs my arm and gives the doors a slight push with his free hand. They noiselessly open inward and we step inside.

After the stark hallway, this is closer to staring into space. A black hole, really. The walls are covered in thick charcoal panels, with a floor and ceiling that are only a marginally lighter shade of slate. A sleek desk lurks in the center of the room with a black leather office chair behind it. The desk top glows with the light of a dying star beneath its transparent surface. An oddly-designed chair, with chrome bars to support the seat and backrest, sits opposite the desk. Next to that is a table with a chess set.

I momentarily forget how hopeless the situation is. "Were they out of twirly mustaches at Villains-R-Us?"

Suddenly, my knee collapses. My face smacks into the floor. Blood pours out of my nose onto the hard tile. It's broken for sure. The kid, heir to the king of dickheads, towers over me, speaking to the air. "He's here, sir. He says he has the data."

"Excellent. Make him comfortable. I will be there shortly. I have a special reward for you, Xamse," replies an almost pleasant-sounding voice. Pleasant with the exception of a peculiar, twisted emphasis on the word "reward". The cadence, the contempt, it all overrides any sort of disguise or distortion his battle armor might have offered. I've heard that same voice in my sleep for two years.

Release the boy and he will live. He can tell your husband what has happened today.

We're about to be face-to-face, again, and none of this is going as planned.

CHAPTER 42

HEAD FORWARD, I pinch my nose, staring at the puddle of crimson as it spreads into the cracks and crevices of the tile. The blood almost glows here, in this odd office, cave, lair; whatever the hell he thinks this is. Either I've walked onto a movie set, or this guy is truly an utter psycho. A voice at the door answers that question and I see Xamse turn to face him.

"Ah, our guest. I see you returned my drone with some modifications." A balding man in a light gray business suit enters. He's about average height, scrawny, and his prominent cheekbones support beady eyes. His mouth is small, almost too small for his face. He strides to his desk practically with a bounce in his step and sits on the edge. Blood drips into my open mouth.

"Now, let's have a look at you," he says and Xamse grabs a handful of my hair. His tiny mouth quirks upward and his pebble eyes move, though it's hard to say where. "The spitting image of your father." His head tilts sympathetically this time as he looks from head to toe. "Well, almost."

This is him? I can't say I'm impressed either.

Sensing my amazement, he grins. "Were you expecting someone else?" The man leans back and speaks to the wall behind him. "Computer, open vault." A panel slides open and red light floods into the room, staining the darkness. In the exposed alcove stands the star of my nightmares.

"This, perhaps?" The beady eyes grow and draw closer while his words slice the air. "Yes. We've met before."

Xamse steps away and I glance after him, trying to keep him from leaving me here, alone.

I swallow and search for my earlier bravado. "My mom."

His strange eyes are predatory cold marbles like I'm at a taxidermist shop, holding a conversation with the mounted head of a wolf. "Oh? You came for her?"

I nod.

"Sorry to say, but I turned her over to my clients. You do know who they are, don't you?"

I nod again.

"And you hoped to trade the data for her life?"

I nod again, helpless. Powerless.

"The laptop so cleverly attached to my drone doesn't have the only copy of the data, does it?"

I shake my head and speak, but I already know what I'm about to say won't have the impact I intended. "One more copy. Ready to go to the media."

The tiny mouth gets larger than it should and yellowed, straight teeth show. "You play games?"

"Not your kind."

Delicate hands reach to the side table, and the chess board glides between us. Detailed pewter pieces are arrayed on the board, each rank in the shape of a different insect. More smart-ass comments die under his withering stare. Xamse rolls the chair from behind the desk and the Black Beetle sits opposite me.

"Your father did say you liked chess."

He reaches out and slides an ant-shaped pawn forward. Any coherent thought I once had, fades. I focus on the board, and heft a knight shaped like a wasp. It's an old school, defensive strategy until I can figure out his weaknesses. Soon, more pieces buzz around the board as the game gets underway.

"Tell me, how often have you made checkmate with a lone pawn?" We're several moves in, and the Black Beetle twirls his own wasp knight before placing it behind an opening wall of pawns which he's aggressively moved forward. He plays chess the same way he hunts Augments.

I reach for a stag beetle rook and castle, hiding behind my defenses.

"I must say, I'm shocked at your technical abilities." Another of my pawns is swept off the board in a sacrificial move he makes with a pawn. "But you couldn't have accomplished any of this without my nanomechs. Their performance has been most remarkable."

They're a serious security problem. That's my take. I don't get how Beetle thinks otherwise, but I can't find the nerve to speak. The battle armor watches from the alcove. I've seen so many bug robots. Disabled, blinded and even rode them. But with the armored suit, every single detail matches my night-mare. I'm starting to see how reckless I've been. How easily any of them could pluck me from this chair and carry me into the sky.

The tap of a piece on the chess board brings me back.

"I never thought they would be so flexible, so skilled at infiltrating other systems and pursuing their tasks, my tasks." My opponent sighs and his beady face is practically beaming.

Xamse slouches a bit behind the desk, his eyes studying the floor.

The change in the gun-happy kid's demeanor loosens my jaw. I say as steadily as I can, "Where is my mom?"

"A shame, that. Your father finally surrendering. Unable, with all his power, to escape the fate that has awaited him for two years now." He holds a praying mantis bishop above the board then replaces it, advancing another knight toward my defenses. I threaten with my own ant pawn and he backs away. "Your mother became another casualty."

"What do you mean?"

"Collateral damage, they call it. When a bomb goes astray or a bullet misses the mark. A tragedy, really, but unavoidable in any war."

"You killed her?" I stare him down, for the first time.

"Hardly. She was of value to my clients. And ultimately, I believe she may have had the information which led to locating your bunker. Given the situation," his head casually tilts toward the board and he moves a piece but I don't see which one, or even care, "it is much too late for her now."

"So where is she!" Out of the corner of my eye, I see Xamse's stance shift.

A wolfish grin appears on the Black Beetle's face. "Your move."

"Fuck your games! Where is she! If you don't tell me, that data is going to be sent to every major news outlet in the world."

The thin lips spread tight as he chuckles, "So much like him. Always trying to do the right thing." I shrink back, confused by the reaction and he looks calmly over my shoulder. "Xamse, please prep the Battle Armor."

"Yes, sir. Will you be going somewhere, sir?"

"Oh, no. Not me, Xamse. You."

"Sir?" A sort of bewildered elation trembles in the kid's throat.

"Educate our guest. What is the right thing, Xamse?"

"Your orders. The programs, sir."

"Good. And you brought Mr. Harrington to me, as ordered. But there is one final mission the Black Beetle needs to carry out, and I want that to fall into your capable hands."

"Yes, sir." With long strides, Xamse crosses to the alcove, his hands shaking and his cheeks struggling to contain a grin. "I will make you proud, sir."

The Black Beetle oozes forward. "Your move."

The confidence and sheer will emanating from those creepy eyes forces me to turn back to the board. I'm holed up in the corner with my king and he has advanced on my position with his knights and a bishop. But there's a weak spot. Right in the center. I move a knight into the gap.

He grunts and castles, moving his own king, some vicious looking bug I've never seen before. It's his first defensive move, and now I see the weakness of his strategy. He's intent on ruthless domination, so much so that he's blind to the fact his pawns need to be reinforced to hold their aggressive center line. More pieces shuffle around the board and while he's clearly ahead on body count, I'm holding the line.

"You see, Mr. Harrington," Drake intones as he sweeps another of my pawns off the board. "I don't care what the world thinks of the Black Beetle or the government. What I care about is whether it can be linked directly to me."

"My friend knows the IP. He knows where the servers are. Knows exactly where I'll be."

"And what does that prove?" He sinks into the chair, his ankle resting on his knee and his fingers once again steepled under his chin beneath a gloating smile.

"They'll investigate." I try my best not to stammer. "The media will be all over this place!"

"Fine. No press is bad press, they say, hmm? Let me enlighten you. Nothing will connect the Black Beetle to me. Worst case, it will be a nightmare for my former client. They'll have paid billions to a defense contractor who had no idea about what his technology was being used for." He leans close as he whispers, becoming a black shadow backlit by the red glow from the alcove. "No clue that they pressed desperate terrorists into service to do their bidding." His eyes flick toward Xamse, who is busy prepping the battle armor. "And they'll deny it all."

I'm frozen in that soul-crushing gaze.

"The right thing is what I say. When I say it. Yes?" He says loudly. I'm not even sure who he's talking to and I don't try to answer. "Your father followed the wrong orders. Look where it got him."

"What, what do you mean?"

"Make your next move."

It comes as a demand rather than a request and I glance at the board. He's made his move for the center with his own knight. I ignore the wasp and threaten a mantis bishop instead with one of my own. He has to choose. More pieces fly, but fewer of mine are leaving the board.

His black widow queen strikes out. He's one move away from check. He scowls as I pin his queen with my own.

"My clients were wasting time, chasing wayward Augments and hoping those under orders would suddenly become oblivious to the gifts they'd been given and voluntarily turn themselves in. I envisioned a better way, and knew I would have one obstacle—the Crimson Mask. It was *my* idea to let him believe the Black Beetle had gone rogue. Of course, our former employer supported this wholeheartedly. So while I used their intelligence to stay ahead of him, I rounded up any Augment not on his radar. He did 'right'. I did 'wrong'. We met in the middle."

I stare at the board. I control that crucial center with a handful of pawns. Soon, however, I find open lines for the stag beetle rooks. Unlike him, I cover my pawn advance, maintaining that control with the weakest piece. His face pinches in exasperation.

"Your father may not have been like me, but you, you most assuredly are. You are the true giant among men. I created the Black Beetle for people like us. You could make a capable assistant." His eyes are glued to the board as he speaks.

I catch the dark-skinned kid looking this way, only half-absorbed in his work at the Battle Armor.

He moves too late to stop me. We trade queens. My rooks advance, forcing his king out of hiding. No longer aggressive, my opponent's face twists in rage as he backpedals. Soon, I'm on the verge. His pieces are leaving the board and his king is stuck trying to clear the center while my rooks circle. I can win this.

"Quite capable," he muses. His offer from earlier rings in my ears.

"No," I say, the refusal building up from a deep, cold place, hidden from the world for so long.

The beady eyes become dark slits. "I'd hoped for a better answer."

"You get off on this, don't you? Playing games with people."

"My, you are dramatic." His tiny mouth shrinks.

"This isn't about me. You don't want me to be your assistant, you want me to be your slave. The Crimson Mask's son, your personal boot licker. One last twist of the knife. You torture everything close to you, for your own gratification, and hide behind a wall of unthinking, unquestioning hardware. *Things*, which you dominate solely because they can't talk back. Can't think for themselves."

"You're pushing your luck, boy." His gaze turns murderous.

I leap to my feet tossing the chess board across the floor. Insects scurry in all directions, several coming to rest at Xamse's feet as he watches.

"*I am not a boy! AND I AM NOT YOUR PUPPET!*"

Without hesitation, the Black Beetle launches over the fallen table. I try to punch him in the face but he bats my arm down with a crazed fury and we're suddenly tumbling backward. My head strikes the tile, and little flares explode in the ensuing darkness. I try to struggle but his fingers dig into my sweatshirt and now the stars repeat, again, again, again. Vicious, incoherent hisses escape the Beetle's stretched mouth and spittle strikes my cheek as he shouts, "Xamse! Bring me the collar in my desk!" He slams me to the tile with a burst of maniacal strength and the world grays out for an instant. "We'll see whose puppet you are, *boy*!"

Thrashing and hopeless, I aim a knee at his groin and he anticipates, jamming his own knee into my thigh. "Xamse! Now!"

I hear a noise at the desk as I writhe in pain. There's no escaping his grip but I struggle and scream, "You took them both! You took them from me!"

"Xamse! Hurry, you indolent fool!" Hot breath and spit scatter as his twisted face rounds on me. "Quit your whining! One brat's parents are a fair price for 'peace'. A fair price for the birth of an engineering miracle which will soon change the entire world!"

I try again to break free, but he has the strength of utter insanity on his side. I keep fighting anyway, squirming, then his grip loosens.

"Xamse? What do you think you're doing?"

I follow his gaze. The dark-skinned boy has Eric's .38 leveled at the Black Beetle's head. Beady eyes flick to the desk and then to Xamse's other hand, which is holding a small black box.

"That's exactly it, sir. I'm thinking."

A flash. A sharp pop. And the Black Beetle's blood mingles with the red light from the Battle Armor's vault.

CHAPTER 43

"YOU... YOU SHOT him."

I stare as Xamse turns to face the suit in the alcove. "I have killed men before. Children. Mr. Drake took me from that. Saved me," he whispers. I glance up, trying to read him. He faces me and the gun hangs limp in his hand, tears clouding his eyes. I don't know what to make of this so I train my eyes on the ground.

Mr. Drake. The bloody mess on the floor has a name. Not Black Beetle. Not the scourge of Augments everywhere. Just Mr. Drake.

Hunched over, bleeding, I wipe the corners of my mouth. I came here thinking I was ready to put a bullet in that man's head. So easy, you just pull a trigger and end the pain. But I can't erase the image from my mind. Chunks of his brain spraying out the back of his skull. My stomach turns.

Djinn's mutilated face. Bloated bodies in the Thames. Arms dangling from crushed cars on a Mumbai highway. I only thought I was free when that pod launched. But the bunker has held me in its icy grip this entire time. Death. I've come so close so many damn times and only now is it all sinking in. Emily was right, I had a death wish. I hadn't cared if I lived or died.

Xamse wanders toward the body and kneels, placing the gun on the ground. With purposeful motions, he straightens the Black Beetle's limp form and crosses the arms on the chest. Gently, he turns Drake's face, painted red by the pool of blood, toward the ceiling. Xamse stays focused, intent, kneeling next to the body and rocking gently on his knees.

The gun is within reach, but, then what? I slip into a crouch and shuffle backward on my palms, leaning first on my toes, then my heels, I raise up, backing away, searching for balance as I inch toward the door.

A strangled cry bursts from Xamse and I drop to the floor again. He's beating his chest, screaming, crying in a weird language I've never even heard. He takes up the gun. I nearly trip over my own feet trying to get to the doors. They rattle in the frame as I yank on the handles.

I want to live. A card reader and electronic lock—no problem, with time, tools. But my backpack is by the corpse and the crazy, gun-wielding kid.

Xamse's screaming stops. I spin, plastered against the door. Instead of shooting me, or maybe himself, he speaks. "My family died. Died at the hands of an evil man." The words tumble out softly, in the wake of his anguish or grief. He sniffs and his eyes drop to the body. "Yours doesn't have to."

"What… what do you mean?"

"I know where your mother was taken…"

"Where? Is she alive?" I move away from the door.

"I do not know if she lives. But she was taken to Killcreek. Your father, too."

"And you know where this place is? You can show me?"

Xamse tucks the gun in his waistband and walks to the desk. The holographic screen springs to life and he taps at the illuminated keyboard. Despite the danger, I cross the room, cautiously slipping on my backpack and moving to stand in front of the screen.

"That's amazing," I say, in awe of the skin of light floating in the air.

He continues typing. Images shift and slide by until a satellite picture dominates the screen. "The base is here. Northern Montana. I monitor the drones that take prisoners there."

Half-awed, half-shocked, I stare at the screen. Montana. That's a long trip, and my bridges with plane-owning friends have been napalmed. It could take me days to drive. "How would I even get there?" I wonder aloud. Cuddles? Not sure I can cling to her back that long.

Xamse steps from behind the desk and crosses the room toward the alcove. He stares up at the Battle Armor. A calmness overtakes him and he says, "This."

My pulse skyrockets. The armor stands empty, but those same eyes from countless dreams stare back. So many thoughts race through my mind. Thoughts and images I wrestled, night after night. But facing this monster again, with Drake gone for good, I can finally see that the fear hid a tiny spark I never wanted to acknowledge.

There was truth to what the Beetle said. I don't have to be powerless anymore. A man was in that suit. An ordinary man.

Flying. Busting down walls and ignoring the existence of doors. Keeping the world's strongest Augment at bay for years.

Not until I feel the cool sensation of the outer shell under my palm do I realize I've crossed the room. Xamse moves next to me, casually flipping open the casing and running through a series of checks. His luminous eyes land on me between routine motions.

"I don't know if I can." I say this and know it's a lie.

"Of course you can." He doesn't stop his preparations. "But you must be careful. We monitored all communications from the base and it appears the facility was compromised."

"Why? Why are you doing this?"

He stops, one hand resting on the Battle Armor's forearm. He sweeps his gaze in the direction of Drake's body lying out of view on the far side of the desk. "He is no different. No different from the man that destroyed my village."

"I thought you said Drake saved you?"

"He did. For himself. He never did it for me. The man who slaughtered my family and called himself a warrior stuck a gun in my hand, told me to fight. Drake asked the same, only we killed from this place. Not in the fields and jungles where there is blood, real blood." He focuses on me. "I heard the things you said. I am no puppet, either. I checked his programs. If I got in the Battle Armor like he asked, I would not return."

"Whoa, not return?" The surge of excitement I felt when he first mentioned test driving my nightmares ebbs.

"Do not worry. I changed the programs. The suit will not destroy itself, now," he says, unconcerned.

"Why should I even trust you?"

He finishes putting a sequence of numbers into the wrist-mounted keypad and the Battle Armor releases a pressured exhale. The front half hinges outward on both sides exposing the central cavity. Wires and hoses form striated groupings along the casing, and booted hydraulics are visible at every joint. In between all of this exists an empty space, a puzzle piece in the rough shape of a human beneath the oversized insect head.

"Go ahead. Get in," he says.

"What about that heir stuff? Don't you need this?" My attention is on the suit. Most likely this is my only chance to save my mother. But this trigger-happy kid scares me.

"I am the only one who knows all of his secrets. I *am* his wäras. This is one secret of many, and one that no longer has use to me."

"But aren't people going to be looking for Drake? Asking questions?"

"Perhaps. That is why I wish you to take the remains."

"The what?"

He disappears behind the desk. "Murder, suicide would cause many problems, and I do not wish to embarrass my new client," Xamse grunts as he drags the body into view. Pausing, the corpse's arms pulled taut between his hands and the floor, Xamse scans the office. "There is the teleconference system, the same one he used to disguise himself as Black Beetle when he broadcast. It can be reprogrammed. Mr. Drake can leave a message, admitting his involvement and that he plans to go into hiding. This will buy time until my new client calls again." A faint red smear follows behind the boy and his burden. As he pulls he speaks in quiet tones, "See, I am thinking. You would be proud."

Leaving the body at the battle armor's feet, Xamse pats the side of the armor and watches expectantly. "You must hurry, our former client, the government, asked for our help. They wanted the Black Beetle to come and regain control of the base."

I crawl inside, crouching and staring into the helmet. A metal claw waits above, the fingers terminating in electrodes. "What the hell is that?"

"The neural cage? It is used for transmitting commands through your skull."

"Uh, no. *Cage* and *skull* don't go together in the same space."

"For movement, the helmet reads neural impulses. Go on. Nothing will happen to you." He sighs as I stare. "If I wanted you to die, I would have shot you."

He has a point.

Once I'm in, Xamse enters a sequence into the keypad and a rush of air coated in the sweet smell of hydraulics fills the compartment as the suit seals around me. There's way too much room in here; a booster seat would be a nice addition. Even as I struggle to reach into the spaces meant for arms and legs, and tiptoe to force my head into the helmet, the suit pressurizes. The empty space adjusts, cocooning me in a gearhead's dream.

"Systems, online." A voice within the helmet sends a shiver up my spine.

I'm now towering above Drake's body. Targeting vectors and data streams flick around the inert form like flies. That corpse didn't move or even flinch, but I'm hearing his voice.

The voice of William Drake. The Black Beetle. The guy whose brains just exited the back of his head.

"Possible threat approaching. Thermal engaged." Drake's voice echoes in the suit.

The visuals change and Xamse becomes a reddish blob, the gun in his waistband blinking a virulent purple.

"He's not a threat," I say. When I speak, my voice comes out distorted and tinny; the signature buzz of the Black Beetle.

"Weapon systems offline." I cringe at the suit's statement and check Xamse's face to see if he could hear.

He's calm and collected in his reply. "See. You trust me, I trust you."

"All-righty, then."

Craning my neck, I see a hatch directly above the alcove. How I can get from here to there isn't exactly clear. "How does this work? Can I pull up a wiki or something?"

"Of sorts. There is a list of commands, but the suit is adaptive and will learn to respond to what you say and do. Just move your arms and legs as you would outside the suit. It will do this."

Before I realize I'm nodding, the head bobs up and down. I step out of the alcove and test the arms, moving them back and forth. Lifting legs, bending knees, finally kneeling, the suit responds instantly with each motion. My freakish bug eyes go to Drake and a targeting reticle appears followed by his voice reporting, "Target has no vital signs."

As carefully as I can, I scoop up Drake's broken form. Xamse turns to the desk, and moments later, light trickles into the alcove. I step backward, bathed in an early morning glow.

Unnaturally pale in the light, the body hangs weightless in my arms.

I peer upward through a haze of blinking lines and crosshairs. They mimic my eye's exact movements. Above, a cloudless sky, orange with the first signs of dawn, caps the long chute. The section of floor I'm standing on starts to rise. Xamse's upturned eyes are the last thing I see before the platform disappears into the ceiling. Before long, I'm on the roof, not far from Cuddles.

"Battle Armor, what is the location of Crimson Mask?"

"Crimson Mask transferred to Killcreek Facility, Montana." Drake's oozing voice sounds almost pleasant.

"Can you take me there?"

No answer.

"Battle Armor, take me to Killcreek Facility."

A freight train rumble shatters the early morning silence. The orange sky expands in brilliant stripes of purple and yellow. Below, buildings shrink away into a painstakingly detailed model, until only a nondescript patchwork of roofs and streets remains.

My undead copilot speaks, "Destination set. Weapons online."

CHAPTER 44

DARKNESS. NO DREAMS. Brain made of Jell-O. Probably orange, I hate orange. How does that make any sense? I'm swimming in a void, again, but no one else is here this time.

Alone. A different kind of isolated. That numb feeling of the bunker has ensnared my senses. I don't care about Mom. Dad. Eric, Emily, Doc. My own messed-up life. I could stay here.

I was headed somewhere moments ago. Flying over the earth, watching the neat squares of green and brown bubble into rough hills, wooded slopes and finally bald peaks. My head couldn't keep up with the surging battle armor's rockets. The world went gray. I kept getting left behind, drifting in and out. I guess staying up all night flying on the back of a robot will do that to you.

A tiny speck of light forms. I fly closer to it. Teetering between reality and a dream, I don't know how I can even move. Asleep but standing. Moving, but stuck in place. A hole pierces the circle of light.

"Estimated arrival in three hours, twenty-two minutes," Drake's voice echoes, shattering the solitude.

"Shut up." I'm trying to make progress toward the speck of light and getting nowhere fast.

"Command not recognized."

"Battle armor, shut. The. Fuck. Up." I growl.

"Spencer. Such language for a child," Drake's voice crawls across the void.

"I'm not a child."

"I stand corrected. You've achieved that glorious milestone of having killed another man in cold blood. A rite of passage in Xamse's savage world, no doubt."

"I didn't do it, but I should have!" Not even I'm convinced. "You kidnapped my mother!"

"You brought the gun. I tried to explain, my clients took your mother. I was simply following orders."

"Don't try to weasel out of this. I'm glad that kid shot you."

"Do you think for a second you'll find her alive?" There's an almost vulnerable quality to his voice when he asks the question. Instead of making my blood boil, I feel a deep sense of regret. "Do you?" Drake's lips move. The Drake in my arms. No-vital-signs Drake, his beady eyes blank. His suit whips furiously in the wind, the tie thrashing against the Battle Armor with rapid-fire snaps.

"I... I don't know."

"Is she the only reason you're coming to Killcreek? What about your father?"

"What about him? He can take care of himself."

"Can he?"

"He's strong, impervious to bullets, plasma, emotions. He'll be fine."

"Isn't that what you want to be?"

"Maybe I did. At one time."

"What if he were all you had?" He sounds desperate now. "Do you want him back?"

"Want him back? I don't think I ever had him to begin with!"

Anger burns past his desperation as he responds, "You don't know what it is to truly be alone, Spencer."

Drake's form shifts and blurs, the suit tearing off in the wind until only a white cloth remains entangled around a tiny form. A baby rests in my arms. I don't know how I can even tell, but I know the bundled form is a girl. No name, no birthday, but all that is irrelevant to what's about to happen.

Images assault my mind, freefalling past memories, only they aren't mine. I place the baby in the arms of a nurse. The same infant morphs into a young girl with a pretty round face set with delicately narrowed eyes. Stubble on her head peeks out beneath a thick layer of gauze hiding a nest of scars. She's escorted by men in blue HAZMAT suits down a hallway and past doors that reel and shake violently amid agonizing screams. Without so much as a shudder or a misstep, she walks that hall to the very end.

"What's going on?" I ask.

And then more images. Growing, living, day after day in the same stark rooms. Those memories merge with mine. I see the bleak halls of the bunker, the loneliness, the emptiness;

but within the child, the feelings magnify to a soul-crushing weight. A weight I can't even begin to understand. Tears trickle down my cheek.

"Who are you?" I look up and find the wheel of light. I call out again, "Who are you? What are you?"

The radiance quivers and the baby squirms. It grows, becoming slim and emaciated, all bones and knuckles. The young girl from the hallway is in my arms, naked, her flesh radiating a pink warmth. Beneath the fleshy glow, I can see the crooked form of veins and the straight lines of her bones. Silvery eyes regard me with curiosity. She opens her mouth.

I start and lose hold as she unleashes an ear splitting cry of devastation.

Awake, alert, I'm in the Battle Armor, forging into a cloud-pocked blue sky. But Drake's tie no longer whips against the exoskeleton. His body is disappearing into a puffy cloud beneath me.

"Shit! Battle Armor, uh, stop!"

"Designate location."

"Screw this."

"Unable to comply."

I lean forward and the armor instantly mimics my movements. Footage of Dad plays nonstop in my imagination. All the hours spent watching the television, trying to keep up with him, becomes time well spent as his movements in flight inform my own. I'm piercing the clouds. Below runs a patchwork landscape of desert and canyons.

The targeting reticle pulls my attention to the left. Drake's body rushes to the earth. Jacket gone, the shirt ripped open, his pant legs flap wildly around his knees. A helpless ragdoll tossed in a wind tunnel. In my mind's eye I can see his lips moving even beneath the congealed blood trailing from the bullet hole, and I shiver. I could let him become a pancake in the desert. Maybe that's good enough.

I swoop towards him, gathering him in my arms.

Flying up into the sky, that was a cake walk. Open space gave little to worry about. But now the ground races toward my face at amazing speeds, and I start to realize that I don't have a clue how to land.

"Battle Armor! Land!"

A wire image of the suit overlays my view and the figure turns upright. "Landing accomplished by assuming a vertical position and pointing toes downward," Drake patiently explains. Sparse vegetation comes into focus. The sky leaves my field of vision. "Shall I do this for you?"

"Yes!"

Blue replaces the sands. I'm upright hovering several feet off the ground with a mangled, half-dressed corpse getting crushed in my arms. I shudder and relax the grip.

Scanning the area, I see sand and rock occasionally broken by a green tuft of vegetation which clings desperately to survival. I pick a spot near a canyon wall and start walking.

Or, well, stomping. Thundering. It's so strange to be in this suit and barely lift my leg only to feel the solid impact of hundreds of pounds crushing the desert floor. In the shadow of the canyon, I place the body on the sand, drop to a knee, and begin to dig.

The enormous pincers claw through the ground with ease,

leaving a steadily growing pile of earth in their wake. I stop and examine the hole they've left—I've left. Not far below is a layer of rock that I've mindlessly shattered. Am I actually digging a grave?

I turn and look at Drake, face down where I dumped him. He appears even more helpless, more broken than before. Half-clothed, thin, and fragile, with the sand gathered in a clump on the blood and matted skin of his skull, I feel more connected to that insane bond he was talking about. Weak and fragile, the suit wasn't a project but a necessity. It's how he survived in a world of super-powered people.

Hound said he was my age when he went to war for his country. Xamse, I don't even understand his story, but he's been someone else's soldier for a while now and he can't be much older than me. Dad, he had to make decisions about life and death every day. Maybe he's invincible, but he can't be unscarred.

"Battle Armor, can you access cell towers?"

"Affirmative. Available communications can be blocked or compromised."

"Any signals in the area?"

A glowing line sweeps across my view, bending and arcing in the outline of each facet until a bright light pings on the horizon. Tower switch codes, distance, and a host of information scrolls underneath the blip. "Weak signal available."

I place a call. Static bathes the ringing. A breathless voice answers, "Hello?"

"Eric, it's me."

"Oh my god! Spencer, dude! Where are you?"

"I'm, I don't know where this is…"

The Battle Armor responds instantly, "WGS84 Latitude 44.121360 Longitude – 108.468416."

"Who's that?" Eric asks and the static fills with the rhythm of a keyboard in the background. Before I can think of how to answer, he interrupts, "Wyoming. You're in like Nowhere, Wyoming. How the hell did you get there?"

"Long story, but listen, don't send that video to the press. Not yet."

The connection crackles. "Did you say send it?"

"No, *don't* send it."

"Your connection blows. Why not?"

"It doesn't matter. It's not gonna hurt the Black Beetle anyway."

"Beetle? You found him?"

"Yeah, some business guy. Drake."

"Holy shit!"

"What?"

"I should have put it together. The nanotech. Guy's been all over the techie blogs. William Drake?"

"I wasn't formally introduced, man."

"He's about to go public with some revolution in nano-tech. He's looking for investors. That's the Beetle?"

"I guess. Sorta. Was."

"I can't hear you. Man, we could wreck him with this stuff. Who in their right mind invests in a company even remotely associated with the Beetle? You sure we don't send?"

Drake was bluffing about the data not being impor-tant. Why else chase me around the country with drones?

Effortlessly, he put me off guard, almost controlled me, except for his little friend going postal.

"Spence? You there?" He can barely be heard over the increasing static.

"Yeah. Look, don't send it. Not yet. I need to give someone else a chance to respond first."

"If you say so. But now what do I do?"

He's willing to do whatever I ask. I just want him safe. "Man, I want to tell you you've been one hell of a friend. You're like a brother."

"You found your mother!?"

"Maybe." Not that speaking loud and slowly will clear the connection, but I do it anyway. "Look, *you're like a brother.*"

"Don't get all serious now. Your smart ass doesn't do serious well. You okay?"

"Well, no. I did something wrong." Drake's vacant eyes sear into my mind.

"Apart from riding a blender with legs?" A fractured silence sets in, the buzz of line noise fills the gap. Eric's fuzzy voice quietly interrupts again, "My gun was missing. Is he...?"

"Yes."

Another static filled pause and he speaks, "Man, he deserved it. How many more people was that dude gonna kill?"

"I'm not sure."

"We should talk about this later. When I can hear you."

"Yeah, I need to go."

"Don't stay lost. I need a roommate for college."

"Sounds good," I say. Cutting the connection, the static disappears and the Battle Armor falls silent.

I swipe a claw through the dirt and roll Drake's body into the open grave. Dirt and rock cascade around him as I quickly fill the grave. Tears well up in my eyes. I don't know exactly what to do, but I have to finish this. My way.

CHAPTER 45

TOWNS LARGE AND small have zipped past, and even a massive crater I never knew existed, scooped out between a line of mountains and a flat dirt plain. For the longest time, I've been flying over a vast expanse of wilderness. Ridges and scattered trees rise and fall.

"Weapon systems engaged."

"What? Why?"

"Incoming hostiles with acquired target lock, elevation five thousand feet." A targeting reticle appears, and one of the hexagonal facets in the eyes expands. The zoomed-in shot shows the red outline of a pair of jets. Not the Martin kind of jet, but the military, ass-whooping kind of jet. "Initiating evasive maneuvers."

"Hold on!" I shout. A steep descent leaves my stomach a thousand feet up but immediately levels off. "Christ! All this tech and no barf bags."

"Properly suited, the Scarab internal housing can evacuate most incidental biological functions," Drake announces with all the gusto of a used car salesman.

"How far to Killcreek?"

"Arrival in fifteen minutes, forty-three seconds."

In the corner of my eye the hexagonal inset blinks and the focus sharpens as the two jets close. Then, I'm lost in their shadow as they rumble past, the wake of their engines causing the Battle Armor to dip and then surge upward.

I felt big in the suit for a bit. But the jets are massive, their bellies lined with slender missiles. Drake, or the suit, seemed confident it could take them. I've got no interest.

"Monitoring military communications channels," Drake's voice announces.

An unfamiliar, commanding reply comes over the speaker. "Negative. Allow him through." The man's tone becomes almost conversational, "Beetle, I see you got the invitation. You clean this up, there'll be a hefty bonus. You don't, we'll have no choice but to reduce the place to rubble. A note of warning— automated defenses may be active."

I'm still staring after the planes, as they bank sharply into the sky and disappear behind the sun, when the HUD flashes a new warning. Past the trees ahead, I can see the ground drops into a deep gorge. The new target, a battery of missiles, sits on the ridge with a military truck nearby. As I look, the HUD adjusts and begins to magnify.

Then three more targets. A dozen. Hundreds. They're cluttering the view panel, filling all the little hexagonal sections and surrounding my head in a net of light. From tanks to waiting helicopters, more missile batteries, and even trucks with giant guns mounted on the back. Soldiers swarm the hillsides like ants.

Alarms beep in the helmet. "Multiple hostiles. Awaiting command."

"Don't shoot. Don't blink. Don't do anything," I reply.

"Affirmative."

Past the gauntlet, nestled on the valley floor is an installation surrounded by dead space. No brush or trees, only the smooth contoured dirt of what might have once been a creek or small river. Earthen barriers redirect runoff around the base on both sides, but the parched land shows no recent signs of water.

"Arrived at destination."

A high fence topped with razor wire surrounds the perimeter. Buildings the same color of the dirt rise up, defined only by thin shadows. Along the runway, dust and brittle weeds stir. A corporate jet sits idle on the tarmac, completely out of place.

"No way."

I descend toward the runway, taking in every last line of the jet. As I gawk at the numbers on the tail, the Battle Armor locks on and a new information window opens. "Registration current. Holder: Alexander Enterprises."

"Martin?"

Rapid beeping interrupts my shock, and targeting reticles appear around the facility at varying distances. The closest reticle centers on a hatch in the ground by the runway and I watch, unsure what to do next. I'm entranced as a barrel sprouts from the ground and alarms blare in my helmet. This has to be the biggest cannon I've ever seen, maybe as big as a gun on the deck of a battleship. The massive gun wheels with a speed I wouldn't have thought possible. Before I can move, it's bouncing on the ground as the barrel recoils.

Red lights flash on the HUD. A blur like a passing freight train. I skid across the runway on my back as the *thwump* of the big gun rolls past.

"Systems damage, moderate. Status."

"Battle Armor, get me into the air!"

"Airborne evasive maneuvers initiated," Drake says. In one smooth motion, I'm off the ground and soaring.

Above the base, I have a perfect view. More alarms erupt as I lean forward and get more distance, moving away from the cannon on a column of blue-white exhaust. "Incoming threat." The world spins and a trail of smoke streaks across the HUD, trailing into the distance. A red arrow pinpoints the source—a battery sandwiched between two buildings.

"Arming Gravitational Shockwave Cannon. Ready to fire at your command."

I point an arm. "Do it. Fire. Fire!"

A ripple of invisible energy boils through the air, and a second cluster of missiles explodes in-flight or veers off on wild trajectories. The destructive energy wave reduces the launcher into tiny fragments borne away on an invisible current.

I hover, staring at my armored hand through the HUD. So, this is what power is like.

Glowing tracers ignite the air. A warning flashes, "Small Arms Impact", as bullets ping on the outer hull. I follow the arrow again.

Another turret, this one with smaller guns but spewing out a constant stream of lead. Sparks spatter across the armor, but the rounds ricochet harmlessly. The cannon near the runway has repositioned, too, and bounces violently as another plume of smoke erupts. No warning lights this time, but I curl to one side all the same. The shell goes wide and sends a heavy shudder through the suit with its passing.

"You missed, bitches!"

"Trajectory will correct in 5, 4, 3..." Drake's voice calmly counts down as the cannon turret whips into a new position. "2..."

I point my palm and shout, "Fire!"

The same pulse of energy ripples toward the cannon. As the pulse extends, it builds and the air balloons outward, leaving a dark shadow rippling across the earth. The enormous cannon becomes an indistinguishable spray of parts with the bigger pieces skipping away into the compound. I unleash another blast to the side and the whine of the bullet-spewing turret is silenced.

"Threat negated."

"Ho-lee shit! That's the understatement of the year." I stare down at the suit. I see the equivalent of a fairly serious doording and the front is spattered with hundreds of black streaks, probably from the bullets, but seriously, that'll buff out. The base's automated defenses are obliterated, and the Battle Armor looks as if it were hit by a runaway shopping cart.

Alarms inside the visor finally shut up. I land next to the plane and peer through the cockpit window.

"Hello?" I call out.

"Awaiting command," responds the armor.

"No, bug-brain, I mean, 'hello'. To the outside."

"Intercom engaged."

"Hello?" The tinny reverb vibrates my voice in the bug-like chatter. "Battle Armor, knock off the Sith Lord speech."

"Are you sure?"

"*Yes.*"

"Speech cloaking disengaged."

"Hello? It's me, Spencer." I stand nose to nose with the plane, looking inside. Empty. But the controls, the same seat where I sat, this is definitely Martin's plane. Is Emily here, too? How the hell did they know where this place was? How'd they not get shot out of the sky?

I turn toward the complex. There isn't much to this base. From the air, the most promising structure was maybe the smallest, central building. Despite the size, I noticed a massive reinforced door, similar to the one at Whispering Pines. Pointing my toes, I take off skimming across the ground.

The vault door has a security keypad next to it. I examine the oversized hands again and ask, "I don't suppose you've got any tools hidden in the fingers?"

"Negative."

"Can you hack the lock?"

"Negative. That class of breaching software is not currently loaded."

"Can you do anything remotely useful?"

"I am programmed to perform twelve thousand, seven hundred sixty-eight functions relating to internal and external sensors, tactical response, and targeting."

"I don't suppose kissing my ass is one of those?"

"Command not accepted."

"How about 'mute'? Can you manage that?"

No response. At least that works.

Who needs doors, anyway? Haven't seen a killer robot that uses them yet. I cock an arm like I'm going for a heater of a pitch and can't help but smile. I have never felt this much raw power in my hands. Forget tossing a car, maybe I could toss a cruise ship.

Before I can rip the reinforced door off the hinges, I hear a loud clunk followed by the door creeping outward. I'm frustrated and a bit worried. Outside light knifes into the hallway beyond.

Emily steps out of the darkness. Harsh shadows cover her face, but I can tell it's her by the fieldwork cargo pants and the caffeine molecule shirt. Her hair has escaped her ponytail and clings to her face in damp strands. In that instant, I'm ready to forgive her completely. She's a rare piece of what could be considered "normal".

"Don't freak out," I say. She doesn't answer. Doesn't flinch. Maybe forgiving her was premature. "What are you doing here?"

She gets closer, not stopping until she's in the shadow of the Battle Armor. She flashes a playful smile, stolen from another face, and giggles in an oddly girlish way. "Waiting for you."

Confused, I listen close for the trademark little snort that never comes. And then I notice her eyes. Luminous globes of living mercury.

Suddenly, the broad view of the HUD isn't enough. The suit is tight, cramped. I can't breathe. I want to turn and run on my own feet, but I've got to get air into my lungs before I suffocate. "Battle Armor, let me out! Let me out!"

With a hiss, the suit peels open. The chest slides outward, the limbs hinge, and fresh air washes over my sweat-drenched body. The helmet is the last thing to go as I slip to the ground on my hands and knees.

"Spencer, what's wrong?"

I hang my head close to the pavement, gasping for air.

"You. The dreams. Am I awake?"

"You're not dreaming. You never were."

Those silver eyes, they were hers in the dreams. "Where's my mom?"

Just like the forest floor when we first met, she reaches down and hauls me to my feet. "Come, Spencer." She takes my hand and walks ahead, the smile bright and intoxicating.

"I don't understand."

"You will." Her smile never changes as she speaks, never broken by her lips forming the words. Already, as I regain control of my breathing, I regret stepping out of the armor. I still have the urge to run, but my feet won't listen. I must follow her down this shrouded, metal-ribbed hallway to the truth.

CHAPTER 46

AUTOMATICALLY, THE HEAVY door swings shut, and it's like watching the drone rip into the bunker, only in reverse, as the Battle Armor disappears. Everything in reverse, because this time, I'm afraid to have that high-tech killing machine out of reach.

"So you *are* an Augment?" I ask as Emily leads me away from the door.

"I am. She isn't." Her answer takes me by surprise.

"That makes no sense. Why aren't your lips moving, you're..."

"In you?" she says.

"In my head."

"No, I'm inside you, Spencer." There's the school-girl giggle again in a dark corner of my skull. Concern erases her playful smile. "I'm frightening you."

"Can you at least talk out loud?"

"I... 'm... sorrrrr... eeeeeeeeeee!" Emily's voice strains and cracks as her jaw spasms and the apology ends in a piercing wail.

"That didn't help."

"Speaking is difficult." The voice echoes in my head.

"But why…"

"The body has mostly surrendered. The mind has not."

I clench my jaw. "Whatever you are, please leave her alone."

"She is my vessel. Do you disapprove?" Emily's face twists with pain and anger. "Why would you? After what she did to Mother."

Her grip tightens and she drags me down the hall walking at a stiff but steady clip. No more words, in my head or otherwise, but I can still feel her. The sort of feeling you get that someone is watching, creeping up right behind you, breathing down your neck, but when you look, nobody's there. That exact feeling, but it doesn't go away.

"Sorry about your reception," she says as we near the end of the corridor.

"Oh, you mean the BFG that nearly took my head off? You could have stopped that?"

"You had the Battle Armor, you were safe. You needed to feel the power."

She's in my head. But for how long now?

"Weeks."

The entry hall ends at a second reinforced door with a biometric security pad. Emily, or whatever she has become, cocks her head and winks. One silver iris coalesces into solid brown, a stark contrast to Emily's natural color. Flashing a badge at the panel, she presses her face against the eye cup. When the doors open, she pulls me into a room the size of the bunker bathroom. The door slides shut and a sinking sensation accompanies a whine of machinery.

Down we go. Longer than I expect we should.

At the bottom the doors open, revealing the shadow-splotched walls of a tunnel excavated from solid rock. We pass through another series of doors, one of these thicker than my outstretched arms with hinges like tree trunks set into a metal frame. The heavy door glides effortlessly.

On the other side, bodies litter the ground. A dozen armed and armored men in fatigues lay helpless but breathing, their eyes veiled in a milky glow.

"Are they dead?"

"They won't move. For a long time. Come."

She maintains her confident stride past the fallen soldiers. Dark, sterile hallways branch off in several directions. Soon, the halls narrow, and my tour guide's steps falter. Her hand slips from my wrist and into mine. Vulnerable and natural, for a split second I forget about the creepy eyes and the voice in my head.

"What is it?"

"*My* home."

We're facing a narrow, featureless hall where metal plating has replaced the rock. Doors line both sides and a swinging crash door hangs at the far end. It's the same hallway from the dreams I had over the desert. More bodies lie on the floor.

At first, the catatonic soldiers come to mind. But that wishful thinking dies when I see the blood. Everywhere.

People in HAZMAT suits with their brains fanned on the walls and guns in their hands. Men and women in white lab coats, their heads torn open viciously. I turn away and close my eyes but that doesn't help.

I can see the little girl in her surgical gown, her head a crown of scars and gauze. As I recall the scenes, the hallway melts into the tiny spartan space of my bunker.

"We set each other free, Spencer."

"The little girl, that's you," I say, but I really don't want more details. I'm talking only to buy time. She's headed across that hall and I don't want to go.

"This was my home and my prison, too. I couldn't leave, either." She smiles at me.

"I'm sorry all this happened, but I don't know what you want."

"Don't you see? I always thought this place was home. These people," she tilts her head at the carnage, "my family."

"No, sorry, I don't see. I don't want to see."

"Mother loves you so much." Her face contorts and she clutches at her shirt, twisting the symbol in her hands. "Through her I contacted you. I owe her everything."

"Well, you don't owe me." I look frantically down the hall, wondering if I can make it to the elevator. How do you stay ahead of someone who is inside your brain?

"You can't." Tears begin to stream down her cheeks, flowing from a look of utter surprise. "You can't go. We're family, Spencer. I will give you what you always wanted. Family. Powers."

"Please, if you want to help, just show me where my parents are."

She nods and turns. She begins walking down the hall, her

fingers entwined with mine. I follow, watching the ceiling to keep my eyes off the carnage, but spatters of blood decorate even there. The crash doors are within reach, and I see a bloody handprint streaked down the outside.

"He's in here," she says, as she pushes through the doors.

An underground cavern yawns before us that appears part natural, part manmade. The ceiling extends beyond a ring of stark lights that illuminate the room. In the center, giant glass cylinders connect to rigid supports that disappear in the void above. The cylinders are clustered in a circle, and each one holds a swirling fog. From the middle of the cluster another light glows, but I can't see the source. My eyes drift back to the ring of light above.

"No, there is no coincidence." She pulls, and we rattle across the open metal grating that floats over empty space.

We reach the end of the catwalk when Emily stops. My hand slips out of her grasp. No voice in my head reprimands me for thinking about running this time. Whatever has control of Emily is distracted. I can see myself running to the hallway, grabbing a loose gun. I could finish this Drake's way—bloody. Or Dad's—neutralize the threat before saving anyone.

But Emily put a truck through a wall for me. I don't know why, but she did. Even if it was pure guilt, I don't care. Enough people have died. My way. We're doing this my way.

I take her hand. "What's wrong?"

Instead of answering, she stares at the closest tall cylinder. A solid shape hangs in the swirling gray cloud. White wrappings flutter on a smoke-borne breeze. She is a small girl with a round face and delicate, narrow eyes. A little Chinese girl.

Eric was right. Well, almost right, but close enough. His personal story might have been way off, but that foundation must have been involved in these experiments. What better guinea pigs than discarded kids whose families didn't even want them? If I were missing, Mom would've been looking for me. Even Dad. I step up to the glass.

The girl's eyes are closed as if she's dreaming. Wisps of hair flutter between rows of scars on her scalp. A neural cage grasps her skull.

"That's you?"

She shakes her head. "No. That was my prison."

"So, since you, um, escaped, you've been where exactly?"

A giggle crawls through the closed-off spaces in my brain. "Inside people. And inside the people they know. Space isn't the same in here. 'Being' isn't the same."

Okay, no more questions. I step forward and focus on a puzzle I might have a chance of figuring out. There's an instrument panel covered in digital screens and switches at the cylinder's base. Information scrolls by on a central monitor, along with a variety of voltage meters, digital gauges, and diagnostic text. Through openings in the floor, trunks of wire and hoses snake out and disappear into the smoke around the girl.

"Mom? Is she in one of these?"

She sighs and tugs on my hand, following the cylinders in a loose spiral, each one containing another person. At times, the smoke parts enough to reveal tubes and wires crisscrossing into the frozen bodies. In each one, I start to recognize bits of hardware sewn into their skin. The pile of parts and skin that was Polybius, or the neural cage on this girl, they're identical to the internal workings of Drake's technology.

I can see faces in the mist. They're all Augments, I'm sure of that, but without the masks and suits, they're impossible to recognize. Entire lives spent incognito have made them invisible inside *their* glass tombs.

"They live. These weapons were deemed far too valuable to simply disarm."

"Where's—"

"This way."

We follow the cylinders, spiraling to the core. There, a harsh light beams onto a metal table. Scalpels, syringes, various pieces of surgical equipment are scattered about as if dropped in a hurry. A hairy, bloody mass exactly the size of someone's head lies on the table. I look away in horror.

"A necessary test, Spencer. They all were," she brings her hand to her head, her eyes locked in the past, "necessary."

The closest cylinder catches my eye. "Dad!" He's floating in the same stuff with one key difference – he's minus most of the extra hardware. His eyes are sunken pits and pale skin peeks out from the wrappings.

"Get him out of there."

"The facility is locked down. None of them," she gestures to the bloody lump on the table, "could tell me how to bypass the fail-safes."

"Hang on, Dad." This panel is the same as the others— a tiny alphanumeric keyboard for an interface, several touch screens, and a card reader. "Hand me—" The security card Emily was carrying drops into my outstretched palm.

I swipe the card and a red light flares above the reader. *Unauthorized access.*

Couldn't be that easy, could it? I set my backpack on the floor and get my multi-tool. Eric breathes code like air. I just sort of know how circuit boards and modules and a mess of cables works. Like reading a map; some people get lost going to the grocery store. I'm not those people. Maybe these are Augment powers? Maybe Eric is right on some level. As I dig behind the panel, a lifetime of taking apart every piece of tech I could get my hands on reveals the secrets hidden there.

"He is proud of you," she says.

"Excuse me?" I mumble, staying focused on the task.

"He is proud of the things you could do. Things he could not."

"Three-way calling. Whatever it is, I didn't sign up for it on my plan. So stop, just stop."

"At the moment, I can only be inside two minds."

"Don't you think that's two too many?" I mutter.

"Soon, it will be so many more," she says.

Then she giggles.

In my brain.

Whatever that means, I need to get Dad out of here, fast. As I work, the feeling of someone watching over my shoulder grows more and more intense until I can practically feel hot, psychic breath warming my gray matter. I focus on a new panel. When the first screw clinks through the grating, dropping into the abyss below, a deafening alarm dices the air.

"They've already gone to containment protocols. Ignore the alarm," she says.

"Eh?" I mumble, mouth wrapped around the handle of my multi-tool and hands buried in wire.

"Nothing leaves the base. Bombers are scrambling over-head. We need to hurry."

I manage to find the logic board that controls the cylinder retraction. With a few adjustments, I'll have it open.

"You might get… well, move Emily out of the way."

She steps backward. Watching Emily retreat, I try to keep closed thoughts, but whatever it is inside her pries them open. "If this could be dangerous for her, what about you?"

"Yeah, well, I'm an idiot. I unplugged a nuclear-powered drone earlier this week and managed to not become a chicken nugget. I'll be fine."

"But you are uncertain."

"Again, you aren't helping."

I plug in the modified board and scramble out to watch. I do my best not to think of what I'm going to say to Dad, try-ing to find a way to warn him without alerting the squatter in my head.

"He'll be fine, Spencer. He's invulnerable, remember?"

The mist inside his cylinder clears, sucked out through one of the hoses. Surrounded by a metallic buzz, I step clear as the metal arm retracts the cylinder into the void. Dad hangs in midair, his limbs dangling outside the gauzy white wrap-pings like a corpse on an invisible meat hook. He begins to descend; his pointed toes touch first, then fold back gently on limp ankles, next knees, until he lies in a heap on the platform. I rush forward.

Dad's hand shoots out and grabs my shoulder. I grit my

teeth, vowing not to move even if he crushes my clavicle. But his palm relaxes leaving only the dead weight of his forearm supported by... me. His eyes flutter and he mumbles, but I can't understand him.

"Dad. Dad! We're going to get you out of here." The waist-high platform is too high, and I can't even begin to hoist him down. He's breathing in shallow gasps and his eyes flutter. Emily steps forward and we both struggle to place him on the floor.

"Spencer?" he mumbles. "Spencer, is that you?"

"Yeah, Dad, it's me."

"What are you doing here?" He scrunches his eyes and forces them open. "You shouldn't have come. How did you even get in here?"

"Black Beetle style."

"What?"

"He's... he had an accident. I borrowed his formal wear." Dad starts to reply, but I cut him off. "Did you find Mom? I think she's here."

Emily steps forward, her eyes blazing in the sterile light, and her lips part in a sinister smile. Dad registers her presence for the first time. Confusion transitions to tense determination. He tries to rise and balls his fists, but the determination is swept away by a blank stare.

A silver sheen fills his eyes.

At the same time, Emily's jaw quivers and her mouth twists. "Spencer... run!"

"Emily!"

But as quickly as her eyes cleared, they disappear again behind the mirrored surface.

She turns, spreading her arms wide beneath the ring of light. Dad rises, floating to his feet and hovering inches off the catwalk, his face a naked mask. The creature that is Emily reaches out, trying to cradle the entire cavern in her embrace, and shouts, "We're all together, now. We're a family, Spencer. We have a family!"

Between the words, I hear Emily, screaming.

CHAPTER 47

"**Y**OU'LL BE SAFE here," psychic-freak says, flickering in Emily's eyes. Tears roll down her cheeks above the Arkham smile. "When we're ready for you to join us, we'll come for you. We'll make you one of us, Spencer!"

Dad pushes me into a room along the corpse-lined hallway. Fighting his blind, hypnotized strength is impossible, but I struggle and kick anyway, forcing him to expend about the same effort it might take to pick some lint off his costume. As the door closes, I slam against it and keep pounding.

"Stop! Dad! Don't let her do this! You're the Crimson Mask!"

I beat on the door until my fists are sore and bloody, then I collapse with my sweaty forehead pressed against the steel. Breathing hard, I drop to the floor and start to let the bottled emotions run free.

A mindless groan comes from the back of the room. What the hell did they put me in here with?

My back against the solid door, I struggle to stand. "Who's there?"

Poorly lit, the room has a bed, a filthy toilet and a recessed sink. I'm hit by an odor fouler than old gym shorts and thick enough you could wear it. The lump of sheets on the bed stirs.

"Spencer? Is that you?"

"Oh shit, Doc!" I rush to the bedside and stagger as the wall of funk hits full-on. Tucking my nose under the collar of my shirt, I mouth breathe as I get closer to the bed.

Martin coughs, then chokes and begins desperately fumbling with the sheets. I help him sit. One eye is blackened, swollen nearly shut and his lip is split halfway to his nose.

"Ouch."

Doc gingerly touches his face. "Emily. She had a psychotic episode."

I nod, debating about telling him exactly how much worse the situation really is. "How did you guys even get here?"

"I was going to call the cops, file a missing person's report." He's doing his best to examine me through his one working eye. "How are you? What happened?"

"You look much worse than I ever did, Doc. Epic contusions and lacerations."

"Cuts and scrapes," he says, cringing as he brushes his eyelid with his fingertips. "You?"

"Robots. How and why are you even here?"

"Emily. She started having these weird dreams. Telling me she knew where you were."

"You believed her?" I can't help sounding amazed.

Martin sighs and examines the stained sheets he's been laying on. He frowns, stands a bit too quickly, and steadies himself on the wall. Adjusting to the momentary dizziness, he answers from behind the protection of the hand he's using to massage his temples. "Yeah. I did. I mean, I guess she was right about you being here."

"Only you got here way before I did."

Martin squints, "I don't really know what happened. Emily smashed me in the head with, I think, the cabin fire extinguisher."

"She's, uh, not herself. Literally." I shake off the image of Emily pleading for me to run.

As though it's the first time he's acknowledging the fact, Martin nods. "When we flew in, things got intense. Out of nowhere we had fighter jets threatening to shoot us down. Emily took over the controls and I could hear the pilot's chatter about losing contact. They might have fired on us, I'm not sure. Somewhere in there she clocked me. What's going on here?"

"Project Killcreek, and some kind of crazy psychic Augment. She might have gotten through to Emily because of me, or maybe Dad."

I turn to the door. No keypad, not even a handle on this side. The seam around the door is so tight, I don't think a piece of paper could slip between it and the frame. Outside, Dad is playing ass-puppet for an Augment, and Emily is doing a good job as an *Exorcist* stand-in. In here, I've got no tools, no battle armor, and no underappreciated minions on my side.

I slump against the door. "We're fucked."

Martin walks over and pushes against the door. He paces backward into the room and examines the floor, ceiling, walls. He winces when his neck hits the wrong angle. Even locked in a secret military base, with a face that's half hamburger, he's not panicking.

"How is it you're so calm about this?" I ask.

He peers into a corner and the mask of assurance melts but only for an instant. "Believe me, I'm freaking out. The real question is how you're so calm."

"Why's that? 'Cause I'm a 'kid'?"

"Don't get pissed, but yeah. I've got several years on you when it comes to dealing with emergency situations."

"Maybe I… Oh, forget it."

"What?"

"Could be a death wish, but I'm going to stick with my original answer and say, Dad."

"Oh yeah? I thought he wasn't around much." Martin ambles back to the door, rubbing his neck.

"No, but when he was, he'd talk all this hardcore rule bullshit. How to be a badass Augment. And I'd watch him, on TV. Every chance I got."

Martin slides down next to me with a forced laugh and says, "I sorta know what you mean. My Dad, he'd always talk business, even though I've got the worst business sense of anyone I've ever known."

"How so?"

"Too practical. Too matter of fact, I guess. I tried to sell candy bars once. They were two for a dollar, but I made sure there were two people to complete the sale. I figured a person didn't need two candy bars. Not exactly the healthiest snack. Tooth decay, diabetes."

"Are you serious? How old were you?"

"Twelve. It was for the student council."

"This explains a lot, by the way," I say. He huffs a laugh

from the un-swollen side of his face and I ask, "How about you? All that ER craziness prep you for abduction by insane Augments?"

He shrugs. "You learn to cope with desperation and unpredictability. You also figure out who on the team can keep it together when the Trauma Gods strike." I'm examining my sneakers as he talks but I can tell he's looking right at me. "So, how'd you even get here? And don't say 'robots'."

"How does 'cybernetic battle suit' work for you?" When I look up I see the confusion setting in on Martin's face, so I let him off the hook. "The Black Beetle. I borrowed his battle armor."

Martin's already tenderized face goes slack, "Really?"

"Yeah. He had an accident, sort of." I break eye contact while Martin fumbles for a response. "I don't want to talk about it." To change the subject, I bang my elbow against the solid door. "If I would've left the suit on, I could probably smash this stupid door down, or blow it to pieces. Better yet, smash through the wall like a Kool-Aid man on crack. You know? Augment style."

Martin nods and starts into more of his story. "A week before my dad died, he'd been showing me around his office. Kept calling it 'our office'. Never bothered to ask what I wanted. You know the story; I was halfway through college before I figured it out. Took me forever to realize I needed to make that decision on my own.

"The important thing is, I did figure it out. I'm a doctor. I'm good at it. I don't have the business instinct to be a CEO, but I can help people. You, Spencer, you may not be an

Augment, but you're wicked resourceful. Smart." He claps my shoulder as he finishes. "So, what's the plan?"

I do a double take at Martin as he stands, hands on hips, staring at the ceiling. True to his nature, he's calm as can be. Not only that, he's asking *me* for the plan. Not trying to protect me, or tell me how reckless and insane I am, which would be spot-on. No, he's actually deferring to me about this whole giant chunk of insanity.

So far, I've been doing this all wrong. Trying to escape a prison only to end up in another one, not the best batting average. I've been running around numb, pissed off, maybe a bit suicidal, trying to be something I never wanted, an Augment, all to get *his* attention and avoid the pain of losing *her*, when what I really needed to escape was to be *me*.

Seated on the floor, I start searching the room. There's a single bulb recessed into the ceiling, about twelve feet off the ground. Also, a tiny vent provides air circulation. While I'm small, I'm not sideshow small. To my immediate right, salvation catches my eye: a security camera mounted in the corner under a tinted dome. Might be just enough to work with.

"If I can get up to that camera and crack it open, there's bound to be a data cable. You have a phone?"

He digs his phone out of a pocket. He frowns as he checks the display, "No signal."

I put out a hand and he tosses the phone. "Nice model. My bet, you got the optional insurance?"

"Yeah."

"Sweet." I crack the case open because simply sliding the battery out won't give me access to what I need. A pained expression crosses his face. "Signal wouldn't have helped. There isn't a cell tower for miles, Doc."

"How do you know?"

"Robots." I again have to say that as if it were a foregone conclusion. He rolls his eyes. "Any chance you can give me a boost?"

Without hesitation, Martin nods and drops to a knee under the camera. I scramble up his bent leg to his shoulders and he slowly stands. The dome looks unbreakable, and the scratches indicate plenty of people have tried—a dark sooty black even mars one section. I don't want to destroy the camera, though, just get between it and the ceiling.

"Car keys? Plane keys?" Martin passes them up. Within seconds, I've got the metal partly wedged under the casing. Through the dome, I can see where the data cable connects into the camera. With enough luck, I can snap the plastic tab and fish the cable out.

A low rumble rolls in from the other side of the door. I recognize it as the mechanical strain of a cylinder raising off the platform.

"What was that?" Martin asks, breathless.

"Damn it."

"What?"

"She was watching. She needed to know how to do it."

"Do what?" Martin grumbles as he adjusts my weight on his shoulders.

"I think the family reunion's first guest has arrived."

CHAPTER 48

MARTIN'S BEEN A good sport about me grinding my feet into his shoulders for the past hour. So far, I'm getting closer. The keys weren't working, so I've fished out a bit of the wire with a shim we made from parts of the metal bed frame. The whole time, the wall continues to shake with the noise of more cylinders being raised. I don't know how much longer we have until the reunion gets hungry.

"What now?" Martin groans as he shifts and scowls at me through a shoelace.

"Sorry, almost there." I've got just enough cable to work with.

"How long?"

"Not long. Once I access the phone's field test menu, I can get a basic connection running."

Martin only exhales deeply.

There's nothing to this. I use the phone to masquerade as the camera and the network pops wide open. I can see Eric was actually wrong about this place. There is a connection to the outside world. The message I can send is limited to a binary string, but that's plenty. Eric is fluent in not only binary but Klingon and elvish.

A call for help isn't part of the Augment code of badassery. Never once did Dad say, "When you're in deep shit, call for backup." But that's exactly why this is going to work.

"Done."

With a pained sigh, Martin drops to a knee in what's meant to be a controlled descent. His fatigued legs wobble at the last second and I fall in a heap on top of him.

"Sorry," he moans. "You hurt?"

"I'm fine. I didn't crush the good side of your head, did I?" I bound to my feet and put out a hand to help.

Martin misses the offered support and thunks his head on the wall like a ripe melon. He barely registers the collision. "Got to rest a second. What did you do, anyway?"

"Sent an S.O.S."

"To who?" Reading the 'there's nobody left to call' edge to his question is easy. Army, Air Force, Marines, Special Forces, Augments—they're already here, and either nuts or waiting to turn this place into a parking lot.

"A couple of friends," I say.

"Chess club?"

"Nice, Doc! Your sarcasm is improving." I drop to the mattress on the floor beside the disassembled bed and try to ignore the rank stench. "If I breathe through my mouth instead of my nose, am I going to get some kind of disease?"

"Nasal passages humidify and filter air," Martin's voice starts to drift as he schools me on snot. "Your mucous membranes can trap a lot of bacteria and viruses your mouth can't.

You'll produce less nitric oxide as well…" Not only is his voice drifting in volume, but it seems to be getting further away and muffled.

"Never mind, Doc. Rest a bit." I try not to do the same. Unsuccessfully.

Martin's involuntary-response lecture crescendos into a droning buzz. My vision separates like a strip of old-school movie film melting, and the world is left a white smear. All I can see is stark, white light.

I'm drowning in luminance. There's no cold, but the light has the weight of an ocean. Above, a circular band forms and etches ripples across the surface of my skin. The center void becomes an enormous pupil surrounded by glittering water.

"I want to show you something," comes a quiet voice.

The girl from the cylinder has my hand. Paper-white hair flows in a sharp line around her scarred scalp. Veins course through her cheeks. A powerful inner light creates a fleshy pink silhouette with a core of dark bones.

As we ascend toward the ocean, her face becomes a parade of features. Some are people I recognize from the cylinders, winking in and out of a churning crowd of strangers. I should be scared, but I don't feel afraid. I feel hollow.

"Where are we going?"

Her eyes dart away. She continues to lead with an eager pull. As the light folds inward, she glows brighter. The edge of the darkness fades. The shadows melt away and we're standing on solid ground.

Then again, nothing here is solid. This place seems a flimsy, paper substitute for reality. White walls flex and breathe in rolling waves. Even the wooden floor, interrupted by the thick humps of enormous tree branches, gives me the impression I could slip between the boards.

Two hammocks flank a bed with a metal frame with large hearts bent into the rods. Each hammock is attached to a mighty tree trunk which serves as one of the walls. They droop with the weight of bodies, one hanging deeper than the other, but I can't see inside them from here. On the trunk, a large bookcase is carved into the flesh of the tree.

The girl from the cylinder stands beside me, naked, her flesh glowing with a pink aura. Crystalline eyes bore intently into me. I'm having trouble looking at her. I'm both revolted and fascinated. She's a pathetic little girl now, and not a mind-controlling monster. I want to say something that could maybe make things better, but I can't find the words.

"Is this the Falcon's Nest?" I ask.

"Do you like it?" she stares with eager eyes.

I don't answer, but instead ask, "You've read *Swiss Family Robinson?*"

She nods and smiles, her teeth dark shadows against the inner radiance.

I walk to the bookcase, driven partly by curiosity and partly by the need for space. Once her arm is fully extended, she lets her fingers slip out of mine.

"Have you read all of these?" I ask.

Books crowd the shelves, neatly organized. I get to the second row with an unbroken "read it" checklist, when I realize she hasn't answered my question. I brace myself and look back.

She nods her head. "We both have."

Standing farther from her, I can see her pink body has a definitely female shape. She's posed awkwardly, bundled around herself in an impossible attempt at modesty. I swallow and put out my hand.

Head down, she peers up through her lashes and I motion her forward with my fingertips. She practically bounds over, squeezing my hand tight the second she's in reach. After the shock of her bony grip, I try and focus on the good—the warmth of her smooth skin, a bookcase full of shared interests. Whatever I can to stay calm.

"What's your name?"

She pauses and stands on her tiptoes, her bare breast brushing my arm. I try and focus on the book titles. Reaching up, she grabs a book and places it in my hands. She presses in and nestles on my arm. It takes a moment before I remember the book.

"*Charlotte's Web*? I've read this… oh, Charlotte! Is that your name? Charlotte?" In the excitement, we lock eyes again. She's glowing on the inside even brighter now and her eyes, they aren't filmy, but lit from behind with that same effusive glow.

"Charlotte, you never answered me earlier. How long have you been here?"

She bites her lower lip and reaches for the shelf. This book is weathered and old, a tome that might be in the moldering stacks at a library.

"H.G. Wells, huh? *The Time Machine*?" Another book I've read, but not an answer I understand. "What about why? Why are you here?"

Charlotte giggles, enjoying her new game. She bites the

corner of her lip and scans the shelf. Her finger traces the top corner of a book, then she switches and grabs another. *Flowers for Algernon.*

"Yeah, another classic. Oh." She's staring down, drawing circles on the floor with her toe. The light dims and her bony fingers dig into my knuckles.

The small circles she makes with her toes tighten and she pulls her shoulders inward. She reaches forward and removes another book. The title isn't familiar at first, but flipping through the pages, the story springs to mind. I read this one in the back issues of a classic sci-fi magazine: *The Thought Reading Machine* by Andre Maurois.

Charlotte cradles my arm against her smooth stomach, and stares vacantly at the floor. The fleshy aura of her body flares. The insubstantial room loses detail. All except for the books, which stand out in perfect clarity from a lonely past.

My own memories race by. Days spent on the playground of yet another strange school hiding in the pages of a book, the farthest corner of countless public library computer labs, sequestered away in Eric's basement—finding that one perfect spot in every place I'd lived. A spot where I could lose myself in worlds outside the real one. Places where I didn't have to face who I really was or feel pressured to be like my Augment father.

Her form becomes a featureless orb of light. The hammocks thrash along the wall. White hot heat emanates through her hand, but I don't register pain, only a growing sense of isolation. That isolation is my worst days at the bunker, when wandering out into the Arctic waste felt like a good idea. Days where facing death as a Popsicle, cold and numb, would've been a relief.

"Charlotte?!"

She raises off the ground. A tendril of light lashes out in a frenzied swirl and books tumble to the floor.

"I can't... don't..." Books rip past, and with each one my brain thrashes. My skull feels like it has been opened, the nerves steadily plucked and then yanked in fistfuls. "Charlotte! Please!"

One of the books launches past and leaves a psychic smear, replaying over and over in my head. *The Universe Against Her. The Universe Against Her. The Universe Against Her.*

"Charlotte, please stop!" Our hands unlace. My legs feel weak. Whatever supported me in this place has disappeared and I'm falling.

Charlotte's cries of anguish fade away behind the rumble and squeal of a heavy metal plate.

"Mom!"

I'm sitting on a beach. Barefoot, I watch the waves lap against the sand. No sun in the sky, but there's a muted glow that gives the sand a bluish hue, separated from the water only by the wetness left behind in the retreating waves. And then she's here, sitting next to me.

CHAPTER 49

"IS IT REALLY you?"

Mom smiles.

The blue ambient light saps the life out of this tropical paradise. Everything except her smile and her eyes, which are sparkle with no trace of the silvery sheen. She almost replies, but the words catch in her throat while her smile wavers. Those days when Dad was away come rushing back.

She hasn't answered, but I know I'm finally looking at her. Somehow, this is different from the other dreams. It isn't simple intuition, or even the obvious fact her eyes are their normal color; I simply *know*.

I lunge forward and wrap my arms around her. She squeezes and sighs. Her chest quivers. Again, I think she's going to speak, her mouth right next to my ear, but there's no sound.

A long time passes before I can talk. "How did you get here? Where exactly is this? I mean, I know this isn't real, is it? But you're here." Words tumble out, drunk and aimless.

She pushes away, her smile a tight line, and she stares out toward the sea. "It was a terrible book, wasn't it?"

"Oh yeah. Awful. I mean, some asshat of a father going on

and on about how he knows everything. Making fun of his lazy kid because *he's* a know-it-all, and the whole family slaughtering every living creature in sight."

"Spencer," Mom sighs, but there's the hint of a laugh.

When I got older, we spent more time making fun of *Swiss Family Robinson* than reading it. But she was always serious about the message; the adventure, the can-do attitude that was so overwrought in every sentence. It was an antique parody of our situation and we reveled in the awkwardness.

"You never did get me a flintlock like I asked," I say.

"I know." She tucks a dark lock behind her ear. "You didn't need to be shooting anyone."

I nod.

"What's going on here?"

Mom pulls her knees up to her chest and leans on my shoulder. It strikes me how much bigger I am than the last time I saw her. Two years and maybe a few inches to my midget frame, but she can actually do this now, lean on me. "I needed you to see that," she says.

"Charlotte's playhouse?"

She tilts her head in my direction and searches for an answer. "Yes."

I check the beach for prying ears. Too bad I can't check my head. "She's a nutbag, Mom."

No amusement this time. Mom shakes her head against my shoulder. "She's been hurt. So much."

"Yeah, well, she hasn't exactly made my life easy. I think she's been digging around my brain for days now. What about you?"

"Longer."

"Weeks?"

"Maybe longer."

"How long then?"

"I don't even know. Time here doesn't make sense. How long have I been gone?" she asks.

I could break that down to months, weeks, days, maybe hours, but I don't. "Two years."

Mom sits up and straightens into a stale breeze that glides across the ocean. "I'm sorry. This is all my fault."

"How the hell is this *your* fault?"

"I refused to move. I forced him to leave us out of that cloak-and-dagger part of his life."

"No, he wasn't right, Mom. I loved that house, too. I finally had a home."

"It wasn't even about the house." She closes her eyes and digs her toes into the sand. "I was angry. It doesn't matter. A week before I last saw you, your father told me about the bunker. Said we might have to go soon. He was going to leave the program, go rogue himself.

"Somehow they knew, and had their response planned. That was when the Black Beetle showed up to take a hostage, leverage, so your father would turn himself in. But we had agreed, you were our priority. No matter what happened, we would keep you safe." Her face drops. "I never should have told Charlotte where you were."

"I don't understand."

"She wanted to know where the bunker was." Mom locks eyes with me. "At first, it was her handlers that made her ask.

That was her job, to find answers, no matter the cost." She pauses to straighten my hair and touch my cheek. "They were desperate to find Sean. He was the last Augment either not surrendered or in custody or at Killcreek."

"Drake was right."

She nods. "I tried not to tell her." Her eyes well up. "I'm so glad you're alive."

"Watching that place get melted into slag was maybe the best day of my life." I say, no trace of sarcasm.

"The things she did." Mom shivers and I put an arm around her. "But I thought we had made some kind of connection. She always asked about you and Sean, and I always wanted to remember. I knew that was part of her interrogation, but it was different. She really wanted to know all those stories. Those little details about us. I could tell she was looking at those for herself."

"She needed a family."

"More than that."

"Wait. What happened to you?"

"When I thought we'd connected, I... I opened up to her." Again, the ocean pulls her gaze. "I thought it might help me to escape. I didn't understand the cost."

"Was that you, in my dreams?"

"No. Always her. She got to you before I even told her where the bunker was. Through me. I think she jumps between thoughts of those close to each other. You were too far away for her to control so she used your dreams. Then I couldn't fight her anymore. I told her. I told her exactly where the bunker was." She can't look me in the eye.

"But I'm here now. You'll be fine. I'll get you out of this place."

"I'm gone, baby."

Truth rings in her hesitant voice and I start to feel my throat constrict. "You're right here."

She raises her palms helplessly and looks around. "You already said it. Where's here?"

"But... I'm here too, then."

Her eyes glaze over and begin to reflect the endless sea. "You're lying on the floor in one of the prison rooms. A man's there with you, checking your pulse, your eyes. He seems like a nice man—you can get out of there, right? He can help?" The reflection slips away replaced by wild desperation.

"Help's on the way. Don't worry about me. You're going to come with us. You're in another one of those cells, right? Along the hall?"

She shakes her head.

"I came for you," I say angrily. "Not Dad. Not psycho girl. Not the Black Beetle. I came to get *you*!"

Her head drops. "I can see what she sees, it's really strange. I watched them with me. She was crying when they dug the grave."

My mind flashes to a shallow grave scooped out by a robotic claw. But it isn't Drake's broken form, it's hers. I blink away tears. "No, but you're here. I can feel it!"

"Once I opened up to her, she owned me, Spencer. I don't even understand, but this is her place. Her rules. I got stuck here." She clears her throat grabs my shaking hand. "Something has changed. She's distracted or taxed her abilities, I don't know.

I can suddenly bend the rules, but I don't know how long." She keeps speaking even as I collapse into her shoulder, sobbing. "Listen, you need to go back. When I died, it broke her. She's out of control."

"Stop saying that! Damn that freak!" I'm shouting now, and I don't care if little Miss Scrambled Brains hears.

Mom grabs my shoulder and pulls me tight. "Don't blame her. She couldn't help herself. She was only doing what they trained her to do."

"What, like Dad? Doing her job?" I spring to my feet, every word rubbing raw against my throat. "This is their fault! All of them!"

From her seat in the sand Mom pleads, "Spencer, don't."

"Why not? Why fucking not? Don't blame him? Are you serious? It's the damn Augments, the stupid program. You do know Dad was banging Emily while we were at home, right? While we sat there wondering if he'd make it back? While you got kidnapped. Tortured."

"That's the same way she feels. Don't you understand?" She looks away and squints, recalling tears that must have been shed long ago.

The pain lingering in her eyes makes me realize what I just said. "I'm sorry, Mom. I didn't mean to."

She stands and looks squarely at me, an expression I've seen once before, when she was pulled into the sky in the metallic arms of a robot menace. "This isn't about me, Spencer. Or Dad. Or even you. It's about Charlotte. She wants revenge. She's going to kill every last soldier she sees."

"So? Let her!" I manage to say under that heartrending stare.

"Spencer, this isn't you. This isn't the man I know. Kind, gentle. You're every bit the hero your father might have been, and more."

I have to stare at the sand, the rising tide now lapping at my ankles.

"She's lost, Spencer. She has been for a long time. Until she met me, she had nobody. But as she wandered in my memories, she thought she'd found what she had been looking for. And she kept digging. " Mom's voice sounds empty.

I can't look up.

"Deep down, she's sorry for what she did."

"I came to find you."

"You did, baby."

I collapse against her, a bubbling mess of snot and tears. "I'm sorry, Mom! This was supposed to be Dad's job. He was supposed to find you. Bring you back home. What could I do, trapped in a damn bunker?"

"I think we both forgot how grown up you'd become. How much we needed to let you go."

"Did he even try to find you?"

"Of course he tried. Your father had so much working against him." She holds me gently at arm's length. "I'm not happy with your dad. I won't lie to you. What he did was wrong, but he's your father."

We cling to each other for what could be forever, and maybe it is in this strange place. But it isn't long enough.

"I'm so proud of you. What you must have done to get here

scares me senseless, but you did it. You found us both." She steps back to arm's length, keeping her hands on my shoulders. "Now Charlotte's up there, trying to make her own family. And people who have families at home, wondering if they will ever return, are in danger. And I don't know if she'll stop there. If you can't forgive your father, at least go and help them. Find a way to make her understand that what she's doing is wrong. That, or stop her from hurting anyone else. Okay?"

"Yes, ma'am."

Suddenly, there's that smile. Bright enough to once again cast off the dull film that hangs in the air of this place. "Ma'am?!" She punches my arm playfully. "Are you fucking serious, Spence?"

I've got to laugh. Despite the burning tears and the gut-wrenching pain, I've got to laugh. We both do. We laugh until we're back in the sand, gasping for breath and ignoring the waves trickling along our backs. That smile becomes my world, and this time, this time it stays.

CHAPTER 50

"HE'S GONE NUTS." That's Eric's voice, interrupting my laughter.

The beach drifts away, empty, and I'm shooting into the sky. Below, the ocean glows as a solid ring of light around the chunk of rock and sand. A maelstrom, a giant eye, watching as I ascend.

"Come on, man! Wake up!"

I feel a sting on my cheek and Martin interrupts, "That's not necessary."

Eric hangs over me, his open palm cocked inches from my face. Martin's there, too, kneeling by the bedside. By the door, a butt crack peeks out of a tattered hospital gown. Thankfully, Hurricane turns, beaming his gummy smile instead of his weathered eclipse. "Blaise! Ya back with the living?"

"Couldn't you get him some clothes?" I ask Eric.

Eric leans in close to my ear. "Hey, you're not the one that had to hitch a ride bareback. He can't wear normal clothes anyway. I think it has to do with the friction."

With a helpful shove from Eric, I sit up. "You got my message?"

Eric hides his face and focuses on Hurricane.

"Yeah, we got it. We were about halfway here, though, by the time ya sent it."

"What?"

Eric blushes and hauls me off the mattress. "When you called from the Beetle armor, I heard the coordinates, triangulated the signal, and got a solid fix. Calculating a trajectory wasn't too hard after that. Pretty easy to track."

"Wow, thanks," I say with genuine respect. Eric can't make eye contact but he mumbles a "no problem".

"All his idea." Hurricane crosses the room and slaps Eric on the back. "Woulda brought Hound, but there's only so much room on the 'Cane train!"

"I wish I could've kept you guys out of all this. But I'm glad you're here."

"Sounded like you needed help," Eric says, and clasps my arm weakly in what's meant to be a show of bravado. "Hey, you were rolling around cackling. Completely mental. I thought this place," he checks the door nervously and his face drains of color, "had gotten to you."

"Just a dream," I say.

Martin's patient-assessing gaze follows me across the room, and Eric stays close as I cross to Hurricane's post by the door. He puts out a gnarled hand.

"Ready to skedaddle?" Hurricane asks.

"What about Emily?" Martin asks.

I start to peek through the door when Eric pulls me back. "Bodies, man," he whispers. His once pride-flushed cheeks now seem feverish. I pat his hand and the grip loosens.

"Yeah, I know." I check the hall, keeping my eyes up and looking at both ends. It's quiet and the cavern door's windows emit a yellow glare. The exit at the far end is ajar and the remaining cell doors are open as well.

"I checked this place top to bottom when we got here. Place's empty aside from the GIs we found sleeping on the floor. And these poor bastards." Hurricane's reply tickles my ear with the smell of stale mints. Part of me wants to argue with him and tell him he's wrong. I only nod and step into the hall. "Think everyone headed outside for the furball."

"Furball?" Martin asks as he steps out of the room.

"Fight," Eric translates from the doorway. "You should see it, Spencer. Every big-time Augment I've heard of is lined up against the rest of the US military budget. We need to get clear of this place and fast."

"My God." Martin's instantly crouching over the nearest body.

Hurricane pulls Eric into the hall like he's escorting the blind. Eric follows limply with his face frozen in fear. While I'm avoiding the gore, too, Martin's moving among the corpses and checking for signs of life. I start toward the crash doors into the cavern.

"You comin'? I can get everyone clear, one man at a time. Won't take long." Hurricane whispers.

I don't answer and Eric shuffles to face me. "You're going the wrong way!" he hisses.

Martin looks up from a mangled corpse.

"I've got to do something about this. I can't ask you to stay."

A cavernous grin spreads across Hurricane's face. "Hot damn!" Stooped at the shoulders, he lets a hand slip and rubs his palms together. Eric looks pale.

"Hurricane can get you out of here," I say to Eric. "But I need you to come right back, Hurricane. Martin, I'd feel better if you were here, too."

"I'm here to stay, dude," squeaks Eric. Whimpering, he begins a double-time slide along the wall, squealing with every misstep. Finally, he bursts into the cavern room, gasping.

"Hurricane, get ahead of him, check it out."

He nods and a pressure wave rolls by, carrying the condensed stench of death. I choke and Martin appears next to me, ushering me through the crash doors into the cavern.

Hundreds of feet above, the entire roof has slid aside. A warm column of pure daylight pierces the room, wrapped in a translucent layer of dust. The distant pop of gunfire and the pound of larger weapons ripples into the cavern. On the platform in the center, all of the cylinders have been raised, their massive arms pulled high against a support built in the cavern wall. All except one.

"All clear," Hurricane says, then, following my gaze, adds, "Sorta."

I walk past Eric who stands on the edge of the catwalk gaping at the massive cavern. Even with daylight streaming in, there's no obvious bottom. A skyscraper could fit inside this place. I clank across the catwalk and approach the closed cylinder.

Charlotte. She looks so peaceful. Eyes closed, the hoses and bandages dance around her like strands of kelp among the gray smoke.

A deep rumble stampedes down the cavern walls, causing the catwalk to sway. Martin grabs the handrail and crouches as Eric plasters himself to the cavern wall by the door. Hurricane barely moves, keeping his eyes on me in a steady stare. Perhaps a search for doubt, fear, I don't know, but when he fails to find it, his nostrils flare and he flashes fierce eyes.

"Just a little earth-shakin', yeah? Could be Fat Boy if he's still around," Hurricane hobbles toward me. "What's the plan, boss?"

Second time today I've had to field that question and I actually have an answer. Turning, I stare up at Charlotte. I follow the tubes under the glass until I see one that travels up to the neural cage on her skull. "I'm going to have to set up a meeting. Martin, what can you tell me about some of these readings?" I point toward one of the small screens on the cylinder's base.

Martin finishes crossing the catwalk and squats next to the screen. "Vitals. Pulse is bradycardic, but decent. BP low." Hesitantly, he reaches up and taps the screen, cycling through several menus. He stands and strains to examine the girl. Unsatisfied, he climbs onto the lip of the base and leans against the glass. He shakes his head slowly as he scans the motionless figure head to toe. "My God, what did they do to this girl?" His eyes linger on the scar-braided skin of her skull before he hops down to the catwalk. "She's in a coma, I think, but there is some bizarre brain activity I don't understand."

"Is there a log? What about, say, two hours ago? Before I got trapped in that room with you?" I ask.

Martin scrolls through the menus. "Actually, yes." He makes eye contact, a pensive expression on his face. "Brain dead."

"Now we're getting somewhere," I say.

His eyes go back to Charlotte. "The hoses, must feed into that hardware on her head. This system indicates some serious chemicals getting passed around, too. We might be able to revive her, but I'm not sure."

"No. I need her to keep ignoring us. I've got a different idea," I say.

"Any chance this idea involves me gettin' into the action?" Hurricane claps his hands together, palms blurring at the last second, and the sound echoes through the cavern.

"Um, sure," I say. "First, I need you to bring me the Battle Armor's head."

"You mean break that shiny suit out there? That could come in handy in a fight."

"Yes, it does. But there's one way to end this and more fighting isn't it." Hurricane's shoulders slump as I continue, "I left it wide open. Your level of friction should be able to wrench the helmet free. A bundle of wire runs along the back seam. Try to keep most of that intact."

Hurricane nods and the walkway rattles as he disappears.

"Eric, ready to party?"

"Not really," he shouts from the walkway.

"Too bad. Come here, I need you to send out the invitations."

CHAPTER 51

HURRICANE'S BACK WITH the helmet with his traditional speed. Martin is binding a few wires together like I showed him. Meanwhile, I'm trying to convince Eric that *I'm* not crazy.

"So now you're the one with the crazy theories," says Eric. He's crouched in front of an open panel on Charlotte's cylinder, elbows-deep in a spaghetti plate of wires. He glances at the screen. "But you're right, the system is infested with those nanobugs. I'm getting traffic on the same frequencies we used with Cuddles."

"Perfect."

"How did you even know?"

"I saw them. All these guys were riddled with Drake's hardware." Makes sense to me, but he looks skeptical, so I go over more of the facts. "The government wanted a way to control their toys, not completely shut them down. They tried turning Polybius into Robocop in the early days of the program and wound up with Cyber Veg, so they mothballed him at Whispering Pines—"

"Why? Why not leave him here?"

"I, well, I'm not sure." His question is a good one, but I can't let it throw doubt on the whole theory. Right now, it's all I have. "Whatever the reason, at some point, the bugs got here. One failed experiment or another got woken up, Charlotte caught on, and probably steered the whole damn place back on the cyborg agenda."

His gaze floats upward. "But if she can control all those Augments, why does she even need the hardware?"

"I don't think it works that way. She can only control a few minds at a time—a 'vessel' for her brain, that's what she called Emily, and another one she uses as her puppet. And it's localized. She could mess around with my dreams while I was at the bunker, but I was out of her control." Eric is already scowling and shaking his head as I finish. "After she took over Dad, she was having trouble with Emily, I saw it." *And Mom, Mom was able to contact me.*

"What about the walk of death back there?" He points wildly at the crash doors. "How'd she kill all those people?"

"Jesus, I don't know how that happened. Look, somehow she's exploiting the tech. I'm pretty sure she had to use everyone here for their expertise—she isn't a techie. My guess is that, like Emily said, those nanobots have a kind of hive mind going on. Charlotte's plugged directly into it in a way nobody ever anticipated. I'm betting she's here," I gesture at the girl suspended in the cylinder, "in the wired 'vessel', so she has a stronger link to the Augments. This weird cylinder farm might be acting as a psychic repeater."

Eric soaks it all in. His terrified face glows green in the light from the cylinder's touchscreen. It suits him, the glow of pixels.

Maybe the terror, too, brought on by being the smartest guy in the room. "Are you sure about this?" he asks, fingers busy on the touchscreen.

"Fuck, no." I look down and stare into a sea of my own faces, framed by the geometric lenses of the Battle Armor's eyes. Once again, this could be the dumbest idea I've ever had. I seem to keep topping myself as the week wears on. I check the wiring, bound together in a messy knot and fed into the cylinder base. I've got power. The interface is as good as it is going to get. We're ready to go.

"Why don't we just unplug her?" asks Martin.

Practical, might work. But then what happens to Emily and Dad? Are they stuck in Charlotte's playhouse? Trapped, like Mom? Do the other Augments drop on the battlefield and get slaughtered?

"No. Too risky. It has to be this way," I reply.

"You think Hurricane's okay out there?" Eric asks.

"That old goat? He's fine. I doubt they can even see him." And he knows what he signed up for. He went out there with the regular Hurricane zeal, when I asked him to rush into whatever hell was raging above and pull out as many people as he could, Augment or not.

Dad's stupid rules start to make sense. Neutralize the threat first, because there's always more damage to be caused. More lives at risk, until the job's done. You have to accept that. That's probably why he worked alone. But it's a big reason why he kept failing. That, and he couldn't follow those rules when it came to me.

I sit next to the helmet. Martin crouches next to me, his worried face searching mine.

"I'll monitor your vitals. The first sign you're having trouble, I'm shutting this off."

"Okay, but keep an eye on Carrie there and tell me if she starts to wake up." I grab his arm and he squeezes my elbow, then pulls me toward him in a quick bro-hug, patting my back. As much as I hated this guy at one time, I needed that.

"Spencer, I've got a channel open to the bugs," Eric shouts.

"Be ready to use them to lock her down." Too bulky to lift, I slide into the helmet balanced on the floor. "Battle Armor, you there?"

"Armor operational. Power intermittent. Sensors reporting extreme damage. Weapon systems offline." Drake's collected, prerecorded words call out from the blackened visor display. Martin rests a hand on my shoulder.

"Forget all that. Battle Armor, you should detect a new interface. Same tech, different purpose."

A brief pause and Drake confidently replies, "Accessing."

The view screen flickers then projects in harsh edges and shadowy lines. Details are hard to make out at first, until an orange, fiery blast fills the lower corner. Soon after, the cavern shakes in a concussive wave. I must be seeing outside, through the eyes of her current "vessel".

From high above the base on a ridge, destruction rains down on the neighboring hills. Energy blasts and enormous shapes barrel through military machines tucked away in defensive positions. The machines fire back, belching smoke and fire.

Already, the military forces are retreating under the Augments' assault.

The view turns, and I can see Dad's face in the pixelated image. His eyes are globes of mercury. "Spencer. What are you doing?" he says in an empty voice. This must be Emily's view.

"Breaking the rules. Pulling my punches."

"Spencer, return to the room and wait. We'll be back for you, soon."

"Charlotte, we need to talk. We need to talk or I'm going to have to do something drastic." I feel a hand grip my forearm reassuringly.

Emily's cracked voice fills the helmet and I know that again, these are Charlotte's words. "We will punish them. Burn them to dust. Scatter them to the wind. Then, we can all be together."

"Charlotte," I shout, "Mom doesn't blame you for what happened. She knows you couldn't help it."

The untarnished image of Mom's smiling face fills my mind. Dad's jaw flexes and his eyes soften.

"Connie," he painfully cries. Doubling forward, he clenches his muscles and convulses. Dad drops to his knees and a scream of primal rage echoes across the canyon, reaching down to the catwalk.

"Dad! Fight it!" I slide out of the Battle Armor helmet and Martin helps me up. "Eric, are you on the feed? Can you see any links?"

"Yep," Eric replies. "I've got connections looping back here from all over. I can't isolate the one directly to her, it keeps shifting, a single control distributed over thousands of nodes. I can sever them one by one…"

I dig out the remains of Martin's phone and punch in a number. I'm barely finished when the catwalk rattles, and Hurricane zips into view gripping Eric's phone. He's leaning against the rail, wheezing through the goofiest toothless grin he's worn yet. Blood trickles down his prosthetic, and the gown is shredded into a kraut-and-kielbasa number. Martin springs to his feet and begins checking Hurricane's bleeding leg.

"Haven't seen this kinda action since Normandy! Bunch of Augments who ain't never seen a real furball, yeah. And they ain't right in the head, just like you said. Not too hard to keep one step ahead. Whatcha got?" Hurricane asks through ragged breaths.

"I need you to get Emily and bring her here. Charlotte can't afford to let go of my dad, but she might hurt Emily. She's on a ridge. I could see the base from an angle closest to the runway, the end by Martin's plane!" He's gone before I can finish. "Eric, get ready to signal the bugs."

"Right, the maintenance loop command."

"Not exactly. I want you to use the one I used on Cuddles."

Eric's eyes get wide and he stutters out his thoughts, "When you told it to go home for repairs?"

I nod.

"But, they're all going to come here!"

"Yeah, only you'll lock up the signal once they show. What? Close your mouth before a nano flies in there." I fix him with what I hope is a confident stare. "We can't have them drop helpless out there. We need to keep anyone else from getting hurt, okay? And I need Charlotte busy trying to control them."

Eric nods weakly.

"When I give the signal, sever every connection. This helmet, her connections to the others, everything," I say. He nods blankly and I'm not convinced he heard me. "I'm counting on you."

"Okay. But, even the nanomechs might not be able to do it," He says weakly. "If what you're saying is right, she's tapped in through the hardware in some freaky way that I don't get."

"That's why I'm going to knock again," I say and slip into the Battle Armor helmet.

"What if she ignores you?" comes Eric's muted voice.

"I'll go all Jehovah's Witness on her," I shout. "Trust me, people can't ignore me. I'm a pain in the ass. That's *my* power."

Inside the Battle Armor helmet, the screen has cleared, filled with a blue-gray fog that reminds me of television static. "Charlotte. You have to talk to me. You owe me that." I clear my voice and brace for the next words. "My mom. You killed her. I want to know why."

Drake's calm voice breaks the muffled silence, "Warning, neural cage power fluctuation detected."

With a flash of light, the interface is gone.

I'm back on the beach. Like last time, the surroundings are plucked right from my imagination. There's the Bay of Safety, with a dilapidated tent house sitting on the shore. A dense thicket of cocoa plants, their yellow husks bright among the shaded canopy, rises on the far side of a stream trickling down a hillside.

I search the high ground for the treehouse, the Falcon's Nest. I think I can just make out the top of the white sailcloth ceiling and walls. They built other shelters, all over the island, but this one was my favorite. Who wouldn't want to live in a treehouse? Maybe that's why Charlotte picked this place, where she keeps the books and the... the hammocks. I start on a jog through the jungle.

Every known useful plant and animal in existence managed to live on this remote chunk of land. Even if the seemingly infinite supplies of the wrecked ship hadn't clung to the rocks for months, the family had every possible item they needed for survival and comfort. That, and a father with an encyclopedic knowledge of living off the land, which included making rubber boots out of tree sap and the proper way to tame any animal, or, more commonly, the most efficient way to kill them.

Pleasant thought, given that I'm the prey here today.

But I had a father that left home to protect the world. Go on missions to preserve liberty, freedom, whatever patriotic excuse he was fed. When I was really little, it was the fictional character, William, that was my father. Always there, sharing his boundless knowledge, encouraging my accomplishments and misadventures.

I don't recall exactly when I figured out he was a jackass.

Soon, the stream trickles behind me and broad palms sway in a gentle breeze. As a kid I dreamed nightly of exploring this place. But in those dreams, it was always just Mom and me. Isolated and lost seemed a better alternative to the chaotic life I lived. Now, I'm positive that it isn't.

Somewhere down the line, the book became a running joke. Maybe it was the way I would notice Mom cringe at the old-fashioned ideals. Stuff like the kitchen, made especially for the mother. The father's "thoughtful" gift of sewing supplies.

Or the Robinson mom, almost always left at home during all the adventures. She got tired of that.

And then there was the incredible indifference to escape shown by the family. By the middle of the book, two years had passed and nobody had explored the extent of this so-called island. Nobody had peeked over the farthest hill to make sure there wasn't so much as a ticket booth for the zoo, which would explain the variety of animals they found to slaughter.

Two years is a long time.

I'm trudging up the hill toward this, the first real home the stranded family built—a treehouse made of spare planks and sailcloth in the branches of a giant fig tree. It was a home they abandoned during the first rainy season, because the wind and rain poured in through the large flap of cloth that served as their door. It no longer protected them.

The canopy of the fig tree looms above the thin palms. The roof of the Falcon's Nest isn't sailcloth at all, but a distinct red tile. It slopes down above a stucco wall, ripped open and filled with crooked chunks and shredded wire that form a fanged maw.

I'm home.

CHAPTER 52

THE ROOTS OF the fig tree stand twice my height, rippling out in wavy lines before tapering into earth. A length of rope knotted with debris hangs down from a gash in the stucco tree house. Woven into the rope are irregular wooden planks, evenly spaced to form a ladder.

"Incoming threat." I spin in circles trying to pinpoint the source of the statement. Drake, again, but this time the calm voice-over has an edge of anxiety.

I try and will my heart to stop hammering so damn hard. Focus on the tree.

Even in my imagination, the tree wasn't so freaking huge. I mean, it must've been—they built an enclosed staircase that wound down through a cavity in the trunk, and used the space between the tall roots as livestock pens. Livestock, no. More of a menagerie. They kept kangaroos, ostriches, jackals, monkeys, wild donkeys, pigs, birds of every imaginable type. But here, there are no animals and no open cavity for the stairs, so I reach for the rope.

The homemade rope ladder feels rickety and unstable, a bit of accuracy I don't quite appreciate. The whole reason they built the staircase was to keep from falling to their deaths, because the sturdy branches that form the foundation of the treehouse are way the hell up there.

Climbing on, the ladder twists and squirms. A faint buzz brings the still air to life. I try to relax and let my weight even out. The ladder settles into a gentle swaying motion and I start to climb.

Bees; that's how they made the interior staircase. The trunk was hollowed out and inside lived a massive hive of bees. The family laughed off getting stung by an angry swarm as they relocated the colony. I thought I had a weird sense of humor. Guess they hadn't heard of anaphylactic shock back then.

A scream pierces the buzzing. I tense, and the ladder twists wildly, putting my back to the tree. I struggle with the planks and hook my forearm around one. Below, the ladder thrashes like twenty feet of wounded snake.

Not sure what'll happen if I fall in this place.

I lock my legs around the rope, trying not to move until the twisting stops. The rope swings free and my shoulder collides with the rough bark of the trunk. Another scream sounds. A scream from inside that cavity, blanketed in the droning hum.

Sweat trickles down my face. This can't be rushed. One rung at a time. Slow, steady, to keep from falling. The freakish cries follow and intensify with each rung. At the top, I flop onto the floor and lie in a pool of sweat.

The hammocks sway gently, flanking the wrought-iron bed that was never part of the book. Of course, neither was the bookcase carved into the tree trunk, or the stucco walls. At least

Charlotte isn't here this time, but I have the feeling it won't be long before she shows up. She brought me here, for a reason.

I stand and walk toward the bed and reach out to feel the cold, slick bars. The frame resembles a cage, vertical metal rods feeding into an arced crossbar. Chips and dents cover the unpainted surface.

The mattress has a blue striped pattern on the fabric, splotched with stains. Each bar of the headboard has been crudely bent into a half heart with a parallel bar forming the matching half. The shaping looks crude. Maybe done by hand.

Standing at the headboard, I can see into the hammock with the largest form. Dad's lying there, eyes closed, his normally furrowed face relaxed and peaceful. I don't think I've ever seen him asleep. Emily's in the next one.

Far from peaceful, her jaw is tight and eyebrows gathered. I reach out to touch her hand. She's at the most risk here.

"Emily. Snap out of it."

She twitches and lets out a soft moan.

"Such a clever boy." Droning of bees, the creak of the hammock, it all tickles my ears, but this voice never lands there. "You found your own way home."

I don't turn. "We need to talk," I say.

Charlotte's next to the bed, never having crossed the space between the entrance and here. Her hand touches my shoulder and she pushes me away from Emily's hammock and onto the bed with an effortless motion that I can't resist any more than fighting Dad's brute strength. "So impatient. I have to finish with them before we can be a family."

"I don't think what you're doing is right."

She quirks her head at an alien angle and her eyes, a sliver of sunrise behind cloudy quartz, narrow. "Right?"

"Hurting people." I try to scoot away from her, propelled by the intense gaze, but she matches every move. I look away as I reach the far side.

She leans forward, searching my face with a flat expression. I freeze as the hardened tip of her breast brushes my arm. Her eyes, her naked form; with nowhere safe to look, I stare at the open hole in the wall.

"What you did to my mom was wrong."

"Multiple targets inbound. Weapon systems offline." Drake's frantic voice shatters the air, but Charlotte seems oblivious.

"Mother? I did nothing wrong. I made a place for her. Here." Anger surges in her reply but her face stays placid. "She's right here."

"No, she's *my* mother. Why? Why would you do that?"

"She's safer."

"She's dead!"

"Death?" A tear drops from a glowing eye, but her face remains distant. She lowers herself and brushes her lips against my cheek, whispering, "There is no death here."

Her skin is smooth and warm, and she's so close, I can almost hide the image of her radiant flesh wrapped around dark bone. She seems human again.

"Targets identified. Crimson Mask. Hurricane. Female civilian." The audio feed in the helmet cuts through my subconscious loud and clear.

Charlotte continues talking as she creeps closer. "I made this place for you. I found Father, brought him here, for you."

"What?"

"You wanted him to yourself. You were jealous of normal lives. You wanted a family."

"You're not making sense. I don't want any of this."

"Yes, you always did." Charlotte shifts, raises on her elbows, and I turn again to stare at the opening as a knotted finger traces my cheek and settles in a heated point on my forehead. "Make a family with me, Spencer."

Woah. This, I did not anticipate. Anything I try to say comes out as an incomprehensible grunt and I claw my way off the bed, striking the wooden floor. The buzzing beneath intensifies and the vibration of the bees radiates through my palms.

Charlotte scurries forward and hangs over the edge of the bed, her shoulder blades pointed sharply against her skin and her forearms bent at an odd angle. "Mother was ready to give everything to protect you. Father, he was the same, but he had forgotten who you were and strayed from his family. But now, I'll keep him here with us forever."

"Charlotte, please, this isn't real! None of this!"

"It's more real than you know." She's perched on the bed, a hungry spider, staring down with glittering eyes.

"Targeting data insufficient. Crimson Mask and Hurricane engaged at close quarters. Specify target." Drake sounds manic.

"No! Make them stop!" I call out.

Charlotte absently traces a stain on the mattress with her finger, "I can't let them have my vessel, Spencer. I'm not done with her yet."

Emily's hammock twitches as she struggles within.

"What do you want?" I ask, not expecting an answer that makes any sense.

"I need to punish those that hurt us. Then we can be together."

"But you're hurting me! All of this. I never asked for any of this, but if it's what you want, let them go. Let them all go and I'll stay here with you."

She's visibly confused. As she continues to try and understand or maybe weigh my offer, the buzzing grows stronger. She snarls and her eyes expand across her face, each lens from the center until they fan out across her cheeks. Her body contorts and her limbs twist at inverted angles.

I can hear voices, shouts. Hurricane's banter and chest-thumping "pop" as he speeds around the echoing cavern. Eric's fearful cry rises above the rest, "Here they come! It's working! They're following the signal! Oh, shit… it's working! Spencer, gonna lock them down when they get here!"

The real world is breaking through.

Dad's form thrashes in his hammock. Emily moans. The buzzing peaks. They're all trying to escape this place. Dad, Emily, the bees. The treehouse sways and the rattle of the iron rails on the bed joins the frantic hum. A loose rod clatters to the floor and rolls out of reach.

"Target terminated." I can practically see the sadistic smile drawn across Drake's tiny mouth as the words sound.

A piercing wail erupts from Emily's hammock.

"Please stop this. I'll do whatever you say."

"As soon as we're done," her eyes glow, "as soon as they pay."

Charlotte's dangling over me and more bug eyes continue to sprout in clusters around the first two. Fangs peel back from her mouth. My eyes go to the iron rod lying out of reach on the floor. Emily, tear-streaked and hair matted, wrestles out of her hammock. Her slender fingers with dirt-stained nails wrap around the bar. Charlotte quirks her head, following my gaze and watches as the iron rod smashes into her skull.

"*Get...*"

I roll away from the bed. A sickening wet thud echoes as the rod connects a second time and Charlotte slides off the bed.

"*Out...*"

Emily's face is drained of color and pure madness fills her eyes as the bar cracks again somewhere along Charlotte's spine.

"*Of my...*"

Charlotte's head bounces on the wooden floor and the bees wail in fury.

"*HEAD!*"

Emily stands panting over the limp, naked form, the bar poised for another swing. Floorboards pop and strain as the swarm beneath rages. She turns, letting the slick metal rod clatter to the ground. Her shoulders slump as she walks toward me with a blank expression. "We have to go. Get you out."

I shake my head and she grabs a fistful of my shirt, hauling me to my feet. She drags me toward the exit, which is now a blinding white hole. My eyes go back to Charlotte and I see her head twitch, her arm raise.

"No, Emily. That didn't work. It can't work. Not here."

Emily stops. As if she understands, she turns to face Charlotte and a whimper of resignation escapes her lips. "What is she? Where are we?"

"A mental snow globe inside a completely mental bitch," I whisper. I scramble to my feet and put a hand on Emily's arm. "I tried talking, but I've got another idea."

Charlotte's pale form rises. She snakes her spine in a crooked stretch and utters a repetitive clicking sound. She turns to face us, her insect eyes blazing with rage.

Emily moves to stand between us, clenching her fists. She's exhausted. Slow. Off-balance.

It makes it easy to push her out the treehouse door. With a gasp of surprise, she tumbles into the light and disappears. Whatever happens to her, it can't be worse than what's about to happen here. Charlotte eyes me again with the hungry-spider look.

"She can't escape me. She deserves to be punished. Poetic if he does it, no?" Charlotte hisses in a deadly whisper.

"Crimson Mask engaging female target," echoes Drake's voice. "Male civilian has entered the crossfire. Awaiting command to engage."

This has to stop.

"Charlotte, what does "KUBARK" mean?"

She recoils, and a dense sadness pushes through me that's so raw, I'm nearly reduced to a quivering mass of tears. A hiss escapes her lips, "That is not here."

"Tell me. I want to know. Did you kill my mother? Our mother?"

She rises to her feet and floats above the quaking floor,

hands spread open at her sides. The light, her light, begins to burn bright. "There is no pain here. No death. That is *not here*!"

"Spencer, she's fighting the lockdown! Your Dad, he's after Em—oh God!"

"Civilian target critically wounded," chortles Drake and tears burn my cheeks. "Multiple Augment signatures entering range."

I pick the metal rod up off the floor and face Charlotte. "You don't have to do this! You said it yourself, the government, your handlers, they lost you. You're free from that prison, don't make a new one!"

The entire room is shaking now, and large chunks of debris fall from the gash in the stucco wall. Charlotte burns a virulent pink, unaware of the world falling apart around her as she screams, "Mother! Her strength! She gave it to me and I escaped! I promised to find you! I promised to love you!"

Shaking my head, I jam the rod between two planks and shout, "Eric! Kill the connections!"

"What are you doing?" Charlotte cries.

"Don't worry." I stomp on the angled rod and the plank creaks. "In the book, they laughed about this later."

Charlotte lunges forward, her face twisted in anguish. With a shout, I throw all of my weight onto the bar. She slams into me and the plank pops loose as we tumble toward the exit.

A scream issues out of the gap, high-pitched and angry. The buzz is no longer a sound but a force. It shakes the entire tree house and rattles my brain as Charlotte straddles me, her face turned back to the gash in the floor with a look of surprise. Bees explode from the gap in a glittering cloud, which rises like the tentacle of a great beast. Planks pop and strain as the swarm separates, and the solid column becomes a cloud, filling the air.

Crazy, trapped Augment hive mind, meet crazy, psychic bug queen.

Charlotte stands and I scramble toward the wall. She screams, her pink light buried by the swarm. The tree house pitches and more boards tear free. Both hammocks flop wild and empty. Tiny bees, glowing green with circuitry, issue out of the void between the floorboards.

With a final effort, I lunge toward the blinding white of what used to be the entrance to the treehouse.

Drake shrieks, "Target terminated! Target terminated!"

CHAPTER 53

I'M SITTING ON the beach again. That was one hell of a jump. Never once did I see the ground rushing up to punch me in the face or the rope ladder whipping as the tree shook. Nope. White light, beach, done. Or maybe it was extreme terror, white light, beach, done.

My clothes are completely different. The borrowed sweats have somehow morphed into poofy-thighed breeches, and the oversized polo shirt has ballooned into an airy white number with a ruffled collar. Nice, but why no powdered wig?

I scan the horizon for Emily. Further down the beach, a little girl plays in the mirrored sand. She's young, with a full head of dark-hair, and she's crouched in the surf trying to build a castle that keeps washing lazily away into the sea.

"Hello."

Even though I'm lost in thought, the voice doesn't startle me. Mom stands behind me. She's also wearing something other than her trademark jeans and blouse—a simple blue dress with ruffled sleeves and little white ribbons around the cuffs.

"I say, dear Mother," I attempt a terrible English accent but give up on it, "who's the asshat that came up with this? I think your house is supposed to be on a prairie, not a beach."

Mom laughs. "My beloved son," she says, crossing her hands and walking primly toward me, "this wasn't your idea?"

"Considering I look like a complete idiot, I'd say, no." I try to itch under the tight hosiery on my calves. "But you look… good."

She shakes her head. "I don't do dresses. You know that."

"I was only trying to be nice."

She walks barefoot across the sand to sit next to me. As she smoothes her dress out, I notice the lack of footprints.

"What's wrong?" she asks.

"Oh, nothing." I focus on the water lapping against the sand. "Absolutely nothing."

"Really?" She sounds unconvinced. "Well, *I* think something's wrong."

"What's that?"

"You're here."

I can't answer right away and instead, I start building a little igloo-shaped house with my palm and watch the girl as the relentless waves keep destroying hers. "Maybe I like it here."

"You can't stay."

Why not? I've fought so long, inside and out. Every effort has dragged me to her. I know that now. My brain's gotten drilled in a serious way by psychic bug chicks, out-of-control escape pods, and flights from angry robots. A bean ball, Ray Chapman style. At least he died after taking that pitch. Ever since this began, I've been drifting between reality and a dream anyway. Haunted in the world of the waking, no matter what I do.

"I'm staying. Right here. With you."

"You can't," Mom says.

"Why not?"

"You know why. This is another prison, Spencer. She made it to be a home, but it's not." She pauses and grabs my sandy hand in both of hers. As she continues, I can tell she's watching the little girl in the distance. "And you don't want to surrender yourself to her."

"This isn't so bad. Ocean view. Treehouse full of bees." I strain to see inland and avoid her gaze. "I wonder if Felsenheim is up there. That cave they lived in? Sounded creepy but cozy. I'd love to see it."

Her hand brushes my cheek and sternly turns my face to hers. Such a mixture of sadness and joy, I can't even for a second hold on to what her eyes are saying. They encompass every bit of love—the hurt and the happiness; the elation and disappointment.

"You can't stay here."

I know she's right.

"I did what you said. I kept everyone from getting massacred... I think." I fight back tears. "What if I stay for a little while?"

She shakes her head.

I start to argue but she lays on the "Mom stare". "You need to live. Out in the real world. Whatever makes you happy."

I want to tell her I would be happy here. But she'll see right through the lies. We're both aware she's accepted a fate that she doesn't want to share. Drifting away. An angel.

"I'll find a way to get you out of here."

Her expression softens and she sighs, "Fine. Try. But you can't do that from here."

"I'm not kidding. I'll find a way."

"I know, even if I tell you not to. But Spencer, live your own life. You've earned that for yourself."

I stand and help her to her feet. I force out a breath, promising myself not to cry, ever again. "I will, Mom."

She pats my cheek and smirks, "Now get out of here."

"Your fancy clothes didn't come with the ruby slippers, did they?"

"No. But we have that." She points up the shoreline and bobbing in the surf is a small boat which wasn't there before. Its mottled gray exterior is bright against the blue sea.

"Oh, come on." I turn with a rapid-fire quip about a whale intestine dive suit loaded and ready to fire.

She's gone. So is the girl.

I breathe. Again. Deeper this time. I trudge toward the craft, not looking back.

The outer hull is rough and weathered, the skin of who knows how many otters sewn together. William could tell you the exact number required. Ribbed with whalebone, that was maybe the one animal they scavenged instead of shooting, waterproofed with tree sap and a good degree of pure bullshit, the little canoe never sounded ocean-worthy.

I hop in anyway. Mostly to keep moving, away from where I saw her last, and I launch into the sea.

*

The sea wind blows with steady, regulated gasps.

Gasp, click.

Gasp, click.

Wait a minute.

"Sean." A mechanical intake of air follows the strained and monotonous call. "Someone get Sean."

"How are you, son?" Another familiar voice, and... fluffy clouds on the horizon? No, bushy white eyebrows and a sea breeze of tobacco. Hound leans in close.

"Where am I?"

"Whispering Pines," Hound says. "Didn't have a lot of other options."

The discolored ceiling panels and cinderblock walls painted institutional green should have been a clue.

Polybius stands next to Hound. He's a wasted figure, riddled with cybernetics, supported by a walker and dragging a forest of IVs and medical equipment. But his eyes are alert.

"Where's Hurricane?" I wait for the air to form that solid fist and punch me in the chest.

Hound shakes his head.

I breathe. Again. And nod.

A flash of crimson flutters in the doorway. His mask is clenched in his fingers. Solid and callused, the hands made to transfer unimaginable power twist the cloth into a wrinkled mess. He moves to the bed quickly and I look away. Those same hands touch lightly on my arm and I shrug them off.

"We'll give you some time," Hound says. He escorts

Polybius and his train of equipment into the hallway closing the door behind them.

"What happened to Hurricane?" I demand.

"She was in my head. Nothing seemed real."

"You killed him?"

There's a long pause before he answers. "Yes."

"Eric? What about Eric?"

"He's fine. Sharp kid." He speaks with genuine admiration as he clears his throat.

Drake's final taunt fresh on my mind, I press for more details. "Emily?"

Dad breaks eye contact. "She's outside."

That leaves Martin. Tears trickle down my cheek, hot with anger. Our eyes meet and mine aren't the only ones swimming in tears. The accusations die in my throat.

He speaks. "God, Spencer, I'm sorry. I couldn't break free of her. I never meant to hurt them. You. Anyone."

My tears have stopped, dried by the shock. The Crimson Mask, my dad, crying. All the expectations, all the isolation, all the missed childhood moments seem to come together all at once, and I don't know what to say anymore.

"I understand."

But I don't want to forgive. Not yet. Not with Hurricane dead. Martin.

"Hurricane wouldn't back off," Dad tries to explain. "He was fast, but he got tired. And Martin. I didn't even know his name."

"He was a doctor. Doctor Alexander."

Dad sits up and wags a weary head, "Emily broke free

somehow. Charlotte sent me after her." He stares into the distance replaying every detail. "That's when he tried to stop me."

"Dad, I can't listen to this right now."

He nods. "I'm glad you're okay."

"How long have I been out?"

"Three days."

"Are you kidding?"

"I was worried you weren't going to come back."

"Almost didn't."

I push back the covers and swing my feet off the bed. My pasty legs stick out from a Whispering Pines-issue gown. Dropping to the floor, I wobble and Dad's hand engulfs my shoulder to steady me.

"Ready for a walk?" he asks.

"Yeah."

"I've got some clothes for you in the closet."

"Nah. I'm good."

Unfamiliar faces line the halls, each sporting implants hidden under a crazy collection of scrubs, scavenged clothes, and a few more hospital gowns. They all watch with grim faces. One, a woman who's more flesh and bone than tubes and chrome, steps up with her arm extended. She's got close-cropped hair with an orange mohawk down the center. Her skin is ashen white, and a subtle warmth radiates from her body. I hesitate but take her hand anyway, and the touch sends a hot sensation up my arm.

She smiles wryly as I squirm and says, "Thanks, kid."

I wait to roll my eyes until we pass. I'm never going to shake the nickname. Kid.

"Ember?" I ask. "Are they all here?"

"No. Many went their own way. Some weren't so appreciative." He keeps his eyes straight ahead. I imagine that the ones Dad captured are on that list—whether he knew what was going on at Killcreek or not. "But you and Eric. You're the only reason they're all free. The ones that stayed, stayed because of you guys."

"Eric? My friend, Eric?"

We walk down the compound's halls and out through the reception area. The space has been cleared except for the deep gouge in the floor where Cuddles tried to skewer Hurricane. Outside, the sun shines down on a no-longer-empty parking lot. A black SUV, a few sedans, and then there's Eric's car.

"Hey! Spence! Dude!" His voice drifts down from the sky. I turn, backing away from the building to scan the rooftop. My involuntary smile is lost as I take in the scene.

Eric is perched on the roof in some kind of black unitard and a belt full of tools. He looks like an eight-ball collided too hard with a stripe and had a baby. His broad belt sports an assortment of wire cutters, cables, spools, and a tablet tucked in the front of his waistband. He's scrambling down a metal platform that definitely wasn't part of the retirement home before. It takes me a minute to grasp that this is the enormous platform from the cavern, studded with cylinder bases.

"How did that get up there?" I ask.

Dad shrugs, "I needed a way to carry everyone out of there."

Overwhelmed, I examine the scene again. What I see next causes two reactions. First I stagger blindly backward to get a better angle, and then I wonder how far away I can get in the nearest car.

Charlotte. She's wrapped loosely in a collection of sheets in the chilly air. The array of flexible hoses and tentacles sprouting from her are entwined around a building antenna sticking through the center of the platform. Motionless, her back arches to the sky and the wind whips her ghostly hair. She seems inanimate. Just another fixture amid the straight brick edges of the building or the bristling antenna array.

"Holy…" I start but never finish.

"He's alive!" Out of nowhere, Eric wraps me in a hug and lifts me off the ground. "I thought we were gonna have to sew some robot parts on you!" I wiggle free with my hands up defensively and he laughs, "Just kidding, man! Cyrus said you'd be fine."

"Cyrus? The Augment?"

"He used to be a doctor," says Dad. "He's been checking up on you."

"What's going on here? Why is," I swallow, watching the loose cables around Charlotte's form sway, "*she* here?"

Eric lets out a heavy, "Oh," and tries to explain. "She did that herself. We didn't have time to dump her during the evac. When the Augments all grouped at the cavern, Uncle Sam – no, not the Augment, he died a while back – decided to call in the air strikes. Bombs were falling, the whole damn place shaking, it was FUBAR! So we left her on board and your Dad gave us a lift. Dude, I didn't open my eyes until we were back on solid ground."

"All the way here?" I stammer.

"Had to take a breather in Northern Utah," Dad adds.

"But why come here?"

"Eric's suggestion," says Dad, like it's a normal everyday thing for him to take my slightly nutty friends seriously.

Eric appears to blush again but maybe it's just the heat in his unitard. "Yeah, I guess I did. We needed a place with medical facilities, and I didn't think a public hospital was going to work."

"The government just let you guys move in?" I'm slack-jawed, standing in the fluttering breeze with my ass sticking out of my gown, but I couldn't care less at this point.

"No, dude, better than that. We weren't gonna stay this long. But Charlotte, who we all figured had a skull full of V-8 after whatever you did, made her move. She walked over and latched on to the antenna with her freaky tentacle shit. I think Pops here," Dad doesn't even cringe at the pet name, "was going to, well, finish the job. But he asked me to find out what she was doing first."

I'm speechless. Probably still asleep in a hospital bed. That's the only explanation.

I eye Dad who gives a tight nod. "Pulling punches," he says.

Too bad he couldn't do that before now.

"Where's Emily? You said she was out here."

Dad eyes the edge of the parking lot and a stand of pines. "Just past the parking lot, other side of the ravine. C'mon, I'll take you."

"No thanks," I brush his hand aside. "I can find her."

I can feel both of their eyes on me as I walk away. Eric starts to speak but falls silent. Barefoot, I relish the feel of the rough concrete of the parking lot, and then the soft bed of fallen needles. A light breeze is shuffling the pines and the fragrance reminds me of the night I flew on the Cuddle's back. Why am I even still alive?

It strikes me: in Charlotte's snow globe, I could never smell the world around me. The fabricated ocean breeze was the closest thing, but now that I'm wandering with nothing between me and the woods but a flimsy hospital gown, I realize how immaterial that place was. That same place where I left Mom.

Emily's there, on the other side of the ravine. The pines grow tall and in nearly straight rows. The lowest branches are far off the ground, creating ordered lines of bare trunks. Except for where she sits.

There is a circle of sorts among the trees, and Emily is sitting cross-legged at the center. Stuck in the ground in front of her is a chrome IV stand, bent into the shape of a cross. A stethoscope is draped across the bars along with a surgical mask.

Another cross is next to that one. A worn prosthesis, the foot melted and mangled, lies on top of a folded flag in front of that one.

I don't know how long I'm staring before she turns to face me.

"Spencer!" Her puffy eyes fly open and she scrambles to her feet. I smile weakly as she rushes over and throws her arms around me. I close my eyes and bury my face in her shoulder. Wood smoke. Pine. I look to the side and see a makeshift tent and a fire ring.

She steps back to arm's length and tries to smile. "I'm sorry

I wasn't there when you woke up. I've been checking on you. I told them to come and get me. They knew to come and get me."

"Don't worry. I came to you."

She tries to smile again but it's a wounded look. I don't know if I'll hear that awkward snort anytime soon. "I'm glad you're okay."

I flick my head toward the tent. "Been out here long?"

She scrunches her lip and follows by motion. "It feels so, so real out here, you know?"

"Yes." I don't know how to say what needs to be said. We stand there, checking out the woods for far too long. I'm staring at the needles between my toes when I finally say, "He wasn't a douchebag. He was a really great guy."

She bites her bottom lip and swallows, nodding in short bursts. I feel my throat constrict and tears start to form.

"I'm sorry."

"So am I."

She turns to the graves and walks toward them. I follow and as I approach, my head goes numb. Lying on my back for days hasn't done me any good. I press forward anyway. I should pay my respects, or say something. The people there... they deserve it... for... Wait... what am I doing here? Why did someone jam a couple of metal bars in the ground?

Emily plants her hand on my chest and draws me back a step. The feeling returns to my brain, and the chrome grave markers glare against the brown carpet of needles.

"What was that?"

Her voice cracks. "I put them there. I don't want to remember." She clears her throat.

I nod sympathetically, hoping that Emily hasn't been permanently damaged by Charlotte, but I can't tell.

"What do you do now?" I ask.

"I want to go home. Stuff my head into some research back at the university."

"That actually sounds good." I stare into the canopy, imagining a ring of light I hope to never lay eyes on again. "Fuck computers and robots, though. How's the neuroscience program at George Mason?"

She almost smiles. "Not bad. I could use some help in the lab if microbiology is ever on your schedule. And you could use someone to keep you out of trouble."

"Me?"

"Yeah, you."

"Homework, cheeseburgers, girlfriends; I can handle college."

"Please, Spence, you have the social skills of a—"

"Teenager? Child? Kid? Go ahead, say it." I can almost laugh at it now. "Yeah, I need help. I could use a big sister."

We talk by the gravesites for a long time. She tells me stories about her and Martin, slogging their way through undergrad at George Mason. I regale her with stories about my short experience with Hurricane and finally get a snort out of her, imitating Eric's face when he and Hurricane first met. When the chill finally starts to sink in, I turn and hold the gown closed and make my way back toward the retirement facility. She stays behind. "A few more minutes", she says.

Dad and Eric are still outside. Eric stands tall and proud, and despite the ill-fitting costume, he doesn't appear to be the translucent hermit living on microwave cuisine that he really is, or was. He waves when he sees me coming.

"Found her?" asks Eric. Dad clears his throat.

"Yeah."

"Good," Dad says.

"I might need to talk to Cyrus. Got a little head rush walking around out there."

"Oh no. I bet you're fine." Eric continues under my skeptical gaze. "Turns out, Char is cloaking the place. She's somehow deflecting every kind of signal you can imagine. Polybius and I are pretty sure she's still using the antenna and the metal in the platform as a dish. It's freaking amazeballs."

I nod and stare up at Charlotte, planted on the roof. "What does that have to do with me being fine, Doctor?"

"Get this—she's messing with people's minds, too!" says Eric excitedly.

"What he means to say," Dad interrupts, "is that nobody knows we're here."

"Yeah, you can't get close to this place or even leave without hitting some serious brain fog. I can't explain that. Way outside my pay grade," intones Eric in a voice of quasi-authority.

I don't want to question the suit. The lingo. I mean, I really *want* to sling a heater in that direction, but not today. Eric's face is beaming. And Dad, despite the red-rimmed eyes, they're showing a new emotion as he waits for me to speak.

Pride.

"So if I go too far from here, I'll forget about it?"

Now I understand what Emily meant, when she said she put the grave markers *there*.

"Well, maybe," Eric says, then whips his face toward Dad and back again. "What do you mean, leave? I mean, you could leave, and I guess we could write a note. I don't think we can call you 'cause there aren't any signals going out, or in. Not even the radio in my car, which sucks because the Giants—"

Dad places a hand on Eric's shoulder. "As far as we can tell, you *might* not be able to get back here. She's selective about who she lets in. It's between the two of you, but so far, everyone here has been cleared."

"I imagine the government is out looking for a bunch of escaped Augments again?"

"Not yet. They're still trying to explain to the world what happened." Dad looks at Eric and he continues, "Eric sent that information to the press and blew the lid off the 'military exercise' at Killcreek."

I take in his words, Eric's expectant face, the fierce shine in Dad's eyes. It's a look so genuine I can't watch him with the balled-up pain and anger burning inside. I could tell him off. Make him apologize for all the shit he put me through. For Mom. But this is so different now. I'm the one in control. I'm the one who saved his ass, when all that time he wanted to keep me locked away for my own good. I'm free.

"I might need those clothes after all," I say. "I was talking with Em. College doesn't sound half-bad right now."

"Whoa, Spence! Hang on!" Eric grabs my arm as I turn back to the building. "I mean, we just got here. College is cool and all, but, um, I think they need some more help around here."

"You'll be fine here. You're the Augment. Not me." Eric starts to protest but I interrupt. "I made a promise. A couple, really, and I intend to keep both of them."

"He's right, son. You could stay," Dad says. "These men and women here, these heroes, they'd be willing to follow you. There's a lot to be done. Not everybody walked away from Killcreek without revenge fresh on their mind."

"Yeah, I guess I could stay, but I'm not going to." I turn and look Dad straight in the eye. "You're family. I really care about you. I love you. But you're an asshole. A self-centered son of a bitch." He lowers his head and starts to apologize but I cut him off. "There were heroes at Killcreek. Normal people, like me, who didn't have powers to shield them." I throw an arm around Eric's shoulders as I continue. "So pay attention. You might learn a thing or two from this guy."

Dad seems to swell, from his jaw to his pecs. He isn't about to explode in anger, though. A look of resignation sets into his features. "I'm going to make this right, Spencer. As best as I can. I want to have you here with me. This won't be like the bunker, I'm not going to be that same person. But I understand if you've got your own plans."

I try to smile but it's hard. I have to step away. "Yeah. Cheeseburgers. Ball games. Girlfriend. More girlfriends. A little homework here and there."

Walking toward the building, I make sure to let the gown flap freely in the breeze. Sure it's cold, but it ain't arctic, ball-numbing cold. Not here. Not ever again.

Thank you for reading Crimson Son. To find out more about the author and follow his mad scribblings, visit www.russlinton.com. For notices about new releases, and free books, please join our mailing list online at:

https://landing.mailerlite.com/webforms/landing/d4i4d9